SINS
of our
FATHERS

a Jonathan Thorpe novel

GARY NEECE

Perthshire Press

garyneece.com

Printed in the United States of America

First Edition: June 2013

Library of Congress Cataloging-in-Publication Data

Neece, Gary.
      Sins of Our Fathers / Gary Neece. – 1st ed
         p. cm.

   ISBN-13: 978-0615811109
   ISBN-10: 0615811108

   1.   Sins of Our Fathers—Fiction. 2. Fiction—Crime
   3.   Fiction—Mystery & Detective: Police Procedural

For Bill

For he is the Minister of God to you for good. But if you have done evil, be afraid, for he does not wear the sword for nothing, for he is the Minister of God and a furious avenger to those who do evil.

Romans 13:4

Armed, say you?
Armed, my lord.
From top to toe?
My lord, from head to foot.
Then saw you not his face?

— **Shakespeare,**
Hamlet

ONE

JEREMY JOHNSON—SMILE ON HIS face, burning in his lap—sat behind the wheel of his Chevy four-wheel drive. He fought to keep the beast of a truck below the speed limit, and the beast within, under control. Not three feet behind Jeremy, in the camper shell of his pickup, lay the object of his ghoulish desires.

In high school Jeremy was the smarter-than-thou, overweight, ungraceful, creepy guy few people bothered getting to know. Those few who did quickly realized Jeremy wasn't just creepy, he was downright spooky. That was then; today he was all those things and more. Now, he was a traveler. He didn't want to be, but several regrettable incidents dictated a change in method, *or as detectives liked to say, modus operandi—no doubt to make themselves sound smarter—the stupid bastards.* After all, he was, *is*, a killer of children and the scourge of his community, currently a sleazy trailer park a beer bottle's throw outside Coffeyville, Kansas. The burning in Jeremy's lap diminished as he shook his fleshy head in disgust.

Every time he uprooted himself, detectives with the Tulsa Police Department made sure his new community knew who he was

1

– *what* he was. It didn't matter where he moved, TPD "dicks" kept tabs on him through whatever backwater jurisdiction he happened to reside. *What a joke. If the big city cops couldn't catch him when he was a mere teenager, what'd they expect Barney fucking Fife to accomplish?*

When Jeremy was just sixteen years old, he killed a young neighborhood boy and buried him beneath his midtown Tulsa home. Not yet a seasoned killer, a nervous Jeremy murdered the boy well before having satisfied his ravenous appetite. But the images he'd created in the process were scorched into his memory: the anguish on the boy's contorted face, the fear in his pleading eyes. *Yes, his eyes*—life's burning flame deprived of oxygen, waning until it was no more, snuffed out. Gone forever.

Jeremy was hooked. Every day following the murder, he masturbated; aroused at having his prize entombed just a few feet below his bedroom's gummy carpet. For the most part, he even enjoyed his subsequent arrest, interrogation, and press coverage. He enjoyed the shock in people's eyes when he gave them a wink or thin-lipped smile. He enjoyed being feared.

Jeremy, diagnosed with an array of dissociative disorders—*a fine piece of acting even if he did say so himself*—spent six years in "custodial counseling." Rehabilitated, Jeremy earned his release back amongst the sheep. He stayed with his mother and took a job at a fast food restaurant where he grew fond of leaving personal condiments in the food of local police officers. *Those pigs earned that half-price meal.*

His flabby butt cheek growing sore from a protruding spring, Jeremy shifted in his seat, pushed wispy brown hair from his eyes, checked his side view mirrors, and felt the burning return as he remembered his second kill three years ago. He'd still been living with his mother and still jerking-off at the burger joint, when another neighborhood boy, Michael, caught his attention. *Oh, how he'd caught his attention.* Drawn, Jeremy needed to turn the tables; he needed something that would draw the boy to him. *Puppies?* No, his bitch mother wouldn't allow pets. Jeremy's boy-bait ended up costing a hell of a lot more than a puppy. He tapped all the money he'd saved flipping burgers to purchase a used Honda Magna. All young boys love motorcycles. So every sunny day Jeremy would roll the cruiser out of the garage, angle it just right, sit back, and let sunshine and polished chrome do the rest.

One day, while Jeremy tinkered with the bike, Michael gathered enough courage to walk up the driveway for a closer look. *It's always easier when they come to you.* Jeremy explained he couldn't get the bike started and—wouldn't you know it—Michael offered to lend a helping hand. Within a week the two had the motorcycle running, which was no huge accomplishment given the bike had never really been disabled.

As payment for his assistance, Jeremy promised to teach Michael how to ride the sparkling machine. But because the boy wasn't yet sixteen, they'd have to keep the lessons secret, *to keep anyone from getting in unnecessary trouble.* A couple of evenings later, with Jeremy's mother away at her weekly bridge game, Michael knocked on the front door eager for his first ride. The boy assured Jeremy no one knew where he was or had a clue of their mischievous plans. Two weeks later, on the banks of a rural creek a few miles outside Tulsa's city limits, a startled quail hunter discovered Michael's headless torso.

Jeremy had been careless in taking a neighborhood acquaintance; that's the only reason cops detected even a whiff of his culpability. Already under suspicion, he even hinted to investigators that he had indeed killed the boy. *And they still couldn't convict him!* Oh he never confessed, but he made sure to smile at inappropriate times, or part his lips and take to caressing the front of his small teeth with his thick tongue while being questioned about a lurid detail. He wanted the ignorant bastards to know he'd committed the murder. He just didn't want to go to jail. Ultimately, Jeremy had to admit his bravado had nearly been his downfall. Two hung juries later, the DA's office refused to re-file without new evidence, making Jeremy a free man—well almost. He was watched everywhere he went: by police, by neighbors, by everyone. The high profile case resulted in Jeremy's image being plastered all over the local television stations as well as the front page of several newspaper editions.

Knowing his need to kill would return, Jeremy was forced to find new hunting grounds. So, following his narrow escape from a second incarceration, Jeremy moved to a small inland town along the East Coast where he hoped to operate with anonymity. He'd learned from his first two kills. He would only hunt strangers.

Just eighteen days after moving to Virginia, Jeremy abducted a child from a playground as the boy's mother—oblivious to her surroundings and her son's activities—basked in the sun. He took the child to his home, used him, and killed him, all on a large sheet of plastic. He hadn't even yet released the boy's throat when remorse soured his mood; his plan had been to keep the boy alive for repeated pleasure, and once again he'd lost control of the moment.

After dulling two hacksaw blades and taking a hot shower, Jeremy backed his Caprice into the one-car garage and slung the plastic-wrapped body parts into the gaping trunk. A half-mile away from his home, he passed two county deputies traveling lights-and-siren in the opposite direction. *Surely they weren't headed to his residence?* Jeremy knew better than to satisfy his curiosity while driving with his trunk full of human stew; *more than likely the dumb fucks were en route to a limited-time-only doughnut sale.* So he continued on, discarding the body parts in a remote lake he scouted earlier in the week. On his way home he stopped behind a strip mall and stuffed the evidence-laden plastic sheet into a large commercial dumpster.

Jeremy returned home to find two deputies waiting cross-armed on the street outside. Tulsa detectives had warned the local pigs that Jeremy's residence should be the first place to visit if any young boys were to come up missing. *Those Fucks!* Had he kept the boy alive like he'd wanted, he would've been incarcerated; *and probably wearing a dirty mop on his head while serving as some behemoth's prison bitch. Too fucking close!*

That's when Jeremy decided to be a traveler. Hunting locally brought too much attention. Since the close call in Virginia he'd moved twice and had never taken a boy within a hundred miles of his residence. Coffeyville was as close to his hometown of Tulsa as he'd been in years, and the proximity had given him an itch. He wanted payback on those TPD pricks who'd forced him to be nomadic. Driving back toward Kansas, Jeremy wondered how long it would take before the stupid fucks learned of the abduction. As Jeremy left the city limits of Tulsa, he thought of the nine-year-old boy gift wrapped inside the camper of his truck, and began to touch himself.

SERGEANT JONATHAN THORPE, SUPERVISOR OF the Tulsa Police Department's Organized Gang Unit, felt the downward pull of a very long day. It'd begun at two this morning when he borrowed an undercover Ford Contour from the Special Investigations Division and drove up to the town of Coffeyville, Kansas. There he'd located the residence of one Jeremy Johnson, former Tulsan, and current piece-of-shit. At around 4:00 a.m., Thorpe crept into an aging trailer park and attached a Birddog tracking device—commonly referred to as a "bumper-beeper"—to the undercarriage of Jeremy's Chevy pickup.

Having attached the transmitter and its battery pack, Thorpe parked the Contour a short distance away hoping to go unnoticed. The tag on his undercover vehicle wasn't on file but Thorpe had removed it anyway, replacing it with "borrowed" plates from a similar Contour in Tulsa. A cooler filled with sandwiches and drinks took up half the back seat. A large duffel filled with equipment sat beside the cooler. Between periods of bored grazing, Thorpe tried, unsuccessfully, to find sleep in the reclined front seat. He hated surveillance, but given his current assignment, surrendered himself to this occupational reality.

When daylight peeled back the eyelid of night, sending people to and fro, Thorpe moved his car to a busy parking lot and placed a sunshade against the windshield. With the limo-tint, it was impossible to see inside the Contour. Hopefully, passersby would assume the car was unoccupied and belonged to an office worker. After twelve hours of cursing Jeremy, the car, and the Gatorade bottle he'd been pissing in, the Birddog's receiver finally indicated movement. Thorpe capped his urine specimen, zipped up his blue jeans, and started to follow.

The older Birddog bumper-beeper emitted an RF signal that was detected by a directional receiver with a range of two to four miles, depending on terrain and weather conditions. Thorpe could have selected a GPS tracking device, which was much more accurate and functional, but the Birddog had an advantage crucial for this mission: it left no electronic signature. GPS utilized satellites that could be traced back to the particular unit if anyone ever bothered to check. The biggest disadvantage with the Birddog was if you got out of range, the only way to reacquire your target was to drive around until you came back within range of the transmitter. But in this case, Thorpe had no choice. He couldn't use a GPS unit that could be traced back to the police department.

Thorpe trailed Jeremy southbound on Highway 169, surprised, when seventy minutes later it became apparent the man was risking a return trip to Tulsa and his old stomping grounds. Inside the city limits, he lost Jeremy's signal not once, but twice, in the heavy daytime traffic. Both incidents were caused by ill-timed red lights; his quarry made it through the intersections, Thorpe didn't. The first time this happened, Jeremy fell off the radar for only a few seconds, Thorpe finding him in the parking lot of Promenade Mall. The second time, he almost lost the signal for good. Several disregarded traffic signals and near collisions later, Thorpe still hadn't relocated the fat bastard. Because he'd located him at a shopping center once before, Thorpe gambled and drove toward Tulsa's Woodland Hills

Mall. He'd gotten lucky. En route, he reacquired the signal near Lafortune Park. It was a good thing too, because shortly thereafter, Jeremy left the city.

Northbound on Highway 169, Thorpe followed the Chevy back toward Kansas. Unless it'd happened when Thorpe lost the signal, Jeremy never stopped in Tulsa for any discernible length of time. Perhaps Jeremy had only suffered a bout of nostalgia and decided to take a quick tour of his hometown.

Jeremy's perpetual motion limited Thorpe's opportunities for contact and he began to nod off, jerking awake as he drifted onto the shoulder's rumble strip. Thorpe had to let Jeremy go. He wouldn't accomplish anything by falling asleep and plowing headfirst into oncoming traffic. He'd have to return to Coffeyville at a later date in order to retrieve the transmitter.

Thorpe spotted an area to conduct a U-turn and eased the Contour over onto the left shoulder. He turned onto a graveled pad, unaware he was letting Jeremy drive away with a new plaything.

JEREMY NEEDED A TASTE RIGHT NOW. He couldn't wait till he got all the way back to Coffeyville, but he also couldn't just pull onto the shoulder, climb into the camper shell, and have his fun. *Some dipshit highway patrolman might stumble across his private party.* Looking for an acceptable place to go off-road, Jeremy slowed the Chevy and scanned the side of the road. A mile later, not seeing any approaching headlights, Jeremy drew near a bridge and pulled off the blacktop onto dormant, foot-high grass. He flipped on his K.C. spotlights, jumped out of the truck, and jogged down the embankment, *perfect.* Jeremy returned to his truck, manually locked in his front hubs, entered the cab, giggled, put the Chevy in four-wheel drive and descended into paradise—and the boy's personal hell.

Jeremy found himself so completely aroused he was afraid he'd ejaculate even before he entered the camper shell. He needed to calm down. Jeremy climbed out from his truck into the darkness. It was March and still cold, especially at night. Hoping the chill would stave off his condition, Jeremy stripped naked and tried to think about anything other than the package giftwrapped in the back of his pickup.

Desperate, Jeremy laid his genitals on the ice-cold front bumper of the Chevy. That helped, but he knew his flaccidity wouldn't last long. *Oh well, he'd use the boy repeatedly; a quickie won't hurt.* Jeremy walked to the rear of his pickup, lifted the glass door to the camper shell, and climbed inside, his erection having already returned. Jeremy probed the darkness with his hands, found his present's duct taped ankles, and heard the muffled cries of his victim.

Evan, nine years old, was the only child of Scott and Lauren Birchfield. He loved fishing with his father, playing "Where's Evan" with his mother, and tug-of-war with Smoot, their two-year-old Rat Terrier. His favorite cartoon was SpongeBob SquarePants and he already had a wicked midrange jump shot on his eight-foot basketball goal. But Jeremy didn't know or care about any of that. The boy had no name, no life, and no worth. Nothing existed outside of Jeremy's world. The boy wasn't someone, he was something; something for Jeremy's twisted entertainment.

THORPE WAS TORN FROM HIS sleep by the blaring horn, and blasting wind, of a southbound tractor-trailer rig. *Son-of-a-bitch!* He'd fallen asleep in the middle of the turnaround between the highway's north and southbound lanes, fortunate his foot hadn't slipped off the brake pedal. *Shit! How long was I out?* Thorpe looked down at the car's illuminated digital clock for the time but found something else of much more interest. The transmitter attached to Jeremy's truck had stopped moving. This might be his chance.

Thorpe reversed the Contour off the gravel pad, jammed the gearshift into drive, and sped north hoping Jeremy remained static.

Two miles later the audible signal was humming and Thorpe slowed. He should be able to see Jeremy's truck, but couldn't. He continued on, creeping across a bridge, the signal losing strength. *Shit, the bastard's ditched the transmitter in the river.* Thorpe performed two more U-turns and again approached the signal from the south. Retrieving a flashlight and a pair of night-vision goggles from his gear-bag, Thorpe turned off the car's headlights and stepped out onto the shoulder. With any luck the transmitter hadn't landed directly in the river. Stepping off the blacktop, he noticed a beaten-down trail in the shin-high grass. Tire tracks. Thorpe knelt and shined the flashlight in one of the ruts. Here and there a blade of grass popped up or a surface runner rose in an attempt to gain its previous posture. The tracks were fresh. Thorpe snapped off the flashlight, donned his night-vision goggles, and unholstered his Sig Sauer .45. Crouching, slowly following the tracks down the embankment, finding his way with the goggles, objects highlighted in hues of greens and black, Thorpe found Jeremy Johnson.

The pudgy bastard was buck naked and looked to be humping the front grill of his Chevy. *What the hell?* Thorpe's view was from twenty-plus yards away and from the passenger side of the truck. He watched as Jeremy ceased violating the Chevy, disappeared around the far side of the truck, reappeared at the tailgate, and lifted the glass to his camper shell. The goggles prevented Thorpe from rubbing his eyes in disbelief; it looked like Jeremy had a hard-on as he oozed into the rear of the camper. *Shit. He has someone inside!* Thorpe hurried toward the truck, the tics and pings of the Chevy's cooling engine and a vehicle passing overhead, helped mask his approach. He took a position just aft of the cab and heard the stifled cries of Jeremy's victim.

Thorpe pulled a large serrated knife from its Kydex sheath and slid it into the sidewall of Chevy's right front tire. Hissing like an angry snake, the deflating thirty-three inch tire caused the truck to dip catawampus. From inside the camper shell, a flurry of profanity drowned out the escaping air.

Jeremy would investigate the flat. Thorpe pulled the goggles away from his eyes and up on his forehead, filled his lungs with crisp night air, and steadied himself. He listened as Jeremy, clueless as to what awaited him, spilled out of the camper. Jeremy stepped around the side of the truck, a look of frustration painted on his greasy face. Thorpe struck him in the throat with the butt of the large knife, knocking the fat bastard to his back, lard jiggling like ripples on a pond. Blade still in hand, Thorpe looked down at Jeremy Johnson, his turgid penis like a chubby little flag pole. *How fitting.* With one nimble swipe of the razor-sharp blade, Jeremy was emasculated.

Something guttural loosed from Jeremy. Not a scream; his windpipe had been crushed by the initial blow. Thorpe was reminded of grinding gears and the wet, sucking sound one hears when pulling the hide off of a rabbit. Jeremy stared up with eyes full of pain, terror—and something else—*a plea for compassion?* Thorpe would afford the same compassion Jeremy had given to so many of his young victims. None.

The pedophile clutched his blood pumping stub with his left hand and dug his right elbow into the ground. He pushed backwards with his heels while Thorpe, unmoving, silent, loomed above. Jeremy rolled over to his stomach and like an insect, began scurrying up the embankment.

Thorpe turned away from the fat, naked, emasculated piece of meat leaving a trail of blood across the brown grass, retrieved his flashlight and shined it into the camper. There he found a boy, bound, eight to ten years old, with haunted eyes. *Still clothed, thank God.* Maybe, just maybe, Thorpe had gotten to him in time.

The boy presented a problem. Up until a few minutes ago Thorpe could explain being parked on the shoulder of the highway. Now he had a prickless pedophile and a hogtied child to deal with. If a patrolman rolled up behind his Contour, he'd be all kinds of screwed. He needed to act fast.

"Hey kid, I just killed the fat bastard who kidnapped you. He's dead you understand?" Thorpe kept the flashlight in the kid's eyes; he hated doing so but he couldn't risk being seen. Eyes wide despite the beam on his face, the kid stared back into the light with no response. "I need you to understand, I just killed that fat asshole who kidnapped you. You're safe, do you understand?" The claim was a slight embellishment since fat asshole wasn't yet dead; the man continued to crawl forward, seeking an illusory refuge.

Thorpe's words eventually found their way through the shock. The boy nodded.

"Look, I'm going to drive this truck back up on the highway, then set you free, okay?" The kid nodded again—*good sign.*

Thorpe jumped into the cab and checked the ignition for a key. Empty. He saw Fat Bastard's pants lying on the seat and searched the pockets. Keys. Thorpe found the proper one, inserted it, and started the engine. He ensured the Chevy was in four-low, four-wheel drive, flipped down his night-vision goggles, and drove forward cutting the wheels to the right. Thorpe headed straight toward Fat Bastard who was still crawling up the hill. Thorpe slowed as the left tire climbed onto Jeremy's back. Then he stomped on the gas. Tire flattened, the right wheel threw mud and rubber. The good left tire, perched on Jeremy's back, threw God-knows-what as it tried to find traction on its mushy terrain. The truck lurched off Jeremy's body and Thorpe slowed as he felt the rear tire rise. He repeated the process, throwing mud, blood, fat, and muscle, catapulting off Fat Bastard up the embankment. If by some miracle Jeremy was still alive, he'd be damned sorry for it.

TWO

780 MILES TO THE EAST, sweating on the polished bar of a downtown Atlanta nightclub, sat a half-full alcohol-infused concoction known as "Sex on the Beach." A red straw connected the peach drink to a set of pink lips. Those full lips belonged to Ambretta Moretti, or as Jonathan Thorpe once knew her, Ambretta Collins—though both names were equally bogus.

Lips to straw, Ambretta's elbows rested in front of her drink, her back arched, her ass stuck in the air like a cat in heat. Her cheeks pinched in as she sucked at the thick concoction. She tossed her silky black hair behind her bare, olive shoulders, while looking up, doll-eyed, at her audience. Much to the delight of Saeed al-Haznawi, her date, she and her white, skintight mini had the attention of every man in the establishment.

Ambretta had many talents, careers, and names. For the last few months, interrupted by a brief stint posing as an FBI agent, she'd been Ambretta Moretti, party planner. Her current cover required little research, especially since her date was not the least bit interested in her supposed employment. What interested Saeed *was* the ass she so prominently displayed. He'd been after it for weeks and was growing irritated with its illusiveness.

For someone who claimed to be an Islamic Fundamentalist, who wished to force Sharia law on the western world, Saeed was a bit of a pervert. On the other hand, many analysts believed that women in short skirts and push-up bras were our best defense against future terrorist attacks. The righteous bastards often succumbed to America's sinful ways as soon as they found themselves "in country."

Saeed was not an attractive man, not by anyone's standards. Nor was he a man of substantial means. If the asshole had any brains at all, he'd realize no woman of Ambretta's caliber should be giving him a passing glance. But like many men, particularly those of his culture, he thought more of himself than he should. In Saeed's world women were something to be possessed, not courted. In his mind, she'd be lucky to spend one night with him, this warrior who'd dare strike the heart of the beast.

Thus far, Ambretta had little to show for her efforts. Having accomplished her basic objectives, she was nearing the end of her assignment. The investigation would soon be in the hands of technicians and analysts. Most of Saeed's known associates had been identified; their residences, storage buildings, and vehicles located. Listening, tracking, and video devices were in place. There wasn't much left for Ambretta to do. And, Saeed's lack of progress in getting her bedded was making him more aggressive. Options dwindling, he'd soon call off the relationship, or worse, he'd take what he wanted by force.

Ambretta first made contact with Saeed in this very bar. It wasn't difficult; it never was. With her natural beauty all she had to do was pose and make incidental eye contact from time to time. The marks came to her—even the shy ones. Ambretta spoke Farsi and Arabic, not well enough to pass herself off as native, but she could serve as a translator in a pinch. Of course Saeed never heard her speak anything other than Teenglish—*I know, right*—allowing her to be privy to Saeed's most private conversations.

Unfortunately, neither Saeed nor his associates had ever spoken of any operations they may, or may not be, planning. Unless drunk, Saeed only spoke English in public, as the general population is distrustful enough of English-speaking Middle-Eastern males, let alone "real Arabs." The men did have the occasional clandestine conversation in Arabic, which generally consisted of nothing more than Saeed boasting about his sexual conquests of Ambretta. There hadn't been any, but his associates didn't know any better. Or maybe they did; Saeed did not command much respect amongst his peers.

So, as they stood at the bar, she smiled like an unsuspecting dolt as Saeed used the cover of the club's music to brag in Arabic how hard he'd screwed her the night before. Ambretta was tiring of this assignment and tired of the man next to her with lust in his serpent-like eyes.

Thirty grueling minutes later she found herself in the passenger seat of Saeed's newer Nissan Altima. Her date slurred when he spoke, drooled when he didn't, and smelled of whiskey and trouble. Alone in the car, he'd become rude and condescending. He'd dropped all pretenses of being a nice guy. His patience with the pursuit of her body had waned and thus her usefulness to him was nearing an end.

Without discussion, Saeed had begun to drive to an apartment he shared with another man. She didn't relish having to fend off his advances and possibly those of his roommate, so she convinced him to drive to her loft by suggesting his patience might at last be rewarded. Saeed would not be happy when things didn't go his way.

As her date worked the wheel, studying his rearview mirror with glassed-over eyes, a ring tone emanated from the liner of his brown leather jacket. She'd never seen him use this phone before but had felt it when pressed up against him. Ambretta listened to the one-sided conversation spoken in Arabic.

"Yes, this is he…I'm alone…Yes…Tomorrow…Okay…I'll prepare immediately."

The twenty-second call was the first semi-interesting conversation Ambretta had overheard in the presence of this man; alcohol likely impairing his discretion. Ambretta, knowing the relationship was at an end, decided to push. She leaned over and put her hand on Saeed's right thigh, a little higher than she would have liked, a little lower than he would have preferred. She breathed into his ear, "What was that about, baby?"

"Nothing. Just business," he said, sliding down in his seat.

He enjoyed being mysterious, she thought.

"You know, I was thinking," Ambretta started. "It's time. You've waited long enough. How 'bout we go away for a few days, find a hotel, never leave the room."

Saeed looked at her with vacant, film coated eyes, "I cannot. I have a business trip."

Ambretta caressed his thigh, "Let me come with you, I'll make it worth your while."

"Impossible, I must go alone," Saeed said, lowering his gaze; her skirt had crept up high on her thighs. "But you're right, I have been very patient." He licked his lips, tongue darting out. Snake like.

Whatever Saeed's plans, they were important enough to ignore Ambretta's declaration of future sex; a goal that only a few minutes ago seemed to be number one on his bucket list. They were also clandestine enough he wouldn't allow Ambretta to accompany him on his trip. Most men would have no problem mixing a little pleasure with their business, especially this man and especially with this woman.

Ambretta leased a flat in downtown Atlanta near Centennial Olympic Park and the Georgia Aquarium. Parking for her unit was underneath a stylish, seven-story, red-brick building. Saeed pulled into the secure garage, bypassed the elevators and stairwell, and pulled the gray Nissan into a darkened, secluded parking space.

"As you said, I've been patient. Let's go up to your place."

It was a statement not a request.

Ambretta pouted, taking on a look of disappointment, "I can't. I told you, I live in a studio with a roommate. We'd have no privacy." Ambretta's loft was furnished with two beds, but no roommate slept there; neither did she for that matter.

"Then we'll do it here, in the car."

"No. Someone will see us."

Saeed undid his pants, "No one will see us; there is no one around."

Time to get out. Ambretta clutched her handbag and reached for the door. Saeed yanked the back of her hair eliciting a sharp yelp as several strands were extracted by the roots. "Saeed, No!" He clamped down on the nape of her neck and pushed her face down toward his erect penis.

Ambretta struggled on a course of action. She knew what she *wasn't* going to do. She almost gagged at the thought. The smell of acidic, curry-enhanced genital sweat didn't help matters.

She carried Oleoresin Capsicum in her purse and considered using it to spray the ugliness just inches from her face. OC spray applied to an erect penis is not an aphrodisiac. She of course could do something more permanent to the prick. Or she could try and reason her way out of this mess. Ten minutes ago she would have just grabbed him by the windpipe, dug her nails in and behind, and yanked with all her considerable strength. But now, *now*, the investigation might actually be going somewhere. She'd just decided to give reasoning a try when glass rained down on her head.

The driver's side window of the Altima exploded, followed closely by the dull thud of a heavy object striking Saeed's head. Then her "date" was sucked through the empty hole like a scene from a horror movie. "Shit." Ambretta leapt from the passenger side of the vehicle, ran to the driver's side as Saeed, belly down, penis out, was dragged across the concrete parking area between a van and wall. She arrived at her rescuer's side just in time to see the serrated edge of a knife flash out to his side. She recognized what her savior had in mind and grabbed his wrist.

"Ben, no!"

Ambretta's grip prevented what would have been the second man this night to have been emasculated by a Thorpe.

THREE

CARLOS BENITEZ WAS A UNITED States Army Ranger…
Hooaa! But before Carlos became a Ranger, he was an Almighty
Latin King. And when you join the Nation, you are crowned for
life…*Por vida!* There was no changing teams—*no set trippin' outta
the Kings*—not with the Vicelords, or Cobras and certainly not with
a Folk Nation set or even the United States Armed Forces. Carlos
couldn't leave the Kings no matter how badly he wanted. He knew
that now. They'd invested too much into Carlos and a few others like
him. He was theirs forever, like it or not.

Carlos was born and raised in Chicago—the Motherland—
amongst a Puerto Rican faction of the Latin Kings. The LKs are one
of the oldest and largest street gangs in Chicago and enjoy the
reputation of being one of the most organized modern gangs in the
world. Puerto Ricans formed the Almighty Latin King/Queen Nation
in the 1970s, and it has grown in size and sophistication ever since.
But times have changed and Puerto Ricans no longer dominate the
Nation. Chicago has the second largest Mexican population in the
United States, outnumbered only by Los Angeles. The influx of his
Mexican brothers changed the dynamics of the city and with it the
Kings. And though any nationality and race is eligible for
membership, the Kings have become predominantly Mexican.

A splinter Latin King chapter started in the New York Prison system before spilling out onto the streets. The LKs are one of the fastest growing street gangs in New York City. Nationwide, the ALKQN membership is thought to exceed 50,000 members with over half of those residing in the Chicago area alone.

The product of a Puerto Rican father and a Hood Rat, his black prostitute mother lost custody of Carlos when he was three years old. He'd never known his father and didn't remember his mother. He didn't want to. He moved from foster home to foster home and when he turned ten, was adopted by a Puerto Rican couple. The husband and wife received government money for taking on their new ward, and unbeknownst to Carlos, they received cash from a benefactor— one Alberto Vega—a high-ranking Latin King. Carlos' new parents had just one obligation, well, only one they knew of. All they had to do was provide Carlos with a stable home, prevent him from getting into trouble, and keep the arrangement with Vega a secret. Vega would be introduced to Carlos as Uncle Alberto. That's the way it started. Now, twelve years later, he had a better understanding of how *everyone* had been puppeteered by Vega—Uncle Alberto.

Carlos' adoptive parents, Esteban and Luisa Arroyo, were a well-meaning, hardworking, immigrant couple who tried to start a life in the great United States, but found the American dream much harder to achieve than they'd anticipated. Esteban and Luisa had been unable to conceive, so when Alberto approached them about "helping the Puerto Rican people" by adopting one of their own— and getting paid for it—they accepted. They grew to love their son, and appreciate the mysterious "uncle" who seemed quite concerned with Carlos' upbringing, making himself a permanent fixture in the boy's life. It was in those early years that Uncle Alberto started shaping the boy's mind. "The Kings have big plans for you. I have big plans for you," Alberto would often say. Young Carlos didn't have a notion as to what those plans might be. Now he did.

Carlos sat, right calf on left knee, in a window seat of an American Airlines Boeing 777 solemnly looking down from the heavens at the mass of lights he once called home. Refocusing, he studied his reflection in the same window. Dressed in a tank top and shorts, his attire reflected the weather of his departure city, Miami, Florida, rather than that of Chicago. His left shoulder sported a distinctive tattoo, the image of a shield divided into quadrants. In the upper left quadrant was the sun, in the lower right a star. A lightning bolt cut diagonally across the shield occupying the two empty spaces. Above the image was one word, a word which meant a lot to Carlos. *Ranger.* Also visible in the reflection was a souvenir from one of his tours in Afghanistan, a deep scar which started on his forehead and disappeared into his hairline. The sight prompted him to shift his gaze to yet another Army memento on his right calf. This wasn't a tattoo, it was a bullet wound he'd earned, and he *had* earned it, in an ambush just outside of Asadabad, not five miles from the Pakistan border.

Carlos shifted in his seat and retrieved a worn photo from his wallet. He looked down at the image that had lifted his spirits out of many a snake pit he'd found himself in while serving his country. Staring at the photo, he felt the lumbering jetliner descend and realized the image wouldn't lift him or his plane from the abyss into which they were falling. The two faces looking back at him were precisely why he had to fulfill a promise he'd made when he was only ten years old and too young to know better.

With the exception of Uncle Alberto, Carlos had been isolated from the Kings while growing up. He had no gang tattoos, engaged in no criminal activity, and had few childhood fights. The neighborhood kids let Carlos be; they knew the Kings had his back.

Carlos made good marks but if his grades slipped it was his Uncle who disciplined him, not his adoptive parents. Alberto encouraged him to participate in sports and he excelled at baseball. When Carlos graduated from high school, his GPA, ACT scores, and station in life earned him scholarships to several universities. Alberto dismissed the idea of higher education. Instead, Carlos was to join the Army. In particular, Uncle Alberto expected him to enter a combat unit. It was then that Carlos got an inkling of what his fate might be.

Carlos took to the Army naturally and its NCOs shaped him into a true DICK—Dedicated Infantry Combat Killer. But they'd also shaped him into something else. A man. He had pride. Pride in his country, pride in his fellow soldiers, and most importantly, pride in himself. Early in his military career, he met the woman staring back at him in the photo, fallen in love almost instantly, and married her two short months later. She too had been in the Army, and was three years Carlos' elder. He never told his wife, Eva, about his gang affiliation. He was too embarrassed. Plus, that part of him seemed like another person and was a lifestyle he never engaged in to begin with. The Kings kept his record clean on purpose—to get first-rate training in the art of killing men.

Shortly after marrying, Eva became pregnant, finished up her military career behind a desk, and mustered out of the army. She returned to her hometown of Orlando, Florida, to live and raise their daughter, Celestina, until Carlos discharged from the Army. Only his adoptive parents and a few close Army buddies knew of his new family. Carlos earned his way into the famed 75th Ranger Regiment where he finished up his stint in the military. Trying to distance himself from Alberto, Carlos made fewer and fewer calls back home to his uncle, making excuses that were not hard to come by when one was busy fighting a war. Carlos had plans and none of them involved the Kings. He would join Eva and their three-year-old daughter in Orlando, work while attending college part-time, and confront Uncle Alberto about his desire to leave the Kings.

Those plans had gone to shit. Two weeks before returning to the States, Carlos received a call from his uncle. Alberto told Carlos his stint in the military had earned him a vacation on his "uncle's dime." Alberto wanted to meet him in Miami, Florida, where they'd spend a week relaxing at the Royal Palm South Beach Resort. Carlos couldn't tell Alberto he was anxious to return to his wife and daughter, because as far as Alberto knew, they didn't exist. And that's just the way Carlos intended to keep it.

Carlos decided Miami would be the perfect place to tell Alberto he wanted out of the Kings. They'd be far from Chicago and away from Alberto's minions. If a physical confrontation ensued, Carlos was confident he'd win the contest despite being seriously outsized. Big for a Latino, Alberto stood an inch or two over six feet and probably weighed around 220 pounds. His short arms and legs didn't harmonize with his long torso; he was one of those guys who, when sliding off a barstool, actually shrank in height. Large but soft, he had fleshy cheeks, another half a chin and a small potbelly, yet managed to maintain a youthful appearance. His full head of thick black hair helped but it was more than that. A stranger would probably guess Alberto to be in his lower thirties but Carlos figured him to be at least a decade older. It didn't matter. Even if Alberto was twenty, Carlos could pull that bar stool out from under his fat ass and club him over the head with it.

Alberto left instructions for Carlos to meet him in room 122 of the Royal Palm. Upon arrival, Alberto would take Carlos to the lobby and get him situated. Carlos had no intentions of staying. He rented a car and parked it outside the hotel, leaving his luggage inside the vehicle. From there, he would go straight to the room, tell Alberto to go screw himself, and explain he was a grown man who would no longer be exploited.

Carlos marched forward prepared for a confrontation. He pounded on the door and was startled when his wife, Eva, yanked it open and jumped into his unsuspecting arms. Carlos stood there in stunned silence as his wife embraced him with kisses and sobs. Then Celestina padded out of the room and said, "Daddy." Carlos dropped to his ass, his wife's legs still wrapped around his waist, as the three of them sat in the hotel's hallway. Eva smothered him with affection as his precious daughter clung tightly to his neck.

When the greetings subsided a shocked Carlos questioned his wife's presence. After admonishing Carlos for not letting her know of Uncle Alberto's existence, she explained how she received a card in the mail complete with airline tickets and hotel reservations.

Alberto followed the letter with a phone call and apologized for not being in contact earlier. As a "delayed wedding gift" he'd arranged for Eva and Celestina to meet Carlos in Miami for a week's vacation, telling Eva the arrangement would be a surprise to Carlos and asked her to keep it a secret.

How had Alberto learned of his wife and daughter? It didn't matter. Uncle Alberto had sent Carlos a pimp's message. A not-so-subtle warning disguised as a gift that told Carlos he and his family could be found—anywhere. Alberto was a pimp of men, and Carlos was his whore.

The 777 touched down on one of O'Hare's six primary runways, indicating a new tour of duty. Unlike his time in Afghanistan, this tour didn't have a predetermined expiration date. This tour would last a lifetime—as brief as that might be.

FOUR

WEARING A SET OF BLACK thermal sweats, head back, eyes closed, soaking in the noontime sun, Thorpe sat on an unattached wooden deck perched over a creek running forty yards behind his home. He'd killed Jeremy Johnson less than thirteen hours ago, disposed of his tainted clothing, returned home, and fallen asleep, instantly.

He sat among the oaks and towering pecans, with the soft gurgle of the creek in the background. Something less peaceful rested on a small wooden table next to his elevated, Adidas-clad feet: a well-oiled, 9mm Beretta, lying on its right side, ejection port down. Thorpe wasn't a fan of the 9mm Parabellum cartridge (it didn't pack much punch), but since it was one of the most popular rounds in the world, he thought he should be familiar with the way the pistols handled.

But Thorpe wasn't concerning himself with principles of hydrostatic shock, he was trying to uncover any mistakes he might have made the night before. While there were many, none had been entirely avoidable. He hadn't known he'd catch Jeremy in the act; hadn't known he'd be saving little Evan Birchfield—only that he'd be saving some young boy, somewhere, sometime. Jeremy was a pedophile of the worst sort; and once a pedophile, always a pedophile. In rescuing the boy Thorpe also saved the child's parents, for no mother or father should have to outlive their children, especially through an act of violence. Thorpe knew that first hand.

Sipping hot coffee from a mug, Thorpe considered the TPD-issued Ford Contour he'd left parked on the side of the highway as he killed Fat Bastard. The plates were bogus and he'd chosen the car because it was nondescript; it'd take more than someone remembering a Contour parked near a murder scene to make a connection to Thorpe. *Murder.* Murder seemed a harsh word for killing a monster. Thorpe felt the word "execution" more appropriate. "Extermination" better yet. *Is that why he'd begun referring to Jeremy as "Fat Bastard"—to dehumanize the man in order to trivialize his own actions?* Thorpe shook his head. He'd wrestle with ethics later. He always did. Right now he needed to concentrate on external repercussions.

Thorpe pictured the bumper-beeper's battery pack when he'd pried it loose from the Chevy's undercarriage. It'd been covered with blood, hair, skin, and fat, and would require multiple cleanings to remove DNA evidence. But the bumper-beeper wouldn't be a problem unless authorities developed Thorpe as a suspect. And really only one person could begin to point investigators in the right direction: nine-year-old Evan Birchfield.

Thorpe had donned a black balaclava before releasing the boy but certain characteristics would have been noticeable. Evan, if he were observant, would be able to describe his rescuer as white, around six feet tall, with an athletic build. And of course there were Thorpe's unnaturally bright green eyes. *He really needed to invest in a set of colored contacts.*

Thorpe could have avoided contact with the boy if he'd left him tethered in the back of the camper. Less interaction would have been more prudent, but the boy had been through enough. Instead, Thorpe risked much by parking the Chevy on the highway, doing away with the flashlight, climbing in the back, and releasing him. Having learned his name, Thorpe asked young Evan for a huge favor.

Explaining his need for autonomy would have been too

complex for a boy experiencing a colossal amount of stress. Instead, Thorpe put himself on the nine-year-old's level and told Evan that he, Thorpe, was a lot like Batman. No one could know Batman's identity, or he wouldn't be able to do his job. "The investigators will want to talk to you. They mean well but they'll get real tricky trying to find out who I am. Maybe they'll even tell you I was with the fat bastard who took you. Can you remember three things Evan?"

In the two minutes he spent talking with Evan, the boy promised to describe Thorpe as black, skinny, and driving a dark two-door vehicle. Thorpe doubted the description would last long. Kids are easy to crack but sometimes the hardest to tell if they're lying to begin with, particularly following a traumatic event. Promise made, Thorpe left Evan with the truck and Fat Bastard's cell phone, which Evan proudly announced he could operate.

His recollecting interrupted, Thorpe was brought back to the present by the nose of one of his best friends nestled in his crotch.

"What the hell are you sniffing? I haven't been cheating."

Trixie retracted her head, walked over to Al and licked him on his nose. Al and Trixie were German shepherds, guard dogs, family. They were two of several friends who had helped Thorpe survive a bloodbath on his property.

A few miles outside of Mounds, Oklahoma, Thorpe's twenty acres was a twenty-minute—fifteen if you were in a hurry, twelve if you were a cop in a hurry—drive from downtown Tulsa. West of his deck sat a newer barn Thorpe had converted into a gym—a place where he'd once killed a man. In front of Thorpe's house ran a seldom-traveled gravel road—a road on which Thorpe once killed a man. Across the road lay a vast expanse of wooded property. And yes, he'd also once killed a man in those woods. That was just a month ago; seemed more like a year. The events of February began crowding Thorpe's mind and he fought to push them back. Many questions remained unanswered and he doubted he'd ever find the answers. His thoughts turned to Ambretta, hoping one day...

Thorpe's cell phone chirped on the deck beside his chair

prompting him to sit up and retrieve the burdensome piece of technology. It was Robert Hull, the sergeant over TPD's Homicide Unit. Last month's events had forged a tight bond between the two. Now Thorpe considered Hull to be one of his two best friends—Al and Trixie excluded.

"What's up, Bob?"

"You hear about Jeremy Johnson?" Bob sounded like a kindergarten boy who'd just gotten a Red Ryder BB gun for Christmas.

"Yeah, caught it on the morning news. Didn't learn much from them though. You got the scoop?"

"I do indeed. Crazy shit. The sick fuck had a nine-year-old boy in the back of his camper shell. Snatched the kid in Tulsa and was headed north on 169 when he pulled off the highway, probably to take the kid right there in the back of his truck, when some dude showed up and cut off his dick."

Thorpe used his best surprised voice, "Cut off his dick?"

"Cut his dick. The. Fuck. Off." Hull confirmed.

"No shit? Who says there's no justice in this world?"

"Justice found his ass for sure. The news reported he was stabbed and run over. That ain't exactly how it went down. Like I said, someone cut off—not stabbed, but *cut off*—his dick. Then as the fat fuck crawled away on his belly, Batman took Jeremy's own truck and..."

Thorpe interrupted, "Batman?"

"That's what the kid called his rescuer...the name kinda caught on. Anyway, Batman drives Fat Fuck's own truck up on Fat Fuck's back. Then he hits the gas. Man, I guess there's pieces of Jeremy meat over half of northeastern Oklahoma...but you know what the coolest thing is?"

"Can't get much cooler," Thorpe argued.

"Oh, but it does...the fat piece-of-shit crawled another twenty yards after his back was peeled off 'im. He lived a good while...that cocksucker suffered!"

"Huh, wild shit."

"That's it? 'Wild shit?' Come on, a child-killing pedophile got exactly what he deserved and you say, 'Wild shit?' Bunch of us are going out tonight to celebrate his demise. You in?"

"I'm working tonight, but I might catch up with you guys later. By the way…who's Batman?"

"Don't know. All the kid says is the guy who saved him is Batman. Says he drove away in the Batmobile. I'm not so damn sure the kid doesn't believe it. Stress does some crazy shit. Just in case, I'm going to find Christian Bale and shake his hand," Hull joked.

"How do you know you're not looking for Val Kilmer, George Clooney, or Michael Keaton?"

"What are you, some kind of Batman nerd? Besides, those guys wouldn't cut off a guy's dick. Only Christian Bale is dark enough to do that."

"Good point. I'll catch up with you tonight."

"By the way, you forgot Adam West."

"Who?" Thorpe asked mockingly of the older man.

"Fuck you."

He suspected when Hull had him alone, the detective would ask where he'd picked up a Batmobile. He'd be joking…somewhat. Seemed like every time a shitbag got killed in or around Tulsa, Hull peered at him with arched eyebrows. He knew of Thorpe's capabilities, though February's events had left Hull more than a little confused.

Just over a year ago, Thorpe's life had been forever altered. He'd come home from work to find his wife, Erica, dead— murdered, then charged upstairs to his daughter's bedroom to discover Ella's cold and lifeless body.

Thorpe trembled as he remembered rolling his daughter over. Her beautiful face in ruins, the exit wound from a bullet having removed her lower jaw. He'd smoothed her hair away from her vacant eyes, closed the lids, and pulled her in tight. He sat on the bloody carpet rocking Ella in his arms. Whoever Thorpe had been then, died the same night as his wife and daughter.

Drowning in memories, Thorpe looked at Al and Trixie and said, "Earmuffs." The two dogs tore off toward the road. Far enough away he didn't fear for their hearing, Thorpe sprang from his chair, and though right-handed, he grabbed the Berretta with his left. He swung the weapon in the direction of the creek and emptied the magazine into a silhouette target posted thirty-five yards distant. Eyes refocusing from sights to target, Thorpe was pleased with his accuracy. He bent over, retrieved a heavy nylon "go bag" slung it over his shoulders, jumped the railing of the creek, and started down a jogging trail he'd carved into his property and that of several neighbors.

Legs pumping, he fought to push thoughts of his family out of his mind. Physical pain battled his emotions for dominance. A mile later he jumped up and grabbed a tree limb for his first set of twenty pull-ups and felt his head clearing. Two and a half miles of trail behind him he reentered his property and scaled a six-foot wall he'd erected in the middle of the path. Landing on the other side of the barrier he knocked out fifty pushups, slipped off the heavy pack, withdrew a Sig Saur .45 and an extra magazine, reslung the weight, and charged ahead. Two hundred meters farther along, he encountered the first of ten cans dangling from ropes and spaced along the path at varying distances. Anyone can shoot while stationary and rested. His heart rate in the 150s, his arms like lead, he shot the cans on the move. The last two hundred meters brought him back to where he'd started. Sprinting out of the creek bed, Thorpe dumped his pack, collapsed, and vomited on the ground. It was the best he'd felt all morning.

FIVE

CARLOS LEANED AGAINST A FILTHY living room wall. The bleak space was part of a blighted house in the Lower West Side of Chicago near an area local gangs referred to as "Chi Town." He stood, back to the wall, watching two Latin Kings he didn't know and didn't want to know. The men were seated on a crusty, 1980s era couch. Its upholstery depicted wagon trains and stagecoaches of all things.

Made obvious by the greetings they'd given one another upon arrival, the two men were, at the very least, acquaintances. However, their apparent familiarity hadn't inspired much conversation; the room was as silent as a church on New Year's Eve.

Carlos had been ordered to be at this address at 7:00 p.m., on time, and to stay until he received further instruction. He'd been here an hour now and hadn't been told shit. He didn't know why he was here, or what would happen next—things he'd gotten used to while serving in the military. Hurry the fuck up. And wait.

The poorly insulated house allowed him to hear an engine idle into the driveway followed by the thud of a car door slamming shut. Carlos readied himself as he watched the front door swing open. A dark-skinned male walked into the house, thumped his chest, and "represented" with a closed fist—thumb, index, and pinky finger extended—the universal hand sign for the Latin Kings. It also happened to mean "I love you" in American Sign Language. Along with the gesture he stated, "King love," and gave the other men knowing smiles. Carlos only received a hard stare.

Like Carlos, the man had a complexion that made it hard to decipher if he was black, Latino, or some combination of the two. Judging by how the other two scrambled to their feet, Carlos figured the man possessed a higher rank in the Kings' hierarchy. The newcomer dropped a black Nike gym bag on the couch and approached the larger of the two underlings, "King Loc! Nigga it's been a minute," he said.

"Fo sure, King Ghost, fo sure."

King Loc obviously wasn't black, but every gangbanger these days addressed one another as "Nigga" no matter what race they were.

King Ghost turned and greeted Loc's partner, King Speedy, with a shoulder slap before turning his attention to Carlos. "You ready to serve, Soldier Boy?" he asked. His insides full of dread, Carlos nodded dutifully. It had begun.

Ghost ordered Carlos to strip, passing his clothing on to Loc and Speedy who searched his pants, shirt, jacket, socks, and shoes, with a cursory check of his briefs. Ghost kept Carlos's Tag Heuer watch, slid it on his own wrist, and told him he'd get the timepiece back "after."

The watch was more than expensive jewelry. It'd been a gift.

"You're not taking the fucking watch."

"What'd you say motherfucker? You giving me orders, Soldier Boy?"

Ghost closed the distance fast. He leaned down and pressed his forehead against Carlos', trying to intimidate him.

"I'll kill you right here motherfucker," Ghost hissed, the veins in his neck appearing like highways on a roadmap.

Carlos didn't back down, "I'll be shittin' down your throat before you can order your goons to do the heavy lifting, pendejo. Now give me that watch back before I take your whole fucking arm."

Ghost kept his head pressed against Carlos'. He'd been put in a jam. If he walked away he'd look weak in front of Loc and Speedy. "You lucky Alberto ordered me not to beat you. Not till after anyway. 'Sides, I don't want to fight a naked little bitch like you, you'd probably like it." Ghost took a step back and continued, "Alberto said to take your watch; half the fucking things have GPS anymore and he don't trust you. You get it back after. You don't like it, tough shit." Ghost turned on his heel, headed for the door, and spoke over his shoulder, "When this is done I'm gonna fuck you up."

Ghost had backed down. Carlos knew it, Ghost knew it, everyone in the room knew it. And even though he he'd pay for it later, Carlos couldn't help but get in one last parting shot as Ghost stormed out the door. "You put a scratch on that watch and they'll be scraping pieces of your pussy off the floor. Bitch."

Carlos would undoubtedly come to regret his disrespect. He'd half expected to be given a "violation" for keeping his marriage a secret from Uncle Alberto. To Latin Kings, a violation wasn't something one committed, it was something one earned. Violations, punishments doled out by fellow Kings, usually involved a beating with a predetermined time limit. Minor violations lasted anywhere from a few seconds to a couple of minutes. Major violations lasted three minutes and sometimes longer. A "head-to-toe" violation—for the most severe infractions—meant the punished could be hit in the groin, head, joints…anywhere. Members have died from head-to-toe violations and many more have been hospitalized. The worst thing: you weren't allowed to fight back. The condemned stood against a wall while his liver was beaten into hamburger meat. Carlos doubted he'd receive a head-to-toe. Alberto had invested too much time and money to risk killing him. Not yet, anyway.

Carlos barely stood an inch or two over five and half feet and probably weighed less than a hundred and forty pounds with his boots on; all muscle and grit. He had no doubt he could kick Loc's and Speedy's asses up one side of the squalid living room and down the other. Still, he'd have taken his beating like a good little whore.

Not yet fully civilianized, Carlos' hair was just shy of being shaved. The short haircut exposed the scar that ran from his forehead back into his hairline. Though he'd received the scar in combat, the wound wasn't worthy of boasting. He'd been taking small-arms fire and been in full tactical retreat—AKA sprinting for his damned life—when he didn't duck low enough while running through a blown out hole in the side of a building. A piece of reinforcing metal went up and under his Kevlar helmet peeling off half his scalp.

The wound bled profusely, as head wounds do. His face became a blood waterfall and every time one of his buddies caught a glimpse of him they thought he'd been shot between the eyes. He probably could've made up a good story about the wound, but alas, the event had been witnessed by his fellow Rangers. After getting stitched up, Carlos caught a lot of shit over the incident, and was tagged with the nickname "Too Tall" despite his diminutive stature.

Speedy tossed back Carlos' clothing, as Loc retrieved the gym bag from the couch and placed it on an old laminate kitchen table. Loc opened the bag, reached inside, and pulled out three semi-automatic pistols.

"You know how to use one of these, Soldier Boy?"

Carlos nodded and thought, *a hell of a lot better than you ever will,* as Loc returned the weapons to the bag, zipped it shut, and headed for the door.

"Let's go," was all he said.

SIX

SOUTHEAST OF DOWNTOWN TULSA, NEARING 12th and
Quincy, Thorpe passed a prostitute picking at pus-filled sores. With
her free hand, she tried in vain to flag down customers. The woman
elicited a memory and disquieted laugh from Thorpe, though the
incident hadn't been too damned funny at the time. On that earlier
occasion, Thorpe had spotted a particularly enthusiastic prostitute—
waving him on like a third base coach to a Little Leaguer streaking
around second—and even though he didn't work Vice, thought he'd
perform his civic duty and remove a public nuisance from the streets.

He'd picked up the woman and in the process of "making the
deal," she'd used her forefinger and thumb to pull out a rancid pair
of dentures. She set her saliva drenched falsies on the dash of his
pickup and proceeded to tell him how good it was going to
"sssfeeel." Thorpe shivered at the memory; *sometimes those Vice*
guys earned their paychecks. He hadn't picked up a prostitute since.
Besides, as the Vice guys with their twisted humor liked to say, "It
doesn't matter how many arrests you make, the pussy will continue
to flow." No, he'd rather stick to arresting gangbangers. And
gangbanging is what'd brought him back tonight.

One block away from ground zero, Thorpe eased his truck to
the side of the street. He didn't have to worry about blast waves, but
a crackhead or two, might, at subsonic speeds, be cast his general

direction. The area, comprised of apartment buildings and single family homes with a mixture of blacks, whites, Hispanics, dealers, whores, and homeless, was in no real danger of being flattened by flying crackheads. The place had been a shithole for years but new businesses had sprouted in the area and with them came a classier brand of citizen. Like wildlife on the edge of a sprawling city, the local dopers were slowly being pushed out of their natural environment. Thorpe's crew was here to facilitate their migration.

A small group of black males, all known gang members, had been standing outside a red brick apartment building slinging rock on a dimly lit corner for the last two hours. Well, the bangers didn't involve themselves with direct transactions; they let the smokers take all the risks.

The plan was for one of Thorpe's investigators to drive up to the group and buy crack cocaine, being careful not to call it by its name or be quickly identified as an undercover officer; he'd ask for some rock, hard, cavie, or simply a twenty. The investigator in this case, Jake Holloway, excelled at buy-busts because of his looks; at twenty-six years of age, he could easily pass for nineteen. Tall, skinny, with long greasy, unkempt hair, complete with a frugal attempt at a beard, he didn't look like a cop. He looked like he belonged on a skateboard.

Hidden in the rear passenger area of Jake's Ford Explorer was Jack Yelton. Jack would be lying on the floorboard underneath a blanket. He'd have a shotgun pointed toward the driver's side of the Explorer in case the gangbangers decided they wanted to rob Jake instead of sell him dope. Sometimes that happened, especially to white boys. Crack-seeking robbery victims tended not to make police reports. At the very least, Jake would probably be sold "Turkey-dope," or fake crack cocaine. Caucasians were often sold a small chip of disguised soap or other material, passed off as crack. Easy money. A one-dollar bar of soap could be cut up into five hundred dollars' worth of fake dope. Selling fake drugs is still a felony, the official charge being Unlawful Delivery of an Imitation

Controlled Drug.

Thorpe stationed himself in an area where he thought runners would be funneled—the path of least resistance. As sergeant of the unit, he could do what he wanted. Prudence would suggest he place himself in an area where he could oversee the entire operation and not become too personally involved, but one of his biggest weaknesses as a supervisor was his need to be "in the shit."

Another of Thorpe's investigators sat in the alley just north of his position. Together they constituted "containment."

Using a secure channel, which would be scrambled on public police scanners, Jake broadcast to the arrest team and to containment that they were about to "make the corner."

A minute later, Jake stated, "It's a good deal," and went on to describe the seller and likely stash place for the rest of the dope. The arrest team, five GU investigators in an old and green Aerostar van, acknowledged the transaction and announced their intent to approach. The members of the arrest team were dressed like Thorpe—black football-style raid jerseys and nylon drop-down holsters.

Thorpe watched the "jump-out" van turn north on Rockford Avenue. The driver, Officer Tyrone Benson, had his raid jersey concealed beneath a jacket. He would pull up to the dealers pretending to be a new customer, then the three men and one woman would bail out of the sliding rear back door and take down the group.

Thorpe exited his truck, took a deep breath of nighttime air, and prepared for the inevitable. The radio crackled and a breathless Tyrone advised two "runners" were headed west toward containment officers. *Game on.* Thorpe jogged north down the short alley with hopes of intercepting one or both of the westbound rabbits. He braced himself with his right hand behind a six-foot wooden privacy fence and waited blindly at the corner.

Thorpe heard the distinctive sound of rubber soles slapping pavement and readied himself to deliver a pursuit ending blow. Just prior to the footsteps reaching Thorpe's place of concealment, he heard them slow, stop, and felt the fence shake. *The asshole jumped a fence into someone's back yard.* Thorpe stepped around the corner and almost collided with the second runner whose steps had been much quieter. The banger tried to stop. Instead, his feet went out from underneath him and he skidded on his ass. Thorpe, smiling, hovered over him and pointed his Glock between the man's eyes. The banger didn't see the boot coming. It wasn't Thorpe's boot; Donnie Edwards came up beside the seated man, whose eyes were focused on the pistol in his face, and Charlie Browned his head. But unlike Charlie Brown, Lucy wasn't there to play the spoiler and Donnie didn't miss.

Thorpe holstered his weapon, assisted Donnie with securing the half-conscious prisoner, then scaled the fence in search of runner number one. The suspect, unaware officers had detected his entrance into the yard—probably hadn't gone far. Thorpe hit the ground, withdrew his Glock, and activated the attached M6 light. A driveway led to the back yard and to an old rusted Oldsmobile. On the other side of the Olds, in the southwest corner, stood an open storage shed. Thorpe performed a quick peek under the abandoned car then headed for the shed, which was full of junk but easy enough to clear.

Noticing the house didn't have an accessible crawl space— always the favorite hiding place for rabbits—Thorpe turned his attention to the abandoned car and found the driver's side door wasn't flush with the body. Car doors are difficult to seal if you don't slam them. Perhaps his missing runner had tried to silently pull the door closed, leaving it slightly ajar.

Thorpe cast his light through a window noting the rear seat of the two-door car was full of trash, covered with dust, and being used as a makeshift storage shed. On the inside, stamped in the dust surrounding the driver's side door lock, four perfect finger impressions offered a clue even Doctor Watson could follow. Thorpe tried the door and despite it not being sealed, found it locked.

Thorpe thought for a moment, retrieved a canister of pepper spray from his belt, and used his ASP baton to knock out the driver's side wing window. He filled the interior of the Olds with the chemical irritant. Canister emptied, Thorpe took a position behind the trunk, and waited.

"Sarge, you alright?" Donnie yelled from the other side of the fence.

"Yeah. Should be finished here in just a sec."

Thorpe, watching the ineffectual workings of his human bug bomb, and beginning to doubt his investigative talents, smiled when the Cutlass started rocking. Thorpe illuminated the interior and saw a black male pawing in the fog. Runner number one had risen from the debris in the back floorboard like a blind and rabid prairie dog from his burrow. The man fumbled for the handle, rolled over into the front seat, and stumbled out the driver's side door, eyes closed and foot-long strand of snot hanging from his nose.

Thorpe delivered an elbow just below the man's armpit, dislodging the strand of snot, and sending its owner crashing to the ground. Focused on the suspect's hands, Thorpe lost track of the mucus as it arced through the air, but was relieved not to have felt something warm and wet land on the back of his neck.

Thorpe secured his prisoner and searched him for weapons. Finding none, he stood him up and walked him down the drive and around the fence. By the time they reached Donnie, a new snot-pendulum swung well below the cuffed man's chin. Donnie and Tyrone took control of his prisoner and Thorpe returned to the Cutlass.

After opening its doors and allowing the car to air out, Thorpe went to work finding a loaded Smith and Wesson .40 caliber pistol and a fat sack of dope on the rear floorboard. Thorpe wished he could keep the weapon for his extracurricular activities but they needed it to accentuate the prisoner's charges, namely, being in possession of a firearm during the commission of a felony. The Tulsa County District Attorney, however, would probably dismiss the gun charge if the suspect agreed to plead to simple possession of a controlled drug. Thus, the DA's conviction rate would remain impressively high and he'd be sure and use those numbers during his re-election bid.

Thorpe had made thousands of drug arrests, and out of all those cases he'd testified in a jury trial fewer than ten times. Snot-man had earned a twenty-year sentence. But elections needed to be won and caseloads needed to be reduced, so in all likelihood, the suspect would be given a three-to-five year sentence and would be out in less than two, once again preying on the citizens of Tulsa. Thorpe looked at the pistol and sighed. If snot-man didn't have an extensive criminal history, and Thorpe didn't turn in the weapon, he might not see prison at all.

Thorpe's penchant for collecting untraceable weapons began after finding his family slain inside their South Tulsa home. Evil had entered his house and slaughtered his wife. His daughter witnessed the killing of her mother and had run upstairs in a feeble effort to flee. She'd been caught in her bedroom and shot to death. Thorpe returned home from work to discover the bloody aftermath. Something deep inside him cracked that night and a malignant tumor breached the fissure; the tentacles of which eventually reached his family's killers and left Thorpe a broken man.

As supervisor of TPD's Organized Gang Unit, Thorpe thought the murders might have been related to his position on the department. After all, he and his investigators were responsible for putting many of Tulsa's "worst" behind bars. The list of potential suspects seemed endless. Thorpe waited for homicide detectives to catch a break in the case and develop viable leads. While in limbo, Thorpe amassed a collection of weapons that couldn't be traced back to him or his unit. Had suspects in his family's murder ever been identified, they never would have made it to trial. Thorpe had been prepared to kill everyone involved, even if it meant his death or a life behind bars.

Ultimately, the investigation stalled and Thorpe decided to handle matters himself. He compiled a list of known killers and associates of killers who operated in Tulsa's gang-laden underworld.

His plan had been to capture these men, ignore the niceties of interviewing them with their attorneys present—or, for that matter, the niceties of any human compassion—and identify suspects on his own.

Thorpe had gotten lucky with his first target, Marcel Newman. Newman hadn't known much, but he'd known a name. The name led Thorpe to a man who provided him with information that sent him spiraling even further into despair. The two men who killed his family had been slain the same night they perpetrated the murders. But what shocked Thorpe to his soul, was the senseless murder of his wife and daughter had been the direct result of a plan orchestrated by fellow police officers—his brothers in blue. A small group of officers who referred to themselves as "The Band" had let paranoia ravage their minds. When Thorpe's unit inadvertently arrested several of their associates and family members on drug charges, they feared discovery and feared for their freedom. In response, two gang members were enlisted to plant drugs in Thorpe's home, a plan that had gone horribly wrong.

Thorpe uncovered the officer who sent the two gang members to his home, isolated him, and plunged a hunting knife into the man's throat. The other collaborators correctly surmised Thorpe's involvement and countered. The end result was an abstruse bloody war which left several Band members—and a part of Thorpe—dead.

During the incident, Thorpe spent a few short days with an attractive FBI agent, Ambretta Collins. His partnership with her had been forced. His feelings for her had been a mixture of resentment, fear, and distrust. But in the end, he'd fallen in love with Ambretta—or whatever the hell her real name was. He knew now she wasn't really with the FBI. For reasons still unknown, she'd helped Thorpe evade those trying to kill him, and had provided misdirection so that he wasn't a suspect in any of the Band member's killings.

Who she was, and why she'd done these things, were questions constantly gnawing at Thorpe, secondary only to whether Ambretta's feelings for him were genuine. He might never know; it was unlikely he'd ever see her again. But he held hope. And hope was in short supply these days.

Thorpe had lost faith in the justice system and in humanity. Countless shitheads breezed through this world without an ounce of compassion. Some disguised their true selves, amassing fortunes or political power at others' expense while being sure to dole out a few funds to charitable organizations for a nice tax deduction and personal acclaim. Others didn't bother hiding their self-serving interests. Sociopaths like Jeremy Johnson who took satisfaction in the ruin of innocents. Those were the people Thorpe had recently vowed to eradicate.

Justice system beyond repair, it allowed predators free range on the sheep of the world. Thorpe would protect those who couldn't protect themselves since the liberal lobbyists, judges, lawyers, and politicians didn't allow police officers to adequately perform their jobs any longer. The sentences Thorpe dispensed wouldn't be shortened for good behavior, overcrowding, or so-called rehabilitation; they were permanent.

It was his religious beliefs that left him conflicted. Most modern-day Christians preached the "turn the other cheek" philosophy, conveniently ignoring Bible passages much less forgiving. Thorpe figured if every Christian simply turned the other cheek, there wouldn't be any Christian cheeks left to turn; they'd have all been slaughtered long ago.

Praying for men like Jeremy Johnson was pointless. Jeremy would not stop. Ever. And Jeremy was just one of a multitude of monsters prowling this earth. Maybe, just maybe, Thorpe thought, he could be God's answer to some parent's prayer: "Don't let anything bad happen to my baby."

Thorpe shook his head. *When I start thinking I'm heaven-sent is when I know I'm full of shit.* He'd leave philosophy to men who could afford such privileges. But he did know this: Jeremy Johnson destroyed innocent lives and Thorpe couldn't stop him legally; but he damned sure stopped him his way. Better some piece-of-shit die than an innocent child be raped and murdered. Thorpe also knew in the end God might judge him with equal ruthlessness. If that was the case, his eternity would be spent in a place he'd helped send others.

SEVEN

CARLOS SAT IN THE BACK SEAT of a rented four-door
Chrysler with the metallic taste of stomach acid percolating in his
throat. He and his two new "brothers" had been on the road for three
and half hours and Carlos didn't know any more now than when
they'd left Chicago. The two men in the front seat weren't exactly
forthcoming, and Carlos wasn't going to give them the satisfaction
of asking. Besides, he knew what their response would be. They
didn't trust Carlos and he didn't blame them; if he could extricate
himself from this predicament without endangering his family, he'd
do it.

Road trips will force conversation, and even though the two
men had been talking with each other, they hadn't said anything
pertinent. Yet, Carlos had learned a few things about the men with
whom he shared the car.

The man behind the wheel, Loc, demonstrated an affinity for all
things "gangsta." He expressed his desire for a popular Hispanic
television starlet but couldn't believe she'd "settled for a darkie." He
also liked to finish every sentence with, "you know what I'm
sayin'," when of course everyone did; he wasn't very bright.

Loc was missing half of his left pinky finger. Carlos watched
the stub dance up and down on the steering wheel, keeping beat with
the nasal lyrics of Cypress Hill. The bobbed digit didn't look to be

42

the result of a genetic misfire; it'd been severed, probably violently and with purpose. How, Carlos didn't know, nor did he care.

Three or four inches taller than Carlos, and much heavier, Loc's weight wasn't solid muscle but wasn't all bacon grease either. He probably lifted weights on occasion, but wouldn't know how to perform, or spell, "cardiovascular" activity. Loc looked to be in his early twenties, though health-wise was likely nearing middle age.

For reasons unknown to Carlos, the front passenger went by the name, "Speedy." Shorter than Loc, taller than Carlos, Speedy was in his late teens, bone thin, with a pockmarked face and razor-sharp cheekbones seemingly anxious to slice through his skin. Carlos couldn't tell if Speedy was naturally emaciated or if he'd become addicted to one of the many drugs by which the Kings earned their living—an addiction that was perhaps the source of his nickname. He parted his sandy blond hair on the side and his fair skin could pass as Caucasian at a distance. Speedy's elevator traveled a floor or two higher than Loc's, but he wouldn't garner much respect in a gang unless he attained it with a gun, which was how most earned it anyway.

Carlos suppressed a shiver, a symptom of anxiety he'd never before experienced. Not even in battle. The fact was, the three of them were en route to perpetrate a criminal act and it would most likely be violent. He'd been funneled through combat units to learn how to effectively kill people, not to gain accounting skills. And if he put those talents to use by killing innocent citizens, well, once he crossed a bridge so broken, there'd be no turning back

If he'd been recruited by the Kings to gain military tactics, why keep him in the dark when it came to planning? He could think of only one reason: they were en route to do something so egregious Alberto knew Carlos would refuse to go along. He'd killed before, for his country—not for the ALKQN, the Almighty Latin King Queen Nation. Carlos wouldn't kill an innocent person. *Another gangbanger?* Even that would forever link him to the Kings. He'd be theirs forever. And if an innocent bystander became collateral damage because of the ineptitude of his *brothers*, he'd never be able to live with himself.

He was aware his "fellow" Kings saw things differently. If they accidentally shot a child while pulling a drive-by, they chalked it up to killing a future rival. They simply didn't give a shit. But if someone on their block caught a bullet in the crossfire they took it personally and vowed revenge, and the result was an endless cycle of violence.

His stomach a sour, bubbly, pool of tension, Carlos bled off a cubic foot of nervous gas which finally got the attention of his new brothers.

"Fucking pendejo," Loc said as he rolled down the window.

Carlos allowed himself his first smile in days.

ALBERTO VEGA, AKA UNCLE ALBERTO, aka King Slick, parked his black Mercedes-Benz CL500, outside his suburban Chicago home and thought it was time for a new car. He'd accumulated 24,000 plus miles on the Benz and deemed it too high mileage to fit his considerable stature. Alberto owned a used car lot and two out-of-state massage parlors, which, as far as the United States government knew, were the sources of his income. In reality he had amassed his small, but growing fortune, by the blood of his brothers.

The Latin Kings were like any other gang. A large portion of the membership took the risks and spilled the blood so a select few could live in relative luxury. The Kings separated themselves from other gangs by the level of success one could achieve.

Success, as measured by Bloods or Crips, might include driving a new Cadillac Escalade while donning a few gold trinkets. Between stints in prison, they bounced from one section eight apartment to another, no doubt rented by their "baby mommas." *Those stupid motherfuckers.* The real money from black gangs went straight to the Latinos. At least the Kings were organized well enough they kept a good share of the profits for key members of the organization. Though—just like their African-American counterparts—the vast majority of Kings barely scratched-out a living.

Alberto considered today's Latinos to be what Italians were in the 1920s, rulers of America's underworld. Over fifty percent of all gang members in the United States were Latino. That percentage grew daily. And like his Mexican brothers south of the border, one day they'd own this country. The way the Hispanic population was booming it wouldn't be long—if they would just unite. Hell, over 25,000 Latin Kings resided in the Chicago area alone. The ALKQN was taking over New York and new chapters were starting in states all over the country.

Organization was the Kings' greatest asset. Their manifesto rivaled the policies and procedures of federal agencies, and just like the feds had many working parts. Even the street chapters had complex ranking structures: from the rank and file member to throwers, cleaners, secretaries, investigators, treasurers, enforcers, with the Cacique and the Inca sitting on top. Above the street chapters was an abundance of mid-level "management types:" advisors, executive assistants, additional secretaries and treasurers, chiefs of security and on and on. There were even finance and business committees. In charge of it all were the Coronas and finally the Sun-King.

The Kings were a business, it's just that their commodity happened to be drugs, extortion, prostitution, and gun running, to name a few. At times they'd even tried to portray themselves as a civic group with the goals of promoting the Latin cause. If the cause was getting them stoned and killed, then Alberto guessed that might be an accurate assessment.

The Kings were a business and Alberto a businessman. He thought himself no different than any other capitalist and figured he had more morals than your average politician. At least he didn't pretend to be a baby-kissing Christian. He had no doubt if you put a gun in one of the Clintons' hands, stood them in a dark alley with someone of little importance, and told them the presidency was theirs if they pulled the trigger—there'd be one dead motherfucker in that alley and it wouldn't be a Clinton.

Politicians wanted the power, *craved* it, just like a gangster. Alberto felt himself above all that. He liked the power sure, and the money, but had no desire to rise any further in the Nation. Rank only brought increased attention from law enforcement and jealousy from peers. Let someone else rise and fall. The people at the bottom always took it in the ass, and the ones at the top always got their heads lopped off. It was good to be in the middle. The Sun-King might be running the entire KMC (King Motherland Chicago), but he did it from the supermax prison in Florence, Colorado, looking out a four-inch wide window while sitting on a poured concrete bed. *Fuck that bullshit.* Besides, Alberto was a smart man. He had businesses on the side—massage parlors and such—that even the Kings didn't know about. If they did, they'd stick their greedy little fingers in his pie.

The road to power in the Latin Kings was paved with violence but Alberto was not a hands-on kind of guy. He'd perpetrated enough violent crimes to earn respect and a couple of stints in the county jail but he'd never done hard time. Where some guys didn't mind prison—enjoyed it even—the prospect of incarceration terrified Alberto. Truth be known, he was a claustrophobe.

Lucky for him, Alberto possessed the uncanny gift of getting others to do his dirty work while he reaped the rewards. His unequaled ability to manipulate made him one hell of a recruiter, not that the task was a difficult one. There were plenty of forsaken youth looking for someone, anyone, to show them a sense of belonging. Still, Alberto had taken recruitment to a new level.

Despite the significant organization of the Kings, its members had zero tactical skills. The fact most gang members didn't understand how to properly maintain, operate, and fire a weapon wasn't lost on Alberto. He'd recognized what a properly trained fighting force might achieve and approached top leaders in the

Nation with an idea. It'd been an easy sell. He'd appealed to their machismo; had set them to fantasizing about small units of expertly trained warriors taking down armored cars and defending the organization. Yes, his concept would require funding but those monies would be returned tenfold.

At first Alberto tapped current Kings and had limited success getting a few into the military. Most had criminal histories, gang tattoos, poor academic records, abused drugs, mental illness and a slew of other problems that'd kept them from being accepted. Those who managed to slip under the wire didn't make the best soldiers and didn't receive the best training. Regardless, they'd all resumed their dipshit gangbanging ways once they returned to civilian life.

So Alberto convinced the leadership to find abandoned but intelligent youth and provide them good homes that would dissuade them from the gang lifestyle. The boys would be funneled into the armed forces, made to apply for combat units, and if need be, forcibly integrated into the ALKQN following their military commitment. As a result, the Kings would have an expertly trained fighting force courtesy of the United States government. After years of grooming, Alberto's plans were finally reaching fruition.

Alberto had eight such men under his control. Somewhat. Five had entered the Nation with little fuss. One had outright refused to join, instead thinking he'd found a home in the U.S. Army. That man was about to have his world turned upside down. Another, Carlos Benitez, had been taking measures to leave the Nation, but was about to be shown the consequences of those actions. The last recruit was still in the Marine Corps with a year of service left. Alberto had big plans for seven of the eight men. Soon, great sums of money would be the reward for a lot of hard work. The portfolios of Alberto and those in his chain-of-command were about to see significant gains.

EIGHT

LOCATED IN DOWNTOWN TULSA ON the corner of 2nd and
Elgin, a relatively new bar had become a favorite of off-duty police
officers, especially members of the Special Investigations Division.
As a consequence, it looked like a place where a bunch of big, mean,
bearded, vile men came to imbibe. In reality, all the roughest looking
people in the bar were undercover cops. Badge-bunnies liked to
wiggle their tails here. Women, who for one reason or another, were
attracted to men with ample supplies of testosterone and carried guns
for a living.

At 190 pounds, Thorpe's medium frame bore an assemblage of
stringy muscle sure to make any professional boxer blush with pride.
Despite his baggy long sleeve t-shirt, Thorpe's muscle mass revealed
itself as he worked his way through the room, pausing here and there
to acknowledge fellow officers.

In the middle of a handshake, he noticed Robert Hull at a
corner booth with two other homicide detectives. Thorpe gave them
a nod, indicating he'd be over in a minute. He stopped at the bar and
ordered a bucket of Stella before making his way through the crowd
toward Hull and his associates. Along the way, he gained the
attention of two blondes gyrating on the dance floor. One was a bit
slovenly in both dress and fitness for Thorpe's taste, but the other
was absolutely gorgeous. His supply of nods undiminished, he

offered them one as well and continued on to Hull's booth. As he approached, Chuck Lagrone slid over making room for Thorpe to sit. Chuck, in his early sixties, his face showing every year and then some, was a thin membrane of skin tightly wrapped around bone. Because of his appearance, he'd earned the departmental nickname, "The Skull." With the exception of his boss, Hull, The Skull might be the best homicide detective on the department.

"What's up Carnac?" Lagrone said, using Thorpe's own moniker.

"Same ole' shit, Skull. What's up with you guys?" Thorpe smiled as he shook hands with the three men seated around the table.

"Just out celebrating Jeremy Johnson's unfortunate death," Skull answered, raising his glass in salute and tossing back the warm amber liquid.

"Only unfortunate thing about his death is I didn't get to watch," Hull added, "How you doing, John?"

"Good, Bob, anything new on his killing?"

"Yeah, they've got a BOLO out for a black car with personalized tags that read, 'Batty,' driven by one Bruce Wayne."

"Kid still sticking to his Batman story?"

"Last I heard," Hull confirmed.

Maybe the kid really believed it. Thorpe hoped he hadn't inadvertently caused additional trauma to the boy.

"Any more information on how it went down?" Thorpe asked, as he dispensed beers from the bucket.

Excited to share the story, Skull began, "From talking to the sheriff's office, they think that someone rolled up on Jeremy when he was about to rape the kid. Fat Fuck's truck was pulled down in a ravine just off the highway between Tulsa and Coffeyville, where that warped shit lives. Guess he snatched the kid here in Tulsa, started driving him home, couldn't wait to break off a piece, and pulled his truck off the highway. A sheriff's deputy said Jeremy's right front tire had been stuck with a knife before he was killed."

"Maybe he stopped because he had a flat," Thorpe suggested,

trying to sound like someone who didn't know exactly what had happened.

"No, like I said he was WAY off the road. Based on the tire tracks, they think Fat Fuck pulled over, got out of the truck, and locked-in his hubs. Jeremy drove one of those older four-wheel drives that require you to get out of the truck and manually lock-in the hubs on the wheels. If he'd had a flat, he would've noticed then. Anyway, he puts the truck in four-wheel-drive, then takes the kid down into the ravine to have his fun…"

"Excuse me; sorry; hi, I'm Beth. Do you want to dance with me and my friend?"

The less shapely of the two women on the dance floor had come over and interrupted Skull's story. Thorpe looked up at the smiling woman who gazed down with glassed-over eyes. The question had been directed at him. He glanced at her more attractive friend, still on the dance floor and grinding on an invisible partner while pretending to be disinterested in Beth's conversation. Thorpe wasn't much for dancing. However, it seemed to be a dating ritual, today's first base, so he occasionally succumbed to such requests. For reasons Thorpe was only slightly aware, he politely declined the offer.

"Beth, why don't you two come over and sit with us. We're telling war stories and the current one involves a pedophile who had his dick cut off," Hull offered with a smile.

Beth giggled and turned; her first few steps took her in the wrong direction and like a top-heavy ship in rough seas, she required a wide berth to right her course. She was plastered.

"Screw you," Thorpe said, directing the remark at Hull.

"Have some fun for once. I hate to think of how much lotion you're plowing through every week," Hull laughed.

"Screw you twice," then to Mike Shute, "And what the hell are you smiling at?"

New to homicide, Mike hadn't yet said boo, but that would change. Mike had a reputation as a ladies' man and Thorpe knew if the two came over, his silence wouldn't last. Short, maybe five and a half feet tall, Mike didn't let his lack of stature prevent him from being a slayer of women. He was often referred to as "The Swordsman" by those who knew him. It was like watching an Oscar winning performance when Mike went to work—truly something to behold. And while Hull and Skull were still dressed in slacks and sleeves, Mike had changed into bar clothes. He no doubt kept a set in the trunk of his unmarked car for emergency purposes.

Beth returned, her friend in one hand a drink in the other. Mike, of course, slid over to make room for the ladies. Despite his actions the two stood beside Thorpe, clearly indicating their desire to sit next to him. Thorpe relented and slid over, with the heavier, less attractive Beth plopping down next to him. The booth sat five comfortably. Six bodies ensured they were packed together tightly. Beth wore a three sizes too small Lycra halter that splayed her damp and ample bosom up and outward. Pressed against his side, her lady friends enveloped the better part of Thorpe's right bicep.

Mike made quick introductions, ensuring the women knew he was a homicide detective. Beth's friend turned out to be Blair. Beth and Blair. Beth, drunk, told everyone her name again, and although Thorpe was sure she had names for them, neglected to introduce her halter top-straining friends.

Mike, bringing the women up to speed on the Jeremy Johnson killing, was interrupted by Hull. "Swordsman, you going to shut the fuck up so Skull can finish his story?" Thorpe nearly blew beer out of his nose, and onto Beth's lady friends. Everyone liked Mike, but Hull clearly had intentions of pairing Thorpe with the two women.

When Thorpe's family was murdered, Hull broke protocol and personally took the lead on the case. During the subsequent investigation he uncovered information on Thorpe's past no one else knew. He also pieced together what Thorpe had done after the case stalled. With this knowledge, and with risk to both his career and freedom, Hull had taken measures to conceal Thorpe's involvement. Even now, Hull probably wondered if Thorpe had a hand in ending

Jeremy Johnson's career as a child murdering rapist.

As Skull continued his story, Beth's hand came to rest on Thorpe's right thigh—*just great.*

"So, judging from the tracks, they believe the tires were still inflated when Jeremy drove the kid down the river bank. What happens next is a bit speculative but is based on evidence at the scene. The kid was bound in the camper shell of the truck—this they learned from the kid—and they found Jeremy's clothes inside the cab. They think Jeremy gets an uncontrollable urge while driving, goes down into the ravine, strips naked, then gets into the back of the camper with the boy. Investigators think someone watches Jeremy drive down into the ravine, and follows. They think this person then sticks a knife in the right front tire, which causes Fat Fuck to leave his camper to investigate. When he does, he gets his penis lopped off..."

This elicited a string of excited comments from the ladies, even from the previously aloof Blair. *Nothing like stories of chopping off penises to get the rapt attention of women everywhere.* Thorpe figured that, internally, Mike was adding this story to his arsenal of woman-getters.

"… so Fat Fuck falls to the ground, and based on the blood trail, looks as though he starts crawling up the ravine in an attempt to get away from Batman…" Beth's hand slid up to Thorpe's inner thigh and was inches from pay dirt. "…then Batman gets in Fat Fuck's own truck, cut the wheels to the right, and heads toward the now dickless, Fat Fuck. Investigators know the tire was flat at this point because of the way the rim dug into the dirt. Batman drives his front tire up on Fat Fuck's back, and hits the gas. Then he repeats the process with the back tire. They said pieces of Fat Fuck were sprayed thirty yards behind. Chunks were hanging from tree branches. The tires peeled off half his back, rolled him over, and tore off part of Fat Fuck's fat belly. They said there was blood, skin, chunks of fat, all over the undercarriage of his pickup. But despite all that, the fucker lived long enough he crawled another twenty yards before he died."

Beth buried her hand in Thorpe's crotch and began stroking his penis. And because Thorpe failed to inform said penis that Beth wasn't the least bit attractive, he experienced a physical reaction. Thorpe turned his head and noticed Blair was doing to Beth, what Beth was doing to him. *What a couple of sick bitches. This crap actually turned them on.* A few months ago he might have ignored his distaste. Instead, Thorpe asked the women if they wanted another drink then had them scoot out of the booth. With a degree of embarrassment, and jackknifed at the waist, Thorpe walked toward the bar, passed it, and went straight out the door, confident that tomorrow, Mike would have one hell of a story to tell.

NINE

CARLOS SAT IN A MOTEL ROOM watching his umpteenth hour of television unable to recall a single program that'd passed before his eyes. He and Loc were anxiously awaiting Speedy, who'd left about twenty minutes ago.

They'd arrived early in the morning, rented a room with two double beds, and backed the rental car outside their second-story accommodations. Loc took the bed closest to the bathroom, Speedy the bed closest to the door, and Carlos the floor in between. He hadn't gotten a wink of sleep. It wasn't because of the arrangements. He'd become accustomed to much worse conditions than this. In Afghanistan he'd slept in Ranger Graves—small dug-out indentations in the earth as protection against mortar rounds and small arms fire—only to awake to heat-worshiping scorpions nestled beneath his body. On one particular mission he was required to sleep in MOPP 4 over-garments in the 100 degree heat for two days. *Good times.*

Carlos couldn't rest now because he hadn't the slightest clue what barbarity his associates were planning or what his role in those atrocities might be. Loc and Speedy had offered few clues.

Shortly after arriving, Loc left to fetch breakfast and he'd taken considerably more time than the task required. When the man finally returned, Speedy asked, "You find it?" to which Loc responded,

"Yeah, Dog." Carlos doubted they'd been referring to McDonalds—the source of their breakfast sandwiches. Then, around 1:00 p.m., Speedy left returning with lunch. Otherwise, they'd passed the entire day sequestered in the minuscule room watching a small, 1980s manufactured television complete with useless rabbit ears. Carlos hadn't left the room since they'd arrived and he was climbing out of his skin.

As the day darkened so did the mood of his two roommates. Both checked their watches obsessively and made frequent trips to the bathroom despite neither man consuming much in the way of fluids. Speedy had begun pacing like a caged animal until twenty minutes ago when he'd uttered, "I'll be back," and rushed out of the room. His two companions were nervous and their anxiety told Carlos a shitstorm was on the horizon.

The doorknob turned, Loc flinched, and Speedy walked into the room with the cool March air. The walking stick of a man jerked his thin hand out of his left pocket and produced two joints.

"Got these from a chick downstairs."

Speedy lit one and passed it to Loc.

Loc hesitated before he accepted then turned toward Carlos. "You say a word, I'll kill you myself. Know what I'm sayin'?"

Apparently they weren't supposed to be getting stoned prior to their mission—sound tactics unless your plan was to fly a machine into a battleship; Japanese kamikaze pilots were some of the first users of methamphetamine. Although, Carlos thought if there was ever a good excuse for drug abuse, purposely ramming your airplane into a ship had to rank near the top.

Whatever the plan, it had these two dipshits spooked enough they had to get their courage through smoke. *Fucking idiots.* Carlos was seriously considering killing Loc and Speedy then racing down to Florida to collect his wife and daughter before Uncle Alberto was any wiser. Loc's ringing cell phone snapped Carlos from his hopeful fantasy.

"Yeah....Found it this morning...I'm sure...We ready...He'll do it…No problem…Got it…We goin' now…King love."

Loc terminated the call, passed the joint back to Speedy, and walked out of the room. A minute later he returned with a grimace and the bag containing the pistols. Loc donned black latex gloves and gave what looked to be a 9mm Glock to Speedy, then handed Carlos, barrel first, a .45 caliber 1911.

As Carlos reluctantly reached for the weapon, Loc withdrew it and smiled. "Not yet Soldier Boy. Don't want you gettin' any funny ideas."

TUNED TO THE DISCOVERY CHANNEL, a 55-inch Sony LCD television overlooked Alberto Vega lounging on a leather recliner. Alberto had a huge grin on his face and a glass of 1999 Chateau Monbousquet in his hand. He didn't know shit about wine but the bottle was somewhat expensive so it must be good…*right?* The smirk on his face had nothing to do with the half-naked man running around on TV relating a self-imposed jungle survival situation. Nor had it to do with the half-naked white woman in front of the Sony snorting a line of coke off the glass and steel coffee table.

Alberto's amusement stemmed from the knowledge that the first of several shipments would soon be on its way to Chicago; shipments that were going to make the Nation a good amount of money, and make Alberto rich. And for a little icing on the cake, three loose ends would be wrapped up very nicely tonight. First, Carlos would be forced to commit a heinous crime that would, afterward, make him Alberto's property. Second, a man would be shown the deadly repercussions of not honoring his commitment to Alberto. Third, a long standing debt would be repaid. Alberto didn't like owing anyone anything and was pleased he'd soon have a clean ledger. Some pissant Tulsa police officer was about to stop breathing.

What was that pig's name? Oh, yeah, Alberto saluted the air with his glass, *rest in peace, Jonathan Thorpe*. Alberto rose from the couch, stepped to the coffee table and set down his empty glass, grabbed his girl by hair, pulled her off the line of coke, and licked white powder from her nostrils. He slid his tongue lower, found her open mouth, gave her a deep kiss, and walked out the door.

TEN

IN A DARKENED CORNER OF his own living room, Thorpe sat on an exercise ball peering through a pair of high-powered binoculars. His line of sight was just above the window sill, across his front yard and into the vast woods beyond. He was concerned.

Thorpe's trepidation was born last night while arriving home from the bar. His flight from the twisted bisexuals complete, he'd coasted in darkness alongside his property, his two German shepherds noticeably absent. Usually, Al and Trixie ran the fence line, paralleling Thorpe's truck until all parties arrived at the gate simultaneously. There, they'd wait for a good ear scratching. Last night Thorpe didn't see either dog until he'd reached his driveway. Even then, their attention had been on something in the woods.

Thorpe had seen the same demeanor on a previous occasion. Then, Al and Trixie alerted on two men meaning to do him harm. The men had been lying in wait across the road with a rifle. Al and Trixie helped save his life; his would-be assailants weren't as fortunate.

Thorpe always minded his instincts and learned from experience. History repeats itself. Last night, having seen his dogs in a state of alert, Thorpe continued on past his house as if he were just another neighbor. He'd driven his truck to the property owned by Thomas and Deborah Jennings. Deborah was currently engaged in a nasty divorce from her millionaire husband. Thorpe had once—or twice—made the mistake of sharing horizontal refreshments with the woman. An error he hoped not to repeat.

Despite the house being on the market, Deborah allowed Thorpe access to a large barn near the front of the expansive property. In hope of avoiding contact with the woman, Thorpe hadn't been using it much of late. When Deborah wanted something, she could be very persuasive, and Thorpe found that even though he was extremely disciplined in certain areas, his ability to say no to attractive women was sometimes wanting.

He'd used a code to enter the property's impressive gate, and managed to tuck away his truck inside the barn without garnering Deborah's attention. Then, he spent the next three hours slowly and methodically flanking the area where Al and Trixie had alerted. Eventually he reached a position where he could see both dogs staring back at him. Not having found anyone or anything, he still felt like something was…off and took a cautious and circuitous route back to his property.

Leery of entering his home, he'd caught a few hours of fitful sleep in his own barn, rose with the sun, slipped out the rear door, and again scoured the area he'd previously searched in darkness. He almost dismissed the whole affair as a fit of paranoia when he spotted something of concern. Though sparse and dormant, Thorpe found a small bit of flattened vegetation beside a fallen log. The log itself had recently been moved so that it was parallel with the road in front of Thorpe's house.

The position offered a favorable view of Thorpe's property, and the log provided both cover and concealment. This discovery caused Thorpe to search the woods even more thoroughly and he came across brush marks left in the sandy dirt. Vegetation had been dragged over the ground. Someone had been in the area and tried—almost successfully—to disguise evidence of their movements.

Game hunters don't disguise their footprints, but hunters of men do; particularly professional hunters of men. Thorpe's unease had been warranted. Men had been in these woods. And those men meant to do him harm.

Thorpe sat on the rubber exercise ball and studied the shadows beyond his property. He wouldn't be going to work tonight. Instead, he'd visit Deborah's barn for an afternoon nap. A long night awaited him.

ELEVEN

HALF PAST MIDNIGHT AND CARLOS sat, sweating, in the back of the rental car. The driver's seat was empty as Loc had set off on foot. Speedy, chewing on his thumbnail and peering out the passenger window, yelped when the driver's side door flew open. Loc reached in and grabbed the keys from the ignition.

"Let's go."

Shit. Shit. Shit. It's begun. Carlos followed the men down a sidewalk and through a neighborhood consisting of small homes on elevated lots. After making two right turns, Loc pointed to a white house and said to Carlos, "Stand at the front door, Soldier Boy. Nobody leaves."

Carlos closed his eyes, let out a long breath, then climbed the yard to the front porch as Loc and Speedy made their way toward the back of the house. He watched Loc pull a pry bar from the inside of his jacket just before the two disappeared around the corner. "Shit."

A minute later Carlos heard a woman's faint scream from inside the home, saw the lights flick on, and the front door swing open. Speedy stood in the doorway, motioning for Carlos to enter. Carlos stepped into the foyer not liking what he found. An elderly couple sat on a couch inside a sparse, yet cared-for, living room. The woman had a red handprint across her pale cheek. She'd probably been the source of the scream and the blow had been to gain her silence. This did not appear to be the house of rival gang members.

Loc shouted at Speedy to "cover them," then disappeared down a hallway. Speedy's pistol was unsteady in his too-tight grip. It jumped all over the room. His sweat rained down onto the cream-colored, vacuum-streaked carpet.

"Take your damned finger off the trigger, Speedy. You're going to accidentally shoot someone."

"Shut the fuck up."

After a few seconds, Loc reappeared with a pair of socks in hand. He pulled them apart and stuffed one into the elderly man's mouth. He then withdrew a roll of duct tape from his coat and wrapped it around the man's mouth. He repeated the process with the woman before binding their hands behind their backs. His work done, Loc backed up and again offered Carlos the .45 pistol. This time Loc didn't withdraw the weapon when Carlos reached for it.

"Smoke 'em, Soldier Boy."

Loc's order elicited a muffled scream from the woman. The old man struggled to get to his feet but Loc roughly pushed him back onto the couch and ordered Speedy to hold him down by the shoulders.

"You're fucking joking?" Carlos hissed.

"Do I look like I'm joking, motherfucker?"

Instead of the couple, Carlos pointed the .45 between Loc's eyes, "I fucking swear I'll kill you before I hurt them. In fact I'll kill you before I let *you* hurt them, you sick fuck."

Loc gave Carlos a casual shrug, almost as though he'd anticipated the reaction. Making a show he wasn't reaching for a weapon, Loc slowly withdrew a cell from his jacket and began punching in numbers. "It's me. Like you said, he won't do it." Loc carried the phone over to Carlos, "It's Alberto."

Carlos kept his pistol trained on Loc as he grabbed the phone with his left hand, put the cell up to his ear, and spoke, "I ain't gonna kill no old man and woman."

His uncle sounded calm, almost jovial, "Carlos, Carlos, you

made a commitment. You belong to the Nation now. You belong to me."

"Fuck the Nation and fuck you. You can't hold me responsible for something you put in my head when I was ten-fucking-years-old."

"I can and I am. Carlos, think of them as enemy combatants…they have to die."

"Enemy combatants? What the fuck could they have done?!"

"Carlos, lower your voice and watch the language. Your parents might overhear. You don't want them to hear that filth coming from your mouth, do you?"

"You're at my parents' house? Don't you touch them or I swear to…"

Carlos heard Alberto yelling on the other end of the line. "Hey Luisa, I'm talking to your boy on the phone." Carlos could hear his mother in the background, "Carlos, really? Let me talk to him."

"He'll call you back in a little bit, I'm getting off the phone with him now—he's very busy." Alberto returned his attention to Carlos, "Don't make me hurt them Soldier Boy. They're good people; not like the ones you're protecting."

"Damn you. Don't you fucking hurt…"

"They'll be fine just as long as you do your job," Alberto interrupted. "I'll tell you what, I'll give you a couple minutes to make your decision. Plus, I'll have someone call you and explain why you should waste those two old geezers."

"I don't need a couple…"

The connection ended. Carlos pressed the muzzle against Loc's forehead.

"Wait for the call, Carlos. You'll see," Loc said in a strangely calm voice; too calm for having a pistol pointed at his face. *Where'd this piece of shit find his newfound courage? Must have smoked something stronger than weed.*

"Fuck!" Carlos brought the gun down from Loc's face and paced the room. He couldn't breathe. It was then he noticed pictures on the wall of a young Latino in military garb. The man was wearing a green beret.

No…No…Oh, no. They were having Carlos kill the parents of a Special Forces soldier. He'd probably refused his commitment to Alberto. They were sending Carlos a clear message. *Well fuck that,* he wasn't going to be their lap dog. Carlos raised the .45, slowly squeezing the trigger at a smiling Loc when the phone rang.

"I ain't gonna do it motherfucker!" Carlos screamed.

"Carlos?"

What? It can't be, "Eva?" *His wife!*

"Carlos, what's going on?" She was crying.

"Baby, how'd you get this number?"

"There are men in our house, Carlos. One of them took Celestina away. They're going to rape and kill her! They said they were going to rape and kill our baby!" Her voice cracked—she was barely holding on. "What do they want, Carlos?"

Carlos felt like someone had reached into his chest and clenched his heart. *They took his little girl. They had his baby.*

His eyes burned as he fought back the tears. "I'll take care of everything Eva. Celestina will be fine. They made a mistake is all. Celestina will be back in your arms in a matter of minutes. I promise…"

His wife was screaming as Loc pulled the phone from Carlos's hand and snapped the phone shut.

Oh God no, not my little girl!

Loc pressed, "You got thirty seconds to brain these two motherfuckers before your girl becomes a dead sex toy. Now fucking waste 'em!"

As much as men make circumstances, circumstances make men. Carlos looked at the couple sitting on the couch and the fear in their eyes. That image was shredded as he pictured his young daughter repeatedly raped and murdered. His wife murdered. His parents murdered. Then came the justifications for the man the circumstances were creating. *This old couple had already led a full life. Their deaths would be quick and painless—my daughter's long and brutal.*

Carlos shrank as he stepped in front of the elderly couple. He looked down into their pleading eyes and closed his own. "They have my daughter...I'm sorry."

In the process of pulling the trigger, Carlos reclaimed his wife and daughter. But lost his soul.

TWELVE

LYING ON THE GROUND IN a conglomeration of burlap and jute with intertwined natural foliage, Thorpe was part of the forest. He'd recently constructed the ghillie suit, thinking it might come in handy given his leisurely pursuit of purging monsters from this earth. Wearing the garment, he was virtually invisible in the woods—even in the daylight. In the dark, like now, forget about it.

The suit hooded Thorpe's face, camouflaged his head, and concealed the soft green glow currently projected on his right eye. Thorpe looked through a weapon-mounted night-vision system married to an Aimpoint Comp M3 red-dot sight. The paired optics sat atop a Rock River Arms tactical AR-15 with full-auto capabilities. A TPD gun armorer had shown him how to convert the weapon—a surprisingly simple procedure.

When one is planning to counter an ambush, it pays to be the first one at the party. With that in mind Thorpe had entered the woods early and spent what seemed an eternity moving to his current position. His internal clock told him it was nearing 1:30 in the morning. Sipping on a hydration bladder, pondering the symptoms of paranoid schizophrenia, he caught movement inside his cupped scope. Afraid he was starting to see things—a common occurrence experienced by soldiers who'd spent too much time in the bush looking for something that might kill them—Thorpe blinked hard and refocused.

His pulse increased ever so slightly as he watched a man pull himself across the forest floor toward his property. *Not a man...two men.* Both camouflaged and both taking a position behind the relocated log Thorpe had discovered the previous morning.

Thirty yards to the east and at a ninety degree angle, Thorpe had an unencumbered view of the men's left sides; they faced his home and were using the fallen log as cover. *What the hell?* Thorpe activated an infrared aiming light on his weapon and silently cursed as he watched the farthest man bring a device up to his eyes. *Son-of-a-bitch.* Thorpe snapped off the light; the man was using night-vision and would have been able to see his beam.

The other man slowly, sloth-like, began working something in front of him and Thorpe knew what it would be even before he saw it. *Sniper rifle.* He tried to unscramble what his eyes were reporting. *What are these men's intentions? Is this an advance sniper-team for a warrant service? Are they here to kill him or gather intel?* Except for a lack of ballistic helmets, the men looked military or law enforcement. Maybe the feds had gotten wind of Thorpe's extracurricular activities and the FBI's Hostage Rescue Team had come to take him into custody? If so, he wouldn't harm a law enforcement officer who was only doing his job.

His mind started to wonder, contemplating surrender and life on the run. *Could he handle prison? If he ran, where would he go? How would he survive?* Distracted by thoughts not helpful to his current situation, Thorpe forced himself to concentrate on the now. And for now he would remain perfectly still and observe. *Hopefully they don't have thermal imaging*; he wasn't dressed to defeat the technology.

Already worried about the men in front, Thorpe heard something at his six, though he sure as hell didn't turn to look. Another twenty seconds passed before he detected the distinct sound of something or someone behind him snaking its way across the forest floor, inches at a time. *Damn, damn, damn!* No stranger to peril, he approximated his predicament to be a ten on the pucker factor. He tried to discern the course of *the someone* behind him but could only determine one thing for certain: he, she, it, or they, were getting too damned close. Suddenly the image of one of Thorpe's favorite teenage movies flashed in his mind—*Predator*. The scene where Arnold forgets he's a Republican and hugs a tree and the semi-transparent form of the creature passes over him. Strange, Thorpe thought, the things that pop into your mind even during life and death situations.

His pulse pounding in his head brought to his attention he was holding his breath and he slowly let it out. Had he held it any longer it would have come out in a gasp. He concentrated on his breathing and slowed his heart rate. Relaxed, he realized the rustling behind him was coming in at an angle. It passed less than ten feet behind Thorpe's prone body and sounded like it'd reached its destination about fifteen feet to Thorpe's eight o'clock.

I'm in a pickle. Thorpe nearly laughed at his own internal dialogue. *Pickle?* He had a sniper and armed spotter thirty yards to his twelve o'clock and who-knows-what less than fifteen feet to his eight. *I'm screwed is what I am.*

"Echo Team in position."

Those words weren't part of Thorpe's internal dialogue. They'd been whispered by the "who-knows-what" stationed behind his burlap covered ass.

"What's your sit-rep?"

The word "shit" now a common mantra of his thought process, Thorpe didn't like anything he was hearing. One, the "team" part of "Echo Team" implied whoever was stationed behind him wasn't alone. Two, "sit-rep" is short for situation report and all but guaranteed Thorpe was dealing with current or ex-military. And three, the "team" behind him moved in unison, which demonstrated a certain level of professionalism—not at all comforting. Thorpe prayed there weren't also teams Alpha, Bravo, Charlie, and Delta, which had required them to use the E in the military's phonetic alphabet.

Only one thing to do now—hump earth and hope to hell his stomach doesn't start growling before these assholes get tired and leave. Yup, sounds like a plan: become one with the soil, concentrate on his breathing, try not to fart, and look for an opportunity out of this shit.

Those hopes were crushed by the words spoken next.

"Roger that. Taking out K-9s."

Kill his dogs? The hell you are, Thorpe thought as his body reacted. *This doesn't have the smell of law enforcement, and nobody is going to kill Al and Trixie— they're family.*

A couple gigabytes of information tore through Thorpe's brain at lightning speed while a lifetime of training told his body what to do. Thorpe didn't care how well-trained these sons-of-bitches might be; when you're sneaking around the forest, whispering into your throat-mic, thinking you *are* the element of surprise, you *will* shit yourself when an automatic weapon opens up on your ass in the still of the night from a mere fifteen feet away.

In one swift motion, Thorpe twisted onto his right side, swung his weapon around and used his abs to rise up on his ass while his thumb found the fully automatic switch and his index finger applied pressure to the trigger. Thorpe unleashed a volley of lead toward the threat, rocked up onto the soles of his boots, and used his legs to thrust his body upward. He did all this while keeping an eye in his optics looking for the movement his booming weapon would surely generate. As expected, two piles of forest floor jerked from the sudden onslaught. Thorpe put a burst into each man beginning where he thought he'd find the chest then moving up toward the head.

Up and running, Thorpe was disappointed he didn't have time to grab one of their headsets, but he needed to create distance before the other two men—the sniper team—stopped shitting their BDUs and started laying down fire. Heading east and peering through his night optics, Thorpe stepped left to dodge a tree and heard a fffft sound part the air and a stinging in his right ear. As he continued to run he felt a warm wetness running down the side of his neck. He'd been hit. He hadn't heard a shot or the supersonic crack of a bullet but remembered the long extension on the barrel of the sniper rifle. They were using suppressors paired with subsonic ammunition. *More than just a suppressor, he hadn't heard shit except for the whisper of the bullet as it tore off half his lobe.* Thorpe felt no pain, but that would change when the adrenaline dump dissipated. He had a decision to make; keep running, or find a place of cover and concealment and stay in the fight.

He simply didn't have enough information. There could be additional men in these woods. He could dig-in to spring an ambush only to be shot in the back by a team of which he wasn't aware. On the other hand, if he ran, he might as well keep running forever. He'd never be able to have a normal life not knowing if and when these men, or others, would return. And he wouldn't be able to take the fight to them because he had no idea who "them" was. There really wasn't a choice. Thorpe would stay and fight.

Night-vision has its limitations, and one is depth perception. It's very difficult to move high speed through the woods without becoming a human pinball. Navigating as quickly as possible by hues of greens and blacks, Thorpe tried to decide on a plan of action. *Am I even being chased?* Thorpe stopped, went to a knee, swung his weapon around, watched and listened. He couldn't see anything but he could hear someone stomping around in the direction from which he'd fled.

Stop acting and start thinking! Using a form of self-hypnosis, Thorpe hit the restart button on his brain. Everything slowed yet he became hyperaware: he felt his breathing deepen and slow, his heart rate decrease, the warm blood running down his neck, cold wet mud seeping through his BDUs, a slight wind on his cheek. He smelled the damp earth, musty leaves, and the dead bark. He became one with his environment.

Thorpe reached down and grabbed a handful of the muck. He packed his mangled ear with the gooey substance hoping to decrease its blood flow. *What to do? The unexpected.* Thorpe gathered another handful of mud and applied it to his face—*may as well go completely Predator.*

With any luck they wouldn't expect him to launch an assault from the direction he'd just fled. Not this soon anyway. *Speed, surprise, violence of action...*Thorpe, silently and unconsciously spoke to himself as he made his way back into battle.

JULIO LOPEZ, AKA KING FUBB, was a Screaming Eagle of the 101st Airborne Division and a willing member of the Almighty Latin King Nation. Mexican-bred, American-born, the son of poor working-their-ass-off-for-shit, Mexican immigrants, Fubb was down for the Nation. The U.S. government never lifted a finger to help his parents, treating them like pond scum their entire lives. Young Julio excelled in school, was a U.S. born citizen, and was going to use his citizenship to pull himself and his parents out of the slums by his boot straps. That was until Uncle Alberto had showed him the way.

Alberto first helped Julio, by helping Julio's parents. He got his father a steady job, his mother a dependable car, and all three of them out of their roach-infested apartment and into a decent rent house. Once Julio was secure, warm, and well fed, Alberto began to enlighten the young man. "Julio, no matter how much you achieve you'll never have the respect of the white man, and make no mistake, it's a white man's world. You'll always be a spic in their eyes. Even if you get a white-collar job they'll secretly be thinking, 'Why isn't that wetback mowing my yard?'" Alberto had been right and Julio started to see things for how they really were—not the pretty little façade the white man wanted you to see. "It won't be their world forever, Julio. I got big plans for you in the Nation."

Nevertheless, Uncle Alberto shielded Julio from gang members and their activities. Instead he encouraged him to study and participate in sports. "You're going to be a warrior for the Nation some day, Julio. Our own Latino John Rambo. You'll be a legend."

But before he could be a soldier for the Nation, he first had to be a soldier for the United States Army. Julio risked his life for the same government that refused to give his parents food stamps in order to survive. But survive they did—thanks to Uncle.

Fubb had inched his way across the gritty loam of an Oklahoma forest to start building a reputation for himself. Fubb had no idea why he'd been sent to Tulsa, Oklahoma, to kill a cop, but if Jonathan Thorpe was an enemy of Uncle Alberto and the Nation, then he was also an enemy of his. Besides, white pigs had worked to keep his people down for years. *Like whites were born on this land—they'd crossed more fucking water to get to America than his Mexican brothers had.*

Accompanying him on this assignment and less than a foot to his right, was King Knuckles. Fubb doubted his enthusiasm and commitment to the assignment but Uncle had assured him that Knuckles was a "down nigga." Two more Kings, "Echo Team," had moved into position forty yards to the east. The plan had been a simple one: wait for the white cop to come home and have Knuckles punch a hole through his cranial cavity.

Fubb was the only actual soldier in the group and he'd been given the responsibility to train-up the other three Kings to the best of his ability. Fubb was, without doubt, the most proficient shooter of the four, having achieved a ninety-five first-round hit percentage at 600 meters at the U.S. Army Sniper School. But the other Kings needed to learn, and the easiest way to learn was by doing. That's why he'd designated Knuckles as the principal shooter and had given him the sniper rifle.

Knuckles had proven to be an adequate shot when firing at paper silhouettes, and he had shot actual people in the past. But those incidents had entailed "spray-and-pray" shooting, not precise marksmanship with a precision weapon. On this mission, Fubb expected Knuckles to be nervous and anticipated the potential for a missed shot. That's why he and two other Kings accompanied Knuckles. They were his safety net.

In addition to spotting equipment, Fubb carried a Heckler & Koch MP5SD submachine gun. By design, standard supersonic ammunition left the suppressed weapon's muzzle at subsonic velocity. Fubb didn't know who supplied Alberto with his weapons, but they had access to some serious hardware. Echo Team was carrying M4s and in Fubb's opinion was complete overkill; four trigger-pullers for one municipal civil servant with a tin badge. Uncle said not to underestimate the man, but shit, *come-on!* On the other hand, his guys needed training and he might as well pop their cherry on a simple job. At least that's what Fubb had been thinking only a few minutes ago.

"Alpha Team in position," Fubb had announced over the radio, letting Echo Team know he and Knuckles were in place. Fubb had retrieved his spotting scope and located two minor obstacles, but neither team had yet garnered the dogs' attention. This time his team had come in much quieter and with a northerly breeze. Their plan had been to kill each dog well inside the property line and away from the road.

Everything had been going according to plan:

"Echo in position."

"Roger that," Fubb had replied.

"What's your sit-rep?" Echo Team had asked.

"Preparing to eliminate two furry tangos."

"Roger that. Taking out K-9s," Echo Team acknowledged.

And that's when Fubb nearly infused his pants with his last meal. The roaring thunder of an automatic weapon opened up a few yards to his left. His instincts told him to stand and address the threat. After the initial shock—and probably a noticeable jerking of his ghillie suit as his asshole slammed shut—his training took over and told him to stay still. The gunfire wasn't directed at him and he'd remain invisible if he didn't move. Besides, maybe one of the idiots on Echo Team was shooting at shadows. The noise definitely sounded like an unsilenced M4, which one of the men was carrying. The deafening booms stopped as quickly as they started and were followed by footsteps falling away from Echo's position. *What the fuck? Were they pursuing someone?*

Fubb hugged the muddy forest completely clueless as to what had just occurred.

"What you got, Echo?" Fubb asked over his throat mic, receiving no reply. "What's your fucking situation, Echo?" No answer. *Goddammit!*

Fubb knew the threat hadn't come from the south because that's where his weapon had been directed. He looked over at Knuckles who was on a knee pointing his rifle east toward all the commotion. Fubb pulled Knuckles back to the ground then spun around so he faced north. He didn't want someone sneaking up on their backside.

"Let's get the fuck outta here!" Knuckles said, breaking the silence.

"We're not leaving the A.O. Now, stay still and shut the fuck up!"

"Echo is that you?" Knuckles whispered into his mic. "Identify." Then louder, loud enough to be heard several meters away. "Identify yourself."

"Knuckles keep your fucking mouth shut." At the same time Fubb told his partner to be quiet, he heard the rotating bolt on Knuckles SPR Mark 12 sniper rifle slam forward. Knuckles had fired his weapon. Now it was Fubb who broke the silence, "What the fuck did you just shoot, Knuckles?"

"Nigga walking right at us. I took his bitch head off," Knuckles answered, then, "We was set up, Fubb. Time to un-ass."

Knuckles had a crude but valid argument. "I agree. This is FUBAR. Cover me, I'll go first." Fubb stood, ran thirty yards to the west, and again dropped to the forest floor. There he looked and listened, then called for Knuckles to move.

LIKE FLOWING LAVA, THORPE HAD moved slowly but

fluidly between the trees and back into the fight, prepared to scorch any living thing he crossed. He realized he wasn't using the best judgment as far as surviving the night went, but he couldn't run and spend the rest of his days looking over his shoulder. That would be no life at all. Sights up, crouched, he had moved toward a ruckus ahead of him. Perhaps one of the men he'd shot was wounded, flopping like a fish on the bank of a stream. Rounding a large oak, he'd caught partial movement out of his peripheral vision, swung his weapon to the left, applied pressure to the trigger and spotted a man in obvious distress stomping away from him. Thorpe hadn't fired. The man had been a potentially beneficial distraction and Thorpe hadn't wanted to announce his location.

He'd been considering how he might use the situation to his benefit when he'd heard a half-shouted whisper, "Identify yourself," then the injured man's head had exploded like an overripe pumpkin struck by a Nolan Ryan fastball. Thorpe had dived to the ground, and again feigned carnal knowledge with the forest floor. *Did they just kill their own man?*

A few seconds later, he saw what looked like a chunk of the forest rise from the ground and sprint to the west. Thorpe almost let loose some rounds, but remembered there were at least two assholes still alive in these woods. His volley of bullets might be answered with a well-placed sniper round, and he didn't like what he'd just witnessed with Pumpkin Head.

Then, through his scope, Thorpe watched a second pile of vegetation erupt from the forest floor. This one held a long gun, and as the bush turned to run, Thorpe put a three round burst into the man's legs. He needed one of these bastards alive, or he might never get answers. The vegetation fell to the ground, out of Thorpe's sight, and began screaming. *The Bellowing Bush*, Thorpe thought, and shook his head at himself.

"Help me...Fubb...Fubb, help me, I'm hit!"

Good of the injured man to provide intel. "Fubb," how do I know that name? Despite the pleas for help, Thorpe heard footsteps traveling the opposite direction. Fubb must have decided his buddy wasn't worth dying for.

"Fubb…Help me…Fubb!" The Bellowing Bush continued.

"Fubb," Fucked up beyond belief—FUBB—he remembered it was military slang. Thorpe wanted to get a better view of The Bellowing Bush. He looked to his left and nearly shit his trousers. A foot away, in a ghillie suit of his own, lay the body of a man; a member of Echo Team. Thorpe hadn't seen him when he dove to the ground. This close, he could make out the white unfocused eyes staring back at him. "Jesus." Thorpe slid behind the corpse, and its body armor, for cover. He placed his weapon on the dead man for support--*You don't mind do you?*—and briefly wondered if he was slipping out of reality. *No*, he always found humor in stressful situations; it was a coping mechanism, he hoped—for an alternative diagnosis might not be as palatable.

Still singing his tune, The Bellowing Bush was stuck on the same old chorus which included little more than the words, "Fubb, cocksucker, and help." Thorpe examined his human sand-bag and located the dead man's throat mic. As he worked to free the device he thought about the men with whom he shared the woods. If there were only four, then two were dead, one wounded, and the fourth in full tactical retreat. Thorpe keyed-up the radio, "Warriors, come out to play-ye. Warriors, come out to play-ye." The reference to an old classic movie was probably lost on his retreating adversary. "Fubb, I'm coming to get you, Fubb." Trying something more current, Thorpe lowered his voice, "Fubb, do you like scary movies?" *Nothing.*

FUBB HAD HEARD THE SHOTS and had watched Knuckles go down. Then he'd run another fifty to sixty yards northwest where he'd dug-in and listened to his fellow King plea for his return. *Unfucking likely.* Then he realized Knuckles had the only set of keys to his ride out of this mess and that's when it started, "Warriors, come out to play-ye. Warriors, come out to play-ye."

What the fuck? Who the fuck is this guy? Whoever he was, he'd acquired their communication's gear.

"Fubb, I'm coming to get you, Fubb…Fubb, do you like scary movies?"

Fucking comedian…got a set of balls though…I'll give 'im that. Then it dawned on Fubb that the comedian had used his street name. *Knuckles, you fucking dumb-shit!*

The voice again, "I'm going to find you, Fubb. Might as well come back and end this thing…I'm going to squeeze it out of your little bitch of a friend. I'll find out who you are, then one day you'll head out to your mailbox for your copy of *Playgirl,* and I'll paint the pavement with your gray matter. Use your buddy's sniper rifle to do it with. How does that sound, Fubb? Sound like fun to you?"

Motherfucker! Fubb had to go back and kill this prick, or at least kill Knuckles…hopefully both.

IT'D TAKEN THORPE SOME TIME to peel the Motorola radio, wires, earpiece, and throat mic from his dead bullet trap, then secure the items to his own gear. The process had been nerve-racking; The Bellowing Bush causing such a racket a whole platoon could have walked-up on Thorpe undetected. The radio in his possession, Thorpe moved toward a different location, leaving behind the dead man's rifle. It might be better equipped, but now was not the time to be experimenting with new sights and weapons.

Thorpe worked his way southwest toward the same fallen tree the sniper team had once occupied. He positioned himself on the opposite side with the road at his back. He doubted anyone would dare cross the open expanse, plus, Al and Trixie would announce the presence of any unwanted visitors. Secreted behind the log, Thorpe had a good view of The Bellowing Bush, who was still armed and therefore still dangerous.

Designed so one could speak in a whisper and be heard with

great clarity over the two-way radio, the throat mic was equipped with a push-to-talk (PTT) button which Thorpe hastily attached to his chest. He moved slowly toward the southwest while training his optics on The Bellowing Bush and the woods beyond.

"Whatta you say soldier, you going to come back and fight, or did you get your string caught on a limb running outta here like the little bitch you are?"

Fubb had to be listening, but was maintaining radio silence. *Smart.* If Thorpe were in his position, he wouldn't say anything either. No sense announcing one's intentions.

"You pussy. Can't you hear your buddy crying for you—or has your yellow ass run too far already? Never leave a man behind, remember soldier?"

In fact, The Bellowing Bush seemed to be losing much of his gusto. He no longer shouldered his weapon. Instead, he lay on his back staring up to the heavens. Thorpe feared the man might bleed-out and if the man died, his secrets would die with him.

The Bellowing Bush became the Whispering Bush. Thorpe could barely make out the man's words, "…Hágase Tu Voluntad, así en la tierra como en el Cielo. El pan nuestro de cada día dánoslo hoy, y perdona nuestras ofensas, así como nosotros perdonamos a quiénes nos ofenden, y no nos dejes caer …" Thorpe couldn't speak fluent Spanish but thought the man was reciting the Lord's Prayer. Thorpe mentally noted that if the Bellowing Bush started referring to him as Moses, then he might want to look down and make sure his rifle didn't turn into a snake. Never take a snake to a gun fight.

His only source of information fading, Thorpe felt compelled to take another risk. He slid over the log, and in a crouching position, ran toward the dying man. Thorpe landed on the man's chest, shoving the point of a large knife into his right nostril, flaying open his nose. The man's eyes registered Thorpe's presence but didn't convey pain or fear. He was ready to die.

"You speak English?"

The man didn't answer. He only stared into Thorpe's eyes.

"You want to go to heaven? You speak English?"

"Yes," he answered in a raspy voice.

Thorpe would play to the only fear the man had left. He'd been praying, hoping that God's grace would save him from his sins.

"I've sinned, you've sinned, we're all sinners. You're about to answer for yours. What's the only thing that can save your ass?"

"God's forgiveness. Not yours."

"Don't worry asshole; I'm not forgiving you for shit. But you gotta be sorry for what you've done. You have to ask God for forgiveness."

"I..."

"You gotta make things right."

"I've asked for forgiveness."

"Who sent you?"

"Please forgive me, God."

"Who the fuck sent you?"

"Please forgive me for being a Latin King."

SIXTY YARDS NORTH OF THE dying Latin King, another prayer was quietly being spoken as Fubb inched his way back "into the shit." He whispered a misguided prayer he'd been reciting since the age of thirteen, "I am a Latin King in every moment protecting my crown with all my life. It is my duty in every mission to be readily available until death. Heavenly Father forgive my sins and free my soul. Blessed be The Father, The Son and The Holy Spirit, Amor De Rey."

"You out there, Latin Kooze?"

Motherfucker! The pig is still at it. How does he know we're Kings? Knuckles!

"Fubb – Fucked Up Beyond Belief – more like Fucking Useless Buddy Boner. You know what your buddy's last words were? They were, "Fubb, you fucking pussy.""

Fubb lost his cool. Never had he endured such humiliation and not made someone pay. He keyed-up his own mic, "Fuck you. You're a dead man talkin'."

Overt sarcasm crept into Fubb's earpiece, "Fubb? Fubb is that you? Are you going to cowboy-up and join the party, Fubb?"

"Who is this? This Thorpe?"

"You guys like your cute little nicknames, your cute little initials. You can just call me Double K. That a cute name, Fubb? K.K.—King Killer."

"You're not going to make jokes when I shove a nine mil down your bitch throat."

"I doubt that, Fubb. You incompetent fuck; you shot one of your own men in the head."

"That wasn't me asshole, that was Knuckles," *Goddammit!* The cop had him all twisted around.

"Knuckles? Another cute name. You guys are just so damned cute."

"Fuck you, motherfucker," Fubb replied a bit too loudly.

A few seconds later Thorpe's mic keyed-up but no one spoke. Followed by a full minute of nothing but rustling noises. *The dumbass's mic is stuck open.* Then he heard Thorpe's voice again but this time without the sarcasm and condescending tone.

"Are Rob and Don almost in position?" Then, "They should be behind the asshole by now. Let me know when they got a shot."

Fuck! This motherfucker had help with him. No wonder his whole damn team got wiped out.

"FUCK YOU, MOTHERFUCKER." THORPE HAD heard those words through his earpiece, but, faintly, had also heard them with his free ear as well. Close and pissed-off, Fubb wasn't thinking straight.

Perhaps Thorpe had overestimated the man; apparently, a tightly wired Fubb is a stupid Fubb and stupid people are easily fooled. Thorpe held the transmit button but didn't speak. He kept it in that position for a full minute, acting as though his mic was stuck open. Then he began speaking as if someone was at his side. "Are Rob and Don almost in position? They should be behind the asshole by now. Let me know when they got a shot." Rob and Don didn't exist, but Fubb didn't know that.

Thorpe heard a primal scream, and crashing through the trees. And if Fubb's weapon hadn't been silenced, Thorpe figured he would also be hearing a volley of gunfire. Though suppressed, Thorpe could see the muzzle flashes of a weapon being fired indiscriminately. Then Thorpe saw the man behind the flashes; Fubb, out of control, charged ahead. When Fubb closed to within twenty yards, Thorpe applied six pounds of pressure to the five pound trigger and let loose a volley of rounds. The banshee of a man fell to the ground, and like the rifle he carried, was silenced.

Thorpe had witnessed a common battlefield phenomenon. Fear and anger flood the body with fight or flight chemicals producing a drug-induced soldier. Cracking from the anxiety of when, and from where, death will come, causes some men to seek it out; better to get it over with one way or another than endure another minute of death unseen. More than one combat medal for bravery had been awarded to such men. In reality their unthinkable acts of courage—like charging a machine gunner's nest—were motivated entirely by fear.

Thorpe keyed his mic and borrowing a line from another movie took one final parting jab, "Fubb, if you're still alive …I was just foolin' about."

THIRTEEN

NINE HOURS AFTER PULLING THE trigger on an unarmed
senior citizen and proud parent of a U.S. Army soldier, Carlos was
back in the same feculent house where he'd first been paired with
Loc and Speedy. His two associates slept in the living room while he
sat on the bathroom floor, back against the wall, head between his
knees, weeping.

A day ago he couldn't have fathomed being able to commit an
act half as vile as the one he'd just perpetrated, yet here he sat;
Carlos Benitez, United States Army Ranger, war hero, would-be
murderer.

Carlos didn't remember much of what happened after he pulled
the trigger on the old man. A pop that didn't seem loud enough. No
exploding head. No bullet hole. No blood. It reminded him of his
wartime dreams, the ones where he repeatedly fired on an advancing
enemy with absolutely no effect. He did remember standing above
the elderly couple, pistol limp in his hand, the wife's muffled
screams, Loc and Speedy dragging him from the house. The entire
event like an out-of-body experience, Carlos floating above, only a
witness to the atrocity, not a participant.

It wasn't until they all returned to the car that Carlos pieced
together what had happened. Loc and Speedy howled with laughter.
They laughed about Carlos' stunned expression when the gun didn't

perform; about how the pistol was loaded with blanks.

He might not have murdered anyone—but he'd meant too. And even though he'd done it only to save his own family, it was a decision he would live with with for the rest of his life.

No one had been killed, but two very clear messages had been delivered. To the Special Forces soldier: *honor your commitment to the Kings, or everyone you love will be killed.* And to Carlos: *This can happen to your family too, Soldier Boy.*

Along with the message, perhaps a revelation had also been delivered; Carlos shown what he really was. *A murderer?* Before last night, he would never have thought himself capable of committing cold-blooded murder. Yet with his wife and daughter in imminent danger, he had tried.

His thoughts vacillated from homicidal madness to suicide. Only the images of his Eva and Celestina kept him from turning those thoughts into actions. Once he found a way to keep them safe, the Kings would pay dearly. He'd kill Loc, Speedy, Alberto, Ghost, and any other pussy Latin King he was able to get his hands on. Right now though, he needed to play the part of the good little soldier.

Carlos didn't want to imagine what Eva must be thinking. He'd only been given a minute to speak with her, just long enough to be assured Celestina had been returned—unharmed. He winced as he pictured his wife and daughter, confused and terrified as strange men broke into their house and carried Celestina away. And now Eva knew Carlos was involved in something that nearly got their daughter killed. He might not ever be able to repair their relationship regardless of his explanation. And if she ever discovered what her husband had done to save Celestina, he was sure she would forever despise him. Hell, he despised himself. Carlos might have already lost his family. The only thing he could do for them now was keep them safe.

Sitting on the filthy linoleum, Carlos heard pounding at the small home's front door. Seconds later he listened as Loc welcomed

Uncle Alberto inside. Carlos pushed himself up the wall, looked in the dirty mirror, turned on the faucet, splashed cold water on his face, and took a deep breath before exiting the bathroom. *Be his dog now, bite his hand later.* Carlos walked down the short hallway to his smiling uncle.

"There's my favorite nephew."

Bastard just kidnapped my daughter, threatened to rape and murder her, and he's acting like we're best friends. "Uncle," Carlos greeted. He couldn't muster a smile but was trying with considerable will not to look at Alberto with murderous eyes.

"Heard you did good, Carlos. I knew you had it in you. You're going to go places in the Nation. Maybe be La Corona some day, huh?"

Fuck your Corona. You don't believe in this shit anymore than I do, you fucking hustler. "I'll do whatever the Nation has me do, Uncle." *Good little dog.*

Alberto lost the smile, "Yes you will, Carlos…Yes you will," then added, "Do you know why I chose you to pull the trigger, Carlos?"

Carlos nodded his head. He did know.

"That old couple has a boy who made a commitment to the Nation, Carlos. He didn't keep his promise. We couldn't get to him because he's hiding in the army, but we could get to those he loved. Blood-in, blood-out, remember? If he doesn't come back to us, his parents will pay the blood for him. Man's gotta keep his word, Carlos. Or he ain't a man."

"I understand."

"I know you do," Alberto said with a smile. "This is a momentous day, Carlos. You made your commitment many years ago but today you earn your crown." Alberto gestured to the room, "Usually initiations are a bit more ceremonious but you're going to be an undercover King, like the Insane Unknowns use to be."

In the 1970s the Latin Kings had achieved a certain notoriety; some would say they were getting a little too notorious. The police were forced to respond and increased their efforts to incarcerate the gang's members—especially its leaders. In an effort to avoid heightened police scrutiny, the Kings started a splinter gang and named them the Insane Unknowns. In reality, the **UnK**nowns were **U**ndercover **K**ings. Thinking about it now, Carlos thought the play on letters had a juvenile quality about it. In fact, the more he considered it, gangs in general echoed emotionally underdeveloped twelve-year-olds. No surprise there, because on average Latin Kings join the gang at around twelve years of age.

Carlos did as he was told and stood against the living room wall. Loc and Speedy approached him as Uncle Alberto looked down at a large expensive-looking watch.

"Three minutes brothers…Go."

The blows rained down. Carlos leaned against the wall and took the beating like a man. Initiations were not head-to-toe, meaning Carlos shouldn't be hit in the head, neck, or groin. However, he did have to endure three minutes of getting punched and kicked in the arms, stomach, chest, and legs. Speedy and Loc appeared to be thoroughly enjoying their workout. They pummeled Carlos with enthusiasm and without mercy. At first Carlos recoiled from the intense pain, then, as the assault continued, found salvation in it. It provided relief from his emotional turmoil. He came to cherish every punch thrown. After a minute and a half, he barked at his punishers as they began losing steam. "Is that all you got?"

His baiting caused a brief flurry but after another twenty seconds or so Speedy and Loc were spent. The punches came slower with no snap behind them.

"Time. Carlos has earned his crown."

Following Alberto's announcement, Loc and Speedy embraced Carlos, "Amor de Rey, hasta la muerte"—King love until death. Carlos found the welcome unconvincing. Then, Uncle Alberto approached, put both hands on Carlos' shoulders and said, "King Too Tall. Amor, brother."

Alberto had used Carlos' military nickname. A name he'd

never shared with his uncle or any other civilian for that matter. His uncle was an informed man and he had just let Carlos know it.

Alberto headed for the door, "Don't leave town, King Too Tall. I've got work for you in the next few days. Loc will drive you to your new apartment."

"Uncle, I'd like to call my wife."

"Of course, Too Tall. You don't need permission from me to talk to your own wife. But you might not be able to reach her right now, she's on a flight."

"Flight? Where's she going?"

"Coming, Too Tall, not going. She and Celestina are on a flight to Chicago. I think she was about to pack her bags and leave you. We couldn't have that, could we? You know, you should learn to be a little more forthcoming with your wife," Alberto grinned, getting in one last shot before he disappeared out the door.

Fucking asshole.

"Let's go, King Too Tall. I wanna go home and get some sleep," Loc breathed. He was still panting from his workout.

Carlos was barely able to move his limbs and wouldn't be surprised if he had a couple of cracked ribs. But no way in hell would he let Loc and Speedy see his pain. Carlos followed Loc out the front door, and though wearing the same clothing as when he'd first arrived, he left a much different man.

FOURTEEN

DAYLIGHT HAD BROKEN AND THORPE wasn't far behind.
Having lain motionless for more than three hours the inactivity had
driven him to the cusp of madness. Unsure if others still prowled
these woods, or if Fubb lay dead, injured, or was just playing
possum, Thorpe had made a promise to remain stationary for four
hours. He hoped any living adversaries would be the first ones to
move and pay the price of impetuousness.

Hunters of large game generally wait a half hour or more before
tracking quarry they've shot. Wounded animals will run for short
distances then search for a place to lie down and hide, where they
often succumb to their injuries. If a hunter looks for the animal
before it's dead, the prey will hear the hunter coming and continue to
run. The "shoot and wait" philosophy is even more important when
the hunted is capable of fighting back. You don't want to go looking
for wounded prey and have it kill you from its hide.

Comfort was a commodity which had deserted Thorpe hours
ago. His cocked back neck ached from looking through a scope all
night, his ribs hurt from lying on something rigid, his shoulders from
being extended, and his ear throbbed from the bullet wound. And if

that weren't enough, he'd urinated in his trousers about an hour ago. There are no time-outs for potty breaks during combat. Thorpe was thankful nature hadn't beckoned in other more substantive areas; he probably would have taken his chances with a bullet rather than "drop a deuce" in his BDUs.

Despite his discomfort, Thorpe knew he was better off than anyone else who might be sharing these woods. His woods. If by some miracle Fubb still lived, he was nursing several oozing bullet holes. And if there were gunmen he hadn't yet encountered, they'd be dealing with even more anxiety than Thorpe. The deputy who'd driven by would have been cause for concern. One of Thorpe's distant neighbors had undoubtedly heard the shots and phoned it in to the sheriff's office. Gunfire in this area is not uncommon during all hours of the day and night, but the burst of automatic fire had caught someone's attention. Twice the deputy passed with his car's spotlight cast into the woods, but at speeds much too fast to be able to see anything.

Thorpe didn't blame him. The deputy would have no way to pinpoint the location of the gunfire in these vast woods. Plus, if someone fired at him from the trees, he'd be a sitting-duck behind the wheel of his squad car. The deputy did just enough to avoid a complaint for "lack of police action" then got the hell out of Dodge, probably attributing the call to nervous neighbors mistaking firecrackers for a gun battle.

Thorpe switched off the night optics an hour ago. The green and black hues gave way to the grays, blacks, and browns of a leafless sunrise in the wilderness. Through the morning three cars passed behind him; he hadn't risked turning to look, but none slowed significantly. An occasional whimper let him know his dogs were still alive. Their master was out in the woods and something wasn't right.

Having made his four-hour goal, Thorpe slowly rose from the forest floor to one knee. Prickling sensations swam over his body as blood rushed back into oxygen-starved muscles. He remained still for two reasons; he was looking for movement in response to his own, and he didn't quite have his legs back underneath him. As he kneeled, he looked down on an exposed root and the source of much of his discomfort, and thought *I'll be back for you later*. Thorpe stood, then took a circular route to where he'd seen the charging Fubb make his last stand. Behind him, Al and Trixie upped their whining as they sensed their owner's movements.

Thorpe spotted Fubb's boots first, then the man's optics. The optics were attached to a suppressed MP5 and was pointed toward where Thorpe had spent the last four hours. Behind the optics lay the man formally known as Fubb, who had died true to his name; he was Fucked-Up-Beyond-Belief. He had apparently lived long enough to get his weapon out in front of him in hopes that Thorpe would come investigate—if Thorpe could move his arms right now, he'd pat himself on the back for his patience.

Fubb died looking through his optics ignoring the fact his lower face was missing in action. Thorpe wasn't worried about Fubb's three associates either. Pumpkin Head could not have survived the high-powered round that nearly caused his decapitation. He'd watched The Bellowing Bush die. And he'd looked into the lifeless eyes of his human sandbag.

Thorpe checked the area around Fubb's corpse then carefully checked his sides before rolling him over. He'd really be pissed having survived the ambush if he were to lose an arm, or worse, because Fubb had booby-trapped his own body with a fragmentation grenade. Thorpe peered down at Fubb's mangled face, *Who the hell are you, Fubb, and why do you want me dead?* Thorpe looked up to the sky with tired eyes and knew it was going to be a long day trying to find the answers to those questions.

FIFTEEN

SAEED AL-HAZNAWI SHOULD HAVE BEEN in a much better mood. He'd pledged his commitment to jihad many years ago and hadn't once been called upon to exercise his—what he considered to be—immeasurable skills. But now, *now* he was doing something for the cause. *What* he was doing, he wasn't entirely sure but it must be monumental considering all the misdirections and feints that had been implemented over the last few days.

Only one thing dampened his spirit. *Soaked* his spirit. If one was to examine Saeed's manhood he or she might think they were looking at a recently grated beer brat. In fact, Saeed had packed his underwear with tampons to keep from bleeding through his pants. For three days he'd been suffering, unable to seek medical treatment. Saeed shuddered at the thought of infection. *Would they amputate? Ambretta, that fucking bitch!* He still wasn't sure what had happened.

He remembered sitting behind the wheel, watching those full lips of Ambretta's just inches away from his healthy penis. Then darkness. He woke behind a van on the filthy concrete floor of the parking garage, his head throbbing. Lightning bolts of pain from his groin quickly overpowered his headache and he looked down to see his penis reduced to a few ounces of raw hamburger meat. He lay there weeping, his once-white linen pants around his ankles.

After gathering himself, he returned to his car finding the driver's side window completely obliterated and Ambretta gone. *At least the police hadn't been summoned.*

Had someone come to her aid? Had he been robbed? He checked for his wallet and found it missing as well. *He'd been robbed*; his wallet, IDs, and a couple hundred dollars all gone. *But what had happened to Ambretta? She hadn't called the police. Kidnapped?*

Then, for the very first time, it occurred to Saeed that Ambretta might be law enforcement. *What if he'd been under surveillance? If so, he'd be in custody already, yes?* Saeed knew he should report the incident to his superiors. But then he wouldn't be able to participate in the jihad—and Allah had plans for him—he was sure of it. *No, he'd been robbed. It was that simple.* Besides, if his superiors discovered he'd been dating a possible law enforcement official, he would be shown no mercy. And death would come behind a friendly smile, and at the hand of one of his "brothers." Saeed would tell no one. He cleaned his wounds as best he could and hoped for Allah to take care of the rest.

That night he'd driven back home, and even though the driver's side window was permanently open, he vomited on the passenger seat. Once inside his apartment, he walked straight to the bathroom, locked the door, took six extra-strength Tylenol, sat naked in the bathtub, placed a rag between his teeth, and dumped the entire contents of a hydrogen peroxide bottle on his mangled manhood.

The pain crashed over him like a giant wave, sweeping him under and into blackness. He woke slathered in sweat, not knowing how long he'd been out. Lying in the tub, Saeed retrieved a chunk of glass from a slightly torn left testicle, which must have gotten snagged when he was pulled through the car window. He slept in the tub that night; the absolute worst of his life. The next morning his roommate pounded on the bathroom door. Saeed screamed that he was ill and pleaded to be left alone. His roommate muttered something about the evils of alcohol before slamming the apartment door as he departed.

Now, three days later, perspiring from the relentless pain in his lap, he drove a blue Ford F-150 on Interstate 75 headed toward Chattanooga, Tennessee. He'd twice switched cars before meeting the man who'd given him this truck, its papers, a map, a pre-programmed GPS navigation device, and a new cell phone. He'd also been provided a cover story in the event he was pulled over by police. Otherwise, the instructions were brief: *Adhere to all traffic laws. Remain calm and comply with commands if you are stopped by the police. We will be following you. Don't search for us with your eyes; you won't be able to see us but we are there. If we need to intervene, we will.*

His first indicated stop was a motel in Louisville, Kentucky. Driving, and in spite of the man's implicit instructions, Saeed couldn't help but try and locate his tail. A few times, and at considerable distances, he thought he'd noticed the same black sedan in his rearview mirror. But often the sedan fell so far behind that he'd lose visual contact for several miles. He questioned how they could effectively follow him at such long intervals, and reached the conclusion the truck, or his new cell phone, was most likely equipped with a tracking device.

He also wondered what the man had meant when he said they would "intervene" if there was a need. *Would they kill a police officer right on the side of the highway, or simply drive on and let Saeed take the fall? And take the fall for what? He'd searched the cab and cargo area of the truck and both were empty, and he didn't know shit about shit.* If he were questioned, he certainly couldn't jeopardize the mission because he didn't know what the hell the mission was.

SEVEN MILES BEHIND SAEED, AND six miles behind Saeed's babysitters, Ambretta reclined in her leather bucket seat. She adjusted the mirrors on her slate-colored Nissan Pathfinder to accommodate two more inches of slant and settled in for a long drive. She hadn't the slightest clue of her destination.

Ben had called in additional manpower three days ago. He'd anticipated an increase in activity based on chatter they'd picked up through an array listening devices put into place the last few weeks. And it's a good thing he did. Nearly every car they'd identified and wired went into motion early this morning. All of Saeed's associates were on the move. No less than thirteen surveillance personnel were currently involved in the follow. And they needed every single person. The morning had been a game of musical cars, many of which had been switched with previously unknown vehicles, including rentals.

Four hours after rats began jumping off the USS Atlanta, surveillance teams knew of at least three pairs of vehicles taking various routes out of the city. The first pair to move was a blue Honda minivan northbound via Interstate 85, being loosely followed by a white Chevy Malibu. Forty-five minutes later, a blue Ford F-150 driven by Ambretta's wannabe lover left the city followed by a black Honda Accord, all northbound on Interstate 75. Thirty minutes after that, another set of cars left the city also traveling northbound on 75.

Every vehicle was a potential threat. It could also be a shell game where only one of the six vehicles carried anything of significance. Or the entire operation could be a complex misdirection aimed at diverting manpower from the real threat—assuming there was a threat at all; an assumption they had to make.

Whatever the suspects' intentions, the surveillance teams were now divided into four groups. Most were following the three pairs of cars headed out of the city. Five remained in Atlanta, pinning down new developments and keeping an eye on abandoned vehicles in the event they started moving again.

Directionally, Interstate 85 took a northeasterly route, while Interstate 75 followed a northwesterly course. A state-of-the-art helicopter, outfitted with rotors and technology that minimized blade-vortex interaction (it was quiet), followed the Interstate 85 targets.

Ben, responsible for monitoring the entire complicated affair, provided feedback on the vehicles' movements. If the groups continued in different directions, those responsibilities would eventually have to be divided.

Ambretta's current assignment was a simple one. Stay away. Too many of Saeed's associates knew her face and would find it more than a coincidence if they encountered her outside Atlanta.

SIXTEEN

WEARING A WHITE, STAY PUFT Marshmallow suit, Thorpe stood inside his barn overlooking four nearly naked cadavers growing stiff on a sheet of plastic. Seeing the bodies this way—in various stages of *rigor mortis*—brought home the finality of his actions. Yet he felt no remorse. It was kill or be killed, and instead of these men, it could very well have been him growing cold on the concrete floor. Still, the scene sickened him. Even more disgusting was what he proposed to do with them.

The suit Thorpe wore was one of many issued to all members of the Clandestine Lab Investigation Team. Thorpe shook his head in disbelief at whoever concocted the title. The name became official before management realized what the acronym would most assuredly become. More than a few "C.L.I.T." emblazoned t-shirts hung in the closets of SID investigators.

Designed to keep harmful biological and chemical elements away from its occupant, Thorpe donned the suit to keep evidence off his skin and clothing. Of course, the "theory of transference" ensured he would leave behind traces of the Tychem suit on the bodies. Not a common garment, but still a far better choice than leaving behind hair, blood, spit, or a plethora of other physical evidence. Besides, anything transferred to these cadavers wouldn't be usable in a few hours. Not with what he planned to do to them.

Hauling the four bodies to the barn in the middle of the day hadn't been without stress. He'd dragged them to the edge of the woods, fetched his truck from Deborah's barn, laid plastic down in the bed, and loaded them directly in front of his house. That had been a nerve-racking experience. On top of the possibility of being discovered, he was further cognizant he could be the unwilling recipient of a bullet from unknown associates of Fubb and Friends.

Once in the barn, Thorpe arranged the men in order of their demise, stripped them of equipment, and searched their bodies and belongings. None of the men had been carrying identification or cell phones. Only one, The Bellowing Bush, possessed keys.

Thorpe used a digital camera to photograph the four dead men. He began with the body on the left—the first killed—Human Sandbag. Mr. Sandbag wore two full sleeves of tattoos. In the midst of all the ink he found a five-point crown. To the left of the crown was a large "L," to the right a large "K;" between each point in the crown a letter, "A, L, K, and N." The man was a Latin King. The second cadaver, Pumpkin Head, also sported several tattoos; the most distinctive being a marijuana leaf on his abdomen and a lion wearing a crown on his chest. The third man, Bellowing Bush, displayed one simple King tattoo on his right bicep and an intricate Virgin Mary that covered the entirety of his back.

The fourth body, Fubb, wore no gang-affiliated tattoos whatsoever. All of his body art appeared to be military inspired, including one indicating he served with the 101st Airborne. It looked to Thorpe that Fubb was the only true soldier in the group. It made him curious as to the men's relationship. *Had the Kings enlisted Fubb? Had Fubb sought-out the Kings?* He doubted the latter; Fubb probably would have been successful had he come into the woods alone. Thorpe had barely recognized the signs of four men skulking around his property. He might never have identified one lone professional soldier.

Luck. Thorpe had it. He stepped left when the bullet went right. Always yinged when peril yanged. Not his family. Those he loved met the bullet head-on, leaving Thorpe to wither in the aftermath. *Luck? More of a curse. How many times had he asked God to take him instead of his wife, daughter, father, and mother?* Even worse, Thorpe felt responsible for each and every one of their deaths. His wife and daughter were killed because Thorpe's profession found him at home. His parents were dead because Thorpe had, at only 16 years of age, killed a man.

His father had taken him on one of their regular "fishing trips." The trips had nothing to do with fish, they were training missions. His father passed down the only skill set he possessed to his son. Instead of team sports and go carts, his father taught him the finer points of armed and unarmed combat.

On one particular outing Thorpe's more-than-willing-opponent produced a knife, turning a simple fist fight into a life-threatening encounter. In a matter of seconds, Thorpe sustained several stabs and slashes before securing the man's wrist and burying his thumb into his eye socket. A few twists and scoops later the man lay on the ground, body convulsing.

Thorpe thought about that night often. *Once he'd secured the man's wrist, could he have subdued him without using deadly force? Maybe.* His split-second decision as a threatened teenager completely altered his life's course. Had he restrained the man, there wouldn't have been a need to avoid police scrutiny. His father could have taken him to an emergency room instead of home. Home, where Thorpe's father treated his injuries with a simple combat medical kit; home, where his mother learned what their "fishing trips" were really about; home, where, because of Thorpe, his parents separated; home, where his father left for duty never to return; home, where a short time later his mother died; her body ravaged by cancer in a matter of months. Home.

And home was where his wife and daughter had been killed; murdered because Thorpe had gotten unwittingly close to uncovering a small band of corrupt officers. "The Band," that's what they called themselves.

A confidential informant provided the spark that ultimately killed his family; one maggot selling out another maggot to save his own skin. In the process two precious innocent lives were caught in the crossfire. Thorpe's wife and daughter died because of his efforts to make Tulsa a safer place for a bunch of citizens who didn't give a shit about him to begin with. All of them shocked when some jobless, "occupy" asshole is sprayed in the face with pepper spray. *OMG, that poor man who spit on that cop and told him go fuck himself might be uncomfortable for twenty minutes!* But none show a sliver of outrage whenever a police officer is gunned down on some lonely street, leaving a family fatherless or motherless forever. Thorpe willingly put his own life on the line for strangers. It was the vow he'd made. He never thought his family would be the ones to pay the price.

The catalyst to his family's demise—the confidential informant (CI)—had arranged for a man he only knew as "Rocc" to deliver an eight-ball of crack cocaine to an East Tulsa convenience store. In order to protect the identity of the informant, Thorpe and his OGU investigators planned to stop the suspect's car before it arrived at the prearranged meeting place. Rocc's real name a mystery, officers only had a physical description and information he drove a newer, white, Dodge Stratus.

As is generally the case, the deal didn't go according to plan. Investigators and marked takedown units were twisted around by ever-changing plans and meeting places. It took an hour before Thorpe and a couple of OGU investigators finally located and stopped the Stratus.

Thorpe wished they had never found the car. Inside the vehicle were Lyndale and Leon Peterson, sons of Charlie Peterson, a notorious black activist and fellow TPD officer. A racial profiling complaint imminent, it didn't matter how much probable cause they articulated. If the two sons had been driving down the street tossing dead bodies out of the car, they still would have filed a complaint. That's just the way things were, and everyone knew it.

Thorpe briefly felt like a professional bass fisherman because the phrase "catch and release" kept repeating itself in his head. But releasing the men was not the right thing to do and wouldn't have stopped a complaint anyway. He might as well locate corroborating evidence—though anything he found would later be alleged as "planted."

Charlie's eldest son, Lyndale Peterson, sat behind the wheel and his younger brother, Leon, in the back seat. But the thing Thorpe found interesting then, and even more so now, was the Hispanic gang member riding shotgun. The man was a Latin King out of Chicago. Tulsa drew its fair share of Hispanic gang members like MS-13, the Surenos, and the Nortenos. But that had been the first Latin King Thorpe had ever encountered in Tulsa. Though now, just over a year later, LK's were not uncommon.

A subsequent search of the vehicle yielded two loaded handguns under the driver's seat, an eight-ball in Lyndale's sock, additional cocaine in the engine compartment, and a small amount of marijuana in Leon's pant pocket. The three suspects were transported to the Mingo Valley Division for interviews. Surprisingly, Lyndale manned-up and took responsibility for the weapons and all the cocaine. Unfortunately, the confession led to the release of the Chicago Latin King—who kept his mouth shut during the entire incident. Leon received a month in County because the marijuana charge was a second offense, but Lyndale got hammered. A three time loser, he was sent to Big Mac—Oklahoma State Penitentiary—with a lengthy stint. Later, detectives traced the gun to a third-party purchase in Chicago, Illinois. Clearly, for whatever reason, Lyndale had taken the fall for the Latin King's gun. It was possible, probable even, that some of the cocaine belonged to the Latin King's as well.

Coincidence? Thorpe looked down on the three, possibly four, dead Latin Kings who tried to kill him. If Lyndale took the fall for the Latin King, then the Kings owed Lyndale a huge favor. And if Lyndale was aware Thorpe had killed his brother last month, he'd want payback. Perhaps the attempt on Thorpe's life was an effort by the Kings to repay their debt to Lyndale. The thread was thin, but it was the only thing Thorpe could find to latch onto.

SEVENTEEN

ALBERTO VEGA WAS NOT A happy man. Something was wrong and it couldn't be happening at a worse time. He hadn't been terribly concerned when he'd arrived home at three o'clock this morning. On the contrary, he'd still been riding the high of witnessing his once smug "nephew" get a beat down, both physically and emotionally. Plus, the bastard's family was en route to Chicago where they'd all be under Alberto's thumb. He'd even had a good laugh picturing Carlos' daughter being initiated into the Nation in a few years. *Queen Celestina! That would really show the little prick.*

No, last night he'd been in an excellent mood. So much so that he'd had a romp with his girlfriend who he'd found passed out on the couch wearing nothing but a thong. He'd come home, walked straight to the bedroom, retrieved a tube of lubricant, pulled off her panties, and thoroughly roughed her up. He screwed her as she lay passed out in one of her drug-induced comas. Alberto acknowledged his brain, sex-wise, might not be wired quite right. He preferred to have sex with women when they were comatose. *Oh well, everyone has their vices.*

Finished violating his living blow-up doll, Alberto stayed awake a couple more hours hoping to hear back from Fubb and the team's progress in Tulsa. Eventually, he'd given up and gone to bed, still unconcerned. In the event one or more were captured, the team had instructions to perform the hit on the pig without identification, cell phones, or any other items which could be traced. If they were apprehended, none of the men would talk. Alberto was sure of that. Loose lips would mean the total elimination of the snitch's loved ones. It wasn't until Alberto woke at three this afternoon that he'd become concerned.

A microwave clock told him two things: it was 5:03p.m. and Fubb was way past overdue. Alberto sat on a stool at his kitchen's marble countertop hunched over a laptop searching Tulsa's news sites. There was no word of a Tulsa police officer having been killed. Thankfully, there'd been no reports of an unsuccessful attempt on a police officer's life either. *Maybe they killed Thorpe out in the boonies. He supposedly lived out in the sticks. Or, maybe they were having trouble with their...what did they call it? Extraction.*

The biggest score of Alberto's life was hours away and he didn't need this headache. *Where were those assholes?* If he didn't hear from them by tomorrow morning, he would send someone to Tulsa to look for them. Fubb's crew was a big part of his payday and if they went and got themselves arrested he was fucked.

Alberto's bleached-blonde girlfriend slid the patio door open and stepped inside. She'd been boiling herself in the hot tub. She pressed her wet, recently purchased, bare breasts against Alberto's back, and began rubbing his neck as she peered over his shoulder.

"The Tulsa World? Why you reading that, baby?"

Alberto swiveled on his stool, smiled, and slapped her to the carpet. Her floss-inspired bikini bottoms stared back at Alberto's throbbing hand.

"Bitch, mind your own fucking business."

DUMPED OFF AT HIS NEW apartment building in the Gage Park area of Southwest Chicago with instructions to contact the manager and retrieve his keys, Carlos tried the man's door with no answer. Exhausted, he sat beside the manager's apartment and fell asleep atop his rucksack. His new neighbors probably mistook him for a homeless man sleeping in the hallway, especially since he hadn't been able to wash the fear-laced sweat off his body or out of his clothes.

Carlos woke to a fat man kicking him in the thigh and yelling for him to "Get the fuck out." The fat man turned out to be the building's manager. Carlos explained who he was and that he'd been told by Alberto Vega to retrieve keys to his new apartment. The super said, "If I knew you smelled like a fucking dog, I wouldn't have leased you the room." Carlos was too tired to explain or to care. What could he say, he'd been too busy pretending to kill senior citizens to worry about personal hygiene? After busting his balls for a few more minutes, the manager supplied Carlos with two keys, told him his first three months rent had already been paid, then told him to get his stinking body out of his doorway and take a bath.

Carlos located his apartment on the fourth floor, stepped inside, and found a shabbily furnished interior. He'd stayed in worse; so had his wife for that matter, but their daughter deserved better.

Carlos' first order of business was to take a shower but discovered the bathroom lacked soap. Reluctant, but determined to scrub himself clean, he knocked on a neighbor's door to ask for a bar. The woman who opened the door was very attractive, and normally Carlos would've been embarrassed by his appearance, but he didn't give two shits about much anymore. When you were trying to save your family and salvage your soul, everything else seemed frivolous.

The woman stared at him from behind the chain as if he were a dog pissing in her doorway. Without a word, she closed the door in Carlos' face. Undeterred, he crossed the hall to try a different neighbor. He began knocking when the attractive woman again cracked open her door and slipped a bar of soap through the gap and out onto the hallway's wooden floor. Carlos tried to thank the woman who once more wordlessly shut him out. He returned to his apartment, showered, and put on a clean pair of boxers then fell asleep on the cheap, well-worn couch.

He labored through a few hours of daytime nightmares before waking in a cold sweat. With nothing else to do, he sat waiting for his family to arrive home—such as it was—nervous and afraid. *Would his wife's looks of unconditional love and yearning be replaced by those of disgust and regret?* Carlos didn't want to see those looks; he didn't know if he could survive them. The promises he'd made to Alberto so many years ago had come from a frightened, impressionable young boy. Now a man, he'd been held responsible for those promises. The toll he'd paid was steep, and carried out only to save his family. Still, it didn't change what he'd done. Pulling the trigger on that old man had only discharged a blank cartridge, yet still it resulted in a death of sorts. His own. Carlos was tarnished and his wife would surely see the stain.

Carlos' heart lurched into his throat as he heard rapping on the apartment door. His body still reeled from the punishment he'd received from Loc and Speedy. He struggled from the couch and limped barefoot across the gummy carpet. Carlos looked through the peephole at the fisheye image of his wife. Even through the contoured glass he could see the anger radiating from her like heat off of blacktop. Carlos took a deep breath and opened the door for his bride. She stood motionless on the other side of the threshold. In her eyes he saw hatred, and worse, pain. But as her eyes looked upon his body he saw them soften. Anger gave way to fear, concern, *love?*

"Oh my God, Carlos. What did they do to you?"

Dressed only in a pair of boxers, Carlos looked down. His body was one incoherent mass of purple and black. He hadn't noticed before—nor cared. Eva stepped across the threshold, placed her cheek on his chest, and pulled him in tight. And though the embrace stung every cell in his body, it was the greatest sensation he'd ever experienced. And, at least for a few seconds, everything was right with the world.

EIGHTEEN

ANY PERSON WHO WALKS INTO a Tulsa hospital with a gunshot wound, a daily occurrence in the city, is going to get a visit from a Tulsa police officer. Oftentimes the victim doesn't want to make a report and refuses to cooperate. However, when pressed into giving a statement they frequently fabricate the circumstances, the location, and the suspects responsible. Most of these shooting "victims" have intentions of seeking justice on their own without the helping hand of law enforcement. The majority of police officers didn't give a shit about the lack of cooperation. Let the little gangbangers kill each other. It's cheaper than housing their asses in prison for the rest of their lives, which is where they're all headed anyway. The problems occurred when innocent bystanders got caught in the crossfire.

Earlier, Thorpe found himself in a similar situation as he sat in an emergency room waiting to have his ear sewn back together. He'd already concocted a bogus story. The location of his injury made the wound difficult to attribute to a gunshot. His ear was more torn than pierced.

He'd told the medical staff he'd been in the woods where he fell into a ravine. He didn't know what he struck while tumbling down the hill, but it tore his ear. The story also helped explain the mud packed wound. The lie, paired with Thorpe letting everyone know he was a Tulsa police officer, must have been enough to convince the attending staff, because his fellow brothers in blue were never summoned. Or, much like police officers, the doctors and nurses didn't give a shit.

Thorpe stood inside a small bathroom looking in a mirror at his newest damage and thought by the time he was forty he wouldn't have a plot of skin without scar tissue. He had a collection of scars behind his eyebrows from having taken a few too many punches over the years. He suffered a slight case of the cauliflower syndrome in his right ear, the mild deformity now aggravated by a bullet ripping off a chunk of his upper lobe. He might have to look into plastic surgery someday. Not out of vanity, but because the wound was a distinguishing characteristic and therefore highly identifiable.

Thorpe's torso also bore an assortment of scars, the result of numerous confrontations. The most severe of which had come from a man Thorpe killed in self-defense. The fight had been a fair one; right up until his opponent pulled a hidden knife and began treating Thorpe like a carrot in a Ginsu commercial. To save himself, Thorpe drove his thumb into the man's eye socket up to the webbing of his hand, then commenced to scrambling the man's brains with the appendage.

Thorpe's scars were a constant reminder of his history and the violence it contained: like the first man he ever killed and the night that changed and haunted his life forever; a night that cost him his father, and eventually his mother. His scar collection grew rapidly following his mother's lost battle with cancer. He'd acted out of despair—much like he did now—except then his actions were without direction and had far fewer consequences. However, the deepest cuts Thorpe sustained were not physical. The loss of his father, mother, wife, and child left wounds that would never be filled, nor healed, by scar tissue.

Exhausted, Thorpe turned from the mirror. He had much to do. Though he'd once again acted in self-defense, he couldn't possibly go to the authorities and attempt to explain the four men who'd just tried to kill him. If he was right, the investigation would lead to Lyndale, and eventually back to Thorpe and the blood-bath of February.

Thorpe had called in a vacation day, then phoned his neighbor, Deborah, and requested the use of her barn. The barn contained a loft with a kitchenette and bathroom. The bathroom was where he stood now. The loft was designed to house a live-in groundskeeper or stable boy, for which the owners never had any need.

At Thorpe's request, Deborah kept the barn off-limits to Realtors showing clients the property unless they gave ample warning. For the time being he would stay in her barn. He thought it unwise to remain in his home until all threats had been identified and eliminated.

He had dumped the cadavers in an area where two others already rested. Tonight, he would place a screen around the six corpses and burn them; hopefully destroying any physical evidence he had inadvertently transferred to their bodies. He'd be sure to plant additional physical evidence in the dirt surrounding the remains. Evidence which would point to others.

The plants would be hairs and fibers from combs and other items he'd collected while serving search warrants on the scum of Tulsa. Those men would never be charged with the murders, probably, but if Thorpe became a suspect, the planted evidence would be enough to cast doubt on anyone trying to convict him of the killings. Although the gravesite wasn't on his property, it was still much too close for comfort, and eventually the burned remains would need to be moved.

Thorpe pulled a black stocking cap down over his bandaged ear, retrieved the Toyota keys he'd taken off The Bellowing Bush, and jogged down the stairs to his undercover Ford F-150. He planned to search the area surrounding his property for an abandoned Toyota. The men had been careful not to carry anything nonessential to their mission with the exception of the keys. That led Thorpe to believe they didn't have a fifth man responsible for their extraction.

Instead, they had a vehicle parked nearby.

The men who'd come to kill him approached from the north. Thorpe decided to search that area first. He'd drive-out the neighborhoods, if one could call them that, north of his property; they were actually a collection of ranches, farms, and houses, occupied by those who wanted to live near the city but still have the solitude and seclusion of acreage.

The sun having retreated, Thorpe rolled down the windows on his truck to help him spot the secreted car without the hindrance of window tint. Twenty minutes later, Thorpe located a car and knew he had his vehicle. A newer Toyota Camry four door sat on the shoulder of Shortcut Road, the hood raised as if it were broken-down. As Thorpe passed the car, he hit the electronic "lock" button on the key and observed the Toyota's lights flash. The Camry wasn't disabled. It was the King's getaway car.

Thorpe conducted a U-turn and returned to Deborah's barn. He would have a long trip back on foot to retrieve the Toyota, but he hadn't had much exercise today and was looking forward to the run. Once he got the Camry back to the barn, he would thoroughly search the car and hopefully find a clue as to the men's identities.

If the Camry turned out to be a dead end, Thorpe would pursue other avenues to determine the men's identities. His friend, Robert Hull, would be called on to assist once again, though Thorpe planned on keeping the sergeant over the Homicide Unit unaware of his contributions.

NINETEEN

CARLOS COULDN'T FATHOM THE AMOUNT of unconditional love, forgiveness, and understanding his wife bestowed upon him. Two hours ago he'd felt like the most hapless man on earth. Now, he wondered what he'd done to deserve the devotion of such a woman. Carlos explained how he'd been manipulated as a boy. He told of the leverage Uncle Alberto plied to get him to do his bidding. His wife hadn't blamed Carlos, but she was angry he hadn't trusted her enough to tell that side of his life before now.

Eva didn't know what Carlos had done to save their daughter. She told Carlos she didn't want to know. She too would do anything to protect Celestina. Anything. That didn't stop Carlos from thinking of the couple he'd been willing to kill to save his daughter. Those two faces would torment him the rest of his days.

Carlos and Eva sat on their secondhand couch and plotted how to escape Uncle Alberto's clutches. Their plan involved much deception and violence, but both were prepared to do whatever necessary to protect their daughter.

ELISA RUIZ SAT ON HER leather sofa watching a drama unfold on television. Despite living in a somewhat squalid apartment building, her place was nicely equipped and furnished. One of her few complaints would be the occasional cockroach that strayed from one of the other apartments in search of better accommodations. Otherwise, unless she looked out her peephole for a reality check, she could have been residing in a luxury condominium.

Elisa Ruiz was a Latin Queen, a very beautiful LQ; attractive enough she'd caught the attention of Alberto Vega and became his lover. Never truly attracted to the man, she *was* attracted to the man's money. He paid the rent on her apartment and had purchased nearly everything contained within. All she had to do in return was suffer the occasional romp and dole out a little dope from her living room.

Besides, she never remembered the sex. During his visits, she regularly passed out early into the night. The next morning she'd wake up with a sore ass and genitals. She wasn't stupid. She knew Alberto had been slipping something into her drinks, probably a date rape drug. *Whatever*, her lack of consciousness made the relationship with the man that much easier to endure. She gave him what he wanted and didn't have to fake enjoying it.

The drama on Elisa's screen was some of the best reality television she'd ever seen. The program starred her new next door neighbor and his wife. The theme of the show would be quite interesting to Alberto, particularly since the subject of their discussion happened to be his demise. She'd forward the information to help ensure Alberto found her to be useful in areas other than the one-way sex. With any luck he'd continue to be her sugar-daddy for the foreseeable future.

Elisa redirected her attention to another screen. If not for the soft glow of a nearby nightlight, she wouldn't have been able to see the angelic face of Celestina. The young girl looked peaceful in her sleep. Elisa couldn't help but think the girl wouldn't have the same expression if she knew what was about to happen to her parents.

TWENTY

THE SUN YET TO RISE, Hull stood outside an electronics store staring at a banner with unfocused eyes, *NO INTEREST NO PAYMENTS FOR six months*. This was not black Friday, and Hull was not here to add a sixty inch television to his growing credit. The store wasn't even open for business, but it was open. Someone had smashed it that way with a brick. *How is it that people always manage to find bricks in the middle of the fucking city? Or do they carry the damned things around with them?* On the sidewalk in front of Hull's leather-clad feet lay a mound of glass and a small cardboard box. Hull returned his gaze to the box's contents and rubbed the back of his neck. *There is some crazy assed shit going on in Tulsa these days.*

It started last month when TPD officers began dropping like metal targets on a competition pistol course. Hull both loved and hated mysteries; he loved solving them, he hated when he couldn't. As supervisor of the Homicide Unit, he'd seen his fair share of whodunits but the month of February had been something else.

When TPD officers started getting assassinated, Hull took a back seat to the FBI as they investigated the killings. Despite no direct involvement, Hull soon suspected his friend, Jonathan Thorpe, of being the guilty party. He also surmised John's motive: the officers killed were responsible for murdering John's wife and daughter. Put in a difficult situation, Hull decided he would probably react in a similar fashion if his own family were murdered. Rather than pursue John, he'd helped him. Looking back, he still felt as though he'd made the right decision.

But just when he thought he had everything figured out, things got weird. The final suspect in the murder of John's family, Sergeant Carl McDonald, died in Wichita, Kansas, while John remained in Tulsa under the watchful eye of the FBI. Furthermore, before dying of an apparent suicide, McDonald confessed to the murders of the other officers—neatly wrapping up the case and directing focus away from John. All bullshit of course. *But who killed Sergeant McDonald?* Prior to his "suicide" even the FBI hadn't been able to locate McDonald's hiding place. Whoever was responsible had considerable skill and better resources than the Federal Bureau of Investigation.

Hull had his theories as to whom that person might be, but John never broached the subject. Then again, John seemed to keep most thoughts of significance to himself. If the man spoke at all, it was generally a good-natured roast at the listener's expense. Probably a coping behavior he'd acquired during his less-than-utopian life.

When John's family was murdered, Hull had cause to investigate the man's past. John had never truly been a suspect in the killings, but as a matter of statistics he had to be eliminated as part of the investigation—not to mention public scrutiny. History has shown when a wife and child are murdered inside their home, one usually didn't need to look further than the husband/father.

During the subsequent investigation, Hull learned quite a few interesting tidbits about Jonathan Thorpe and his father, Benjamin. Though the younger Thorpe claimed his father went missing in action while serving with the United States Army, Hull found the truth wasn't so simple or easy to come by. Hull did learn Benjamin Thorpe had been a sergeant in a supply company for the Army but was honorably discharged when John was eleven years old. From tax records, Hull determined Benjamin Thorpe then went to work for

USA International, a private security corporation which hired mostly ex-military personnel, particularly ex-commandos. U.S.A.I. gave Hull the runaround before finally admitting it once employed Benjamin Thorpe. Cooperation from the U.S. Army was lacking as well. All set to pay a personal visit to U.S.A.I., Hull's division commander made it clear further investigation into Benjamin Thorpe's background would not be necessary. Explanations weren't forthcoming but Hull figured he'd been poking his nose in unwelcome places and concluded Benjamin Thorpe likely worked in a clandestine capacity for the United States government.

The bigger question for Hull was if Benjamin Thorpe still lived. When McDonald died by "his own hand," neatly wrapping up the deaths of several officers, Hull suspected Ben was still alive. Who else would have the capabilities and resources? More importantly, who would be willing to risk so much for a sergeant with the Tulsa Police Department? Surprisingly, the younger Thorpe seemed not to have come to the same conclusion; not that Hull could see anyway. Perhaps John couldn't conceive of his father willingly abandoning him and his family, never to return. Maybe John's mind wouldn't allow for that possibility. It appeared as if those events would remain a mystery; Hull decided to let sleeping dogs lie—a wise decision when dealing with dogs that could kill you in your sleep.

Hull looked down at his newest puzzle. He loved his work, and he loved a challenge like the one before him now. At 4:13 in the morning someone tossed a brick through the front window of this electronics store. When officers arrived they found a cardboard box sitting on top of the broken glass. Inside the box were eight human fingers.

TWENTY-ONE

THE SPECIAL INVESTIGATIONS DIVISION (SID) is located on the top level of a multistoried office building in east Tulsa. It's an odd place to house the department's vice, narcotics, gangs, intelligence, and other undercover units. Odd, because the building neighbors two robust drug-dealing "whore"tels and resides in the midst of numerous street prostitutes who peddle their wares all hours of the day and night. In an effort to thwart counter surveillance, the division is moved every few years.

Beleaguered by strumpets, junkies, and dope-slingers, the current site of the office remains anonymous thanks to its unconventional design. The structure is three stories high, with half of the third story serving as a parking area. If interested, investigators could peek over the parking lot's walls and witness numerous felonies without ever leaving the property.

The only way to gain access to the parking area is via a concrete ramp located on the south side of the building. At the top of the ramp is a ten-foot electronic gate with a sign that reads, "I.T.P.S. AUTHORIZED PERSONNEL ONLY." Similarly, there is no public access to the third floor from the interior of the building. Signs identical to the one above are posted on sturdy metal doors in the stairwells. ITPS, stands for "It's The Police Stupid," a testament to police officers' humor, which might not always be demonstrated to the public.

The offices of SID are referred to as just that—The Office—by those who work there. The division is commanded by a major with a little-man complex, all the more perplexing since he weighed well over three bills. The second-in-command is a well-meaning but micromanaging captain who shares the investigator's assessment that their major is an idiot and an asshole. For these reasons, and many others, Thorpe chose to work the night shift.

The major, captain, administrative sergeant, civilian personnel, Intelligence Unit, day shift Narcotics Unit, DEA agents, FBI agents, equipment officers, and some of Thorpe's own Organized Gang Unit all worked day shift hours. The only folks minding the store at night were his evening shift gangs investigators and Vice. The evening shift narc investigators usually disappeared by 9:00 p.m., to destinations unknown.

At night no brass was around to peer over your shoulder. More than a few reports had been written with the aid of beer instead of coffee. Evening shift at SID offered investigators more freedom than any other assignment on the department. But instead of seeing the lack of oversight as an avenue to easy street, Thorpe's unit flourished in this environment. Every officer in the squad was a self-motivated, thug-hunting machine. Those who entered the unit and didn't find an inner-drive were quickly weeded out.

Thorpe had just finished giving his investigators a cryptic assignment. He'd passed out color copies of a photograph he'd taken in Deborah's barn a couple hours before. The picture was of a key attached to a large, red, diamond-shaped, semi-transparent, piece of plastic imprinted with the number 201. It was the motel key that Thorpe had found in the Latin King's abandoned vehicle. His squad's assignment was to find out what motel or motels employed similar looking keys.

Several of his officers made inquiries but Thorpe told them the case was a "need-to-know" assignment. It was not unusual for the unit to assist federal agencies without being given the "big picture."

On occasion, the division became involved, sometimes unwittingly, in the investigation of other officers. In some of those instances details of the case, including suspect information, were purposely omitted. Thorpe's investigators would be curious as to why they needed to try and find this motel, but he had little doubt they'd be successful. With enough time, Thorpe could have uncovered the motel on his own, but time wasn't a luxury he'd been afforded.

As Thorpe studied his computer screen, Jennifer Williams walked unannounced into his office and plopped down on the leather sofa across from his desk. Jennifer was one of his top investigators, and like many of the best officers on the department seemed afflicted with ADHD. If she wasn't doing something, Thorpe feared she'd fall on the floor in an epileptic fit. Therefore, she usually had a search warrant to serve every night and if not, she engaged in activities likely to send some shithead to jail.

Jennifer's attributes were also her detriments. She was horrible at surveillance and a true pain in the ass during idle time. Her reports were always late because she flew off on her next caper before finishing the paperwork from the last. Plus, she spoke directly, and either hated or loved you; there were no such things as acquaintances in her life. Therefore, she had friends on the department for whom she would do anything, and who would do anything for her. She also had people on the department who despised her, some of whom worked in the same unit. As a result, Thorpe's biggest challenge was keeping the unit cohesive and working together as a team.

Another of Jennifer's attributes was her figure. Damn near constituting entrapment, she could walk into any bar in the city and find a man willing to give her dope. Her physique more resembled a bodybuilder—minus the testosterone injections—than a cheerleader. She was hard but had curves. And she was tough: she could, would, has, and will, kick the average man's ass.

"What's this key shit all about, Carnac?" Jennifer asked with her usual directness.

"Can't tell you," Thorpe answered, not even bothering to look up from the computer monitor.

"Can't or won't?"

"Yes."

Several seconds of silence passed. In an attempt to avoid spinning lies, Thorpe pretended to read an email and tried to ignore the weight of her stare.

Jennifer broke first, "What if I told you I already know the name of the motel that key belongs to?"

Jennifer liked to conduct "knock-and-talks" on motel rooms. Actually, law enforcement was trying to get away from the term "knock-and-talk" and now utilized the term "consensual encounter." Always attempting to soften their image, "jump-outs" were now "rapid deployments," foot-pursuits now "investigative follows," street crime units now directed patrol units, and don't even mumble the words strike team—way too Gestapo. Thorpe was sure one day his own Organized Gang Unit would be renamed "Disablers of Wayward Young Men's Clubs," then again maybe not—DWYMC wasn't much of an acronym unless they tossed an "A" on the end.

Knock-and-talks, or consensual encounters, are exactly like the term implies. An officer knocks on a door, and without probable cause, "talks" his way to being invited inside. It's an art form. Some officers have a gift for it just like some people were born to be salesmen. If done right, rarely does someone refuse to let the officer in the room...even when fifty bricks of marijuana lay spread across the bed. Been there—done that. Drug dealers and users, generally fall into the idiot category.

Jennifer was one of those investigators who demonstrated a mastery of the consensual encounter. She could approach a number of motels and come away with a fair amount of dope within an hour, a task she performed frequently. As a result, she'd been inside every flea-infested motel in the city.

Thorpe finally looked up from the computer screen, "If you know the name of the motel, I'd appreciate you telling me."

"Tell me what's up, and I'll tell you the name of the motel."

"Maybe an attractive woman slipped me the key when I was drunk and I can't remember the name of the motel where I'm supposed to meet her."

"If you're meeting a woman at *this* motel, you're a desperate man."

"Maybe Jimmy Hoffa is buried there."

"John, are you going to keep jerking me around, or do I have to go to the motel myself?"

Thorpe had made an error; by making the search a mystery he'd garnered too much interest from Jennifer. He should have just concocted a bullshit story from the start. "Jennifer, when have I ever 'jerked you around?'"

"How would I know?"

"Do I treat you well?"

"Yes."

"Between you and me, can I just tell you it's something personal and leave it at that?"

Luckily Thorpe was one of the loved, not hated. After a theatrical sigh she relented, "The Desert Moon on West Skelly."

"Thanks, Jennifer. I owe you one."

"Duh."

"I'll let the others know they can stop looking once I confirm it's the right motel. There may be more than one place using that plastic diamond."

"None I can think of."

As Jennifer walked out the door, Thorpe enlarged the screen he'd minimized when she'd first stepped in. In front of him was a report he'd prepared months ago. In the narrative he found the name of the Latin King who owed Leon Peterson his very freedom.

Luis Carbia. It's time to reintroduce myself.

TWENTY-TWO

THE DESERT MOON MOTEL WAS situated on Tulsa's west side in an area decades past its glory. It sat to the south of Skelly Drive and allowed patrons occupying the northern rooms a view of I-44 through their grimy, 70-year-old window glass. The motel was one of many within the Tulsa city limits that mostly housed dealers and their customers. Crank was this particular motel's drug of choice and most of its denizens displayed the cognitive and physical signs of regular methamphetamine use: decaying teeth, poor personal hygiene, emaciation, and the look of perpetual paranoia.

Having substituted his assigned undercover pickup for a gray Ford Taurus, Thorpe drove past the motel. He parked his vehicle at an office complex to the west, grabbed his equipment, pulled up his hoodie, and set off on foot. Lit by sporadic street lamps in various stages of disrepair, the motel's parking area was interspersed with darkness and a seemingly tactile, yellow, crusty haze. He followed an overgrown easement on the west side of the motel and walked on the outside of a wooden privacy fence toward the back of the property. His pant legs and shoelaces having gathered a half bushel of cockleburs, Thorpe located an area untouched by working streetlamps. There, he peered over the fence.

The motel rarely fluctuated above thirty percent occupancy. Tonight was no different; few cars occupied the expansive lot.

Thorpe spotted his problem within seconds. A black Chevy S-10 pickup with tinted windows sat in a darkened corner of the property. Thorpe recognized the truck, and though he couldn't see inside, had no doubt who sat behind the wheel. He suspected Jennifer would be nosing around; she'd relented too easily. She'd come to snoop on her sergeant. Like him, she'd traded her assigned undercover unit for one of the extras in SID's fleet.

Thorpe was tempted to retrieve his pistol's laser attachment and have a bit of fun with his subordinate by placing the red dot through her windshield. It might be good for a laugh but would be counterproductive to Thorpe's goal. At best, she'd get on the radio and have a bevy of officers flood the area in search of the offender. At worst, she would send lead his direction at about 1200 feet per second.

Thorpe resisted the urge to one-up Jennifer, and instead punched in star 67 on his cell phone, then dialed dispatch's non-emergency number. Once connected, he reported an armed robbery in progress at a nearby "QT" and terminated the call. Armed robberies are broadcast on all radio subfleets. A minute later, Jennifer roared out of the lot hoping to get a piece of some nonexistent robbers.

Thorpe climbed over the fence and quickly found room 201. Located on the southwest corner of the motel's second floor, Thorpe approached by ascending the stairs and stepping onto a four-foot-wide balcony. Alone on the terrace, Thorpe unlocked the room's door entering low and fast. Illuminated by the tactical light attached to his non-issued Glock .45, Thorpe knew one thing already: someone had beaten him here. After clearing the bathroom, Thorpe returned to the front door and pushed it closed. He flipped on the lights, propped a chair against the door, and surveyed the ransacked room. The drawers had been pulled out, the mattress yanked off the box springs and both cut open, the ventilation panels removed and even the smoke alarm had been torn out of the wall. Someone had been looking for something. Whoever sent the Kings sent someone else to clean-up after them. Thorpe checked the door jam. It was obvious the door had been pried open on numerous occasions, and impossible to tell how recently the last burglary occurred.

Having searched countless motel rooms on search warrant services and knock-and-talks, Thorpe knew all the places dealers utilized to hide their contraband. He went about searching these areas hoping the "clean-up man" had left something behind. Finding nothing, Thorpe switched off the light, looked out the window to see if Jennifer had returned, then left the property empty handed. He didn't waste his time checking with the desk clerk. By law, hotels and motels are required to obtain picture identification before renting to customers. The Desert Moon didn't bother, which was another reason criminals stayed in places like this one—to remain anonymous.

TWENTY-THREE

AMID AN OTHERWISE MODEST BUILDING, Alberto sat in the relatively luxurious apartment of Elisa Ruiz like a man who'd found paradise in the middle of hell. Alberto paid Elisa's rent, bought her clothes, supplied her furniture, and provided for the electronics he now viewed with growing interest. Carlos' apartment contained three pinhole cameras and listening devices, the wiring of which led through their shared wall into Elisa's living room. Next to a large flat screen television, sat three monitors. She could watch the network's Big Brother on her flat screen while she enjoyed a local version of the same show on the three smaller sets.

Elisa had called Alberto saying she possessed a recording of her new neighbor that he'd find interesting. Alberto didn't have time for distractions right now and told Elisa as much. Her response: "You got time for this."

Elisa was one of the brighter members of the ALKQN, King or Queen, and if anything, had a knack for self-preservation. Alberto decided if she thought it important, then he'd better have a look. *Maybe Carlos was still considering trying to walk away from the Kings—the fool.* Anyway, Alberto was feeling the stress and might find relief in a romp with the unconscious body of his favorite Queen. One way or another, the trip would be worth his while.

As usual, Alberto arrived at Elisa's door with a bottle of wine.

Invited inside, Alberto walked directly to the kitchen, removed the cork, and filled two glasses. Elisa's crystal received an additional compliment of GHB to facilitate unconsciousness. Elisa always gulped the first glass of expensive wine in a couple of swallows and quickly requested a second. All of this was fine with Alberto. Having to bestow false gestures of affection taxed a man. The sooner she passed out the sooner he could screw out her benumbed brains. Also, though her apartment was nicely furnished, it was on the small side; small enough to stir his claustrophobia if he spent more than thirty or forty minutes inside. Luckily, she eagerly slammed a few chemical cocktails and got down to the business of falling asleep on her couch.

The two lovers, if one dared call them that, went through the pleasantries of pretending they cared how the other was doing while the drug took effect. As Elisa's eyelids grew heavier, Alberto hit play on the DVD. His attention shifting between the monitor and the almost lifeless body next to him, Big Alberto smiled. Little Alberto saluted.

Five minutes into the recording Little Alberto lost his patriotism. Carlos and his bride had not been planning an escape from the life; they'd been plotting to kill someone. *Him. Those ungrateful motherfuckers!* He'd have Carlos and his wife terminated. *And the daughter?* Alberto knew people who'd hand over their life savings for a pretty little girl like her.

Alberto was pacing Elisa's room trying to refurbish his bruised ego with fantasies of retribution when his cell phone rang.

"What?"

"We need to talk," King Ghost replied. "Something's wrong."

Ghost was in Tulsa. Alberto sent him there to search for Fubb and the missing crew. He had driven straight through, located the men's motel room, broke in, and found their sparse luggage sitting on the floor. The men and their weapons were nowhere to be found. Alberto had ordered Ghost to clean out the crew's room, making sure to remove any trace of them having stayed. Then he instructed

Ghost to rent an adjacent room to keep an eye out for the men's return.

"Well, no fucking shit something's wrong," Alberto hissed into the phone. "That's why I sent you there."

"Well, somebody just tossed their room."

"Tossed their room? Are you sure it wasn't one of them? What'd he look like?"

"I don't know. I heard a noise in their room. I didn't want to be seen if it was the cops so I waited till I heard them leave. Waited a few seconds then looked outside. Saw somebody in a hoodie walk away. Jumped the fence and was gone."

"Maybe it was one of them or just some asshole robbin' the place."

"No. I cleaned that room good. They was in there ten minutes. Robber wouldn't stay that long searching an empty room. He was lookin' for something. Don't think it was Fubb or anyone in his crew either. He was too big."

"Shit. Cop?"

"The fuck I know. Didn't walk like a cop. And why would a cop jump the fence?"

"Goddammit, you dumb fuck. I sent you to find answers not ask questions."

Fubb and the three other Kings had vanished. They'd been sent to Tulsa to clear Luis Carbia's debt. Alberto was tired of cleaning up after his half-brother. *What the fuck is going on?* He let out a guttural scream and threw a lamp into the kitchen. Unsatisfied, he straddled Elisa's immobilized body and began beating the hell out of the already unconscious woman. After a good workout, Alberto used the kitchen sink to wash his hands and shirt of her blood. Cuffs stained pink, he dialed Ghost and flashed a quick glance at his once beautiful mistress as he stormed out the door.

TWENTY-FOUR

CAREFUL NOT TO PASS IN front of Carlos' peephole, Loc stood near Elisa's apartment door while Speedy inserted a key into her lock. Prior to their arrival, Alberto had provided both men with four items and explicit instructions. The items included two keys and two silenced pistols. One key fit Elisa Ruiz's apartment, the other that of her next door neighbor. The keys ensured silent entry into Carlos Benitez's apartment. The suppressed pistols ensured his silent death.

They'd been provided a key to Elisa's apartment because, according to Alberto, she'd be "sleeping" when they arrived and most likely couldn't be aroused. Alberto also told them they'd probably find Elisa in poor condition but alive. Just in case, they were to check her breathing.

Otherwise, their instructions were simple: quietly access Elisa's apartment, monitor her surveillance equipment until they found an opportunity to kill both Carlos and his wife, then take the child. It was early. With any luck, the Benitezes would still be asleep.

After killing Carlos and his wife, Loc would take the little girl to Alberto while Speedy remained in the apartment with the two bodies and removed the cameras and audio devices. He would wait until after dark to remove the corpses for future disposal.

Elisa was known to both Loc and Speedy. A well-respected

Latin Queen, she'd been on Alberto's arm at a number of ALKQN functions. A rare combination of long legs, slender waist and large breasts, everyone who met Elisa remembered her. Everyone also knew of Alberto's propensity to drug women and rape their comatose bodies. When one's fetish is that twisted, it's not easily kept secret.

Concluding Alberto had more than likely drugged Elisa unconscious, the men agreed to take turns with her before venturing next door to dispatch Soldier Boy. The opportunity was just too great and what Alberto didn't know wouldn't hurt them. Plus, the exercise would help provide stress relief before killing Carlos, though they were fairly confident he'd be unarmed. They'd been sure to retrieve the .45 that Carlos used to fire blanks at the elderly couple. Still, both men remembered the ex-commando's familiarity with firearms. If he'd gotten his hands on another weapon, it could spell trouble.

Speedy and Loc entered Elisa's apartment and were thoroughly disappointed when they didn't find her inside—unconscious or otherwise.

"Fuck!"

"My Mexican brown snake would'a woke that bitch up anyway," Loc said grabbing his crotch. "No bitch can sleep through that; know what I'm sayin'?"

"Fuck it. Let's do this thing and get the fuck outt'a here."

Following Alberto's instructions, the men switched on equipment that allowed them to watch and listen to live feeds from Carlos' apartment. Happy to see that all three: Carlos, his wife, and their daughter, were still asleep in their beds, their grainy images displayed in black and white.

"The wife's got some nice titties," Speedy commented.

"Maybe we'll get some pussy after all. Fuck her while she stares into her dead husband's eyes."

"You're fucked up," Speedy laughed. "Alberto said not to fuck around with either of them. Kill them quick."

"Alberto's not here."

"Shit. He's probably somewhere watching the same video we are. Have our asses."

"Maybe. Shit. Too bad. She got some nice titties."

This would be easy. Loc instructed Speedy to remain in Elisa's apartment and monitor the screens as Loc slipped in and killed Carlos and his wife. They'd stay connected via cell phones. If Speedy observed movement, he'd give Loc a warning.

Left hand holding a cell phone cocked to his ear, Loc slid the key into Carlos' lock and carefully pushed open the door.

"They're both still out cold," Speedy instructed over the phone.

Loc withdrew the silenced .22 with his right hand and followed it into the apartment.

"I can see you now. They're still asleep."

Loc walked up to the open threshold of the bedroom. The .22 shook in his hand but was manageable. He could see both their forms lying in bed. The wife's dark hair spilled over her face but h full breasts were on display. *Fucking shame.* Loc crept to the foot of the bed and put four rounds into Carlos before turning the weapon on the wife, firing three more. The final round caught the wife in the head blowing brain matter across the headboard and up the once white wall.

Fuck! That's going to be a bitch to clean up!

"DAMN," SPEEDY BREATHED. EVEN FROM the grainy black and white picture he could see the chunks of human tissue spray against the wall above Carlos' bed.

"Guess you weren't so tough after all, were you Soldier Boy?"

Those words—spoken to no one in particular—were the last ones ever to leave Speedy's lips. As soon as they escaped, a hand covered his mouth and the serrated edge of a steak knife slit his skinny throat from ear to ear. The cut was deep. Down to his spinal cord. Speedy fell to the carpet, the world already fading to black. The last thing he saw was the looming figure of one Carlos Benitez.

LOC WALKED OVER TO WHERE he thought Carlos' body lay and threw back the blankets. The suction caused a flurry of feathers to swirl into the air. No body, only pillows. Loc panicked. He'd been set-up. Loc spun and began firing the pistol into the bedroom closet until the slide locked back, empty. He broke into a sweat. His heart thundered in his chest. He ran to the bedroom door, slammed and locked it closed. *Fuck, Fuck, Fuck. Think damn it!*

How could Carlos use his own wife as bait?

Loc peeled himself off the wall, went to the bed and rolled Carlos' wife from her side to her back. Except it wasn't Carlos' wife. It was Elisa Ruiz.

I'm a fucking dead man.

ST NIGHT CARLOS HAD BEEN lying awake when he'd ~~ard~~ a disturbance in the apartment of the young woman who'd tossed him a bar of soap. Carlos was reluctant to get involved given the woman's frosty demeanor coupled with the fact he had enough problems of his own. What motivated him to act was the onslaught of quiet following the disturbance. Carlos had just cracked open his own door when a man stormed out of hers and stomped down the hallway, a phone to his ear. The man had been none other than his Uncle Alberto.

Whatever the reason for Alberto's visit to his neighbor, it couldn't be good. After a minute of indecision, Carlos walked over and tried her knob. Alberto, who'd left in a hurry, hadn't bothered to lock the door behind him. Carlos pushed into the apartment and found the battered woman lying on a leather couch. She was unconscious. Then he'd heard a voice inside the apartment—his own. Against the wall, a monitor displayed images of him speaking with his wife. *Oh God no. This bitch had recorded him!* Carlos recognized the conversation; he and his wife had been discussing ways to kill Uncle Alberto. Alberto had heard those plans.

Carlos immediately returned to his own apartment. He roused

his wife and daughter out of bed and herded them out of the building with nothing but a wad of cash and a hastily stuffed backpack. They were not safe. No one he loved would be safe until Alberto was dead.

He put Eva and Celestina on a bus and gave them instructions to stay out of Chicago, and out of sight, for as long as they could make the money last. He told Eva not to reemerge until she read of Alberto's death in the newspaper. Even then they might not be free from harm. They might be hunted by the ALKQN for the rest of their lives.

After seeing his family off, Carlos returned to the apartment to lay a trap for his uncle. He stuffed pillows under the covers to make it appear he was asleep in bed. Then he'd brought the limp body of Elisa Ruiz and put her beside the pillows. He placed her on her side, spilled her long hair over her face, and pulled the covers up to her neck. He'd taken one of Celestina's rather life-like dolls and placed it in her bed. Then he returned to Elisa's apartment and looked into the monitors at what he'd staged. Through the grainy black and white images, the bodies appeared real enough, especially since one of them was. His bait in place, Carlos took a serrated steak knife from Elisa's kitchen and hid in her coat closet.

He'd hoped Alberto himself would return with a couple of other Kings to make a preemptive strike. Prepared to die by one of his goon's hands, Carlos would go straight for Uncle Alberto. Unfortunately, his uncle proved to be an even bigger coward than expected. Uncle hadn't accompanied the men sent to do his dirty work.

Watching Loc from a black and white monitor, Carlos stood over Speedy's gurgling body. Loc had just discovered he'd killed a couple of pillows and his boss's mistress. The man sat with his back against a wall and looked as though he might shit himself. Carlos was surprised when the idiot composed himself enough to slap in a spare magazine. Then he watched Loc pick up a phone from the floor, fumble with the device, and put it up to his ear. A second later

Speedy's cell began buzzing next to his lifeless body. Carlos bent over, picked up the phone and accepted the call, but didn't speak.

"Speedy? Speedy, you there? Speedy we're in some deep shit man, say something."

"Fuckin' straight, you're in some deep shit," Carlos said, then "You know you're not getting out of there alive, don't you, Loc?"

"Carlos? Oh Jesus, fuck, Carlos. We was just following orders. You don't have to fucking do this!"

"I can't hear dead men, Loc."

"Alberto's the one you want. I'll help you get that motherfucker. Carlos? Carlos? Carlos, you listening to me?"

Carlos moved back into his own apartment. He could hear Loc inside the bedroom pleading into the phone. He kicked open the thin door and found Loc in the same position he'd been in on the monitor. Three miniscule movements of Carlos' index finger expelled an equal number of rounds from Speedy's silenced pistol into the man's face.

Loc never got off a shot.

TWENTY-FIVE

THE STIMULI AT BROOKSIDE BY Day mounted a full scale
attack on Thorpe's senses. An unusually attractive waitress stood
pitched over his table pouring Robert Hull a cup of java. Coffee
beans and hazel nut jockeyed for position with the aroma of bacon.
Falling through nearly a foot of air before striking the ceramic cup,
the sound of the coffee battled with the blanket-like, Saturday
morning chatter of an eclectic breakfast crowd. The waitress'
accompanying smile fought for attention with a middle-aged woman
seated on a stool, her natural breasts spreading out awkwardly on the
restaurant bar.

"What the hell are you smiling at?" Hull asked.

"Just enjoying the little things. And the big things."

"You're in a good mood."

"Don't worry, it won't last."

The restaurant, BBD as the locals referred to it, was located in
the Brookside district, an area punctuated with bars, coffee, cigar, art
and other high-end specialty shops. BBD only serves breakfast and
lunch, always has a good crowd, and drew Tulsa's trendy and elite.
Even the mayor occasionally left the Berghof to grace the
restaurant's patrons with his presence.

BBD was where Hull and Thorpe first formed an unspoken
allegiance and since then meet here regularly. By now, most of the

restaurant's staff knew the men were cops, and referred to them by their first names. The two sergeants sat at a corner table making small talk. Thorpe pretended not to be interested in a specific topic. He hoped Hull would broach the subject on his own.

"So what happened to you the other night? Those two ladies weren't very happy when they watched you walk past the bar and out the door."

Thorpe smiled, "'Ladies' is a bit of a stretch don't you think?"

"Semantics aside, you're avoiding the question."

"Did it ever occur to you that I might have standards?"

"One of them was a knockout."

"Yeah, but I'm fairly certain they were a package deal," Thorpe laughed, "Did the Swordsman make a double kill?"

"No, I think they were pretty embarrassed when you walked out on them. They left right after."

"I have a feeling they'll get over it."

"Well, 'Carnac the Magnificent', you gotta' trust your feelings."

Thorpe held up his coffee, "I'll toast to that." The men clinked their cups together as their waitress sashayed past the table with a little extra swing in her hips.

"Guess what Santa brought me for Christmas?"

"It's March, Bob, probably brought you a damn calendar."

"Smart ass. It may not be Christmas, but this little present came giftwrapped in a box and might as well of had 'For TPD' written on it," Hull added, "You haven't heard about this?"

"I haven't heard shit. Jeff is usually my source of information and that bastard's in Florida pretending to be Tiger Woods. His golf game won't come close but he will probably bag a couple of blonde chicks. "

Hull laughed, "Well, I'm surprised the whole department hasn't heard. Early Friday morning someone threw a brick through the front window of an electronics store at 71st and Lewis. When uniforms showed up, they found a cardboard box sitting outside the broken window. Guess what was in the box?"

"An IOU for the broken window?"

"Eight human fingers. Well, technically four fingers and four thumbs."

"What the hell?"

Hull shrugged his shoulders, "The sergeant at the scene said someone was looking for a five finger discount."

Thorpe laughed, "But you said there were eight fingers."

"They left a tip."

"You find their owners yet?"

"Not yet. Just a box full of fingers," Hull answered.

"Box fulla' fingers. Sounds like an item on the dollar menu. Crazy."

"Very," Hull agreed.

"Theories?"

"Whoever left the box wanted the police to be able to identify the victims."

"What makes you say that?"

"Seven of the fingers were wrapped in a moist towel. A thumb was lying on top of the towel. Whoever left the box on the sidewalk also left the lid open. The first officers at the scene found the box, put a light on it and saw a pretty little thumb staring back at them. Whoever left it probably figured if the box was closed we'd be afraid it was a bomb or something and blast it with water."

Long gone are the days when bomb technicians try to "defuse bombs." Now they blast the suspected device with "projected water disruptors." TPD uses a directional, explosively propelled water jet, to disrupt the possible bomb. Simply described, it's a water missile.

"What was the moist towel for…to help preserve the fingers?" Thorpe asked.

"Probably, if they get dry they shrivel up. You ever see how the lab guys fingerprint shriveled fingers?"

"Can't say I have."

"They soak 'em in water, de-bone them, then wrap the skin

around their own fingers and roll them through the ink."

"That's nasty!"

"Yeah, and the damn fingerprint expert does it for about fourteen bucks an hour. Wraps himself in someone else's skin."

Thorpe altered his voice, "It rubs the lotion on the skin or else it gets the hose again."

"What the fuck are you talking about?"

"Have you ever been to a damn movie?" Then, "Never mind, so where do you go from here?"

"Got good prints off all of 'em; the fingers were in good shape. Musta' been fresh kills. Anyway, two of the guys were in the system. We got names."

"Two of the guys? How many guys are there?" Thorpe asked, keeping up the ruse.

"Four. One index finger and one thumb from four different guys. I'm assuming all four were male. The fingers were thick and hairy. If one was a woman…she was an ugly bitch."

Thorpe laughed, "How the hell have you kept this out of the news?"

"Won't be able to for long. We're hoping to get a little more info on the two known victims and make next-of-kin notifications before a news release."

"Any of the names belong to me?" Thorpe was asking if the fingers belonged to any known gang members. The Gangs Unit investigated gang-related homicides.

"Yes and no. They're bangers but not local. Couple of bad guys out of Chicago with ties to the Latin Kings," Hull explained.

"Latin Kings from Chicago? Something tells me you're going on a road trip."

"That's why they call you Carnac."

After another twenty minutes of chitchat, Thorpe walked out of BBD with what he needed. The pleasant sights, sounds, and smells the restaurant had provided were pushed aside, replaced with the smell of blood, the sound of ligaments tearing, bones snapping, the images of fingers and thumbs being stripped from four cadavers.

He hadn't enjoyed removing the men's digits, not in the least, but he was afraid he'd never learn their identities otherwise. And he'd been right.

TWENTY-SIX

PITCH BLACK. TWO MEN, DARKLY clothed, were holed up in the cafeteria of Faubian Elementary School. The men were well armed and knowledgeable with weapons. Their intentions hostile.

Approaching the large opening to the murky dining area, Thorpe led three of his Gangs investigators toward those armed men and the cavernous gloom in which they were embedded. Thorpe could smell Jack Yelton's beer-tainted breath. Jack trailed less than a foot behind using Thorpe as a human shield—as were Tyrone and Jennifer for that matter. The light attached to Thorpe's Glock sliced through the dark leaving shifting shadows and blackness in its wake.

Music blasted from inside the cafeteria. It masked their movements, and that of their enemies.

Thorpe held up two fingers and pointed to the opposite side of the large opening.

Tyrone and Jennifer performed a slow "step-around" both activating their own weapon-mounted lights. The double-door opening was too large to perform a typical split-door room entry. Instead, on Thorpe's cue, Tyrone curled around the right side of his opening hitting the deep corner while Jennifer split off toward the middle of the room. On the left side of the opening, Thorpe and Jack simultaneously executed the same maneuver.

A few years ago, instructors would have told officers to "run the walls" in a situation like this. Now they instructed them to enter side-by-side with each officer covering different sections. The way Thorpe saw it, one shotgun blast would take them both out. Even armed with a pistol, a marksman could drop both officers in less than a second. Thorpe liked some distance between him and his partner. It created confusion for the bad guys, split their attention, and increased the reaction time necessary to acquire both officers as targets. The trick was to know the location of your partner, and trust him to manage his area of responsibility. Anyway, the experts would be teaching something completely different this time next year; tactics revolved more than they evolved.

As Thorpe stalked the west end of the cafeteria the song changed and "Thank You" by Sly & the Family Stone, cascaded across the vast, tiled room. *Surreal.* He was about to engage in a firefight while listening to classic funk.

Contemplating the hallucinogenic quality of the situation, Thorpe heard shots ring out from the other team's location followed by Jennifer scream she'd been hit. Thorpe directed Jack to break off and head toward the gunfire as he continued clearing his end of the cafeteria. As Jack scurried away, he heard Tyrone shout he was down. Following Tyrone's announcement, Thorpe heard Jack engage a target. Then Thorpe caught movement ahead. Someone lurked in the darkened entryway that led to the kitchen—and that someone let off a volley of shots in Thorpe's direction. Thorpe returned fire, unsure if he'd struck his adversary. Well, unsure until he heard Jake Holloway laugh and yell, "You got me."

Thorpe redirected his attention to the firefight occurring between Jack and Donnie Edwards.

Before reaching the melee, Jack also yelled he was hit, then Donnie called out, "You all dead out there?"

"Your sergeant's still breathing. Come get some," Thorpe jokingly taunted.

"I'm out of fucking ammo," Donnie answered.

"You know the rules. What would happen if this was for real?"

"I'd run out the fucking backdoor, that's what."

"Tough shit. That's not an option for you," Thorpe reminded the investigator. "You can either come out and take it like a man, or I can come in there and give you a contact shot."

"Fuck! Not in the balls."

Donnie stepped around the corner, his left hand covering his crotch, and Thorpe considerately plinked a simunition round off his protective face mask; considerate because while wearing the mask, the face is the least painful place to be shot.

"Hit the lights," Thorpe yelled.

Several of his investigators flipped on battery-operated lanterns giving some light to the cafeteria. Without being directed, the officers walked into the kitchen, opened a Styrofoam cooler and began drinking their assessments. The "dead" had to slam a full can of beer; the living drank at their leisure. Jake Holloway and Tyrone weren't drinkers, instead they sipped on Gatorade. But since the rules required some type of assessment, they both had to bake a dozen cookies each and bring them in on their next shift. Their penalties would most likely be paid by their wives.

Saturday nights were a pain for the Gangs Unit. Guaranteed, somewhere in the city, some gangbanger would get his ass shot— with real bullets. The shootings generally occurred late at night and assured a good dose of overtime for his investigators.

Though it might sound callous to your average citizen, gangbangers shooting each other was a fairly lucrative affair as far as the unit was concerned. Most "victims" had it coming. The biggest exception was when a truly innocent person found themselves between two dipshits trying to kill one another. Gang members couldn't shoot worth a damn. They seemed more determined to look cool—holding their gun sideways and all—than to aim down the sights and actually hit their targets.

Officers' apathy toward gang members was largely a result of their knowledge. If a gangbanger knew he could kill a cop and get away with it, most wouldn't hesitate. In prison, cop killers were royalty.

Though Thorpe and his unit weren't practicing accepted police tactics, the game provided a slight taste of what it was like to be under fire. The mock training also reduced stress. Being shot with hard plastic rounds that drew real blood and left welts for several weeks might not seem like stress relief to the average citizen, but it was to this group. They were all type-A personalities who appreciated the fact they'd be getting shot at with something non-lethal. Besides, after five or six beers the hits lost a lot of their sting.

The elementary school they were using had been abandoned years earlier and the Tulsa Police Department's Special Operations Team (SOT) had been utilizing the building for "active shooter" scenarios. About six months ago, Thorpe acquired the keys to the building from one of their team leaders and used it for search warrant service training with his unit. That training had led to this.

"Sarge, I could have shot you when you first entered the cafeteria," Donnie proclaimed.

"Then why didn't you?"

"I don't like to kill the people who approve my overtime," Donnie laughed. "Shit, it's so dark in here you can't tell who your shooting at. I was mainly going for the light on your weapon."

Donnie, around 6'3" and upwards of 230 pounds or so, kept his hair long and would make for a decent looking biker if he hadn't been in such good physical condition. Most bikers don't have a six-pack, they carry the whole keg. An ex-collegiate defensive end, Donnie had been even bigger in his playing days. His large build—which had been an advantage on the football field—was a disadvantage when framed inside a weapon's sights. The bigger one is, the easier one is to shoot. That's one of the reasons Thorpe usually assigned Donnie to the ram on search warrant services; that and the fact you needed someone of substance to wield the sixty-five pound chunk of metal. If the door gives too easily, smaller guys tend to follow the momentum of the ram straight into the house. Or they let go, and the ram becomes a sixty-five pound unguided missile.

But with Donnie's size, he could knock the door off its hinges, maintain his base, and step aside. He was generally the last one to make entry.

"So you said you were going to be gone the first part of next week?" Jennifer asked.

"Yeah, headed to Chicago with Hull and Skull. I'll be helping them with the 'Finger Basket' case."

"Damn! That's jacked-up. I can't believe it hasn't made the news yet," Tyrone added.

"It will. We're trying to get a jump on it. But Hull can't keep something like that out of the papers forever. This one's ghoulish enough to get the national media buzzards circling overhead."

"Great, those assholes just left."

The "McDonald Murders," as they came to be known, had kept the national networks—along with their outlandish and incessant speculations—in town for weeks.

"So you're flying out with Hull Monday morning?" Jennifer asked; she had to know everything about everything.

"He's flying out Monday morning; I'm driving up tomorrow morning."

"Why aren't you flying?"

"I may turn work into pleasure and stay up there a few more days."

"You fucker. You're just getting a free vacation on the city's dime, aren't you?" Jennifer smiled.

"Not exactly. I'll help Hull with the case for a day or two and then go off the payroll. Besides this is mostly a P.R. thing. People expect it. We won't do anything we couldn't do over the phone," Thorpe lied.

He planned to do so much more than could ever be accomplished over a telephone. Someone had sent men to kill him. Thorpe meant to ensure that "someone" never issued a duplicate order.

"You need someone to watch your pooches?" Jennifer offered.

"Thanks, but I've already made arrangements to leave them at the K-9 center. I think they've made friends up there; it's like a doggie sleepover for 'em."

"I think we should all go to Chicago as a unit," Jack smiled. "It'd be good training."

"Like the brass would go for that, Jack. Besides you're just looking for an excuse to get away from the wife."

"Hell we're all looking for an excuse to get away from Jack's wife; she's wearing us out," Donnie broke in.

This prompted Jack to pick up a simmunition-loaded handgun and point it at Donnie's groin, "I can make sure you're not wearing out anyone's wife for awhile," Jack smiled.

"Let's get back to it. What should we do next?"

"I think we should play shirts and skins. Jennifer and I are skins," Donnie said, looking at Jennifer and smiling.

"I think we should play *pants* and skins. The chances of you getting hit anywhere sensitive would be slim to none," Jennifer added as a retort.

The joke prompted an alcohol fueled group laugh and several fist bumps cast Jennifer's way. Thorpe's pager interrupted the festivities.

"Game over ladies. Got a shooting at Crawford Park; at least two hit. Tyrone and Jake, you two have the lead and do all the talking. Everyone else chew on some breath mints and become a part of the background."

TWENTY-SEVEN

ALBERTO VEGA LOOKED ACROSS A cheap card table at his incessant headache of a sibling. Ten years Alberto's junior, Luis Carbia was his half-brother and full-time pain in the ass. Luis had been in and out of juvenile, jail, and prison. Most his life had been spent behind bars and if authorities had evidence of his other crimes, would have died by lethal injection twice over. Unlike Alberto, Luis liked to get his hands dirty. It was Luis' dirty hands that were responsible for most of Alberto's current troubles.

Alberto had sent Luis to Tulsa, Oklahoma, well over a year ago and was still dealing with the repercussions. He'd tasked Luis to set up new drug markets and to establish roots for fellow Kings. In the dumb son-of-a-bitch's first week, he managed to get arrested by the Tulsa Police Department's Gang Unit. Ignoring Alberto's implicit instructions not to handle drugs directly, the stupid bastard had been caught dirty. In addition to dope, Luis had a handgun on his person, and as an ex-con the firearm charge would've been the final fastball in a lifetime full of strikes. In a heated, ten second negotiation, the driver of the car, a Tulsan named Lyndale Peterson, agreed to take responsibility for Luis' handgun.

Lyndale had been armed as well—so one more gun wouldn't add to his charges. The promise of a $25,000 payoff sealed the deal. Lyndale Peterson took ownership of all the dope and both pistols allowing Luis to walk away a free man. The law states as an ex-con, Luis couldn't even be in a car with a firearm. Lucky for him, Tulsa County's District attorney only filed charges on the most certain of convictions.

Alberto had been trying to decide whether to pay his brother's $25,000 obligation when he'd been given an alternate option. Lyndale Peterson would erase the monetary debt if Luis killed the man who'd sent him to prison. That man was a Tulsa police sergeant by the name of Jonathan Thorpe. Not only had Thorpe put Lyndale in prison but he'd also killed the man's younger brother while Lyndale sat behind bars.

Luis related the proposition to Alberto, who normally would have declined; the killing of a police officer is bad business. Cops tend to get miffed when one of their own are murdered and usually go about making life miserable for anyone they think might be remotely responsible. But Alberto happened to control a brand new group of government-trained killers he'd been eager to see in action. So, he'd agreed to send Fubb and his apprentices to Tulsa to erase Thorpe, and in doing so, also erase his brother's debt.

"They're dead," Luis announced across the padded table.

Because Alberto never conducted business at his own home, the half-brothers sat in Luis' gloomily lit basement. A lone overhead bulb accentuated Alberto's sour mood.

"Bullshit. They're fucking pros."

"We been over this, Alberto, they gotta' be dead. And Carlos—you said yourself, he's a bad motherfucker—should'a sent someone besides those dumb fucks Loc and Speedy to take him out."

"Don't lecture me, Luis, it's 'cause a your stupid ass I'm in this fuckin' mess!"

Speedy and Loc were supposed to have killed Carlos and his wife, and then brought the little girl to Alberto. Just like the Tulsa crew, they'd disappeared without a word. Alberto had refrained from phoning Loc or Speedy fearing they might be in police custody. His calls to Elisa had gone unanswered.

Three hours after having sent the two Kings, Alberto contacted the building's manager and had him check on Elisa. The manager called back saying he couldn't get an answer at the door and had let himself in, finding no one inside. Alberto didn't ask the man to check Carlos' apartment, he didn't need any further connection between potential murder victims and himself. The manager was a "friend" of the Nation and would know better than to mention Alberto's name to the police, but the fewer loose threads the better.

"They're dead," Luis repeated.

"Fuck! I know they're dead."

If Loc and Speedy had encountered a problem and postponed the killing they would have called. If they'd been picked up by the police he would've heard. And if they'd done the killing and gotten caught, it would have been all over the news. There was only one explanation: Carlos had killed them first. *Fucking great, an Airborne Ranger with silenced weapons just itching for an opportunity to put a slug in his ole' uncle's head.*

The men sat in the dimly lit basement lost in thought. To Alberto's left wooden stairs led to the hallway above. To his right and about seven feet off the floor, two windows sat flush with the ground outside.

Both men heard it; something pinged off the plastic window. Alberto froze in his seat while Luis rose and approached, gun in hand. A sudden feeling of vulnerability flushed over Alberto as his half-brother neared the window. His heart thundered in his chest and he cursed for not having armed himself.

"I'm going upstairs to take a look," Luis said.

As Luis turned from the window, he looked toward the stairs, his eyes widening in horror. Alberto saw a red dot appear on his brother's forehead. Both men froze, awaiting death.

Death had a familiar voice, "Relax, Uncle."

Alberto peered at the dark form lying on its side, head down the stairs, right arm extended, pointing a weapon at his brother's sweaty forehead.

144

"Mongoose, that you?"

"Yeah, Uncle. Expecting someone else, maybe?" Mongoose laughed.

"Fuck."

"We good?"

The question came from above Mongoose.

"Yeah, we're good," Mongoose answered.

A pair of tan combat boots and green fatigues descended the stairs behind the ass-over-head Mongoose.

"Just being careful, Uncle. You said you had a soldier off the reservation. I don't want to eat a bullet with your name on it," Mongoose smiled.

What the fuck did the military teach these little bastards, talking to him this way? Weren't they supposed to teach respect toward the chain of command? Now this little fuck was having a "my dick is bigger than your dick" show-off session at Alberto's expense.

Kings Mongoose and Sauce walked down the stairs to where Alberto waited. Both men were short, 5'7" to 5'8", but whereas Sauce had a slight build, Mongoose would be in danger of getting pissed on by stray dogs if he didn't look so damn mean; he was built like a fireplug. His shoulders sloped in resemblance of a recurve bow in the firing position: rigid, quivering, barely restrained tension and power. The man didn't have a forehead—maybe a twohead—two fingers could bridge the gap between hairline and eyebrow. Cro-Magnon epitomized, a bone-tipped spear would look more at home in the man's hand than the pistol he now held.

Alberto stuck his hand out, palm up, "Gun."

Mongoose lost his smile. He reluctantly pulled the pistol from a hip holster and handed the loaded firearm to his boss. Alberto returned the weapon across Mongoose's jutting jaw.

"You think you're fucking running shit, you fucking cocksucker!"

Alberto tended to flip mental switches like a crack addicted five-year-old in a commercial cockpit. It'd been a long time since Mongoose had seen this side of Alberto's bipolar personality but was something he should not have forgotten.

"I could have you erased with one fucking word." Alberto said, snapping his fingers. "You and your family. Don't fuckin' ever forget."

Alberto stormed up the stairs leaving Mongoose to work his jaw open and closed, his tongue tracing a freshly chipped tooth.

Luis smiled at Mongoose, "Cocky motherfucker."

"Fucking snake eaters. They're all alike," Sauce agreed.

Mongoose cracked a crimson-toothed smile, "I guess not everyone shares my sense of humor."

"You dumb fuck."

"Yeah, they forgot to put my brains back in when I left the army."

"Maybe we should split?"

"No, he'll be back down in a few minutes like nothing ever happened," Luis answered.

King Mongoose and King Sauce taped cloth over the basement's windows while Luis sat down at the table and gathered himself. Ten minutes later Alberto descended the stairs with four cold beers. Alberto noticed the covered windows and realized it was a precaution he should have already taken. Pleased as he was to have these men here, the hell if he would admit it.

Mongoose might have taught Alberto a life-prolonging lesson, but the little shit wasn't here to teach lessons. One doesn't disrespect their boss in the gang world—not if they want to live. If a leader shows even an ounce of weakness, an underling will be more than happy to step into his boss's shoes—forcibly.

Lucky for Mongoose and Sauce, Alberto needed the two ex-soldiers now more than ever.

TWENTY-EIGHT

KINGS MONGOOSE AND SAUCE STOOD five yards behind two fourteenish-looking Junior Kings in the hallway of Elisa Ruiz's apartment building. This was the type of housing where just as many residents remained awake at this hour—2:00 a.m.—as were awake in the middle of the day. Several people opened their doors, witnessed the four armed strangers in their hallway, and immediately slammed them closed. "Witnessed," a poor choice of words because if any of these individuals were subsequently interviewed by the police they would claim to have seen nothing.

The hallway's activity unsettled the two soldiers. If Carlos had gained access to any of these apartments, he could easily poke his head out, let off a volley of rounds, and duck back inside.

"Get your ass in that door," Mongoose hissed to one of the scared-shitless Junior Kings.

Mongoose and Sauce, both wearing flak jackets complete with ceramic inserts, were armed with silenced MP-5 submachine guns. The two Junior Kings both had unsilenced handguns. Their lack of sound suppression really didn't matter—the pistols weren't loaded. Not that the two teenagers had been made aware of this fact; they'd been handed the weapons, and like canaries in a coalmine, invited along only as an early warning device. Their job was simple, simpler than they knew. If Carlos waited inside an apartment their job was to enter and die, and thus alert the two real soldiers of enemy contact. If Carlos happened to be gone or dead, well, then,…lucky day for them.

One of the junior Kings fumbled with a key, managed to slip it into Elisa's lock, and pushed open her door. Both teenagers flooded inside as Mongoose and Sauce took a knee in the hall. The kneeling position provided a more stable shooting platform and a smaller target. Mongoose covered the long hallway, including the doors of Elisa's and Carlos' apartments; Sauce covered their asses. Twenty seconds later, the two youths reappeared in the hallway.

"It's empty," a relived junior King announced.

"Back inside," Mongoose ordered.

This time the two ex-soldiers followed the boys as Sauce locked the door behind them.

"Check the closets, under the beds, everything," Mongoose barked.

When the Junior Kings finished searching to Mongoose's satisfaction, he walked over and activated the monitoring equipment while Sauce covered the apartment door. Mongoose couldn't produce anything from the television screens except static. He picked up his phone and dialed Alberto. His uncle had given specific instructions to provide continual feedback; he didn't want any more of his people disappearing into the Bermuda Triangle.

"We're inside Elisa's apartment," Mongoose said, "No one's here. Looks like the surveillance equipment has been disconnected."

"Okay, check out his place. And watch your ass," Alberto instructed.

Mongoose terminated the call and instructed the boys to move out into the hall and repeat the process in Carlos' apartment.

"Alberto said to be careful," Mongoose teased the boys with a smile and a wink.

It didn't matter how careful the two boys were, if Carlos waited inside they'd never see their fifteenth birthdays. Even if their weapons had actually been loaded they wouldn't stand a chance. Not against the soldier.

The two Junior Kings took position outside of Carlos' door. Mongoose and Sauce covered the hallway from the threshold of Elisa's apartment. The same teenager fumbled with the key before both gained entry. The two were frightened; they couldn't have missed noticing the protective equipment the two older men wore, but were more afraid to say no to Alberto than to kill a man.

Thirty seconds after entering, the two re-emerged unharmed. Then all four men went inside as the two Junior Kings conducted a more meticulous search.

"Look at this," one of the boys shouted.

Mongoose walked into the bedroom and saw the kid pointing to a bloody mess on the wall above the bed.

"We're in. Nobody's home; nobody and no bodies," Mongoose relayed to his uncle over the phone. "Loc and Speedy must have got one of them though. Half a brain is plastered above their bed."

"Maybe they got the wife. Look for an answer to what happened then get the fuck out of there before someone calls the cops," Alberto commanded.

Mongoose disconnected and decided he'd only follow half of Alberto's instructions, "We've been here too long. Let's get the fuck outta' here."

ALBERTO GRIPPED THE PHONE AND glared across the table at his ignorant brother. Both men still sat in the same basement. Only three things had changed. One, Mongoose had rigged fishing line from the basement door to a tin coffee can on the stairs. A handful of 9mm cartridges rested in the bottom. A crude but effective warning device, if someone moved the door even an inch, it made quite the racket. Two, before the soldiers' departure, Sauce had provided Alberto with a pistol and an extra magazine. And finally, Luis had added a twelve-gauge shotgun to his armament.

Alberto related his phone conversation to Luis, then added,

"I'm going to send someone to snatch up his parents."

Luis shook his head, "You better call ahead first."

"Why?"

"Carlos is smart. He's already waited inside one place and killed our people. What if he's sitting inside his parents' house with a shotgun across his lap...like I am?"

Alberto nodded; his brother might not be all that bright, but when it came to survival, he was fairly shrewd. Alberto found the appropriate contact in his phone and hit send. His call to Carlos' parents went unanswered.

"Fuck?!"

"What?"

"His parents aren't answering their fucking phone. Jesus Christ!"

"Carlos is inside their house. I fucking know it. Send Mongoose and Sauce over there. They can kill that little fuck once and for all."

TWENTY-NINE

CARLOS WIPED CONDENSATION FROM THE window and looked out into the night. South of his parents' home, watching the front door, sat four men in a brown-over-tan-over-brown, late eighties, piece-of-shit Chevy Blazer. The Kings referred to such vehicles as "rammers." They used old, cheap SUVs to "put in work." The SUVs sat higher and provided better views into adjacent cars. They also had plenty of room for shooters and offered extra oomph when ramming the vehicles or bodies of rival gangsters. In addition to the Blazer, a Lincoln Town Car sat in the alley behind the home. The Town Car was also occupied by four men. Carlos had no doubt of the occupant's intentions. They'd been sent either to kill him or to snatch-up his parents.

If the men were here for his folks, they were too late. Having secured his wife and daughter, getting his parents to safety had been Carlos' next priority. He'd sent them away with instructions to contact no one, going so far as to confiscate their only cell phone so they wouldn't be tempted to make or receive calls.

That left five phones in Carlos' possession. Besides his own and his parents, he also had Elisa's, Loc's, and Speedy's. The dead have little need of cellular technology and Carlos had no compunction relieving them of their possessions. He hoped to use the phones in locating his uncle. But now, as protection for his family, all five phones were powered off. If Alberto did locate Carlos' family first, he wouldn't be able to use them as leverage if he couldn't communicate their capture. Alberto had already used that tactic to force Carlos into pulling the trigger on the elderly couple.

Ultimately, Carlos had to locate Alberto before the snake found his family. But first Carlos had to survive the eight men outside his parents' home. At least he wasn't dealing with professionals; a fact made apparent by their behavior. Both vehicles' engines were running. Plumes of exhaust rose in the frigid air—further announcing the men's presence. Either the men preferred to die warm and comfortable than to live cold and miserable, or they were just plain stupid. Carlos was betting his own life on the latter.

"I DON'T LIKE THIS SHIT!" Mongoose said as he pulled up short of Carlos' parents' home. "Alberto gives us all this training then doesn't fuckin' listen to what we got to say."

"Feels like we're still in the Army, don't it? If Carlos is in there, it's gonna be a fuckin' bloodbath," Sauce agreed.

"We should conceal ourselves. Put a bullet in his head when he walks in or outta the house. Nice and clean."

"Uncle wants this over right now. We got that deal goin' down and he don't want this shit hanging over our heads."

"I know, but there are better ways. If Carlos is in there half our guys are going to get fucked-up. Not us though. You and I are going in last."

"Fuck'n' A."

Having zero tolerance for idiots, Mongoose continued to bitch, "Look at those dumb motherfuckers sitting out in the open. Even got their motors running. So much for the element of surprise."

"Fucking embarrasses me to be a King. Bet the dumb fucks covering the back doin' the same damn thing."

Sauce's assessment garnered a nod from Mongoose, "Retard tweekers is what they are."

Mongoose parked his black Dodge Charger fifty yards behind the Blazer and wasn't surprised in the least when he and Sauce walked, unnoticed, directly up to the four men seated inside. They approached the passenger side and Mongoose rapped hard on the window causing a startled response from all four occupants. After the driver screwed his neck around to see who had scared the shit out of him, the glass slid down.

The front seat passenger tried to save face, "Don't you know I strapped. You lucky I don't shoot yo' ass."

"Get out of the fucking car," Mongoose responded.

The man sat there unmoving, he looked to the driver for guidance.

"Don't look at him. Alberto told you I was in charge. Now get out of the car before I extract you by your fucking snot locker. You know what 'extract' means, don't you, you dumb motherfucker?"

The man opened the door and nervously fumbled out of his seat. Mongoose dug his fingers and thumb around the man's windpipe.

"You stupid fucks. I coulda' put a bullet in all your heads while you sat here, cocks in hand, talking about all the pussy you'll never get. If you want to live tonight, you listen to what I got to say."

Mongoose could give a shit whether or not the men lived except for the fact that the longer they did, the more likely he and Sauce would get out of the house without any new scars to add to their collection.

After a brief conversation with the fantastic four, Mongoose learned that their plan had been to hit the front door at the same time the second crew entered the back. He knew exactly what the result of that exercise would have been. The four entering the back would have eventually run into the four entering the front. Since half of these guys were scared shitless and the other half stoned, they would've started shooting one another. If they were actually disciplined enough to try and avoid friendly fire, their reaction time would've been greatly increased because they'd first have to determine if their target was Carlos or just a member of their crudely assembled assault team. *Assault team*, Mongoose thought, *an affront to the term*.

After an impromptu two-minute briefing, the six men approached the home from the south in a single file. The fantastic four led the charge followed by Mongoose then Sauce, who once again covered their asses. The fourth in line, with fresh fingernail marks on his throat, used a cell phone to communicate with the "team" at the rear.

"Tell them to do it," Mongoose ordered.

A couple of seconds later the faint sound of breaking glass could be heard coming from the rear of the house. The four-man rear containment team had been told, repeatedly, to just break windows and kick in the back door. They, under no circumstances, were to enter the structure.

Mongoose barked, "Go," as the diversion at the back continued.

Alberto had supplied a key and the first man used it to open the front door and begin the assault. Mongoose and Sauce ventured no farther than the front room, found cover, and waited.

Three long minutes later, the rear team was allowed entry and Mongoose barked orders at the eight men, "Search again, under the beds, the closets, the attic—everything! If he's here, I want him found."

Alberto wasn't going to be happy, Mongoose thought. On the other hand, Mongoose felt a tingle. He'd always enjoyed the hunt, and lately had been bored by not having one. This Carlos—King Too Tall—might turn out to be a worthy adversary.

Mongoose covered the front door and sent Sauce to guard the back while the other eight men went about searching the home for a second time. MP-5 trained on the front door, Mongoose felt his cell phone vibrating in his pocket. Never taking his eyes off the potential threat in front of him, he fumbled the device out of his pants and answered the phone already knowing who'd be on the other end of the line.

"Goose."

"Jesus Christ, I told you to call me when you got inside," Alberto demanded, irritation clear in his voice.

The man was losing it, Mongoose thought.

"Been a little busy not getting killed like everyone else you send to do a job. As soon as I know if he's here, I'll call and tell you." Mongoose disconnected. "Fuckin' idiot."

Mongoose knew Alberto was no idiot. The man had proven himself cunning. Mongoose wasn't stupid either. He'd begun his scholastic career with the Chicago Public School system, a system that inflated its performance record via Jethro Bodine-like ciphering. In perpetual reality, fifty percent of CPS's students never make it to graduation day. Despite Neanderthal looks and an environment which included a single mother gasping for air while bobbing above a suffocating poverty line, he'd been a gifted student. Life was hard. Mongoose was harder.

Then along came Alberto Vega. The man struck up a relationship with his mother, and then Robert himself. *Robert*, his mother had given him a white name, thinking it would help him in the white man's world. Anyway, Alberto's semi-regular visits usually resulted in changes around the house. For one, his mother slept-in the next day, the long sleep followed by an evening of shopping for new clothes, food, whatever.

A few months after the relationship began, his mother quit two of her three jobs and stayed home to keep an eye on young Robert with much more regularity. Not long after, his mother didn't have much to watch; she enrolled Carlos in a private military school. The academy's curriculum included soldiering and leadership training.

Over the years, Alberto's relationship with his mother never became serious but neither did she seek out another man. As Robert grew, the more he understood the arrangement. His mother was no prostitute. Those who referred to her as such were quickly introduced to Robert's fists and feet.

If Alberto had wanted to pay for sex, it would have been much cheaper to go through escort services, massage parlors, the internet, or countless other avenues. Alberto had chosen his mother, provided as a father figure to the son, but had no want for a constant family. If his mother and Robert benefited financially from the arrangement, so be it.

It wasn't until Robert began to mature when he realized what the true endgame had been. Alberto hadn't wanted his mother. He'd wanted the son all along. Not for sex—thank God. At first the hints had been subtle, then less so, then not at all. Though there had never been threats, Robert—King Mongoose—knew if he ever refused the wishes of Alberto, his mother would be the one to pay the consequences. And Alberto had many minions who would make sure that payment would be made if Mongoose ever betrayed his "uncle."

In truth, Mongoose had no intentions of leaving the Kings. He liked gang life. Whether for the U.S. Army or for sport, he enjoyed hurting people. He was good at it. But he did have ambitions of which Alberto wasn't aware. Between military school and active service, he'd received nearly twelve years of first-rate leadership training. His uncle had always told him that one day he'd be a big shot in the Kings. On that issue his uncle had been correct. And when the day came that Mongoose ran the Nation, he'd cut the strings Alberto had strung over him and his mother. Until then, he'd do as ordered. But he didn't have to respect the man.

"No one here," one of the eight men announced as they converged in the living room.

Mongoose began pointing and directing, "You two relieve Sauce in the kitchen. You two keep your weapons on the front door. The rest of you cover the windows."

Mongoose grabbed his phone, retrieved his last received call, and hit send.

"He's not here and neither are his parents. The house is empty."

"Shit." Mongoose heard Alberto cover the mouthpiece for a few seconds then came back on the line, "Go to the hallway closet and check to see if there's any luggage."

Mongoose approached the closet and though twice cleared, disengaged the safety on his weapon and pointed the barrel inside as he opened the door, "No luggage."

"That's where they keep it. He's moved them already," Alberto advised.

"What do you want us to do from here?"

"Stay put, I'll get back to you in a minute."

You don't have a fucking clue what to do.

CARLOS WASN'T IN THE HOUSE. He sat in the middle seat of a brown, 1986, GMC conversion van. The van was rough, but the 350 cubic inch motor still rumbled smoothly beneath the hood. Once again Carlos reached between the front bucket seats and pawed away at the heavy condensation.

The van was stolen. Kind of. It belonged to an old high school friend whom he'd given a hundred bucks to borrow for a few hours. If things went south, the friend would report the van stolen. If things went well, the friend would just be a hundred dollars richer.

Carlos considered setting a trap inside his parent's house, much like he did in Elisa's apartment. But as any head football coach will tell you, it's difficult to run the same trick-play twice in a row. They'd be ready this time. Besides, his uncle had already demonstrated a propensity not to do his own dirty work. Instead, Carlos parked nearby and hoped Alberto would do the same. But if Alberto was close, he hadn't yet spotted him.

Carlos had watched the black Dodge Charger arrive. He'd seen two men step out and survey their surroundings. And despite the darkness and condensation, he'd seen how their torso's bulk was disproportionate to their limbs. He'd also noticed the dull gleam on the center of the passenger's chest; the left hands of both men dangling at their sides, their right arms cocked at ninety degrees. *Classic soldier posture*; they both had slung weapons and body armor. These men were Carlos' counterparts. Men who'd been recruited just as he had. Men who meant to kill him.

Carlos had several options. Storming the house to take on ten gunmen wasn't one of them. Ten were way too many, particularly when two were professional soldiers like himself. Perhaps Alberto would show his face now that the men had safely cleared the house. Though, Carlos thought it unlikely. The man was chicken-shit through and through.

Carlos considered sending a message of his own by killing a couple of the bastards when they left the house. As satisfying as that might feel, the act would only cause his uncle to burrow even deeper into hiding.

He also considered secreting himself in the back of one of the King's cars. After leaving his parent's house, they might unwittingly take Carlos directly to Alberto; a Trojan horse of sorts. The most likely candidates for driving to Alberto's hiding place would be the two soldiers. If he was locked in the trunk of their Charger and they became aware of his presence, the small enclosure would become his coffin.

His only feasible option was to follow one of the cars and hope it led him back to Alberto. The soldiers appeared cautiously aware of their surroundings and would likely notice a tail. Instead he'd follow the Blazer parked in front, or the Lincoln Town Car in the alley. The men occupying those cars had already demonstrated their exclusion from the mentally elite.

Carlos exited his van, pulled the collar up on his jacket, and walked down the sidewalk. Across from his parents' house, he took note of the Blazer's license plate. He didn't know if the information would serve him in the future—he didn't have any law enforcement contacts—but gathering available intelligence was always a good idea. Its usefulness could be determined later. Carlos then returned to his van, recorded the plates from the SUV and the Charger, started the rumbling engine and pulled a U-turn. No sense passing in front of the house. The fewer times his quarry observed his vehicle, the better.

The Lincoln faced south in the alley and because of the narrow passageway Carlos thought the vehicle would leave that direction rather than back all the way out. He selected a darkened area where he could see the car exit.

Before Carlos could get settled, the Lincoln peeled out of the alley and headed directly toward his position. Carlos killed the engine and leaned over into the passenger seat. As soon as the headlights washed past, Carlos popped up and adjusted his rearview mirror keeping an eye on the car's movements. Then another car passed by, which, luckily, wasn't the Charger or the Blazer. He restarted the engine, made another U-turn, and began to follow.

If the men he trailed noticed Carlos, hopefully they'd be overconfident in their numbers and abilities. He felt he'd have a better-than-average chance of surviving an ambush from the four idiots.

If the men drove to a remote location, it might be an indicator they were on to him; taking him somewhere they'd feel comfortable piling out of their car and filling his van with bullets without too many witnesses. In the event that happened, Carlos hoped to take evasive action likely to spare his life. *Though, one never really knew—when it's a man's time—it's his time.* Rounds fired miles away at entirely different targets have killed many an unlucky soldier in combat.

The bigger threat was the possibility the men in the Lincoln would notice the follow and call others to get behind Carlos. Aware of the potential hazard, he split his attention between the Lincoln and his rearview mirror.

Fifteen minutes after leaving his parents' house, the Town Car turned left onto a quiet street. Carlos passed on, but watched it parallel park on the north curb line. Carlos turned right, parked, and climbed into the back of his van with a pistol at the ready. He observed four men exit the Lincon. The driver and one of the rear seat passengers began walking toward a house. The front seat passenger and the other rear seat passenger began walking toward separate vehicles. The division forced Carlos to make another decision: *stay on the house or follow one of the two new cars?*

It was possible Alberto, or someone close to Alberto, resided in the house. If so, Carlos could always return. In the gang world, the leader generally rode in the front passenger seat. He sometimes drove but felt it beneath his rank to ride in the back, a concept totally at odds with educated leaders controlling well-funded organized groups—legal or illegal. But these guys were neither wealthy nor educated. Carlos kept tabs on the front seat passenger and liked what he saw. The man shouted something to his comrades, and walked straight to a newer, white, sporty Nissan. Confident and unconcerned with his safety, the man wasn't paying attention to his surroundings. *Stupid.*

The Nissan was parked on the north curb line facing west. The driver cut its wheels sharply, made a five-point turn, drove east and then turned back south heading in the direction he'd just come. Carlos, forced to commit yet another U-turn, noted the location of the house the other Kings had entered, then fed the thirsty eight-cylinder engine and quickly gained on the white Nissan.

At first things went smoothly, then the Nissan turned south on Homan Avenue from 51st Street, and the follow turned to shit. Homan Avenue is one-way and narrow; add to the equation cars parked along both curb lines and one is faced with a very constricted passageway.

In an effort to keep his distance, Carlos paused before following the Nissan into the turn. *Mistake.* The Nissan's taillights had already disappeared. Carlos fed the large motor and propelled the wide van down the precarious street. Passing an alley, Carlos spotted a set of taillights in his peripheral vision. *Shit!*

Carlos slammed on his brakes, turned off his headlights, and backed-up going the wrong way on Homan. He passed the opening, jammed the gearshift into drive, and turned west down the alley. It occurred to him this was a prime location for an ambush and he eased off the accelerator. Then came the fear of losing his quarry.

160

Fuck it. Gas pedal pressed to the floor, by the time Carlos reached the first cross street—Trumbull Avenue—the Nissan had already turned north on St. Louis, heading back toward 51st Street. The circular route concerned him, but he didn't have much of a choice. He followed.

Carlos drove with haste to St. Louis, turned right, and once again didn't see taillights. Accelerating too fast, he almost missed the Nissan. It was parked along the right curb line next to a large building with yellow siding. Carlos gave the brakes another workout, threw the van into reverse, backed-up far enough to get slightly behind the Nissan, and jumped out—weapon in hand.

Pistol pointed at window glass, Carlos discovered an empty interior. Afraid he'd walked into a trap, he spun in a circle, eyes and weapon searching for a target. *Nothing.*

Carlos peered up, guessed the building to be a collection of apartments, noticed several lights on, and decided the man had plenty of time to make it inside. Worse yet, Carlos had no way of knowing which unit the man had entered.

Frustrated but feeling rather conspicuous standing in the middle of the street with a pistol in his hand, Carlos reentered his van, slammed his palm against the steering wheel, screamed an expletive, and contemplated his next move.

THIRTY

LOST IN THOUGHT, THORPE CRUISED along the interstate.
He had lost his way. Not on the road he currently traveled but on the
path from which he'd strayed. If he thought along religious lines, his
soul needed saving. Considering himself a Christian—though an
admittedly poor excuse for one—he realized the depth of his
hypocrisy was unfathomable. Forgiveness no longer resided within
him. People had struck down his family and he'd demanded their
heads in return. *Thou shall not kill?* The commandment offered little
more than a distraction, a suggestion to be considered and dismissed
while exterminating the scourge from the earth. *Judge not lest you be
judged?* Thorpe figured when he stood in front of the pearly gates
he'd be in for one hell of a trial. *And he'd have to serve as his own
counsel since, surely, defense attorneys would be a rare commodity
in the kingdom of heaven.*

Evolutionary lines dictated he be a hunter; not a gatherer;
definitely not a nurturer. His father's son, it coursed through his
veins, framed his very DNA. Like Beethoven was born to compose,
Thorpe was born to kill. Unlike Beethoven, who continued to excel
despite his physical limitations, Thorpe's physicality contributed to
his calling. Like Michael Jordan on a basketball court, Thorpe's
mind and body worked in perfect unison. Except his mediums
weren't hardwood floors and leather-wrapped orbs, they were

sharpened steel and hardened bone. Armed or empty handed, he possessed the ability to think several moves ahead of his adversary.

Thinking along environmental lines, it was in this area where he'd most assuredly become derailed. As a boy, his family would take him to church on Sundays where he accepted Jesus. The other six days of the week his father taught him how to incapacitate, kill, and maim. One day a week learning how to save one's soul, six days a week learning how to take a life. The training had been conducted with good intentions—the safety and protection of oneself and one's family. No, the train didn't come completely off the tracks until other environmental influences flipped the killing switch from a defensive mechanism to an offensive option. Returning home to find the ghastly scene of his slain wife and daughter had been like an earthquake under his moral river. It had forever changed his course.

Environmental influences like the teachings of his father contributed to his evolutionary attributes. He'd been shown how to control elements generally dictated by the autonomic nervous system: breathing, heart rate, sleep cycles, etc. At age thirteen his father would put him on a polygraph machine for an hour and Thorpe could flat line the entire interview. By the time Thorpe turned fifteen he could put spikes on the graph at will—make lies look like truths and vice versa. His father hadn't been teaching him the art of deception, only that he had mastery over his body; self-hypnosis.

"St. Louis 60 miles," the sign snapped Thorpe out of another form of hypnosis. Although he could have reacted to any roadside emergency, would have recognized being followed, and had unconsciously changed radio stations, Thorpe had no recollection of the last hour of driving. It was a condition every driver has experienced; total concentration on a separate matter, yet fully aware of their surroundings despite the eerie detachment.

Thorpe shook his head. He needed to stop reflecting on what he'd become, and begin thinking about what he had to do. Neither of which was pretty.

THIRTY-ONE

LOUISVILLE, KENTUCKY, IS FAMOUS FOR many things, not the least of which are baseball bats and the fine bourbon of Jim Beam distilled in nearby Clermont. The distilling process implemented by Jim Beam is one of experience, care, and patience. Every bourbon made there is aged for a minimum of four years and watched over by skilled craftsmen like nervous fathers at a Michael Jackson sleepover. But the workmanship had been lost on Saeed. Last night he downed an entire bottle of Knob Hill—bourbon which is aged no less than nine years before being made available for public consumption—never once stopping to savor its flavor.

Convincing himself he needed to assimilate with the local populace, Saeed had become quite the connoisseur of various alcoholic beverages. After learning he'd be spending the night in Louisville, Saeed was excited about consuming a bottle of Kentucky's finest so close to where it was birthed. The anticipation of smelling the rich copper colored liquid just before swallowing its warm glow had been replaced with sloshing it down like cheap whiskey for one sole reason—pain relief.

The discomfort Saeed felt in his loins when he'd purchased the bourbon had been steady but controllable. The pain's intensity increased tenfold as he carried the bottle up the motel's stairs while cursing the desk manager for giving him a room on the third floor.

After having made it to his bed, his oozing, constantly throbbing testicles bloodied a once white, motel-supplied bath towel in no time at all.

In addition to the bourbon, Saeed impulsively bought a Penthouse magazine. But, having climbed the stairs, he now realized what a stupid decision the purchase had been and shuddered at the thought of a possible erection in his current condition.

Belly full of bourbon, Saeed overslept and missed his departure time. He'd awakened to two masked men standing over his bed, one holding a hooked knife resembling a Yemeni Jimbia. But this weapon was not decorative and its wielder would not hesitate to bloody its blade. Saeed was smart enough to realize these two were the men who had been following him—his "protectors."

Pleading for his life, Saeed thought he'd taken his last breath. The knifeless man grabbed him by the hair and dragged him off the bed onto the floor. That's when both men discovered the bloody mess between Saeed's legs.

Saeed concocted a story on the fly. He'd convinced the men of his dedication. So dedicated he'd pushed on despite his grievous injury. Ultimately the men saw the warrior Saeed knew he was.

His life spared, Saeed knew no further mistakes would be tolerated. A second misstep would result in his bloody demise. His only hope of survival depended on his total adherence to the mission. So far that mission was to drive an empty truck to yet another motel, and again wait for further instructions.

The pain pills were less than effective; his throbbing, dull but constant. Every time he stood he prayed to have the throbbing back, because it would be replaced by the feeling of a rusty spike being driven up his penis.

He hoped he wouldn't need surgery. He hoped, though his affliction allowed him to fear death less and less with each passing minute, he'd live long enough to discover the answer to that question. Saeed peered hard through his tear-blurred vision and concentrated on his driving. If he were to commit a traffic violation and be stopped by the police, the error would further undermine his position with his handlers.

"WHAT CAN BROWN DO FOR you?" Benjamin Thorpe doubted monitoring domestic terrorist cells fell under the umbrella of UPS' tag line. Nevertheless, he sat in the back of a large, brown, UPS cargo van, doing just that. Surrounded by surveillance equipment and communications gear, the UPS logo provided good cover in a number of environments. The van's dimensions afforded adequate space for Benjamin and three technicians as they bounced along Highway 65.

The van served as the nerve center for several vehicles conducting a loose follow of Saeed al-Haznawi. The operation became much simpler after the game of musical cars in Atlanta. Saeed's truck was not a vehicle Ben and Ambretta had been made aware of during their months of surveillance. Therefore, prior to leaving Atlanta, Ben's team hadn't been able to attach tracking devices. Turns out it didn't matter. Saeed's Ford F-150 was already equipped with two transponders.

Early in the follow the team detected a signal emanating from the vehicle, attached they assumed, by whoever controlled Saeed. Ben's team simply piggybacked the signal. Several hours later the team discovered a second signal. This signal activated once every ten minutes then powered back down. Whatever the significance of this seemingly empty pickup, Saeed's handlers appeared determined not to lose the vehicle or its driver.

Because the pickup was of such importance to Saeed's handlers, it was important to Ben. He'd wanted to attach his own tracking devices, but even when Saeed lay on the floor of his motel room in a bourbon-induced coma, his bodyguards in the black Honda Accord kept an eye on both the truck, and Saeed himself—though the men never made contact. Until this morning.

At 0600 hours Ben's technicians heard Saeed's alarm and a

wake-up call go unanswered. The techs used a "Particulate Flow Detection Microphone." *Whatever the hell that was.* Knowing such things was the job of the geek squad. Once—without prompting—his techs passionately explained how the device worked, "Sound pressure waves disturb the smoke and cause variations in the amount of laser light reaching the photo detector..." *Blah blah blah.*

All Ben knew, and all he cared about, was the device picked up sound inside of buildings as well as in the open air. "Just tell me what you're fucking hearing."

What they'd heard was a piercing alarm clock and Saeed's undisturbed snoring. Thirty minutes later, Saeed's body guards appeared at his door. They knocked a couple of times, then, rather expertly, entered the locked motel room. Their movements spoke of confidence and training.

The techs brought up the audio on the intercom and Ben listened as the men roused Saeed out of his sleep. A slight smile appeared on Ben's lips when the conversation turned to Saeed's butchered testicles. The men did not believe his story and it looked as though Saeed might not survive the morning. One of the soldiers made a phone call. The man on the other end gave instructions to get Saeed moving and that he would be, "dealt with after."

Saeed's mistake had given Ben's team a valuable piece of intel. By triangulating the cell towers, the techs identified the general location of the man on the phone; the one apparently pulling the strings. And it'd come from an interesting locale.

Saeed's associates got him back on the road and Ben and his team resumed shadowing, being careful to stay outside of visual range. The caravan currently proceeded northbound on Highway 65.

The two vehicles and three men they followed would have been a sizeable concern to Ben alone. The fact a similar caravan was en route to the East Coast multiplied his worry. Two of the original vehicles which had gone into motion the same morning as Saeed, now headed northeast. The situation was nearing a point where a difficult decision would need to be made: take the caravans down now and possibly prevent a major event, or let things play out and locate all the players—both options pregnant with potentially disastrous consequences.

Terrorist cells typically operate independently of one another so if one is discovered the others can continue uncompromised. If his team intercepted the caravans, they'd tip their hand that they were on to the operation. With the exception of a possible attempted rape charge against Saeed, the rest of the group had done nothing illegal. And Ben wasn't about to burn Ambretta's cover for that idiot. Plus, the liberal lawyers and politicians would ensure these men enjoyed the same protections guaranteed to United States citizens even though they weren't entitled to those rights. These animals wouldn't say a word unless under duress—and the United States government didn't stoop to those methods even at the cost of thousands of innocent lives. But Ben wasn't part of the government, at least not officially. He operated off the books. Way off.

Saeed and his bodyguards might not even be aware of their ultimate goal. Furthermore, one or both groups could just be a diversion. Ben doubted it though, the operation involved too many moving pieces. Ignorant little Saeed was part of something real. The Ford had been chosen for a reason. The empty, open, cargo area suggested the truck couldn't possibly be carrying anything of major concern—which served to worry Ben even more. The presence of two GPS transponders further confirmed the pickup's importance. It couldn't be the moronic Saeed, who was so precious to his people.

On the flip side, if his team allowed the caravan to continue and people lost their lives because they failed to intercept the players and prevent their plan, the same politicians and lawyers would want the heads of intelligence officials for not having taken preventative action. A no-win situation, these decisions weren't Ben's to make. He fed opinions and information up the food chain and, ultimately, folks in a much higher pay grade made those calls.

AMBRETTA SAT BEHIND THE WHEEL of a silver Nissan Pathfinder. Her mind was not on the road ahead or on the caravan trailing an hour behind. It was on the cell phone lying beside her. She'd twice picked up the phone, sometimes punching in three or four digits before slamming the device back down on the console. The ritual was one she'd performed several times over the last couple of months, usually during moments like this, where idle time allowed her thoughts to wonder.

The first three buttons she pushed were always *67. If she ever completed the entire sequence, the numbers would connect her to the city-supplied cell phone of Sergeant Jonathan Thorpe.

Why did she have such strong feelings for a man she'd known for such a short time? She supposed, the "why" wasn't important. She felt them and they weren't fading like she'd hoped. The connection she'd made had been strong. One she desperately wanted to keep, though she knew any attempt to do so would be an exercise in futility. Her sensibilities battled her emotional desires. She'd picture John's face, his touch, his body, even his vulnerability and would pick up the phone. Then she'd think about her work, her demanded anonymity, her lack of any normalcy, and knew the relationship could never work.

If those problems weren't enough, she also worked for John's father, a man who a month ago risked much for a son who thought him dead. Ben had never discussed those circumstances with Ambretta. Until one fateful day in Tulsa, Ambretta had always assumed Ben to be alone in this world. She didn't know the reasons behind the estrangement but held her suspicions.

Though Ben thought his work of the utmost importance, he carried self-loathing around like a sack of wet flour. She saw it in his shoulders. She saw it in his eyes. *Maybe Ben had done things he thought dishonorable, maybe things he thought his son wouldn't be proud. Or perhaps Ben saw himself in John's eyes; wanted to keep his son from becoming his father. Maybe she was full of shit.*

It added up to an impossible situation for her and John to ever have a relationship with one another. He would always remain a warm yet painful memory of something she once tasted but could never possess.

THIRTY-TWO

ANY FREQUENT FLYER LIVING IN the United States has no doubt spent time in Chicago. Many of those probably never ventured outside the grounds of O'Hare International Airport. Thorpe looked out his ninth floor hotel window at the third most populous city in the country with the sickening realization that, until now, he was one of those people. Not his town, he didn't know her essence, nor did he know his way.

It was eight thirty in the morning and his counterpart with Chicago PD's Gangs Intelligence Section was due to pick him up in half an hour. Today he'd be shown the realm of Chicago's Almighty Latin King/Queen Nation.

Looking across the conglomeration of cold steel and glass, the city seemed empty of humanity, though Thorpe knew millions swarmed in its trenches. Even now its reflective skin appeared to shrug off the warm blush of sunrise. Seven hundred miles to the southwest Hull and Skull might be looking at the same glowing orb, though it'd be a tad lower on the horizon. The two detectives should be boarding a plane in Tulsa. In a few hours they'd land at O'Hare, where they'd meet with representatives of Chicago PD's Homicide Unit.

There were two reasons why Thorpe drove instead of accompanying the men on the airplane. First, like he'd told his squad, he planned to spend some "me time" in Chicago. That time would undoubtedly include violence. He needed to eliminate future threats from treading on his property with deadly intentions. The second and more important reason, he wouldn't have been able to fly with the arsenal of weapons currently secured in the rear of his SID-supplied, Chevy Suburban.

Four dead men missing their index fingers and thumbs supplied much of what he'd brought along. There was Fubb's suppressed Heckler & Koch MP5SD, Knuckle's Mark 12 SPR sniper rifle, a .40 Sig Sauer P229 pistol, an A4, and a flack jacket complete with shoulder guards and ceramic inserts. The men had also been carrying fragmentation and stun grenades. Additional equipment provided by the City of Tulsa, as well as some unwitting donations made by drug-dealing shitheads, complimented his small weapons' depot. In addition to the weapons, recent events taught him the value of a couple of gallons of gasoline-oil mix, matches, and the need for a disposable phone.

Because Thorpe had better than $100,000 worth of weapons and gear along on the trip, he'd traded his assigned Ford F-150 for the Suburban. The Chevy was outfitted with a large lock-box bolted to the rear compartment area and a top-of-the-line Black Dog alarm system. A carpeted retractable cover concealed the lock-box, creating the illusion of an empty compartment. For added protection, Thorpe rigged a flash-bang to the rear hatch. If anyone lifted the door from the outside, the bang would explode. Although the concussion would likely blow out the Suburban's windows, it should also thwart any burglary attempt.

Still looking across the vast city, Thorpe thought the most important piece of equipment in his possession might be the handheld GPS unit he'd updated with Chicago-area software maps. He didn't plan on riding with Chicago officers for long and the device would help him get around. Anxious to get started, Thorpe looked down at his watch. He'd like to get a jump on Hull and Skull before they arrived and began wrecking his plans.

As if on cue his cell phone vibrated in his pocket.

"Thorpe."

"Something's come up and we need to get going early." It was Sergeant James Wyatt, his tour guide. "Hope you've had breakfast. I'm five minutes out."

"On my way down."

"Meet you in front. I'm in a blue Tahoe."

Thorpe grabbed the GPS unit and shoved it in his leather jacket as he mumbled an expletive. He hoped whatever had "come up" wouldn't postpone his intel gathering. Out in the hall, he pushed an illuminated arrow pointed in the general direction of hell and stepped into an elevator occupied by two men and a woman, all smartly attired. The men looked at Thorpe's scruffy beard, ragged leather coat, torn jeans, and Harley Davidson boots, as if he'd lowered the hotel's rating a full star. The three gave him a wide berth.

Thorpe looked at his stitched-up ear in the mirror and understood their concern; he looked like he'd awoken on the wrong side of the tracks. "Relax. My shots are current."

The elevator doors opened allowing three nervous laughs to escape and a curvaceous forty-something brunette to enter. The woman—wearing a snug business skirt—held Thorpe's gaze for a moment, acknowledged his evaluation of her with a smile, approached closer than was necessary, and turned her back to him. Toned ass abutted upper thigh. Thorpe's mind replaced the canned music with Aerosmith's "Love in an Elevator," which in turn was interrupted by a ping as they reached the main floor. Love in an Elevator stepped out, glanced over her shoulder, and sashayed across the tiled lobby, tight skirt oscillating above clicking high heels. Transfixed, Thorpe stood motionless. The closing doors snapped him out of his trance.

Thorpe found a Tahoe occupied by a man in the process of waving off a valet. Average sized, white, balding with a rim of salted black hair and graying mustache, Thorpe concluded the man to be his escort for the day. In an effort to avoid his ear being a topic of discussion, Thorpe pulled a gray fleece beanie over his head and below the injury, then walked in front of the Tahoe, yanked open the passenger door and climbed in.

"I hope you're Thorpe," the man said with a frown.

"Thorpe? Who's that? I just thought you looked kinda' cute."

The man stuck out his hand, "James Wyatt."

Thorpe accepted the handshake, "John, thanks for letting me tag along."

"You armed?"

"Yeah, that a problem?"

"It would be if you weren't."

Thorpe liked the guy already. "So, what has my date picking me up thirty minutes ahead of schedule?"

"Well my friend, you are in luck. We have a brand-spankin'-new homicide and guess what?" Wyatt smiled, "The 'victim' is a Latin King."

During their eighteen minute drive to the crime scene, Wyatt provided a brief synopsis on the current affairs of the Almighty Latin King/Queen Nation. They were headed to an area referred to as "Crown Town." Give or take a block or two, Crown Town filled the space between 51st and 59th Streets, Pulaski Road and Western Avenue. Wyatt, playing the part of gracious tour guide, informed Thorpe that Western Avenue was the longest continuous city street in America. Not yet having a feel for Wyatt's sense of humor, or lack thereof, Thorpe held his thought, *I'll take city streets for one thousand, Alex.*

The Latin Kings had originally formed on the north side of Chicago near Humboldt Park (the Motherland) and will always have a presence there. However, these days most LK action took place in the southwest section of the city either in Chi Town or Crown Town. The two areas accommodated at least twenty-six active Latin King sets.

Westbound on 51st Street, Wyatt passed a cordoned-off St. Louis Avenue and conducted a U-turn in front of a railroad crossing sign. There, he found a place to park along the south curb line. Thorpe climbed out of the Tahoe onto a sidewalk and into an unusually cold morning. Wyatt rounded the front of the SUV, pulled the collar up on his coat, and—turtle like—retracted his balding head inside. Thorpe followed his neckless guide across one of the few uninhabited grassy areas he'd seen in the city, toward a bottleneck of cop cars and plain American-made sedans blocking St. Louis.

Thorpe noticed most of the activity focused around a newer, white Nissan Z parked on the street, and also behind a wooden privacy fence at the back of a three story, shit-hole of a building. Obligatory yellow police tape kept a dozen or so rubberneckers at a respectable distance. One of the uniforms guarding the scene demonstrated uncanny recognition skills when he nodded at the top of Wyatt's bald head, "Sergeant."

Wyatt unsheathed a thumb from his coat pocket and pointed the appendage at Thorpe, "This guy's with me."

The uniform took down Thorpe's information. The fact he hailed from Tulsa raised an eyebrow and a couple more follow-up questions before the pair were allowed to cross under the magical tape.

The uniform pointed a leather-clad finger toward an open and askew gate in the wooden privacy fence. "Body's behind the building."

Before entering the opening, Wyatt and Thorpe paused near the white Nissan and observed a crime scene detective photographing a boot print on the passenger side window glass. Wyatt looked at Thorpe, shrugged his shoulders, and walked through the gate opening. Inside the fence another uniform directed them to turn left around the corner of the building.

There they found a three-eyed, Hispanic male on his back. Well, two eyes and a bullet hole. The body was situated between the building and a tall chain-link fence topped with barbed wire, his head pointed toward Thorpe and Wyatt. On the other side of the body, near the feet of the deceased, stood a trio of large men wearing suits and overcoats huddled together like a corporate football team.

"Who's the yard fertilizer?" Wyatt asked.

Introductions and explanations were traded, hands were shaken, and Wyatt's question finally answered—but not by one of the three men in suits.

"Teicuih Perez."

Thorpe turned in the direction they had just come and found the source of the voice.

A woman wearing blue jeans and a green, army-issued field jacket, stood near the corner of the building. Hispanic and attractive, a black scarf and a brown knit hat framed her face. Even though multiple layers of clothing covered her body, one just knew it was fantastic. How? One just did.

"Who's this?"

The explanations were getting old already and Thorpe had been on the job for less than an hour.

Wyatt saved him, "This is the cop from Tulsa I told you about. The one I'm babysitting for a couple of days."

"Oh yeah, the cowboy. Does cowboy have a name?"

When imagining Tulsa, some people, particularly those from larger cities, tend to envision cowboys, cows, and dust bowls. Thorpe had lived in Tulsa for years and had little experience with any of those things. But he wasn't in Chicago to start dispelling misconceptions.

He extended his hand, "Jonathan Thorpe."

"A cowboy with an Indian's name," she smiled, "Jenna Smith."

Jenna must have been thinking of the late Jim Thorpe, an American Indian from Oklahoma. The state's most famous athlete, among other accomplishments, he played professional baseball and was the first president of what is now the National Football League. Bo might know football and baseball, but he didn't know Olympic gold. Jim did. He's considered by many to be one of the greatest athletes of the twentieth century. The surname is European and Jim Thorpe is actually of both Native American and European descent.

But he wasn't here to provide onomastics lessons either.

"Smith, a Mexican with a British name," Thorpe shot back.

"I'm not Mexican."

"And I'm not a cowboy or an Indian."

Jenna's eyes bore into Thorpe.

"Sarge, I think I like. Can we keep him?"

She'd directed the comment to her sergeant but her eyes never left Thorpe's.

"Jenna's one of my investigators. She's pretty good when she's not fucking with people."

"Correction. I'm pretty good *because* I fuck with people."

"Right. You going to tell us what happened before we freeze our asses off?"

Jenna broke her gaze, took out some notes, and addressed her boss, "At about 0730 hours, a resident of this fine establishment brought his dog out for his morning constitutional. When they walked around the corner here, Fido discovered this," Jenna said, motioning to the dead man lying on the even deader grass. "Person reporting promises he didn't let Fido piss on the cadaver. Our Good Samaritan canceled the bathroom break, returned to his apartment and called 911. Uniforms show up and find our 'victim' here. He has at least five entry wounds: face, chest, and a hole in each leg. Mr. Body didn't have a wallet, ID, keys, or shoes. The responding officers figure—correctly—that he must be a resident here."

Jenna pointed up at the building, "Uniforms perform a canvass to try and get an ID on Mr. Body when they come across apartment 223. The door is wide open and they eventually make entry and find a female asleep in a back bedroom. She has no idea that her front door is open and says she lives alone. Uniforms see a wallet, keys, cell phone, and men's shoes on the coffee table. They have a Sherlock moment, go over and pull out a driver's license, and are not surprised to see the picture on it matches our victim. Girlfriend finally admits the victim lived there after the uni's tell her that her boyfriend is stiff, and not in a good way. Girlfriend says last she knew, victim was playing X-box in the living room, alive and well. Last saw him about ten o'clock before she went to bed. One of the things they found on the coffee table was a remote pager for a car alarm. Apparently someone tripped the alarm around two this morning."

Wyatt interjected, "So victim's playing Grand Theft Auto on his X-box and his car alarm goes off. He bolts out the door, leaving it open, sees some asshole trying to break into his car and chases him around the apartment building. Except asshole car burglar doesn't run far. Instead, he turns and caps the victim?"

"Looking that way," Jenna agreed.

"And Mr. Body's a Latin King?"

"Yeah, old-school. Been in and out of prison," Jenna answered.

"Sometimes justice finds a way," Wyatt remarked. "Doesn't look gang-related after all; some asshole got caught breaking into a bigger asshole's car."

Thorpe nodded at the body, "Mind if I take a closer look?"

One of the homicide detectives answered, "Just don't touch him. We've done all we can with him here. Waiting for the M.E. now."

Thorpe kneeled next to the dead Latin King. There were four obvious injuries. He had a gunshot wound to each leg, both of which had bled through the clothing. A third hole was positioned directly between the man's eyes, and Thorpe could see a fourth wound beneath the victim's thin t-shirt. This injury was directly over the man's heart but hadn't produced much blood loss.

"I thought you said he had five entry wounds?"

"There are. The two to the chest are right on top of each other. Damn near looks like one bullet hole."

Thorpe took a closer look, *yup*, the hole in the t-shirt was misshapen, *probably two separate rounds*. Still kneeling, Thorpe visualized possible scenarios. Sticking with his new persona as a cowboy, Thorpe figured the dead man had definitely been bush-whacked. Nothing about the body added up to a car burglary gone bad; more like an orchestrated assassination. The detectives didn't appear to share his suspicions. Of course, unlike Thorpe, they hadn't just recently survived an attempt on their lives via professional soldiers-cum-Latin Kings. To them this looked like another dipshit gangbanger getting what he had coming.

The victim's bullet patterns had Thorpe thinking otherwise. Two non-lethal wounds: one in the right knee the other in the left thigh. Then at least three perfect kill shots, one of which positioned squarely inside the death band. Snipers are trained to shoot an imaginary band that surrounds the head. The eyes and ears fall roughly in the center of the band. Any shot which penetrates the band has a high likelihood of producing a non-reflex kill. The death band is crucial when engaging a hostage taker with his finger on the trigger. In theory, and proved in practice, the suspect's brain is dismantled before it's able to send a signal to the finger, thereby saving the hostage. Shooting a person in this imaginary band is almost a guaranteed kill.

Thorpe looked up at the gathered detectives, "Any exit wounds?"

"None that are readily apparent."

That meant the shooter used a handgun; a rifle likely would have penetrated all the way through.

"Shell casings?"

"Nope."

A revolver wouldn't expel shell casings, but if the shooter used a semiautomatic, then the perpetrator had collected the casings after killing the man. That'd take a pretty cool customer.

Whoever pulled the trigger had probably been looking his victim in the eyes; the bullet hole was perfectly centered. The other two shots had been fired directly into the heart. The tight grouping suggested a man who remained incredibly calm while taking another's life. Although, the victim was already dead when the suspect fired these last two rounds; despite being centered over a blood pumping organ, the injuries produced little blood loss.

Thorpe figured on one of two scenarios, either way the shots to the legs were the first ones discharged. Scenario one, the suspect shot the victim in the legs as he rounded the corner dropping him to the ground. Then he fired a kill shot to the man's head and followed that up with insurance rounds to the heart.

One problem: if the man had been shot in the legs while running he would have fallen forward on his stomach. He may have later rolled over but his feet would still have been nearer the corner, and his head would be facing north instead of south. That is, unless the victim started break-dancing after having been shot in both legs. Possible, but not likely.

Scenario two, the suspect drove his shoulders into the victim's legs as he rounded the corner causing the victim to flip in the air. This would put him supine on his back with his feet facing north and his head toward the corner, just like the body had been found. *But what about the leg shots? Torture?* If so, the M.E. should find gunpowder stippling around the wounds because the rounds would have been fired at close range.

"You mind if I pull his eyelids down?" Thorpe asked.

"Why would you want to do that? Who the hell is this guy again?"

The questions came from a large detective who'd been paying both Jenna and Thorpe a little too much attention.

"Never mind."

If he were working the case he'd have the M.E. do a GSR test on the victim's face to check for tight rings of gunpowder. He'd also have them check the inside of the mouth. But Thorpe wasn't here to work cases and he could give a shit if they found the killer.

The large detective wasn't finished, "Look Barney, I don't know how many homicides you work back in Mayberry, but I think we can handle it." The man looked at Jenna like he'd just told the joke of the century. Thorpe caught a flash in her eyes. There was history between the two.

Thorpe rose, "What's your name?"

"Nunya. Nunya Goddamned business."

Thorpe, keeping his eyes on "Nunya," nodded toward Jenna, "Look, if you want to mark your territory, why don't you just piss on her leg. We'll all turn our backs so you're not too embarrassed. It *is* cold out here."

The others laughed. Nunya failed to see the humor. He stepped forward, forcing Wyatt to play referee.

"Damn it, let's show a little professionalism. We are at a fucking homicide scene, gentleman. We don't need citizens watching this shit."

Thorpe raised his hands in surrender, "My fault. I asked a stupid question."

Nunya nodded his head in agreement, muttered something unintelligible and walked away, out of sight.

Thorpe, Wyatt, and Jenna poked around the body a little longer, moved on to the Nissan, and then to the girlfriend's apartment. There wasn't much to be gathered from the last two locations, and the girlfriend provided no help whatsoever. She refused to sign a "consent to search" form. Illegal drugs or weapons were probably hidden inside. Officers kept the girl in the front room while detectives prepared a search warrant for her residence.

"Not much else to be learned here. You ready for your tour or you want to stay and make more friends?" Wyatt asked.

"One can never have too many friends."

Wyatt chuckled, then turned to Jenna, "You good?"

"Yeah, I'm good."

Wyatt and Thorpe started heading back toward the Tahoe.

Jenna shouted after them, "Hey, Tulsa."

"Yeah?"

"I'm no one's territory and I don't appreciate you inviting men to piss on my leg," her admonishment was administered with a smile.

"Noted."

Walking back to the car Wyatt looked sideways at Thorpe,

"She likes you."

"So she said. Even wants to keep me."

"I'm serious."

"Well, I'm probably not going to be in town for more than a couple of days."

"Might be why she likes you."

"Love 'em and leave 'em type is she?"

"No. She doesn't get around. She just doesn't date anyone on the department."

"Sounds like a smart woman. Dating fellow cops rarely works out. Eventually you have to marry them or break up with them. If it's the latter, then you have to work with a jilted lover for the rest of your career."

"Yeah, then they go around talking about how small your dick is to anyone who'll listen," Wyatt agreed. "Still, it's a better alternative to marriage."

Both men laughed.

"You married?" Wyatt asked.

"Widower."

"Sorry, man. Kids?"

"Had a daughter; she died with my wife."

"Jesus, sorry. Fucking don't have any more feet to put in my mouth," Wyatt said with sincerity.

"Don't worry about it, you couldn't have known." Thorpe slapped the man's back, "Where to next?"

Wyatt looked appreciative of the change of subjects, "Let's show you where the Kings like to work and play."

CARLOS—STRUNG OUT FROM LACK of sleep—huddled inside the rear compartment of his borrowed van. It'd taken him two nights, but he'd made progress. He was parked along the east curb of South Hamlin Avenue. His van faced north, and was about 60 meters north of his object of surveillance. He waited outside the home of

Luis Carbia, Alberto Vega's half brother and right-hand man. Carlos had met Luis on occasion, though until early this morning, had no idea—or care—where the man lived.

Two nights ago he'd followed the Nissan Z from his parents' house to an apartment building. Unfortunately, the driver had entered and disappeared before Carlos could follow. He'd been forced to return to where the men in the Lincoln Town Car had dispersed. He tried to conduct surveillance on the house they'd entered, but discovered vehicles unfamiliar to the neighborhood came under intense scrutiny. Even at four in the morning, his presence there attracted unwanted attention from unsavory characters. He'd been forced to return to the apartment building on south St. Louis. After having made sure the car was still in its space, Carlos parked about seventy yards to the south and waited for the Nissan to move. It never did.

All damn day he sat. He eventually left to use a restroom and to buy provisions: food, drinks, and windshield wiper fluid. The fluid wasn't essential, but the large container it came in was; he needed something to piss in. While gathering supplies, he'd been a nervous wreck, worried the Nissan would drive off the moment he left his post. His worry had been unwarranted. He returned to find the car in the same parking space. The waiting continued. At four this morning he'd had enough.

The previous night, when he'd jumped out and pointed his weapon at the empty Nissan, he'd noticed an alarm sticker inside the window. A plan had taken root. He would simply walk over to the car, give it a swift kick, retreat through the open gate in the fence, and snatch the driver when he came to check on the car. Then he would drag the guy behind the secluded privacy fence and begin his interrogation.

Carlos had quickly scouted the surrounding area. Once he kicked the car and the alarm sounded, it would attract attention—but not much. People were so used to car alarms they usually elicited a glance and nothing more. Unless it was one's own, no one gave a shit.

Having felt he could trip the device and get to his place of concealment before anyone took notice, Carlos gave a solid kick to the passenger side glass of the Nissan and scurried behind the fence. He'd already secreted himself before he realized the alarm hadn't sounded.

Maybe the driver forgot to set the alarm. Maybe the sticker was just for show. He returned to the car, and in order to see clearly inside, cupped his hands around the glass. That's when he'd heard the bang—the sound of a door slamming against the side of the building as an occupant sprinted outside. The occupant turned out to be his man, and his man held a pistol. *Don't fucking fire that thing.*

Carlos hadn't been too worried about getting shot. Running in a full sprint from twenty yards away the man couldn't have hit a pre-Subway Jared. Carlos worried because a fired shot would attract attention. While car alarms went mostly unnoticed, gunfire still tended to arouse curiosity—depending on the neighborhood of course. Even in this place shots might have caused a few people to stick their heads out their windows to see what all the fuss was about.

Silent alarm. Some devices send a signal to a pager or cell phone. They're more popular with folks who like to take matters into their own hands and confront suspects in the act. Caught in the act, Carlos was chased by his own quarry; the equivalent of hunting deer only to find one of the deer had armed itself.

That thought had actually entered Carlos' mind as he ran through the privacy fence and around the corner of the building, pleasantly surprised the deer hadn't yet fired at him. Even while peculiar thoughts streamed through his mind, so did tactical scenarios. As Carlos made the corner, he realized the location afforded his best opportunity. Given he had a fence to his right, a building to his left, and thirty yards until he reached another tall fence, it was here where his deer would open-up on him. The gangbanger's marksmanship would probably be indicative of possessing hooves instead of opposable thumbs, but nonetheless, Carlos' objective would be lost.

Instead, when Carlos made the corner he dug in his heels. On the other side of the fence sat the empty parking lot of an abandoned business. It was as anonymous as one could hope for given the urban surroundings.

The man-deer would likely do one of two things. If he were a really stupid deer, or a really pissed-off deer, he'd sprint around the corner hoping not to lose any ground on his foe. If Deer Man was smart, he'd slow his pace and "split the pie" with his pistol. Carlos already knew the man was pissed, and confident he would also prove to be stupid; the two traits quite prevalent in the criminal world.

Carlos went to a knee four feet behind the corner of the building. Because, only pissed-off, stupid, deer-like criminals use one hand when the stability of two ensure proper round placement, Carlos held his silenced pistol out in front in a two-hand grip. He used the building for cover. If the man weavered the corner they'd be in a stalemate, except Carlos would still have three advantages: down on one knee he'd be a smaller target and have a more stable shooting platform, he was an expert marksman, and most importantly, he was calm.

If the man bounded around the corner like the idiot Carlos hoped he was, he would collide with Carlos with little to no reaction time. These were a lot of thoughts to go through an average person's mind in the matter of a second. But Carlos was not an average man. These tactics had been drilled into him until not really thoughts at all. They were more akin to how the foot jumps when the knee is struck with a rubber mallet. Similar to the autonomic nervous system; one doesn't hear his inner dialogue telling his heart to beat or his lungs to breathe, it just happens. Carlos barely recognized his brain telling him how to react to the situation…he just did. He'd been an instrument of war when he was born, his training had only honed what his mind and body already knew, and that was how to survive.

As expected, the man rounded the corner at full speed with zero thoughts of an ambush; his pistol pumped from ribs to temple like a baton in an 800 meter relay race. Then Deer Man got the, well, "deer in the headlights" look. Except he didn't freeze. His momentum carried him into the solidly planted Carlos sending him hooves over ass. The man landed on his back, dispossessed of his pistol. But he did have the barrel of another, pressed firmly into the socket of his left eye.

"You even breathe loud and you're a fucking dead man," Carlos said. "I don't want your car or anything in it. All I want are answers. You answer my questions truthfully and you live. You don't, you die. Understand?"

The man nodded as best he could with the silenced barrel pushing against his left eye. His right eye no doubt would have been wide with fear but instead was closed—a natural reaction based on the predicament of its mate.

"You know King Slick, Alberto Vega?"

A nod.

"You know where he lives?"

A shake of the head.

"You know Luis Carbia?"

Another nod.

"You know where he lives?"

Another shake of the head.

Carlos withdrew the silenced pistol from the man's eye as if satisfied—and knee-capped him. Not quite a knee cap, because the man realized at the last second he was about to be shot and began to thrash. The round struck close enough.

Under extreme duress, recognition of pain isn't always immediate. Even though the round tore through bone, cartilage, and muscle, the man was in such a state of shock the nerve messages weren't immediately decoded by the brain. A couple seconds of stunned silence later, he opened his mouth to let loose a scream and Carlos shoved the silencer in the newly exposed orifice. The steel cylinder stifled the scream and induced a gag reflex.

"I told you not to lie."

Carlos had no idea whether the man had lied or not, but he needed to appear convinced that he had.

"Last time, where does Carbia live?"

Carlos made a motion to suggest he intended to repeat history on the man's left knee.

Through gritted teeth, the man managed to get out that he was willing to talk. He hadn't known Luis' address but said he could describe where he lived. Carlos hadn't wanted to drag a stupid, pissed-off, wounded gangbanger around with him for the rest of the morning so instead he'd gotten directions which turned out to be simple. Luis' house sat on the corner of an intersection and the man actually knew the names of the streets. The idiot just didn't know his north from his south but Carlos felt confident he could locate the address based on his description.

"Where does Alberto Vega live?"

The man swore he didn't know.

Carlos whispered, "I told you not to lie," and attempted to shoot the wounded man's good leg.

This time the man knew what was coming and bucked. The movement of the leg and the shoving of Carlos caused the round to go astray and into Deer Man's upper thigh, or hind-quarters, as Carlos doggedly stuck with the comparison—an insult to deer everywhere.

"I'm not fucking lying; I swear I don't know where he lives. I know where his bitch lives, that's it."

His captive went on to describe Carlos' own apartment building when providing details of Elisa Ruiz. The revelation convinced Carlos the man had been telling the truth.

Carlos felt he'd been dealing with matters in the open for too long. Ignoring the promise he'd made, he stood up and backed away from his beaten prey. With enough distance to avoid blowback, Carlos fired one shot directly between the man's eyes. He placed two more into the heart, insurance rounds. Carlos checked for identification, cell-phones, keys, anything, and noticed for the first time Deer Man wasn't wearing shoes. He'd probably been asleep, gotten a page, and had run to his death.

There had been no pager on the body either; all his personal items still in the apartment. Carlos decided he'd tested his luck enough. He straightened his jacket, hitched up his pants, concealed his pistol and confiscated a new one. Then he casually walked to his van as if on an early morning stroll.

Now Carlos sat outside the house Deer Man had described as being Carbia's. It was the shittiest place in the neighborhood—by far. The lack of care made the property readily identifiable. A corner house, its front faced the east/west cross street. Its detached garage faced Hamlin.

Alberto's Mercedes was nowhere to be seen, but if he were here, it'd most likely be inside the garage. Numerous cars littered Hamlin and the cross street, but only one interested him. The black Dodge Charger parked in front of the unkempt yard, confirmed that Deer Man had been telling the truth. The tag matched the one he'd recorded outside his parents' home. This was Luis Carbia's residence and the soldiers were inside.

And it was where all of them would die.

THIRTY-THREE

OAK-WRAPPED BEVELED MIRRORS FRAMED AN image of Thorpe not easily deciphered. Music spilling into the elevator caused neither a grimace nor a tapping of foot. In truth—though he wasn't enthusiastic about attending the scheduled bullshit session— he was in a pretty good mood. All things considered.

Generally, Thorpe's mind rarely strayed from the deaths of his wife and daughter and the guilt those memories brought to bear. When he wasn't what-ifing himself into depression or aggression, his thoughts turned to the brief but intense relationship he'd had, and lost, with Ambretta.

Even those recollections inflicted pangs of guilt, falling in love with a woman so soon after his family's murders. Thirteen months between when they'd been killed and when he'd fallen for the mysterious woman. Thorpe had little doubt he should seek professional help for the unbridled noxious thoughts which ravaged his mind. He doubted however, a therapist could grant him much relief without full disclosure of the things he'd done to secure reparations. And if those deeds were ever revealed, he'd spend the rest of his life in prison. *Maybe that's where he belonged.*

Thorpe didn't bother praying for forgiveness. How could he hope to be forgiven for sins past when he had every intention of continuing with the same actions? If vengeance was the Lord's to have, then Thorpe had taken much from his hopeful savior.

Current circumstances had drawn Thorpe away from his usual brooding. His challenge in this city of nine million was colossal. Find those responsible for ordering him dead and make sure there would be no future decrees. He recognized he shouldn't find the task to be a mood elevator. Nevertheless...

His spirits were also lifted by the nature of the battle. Unlike the events of February, where he'd been under the constant threat of being killed or imprisoned, here he was totally on the offensive. His adversaries didn't know he'd come to Chicago. This time he would be the hunter, not the hunted.

Alone in the elevator, Thorpe studied his reflection. Normally he went to great lengths to conceal his physique. Tonight he'd dressed in blue jeans and a thin, form-fitting, cashmere sweater which revealed the chiseled musculature within. After all, he was in a city not his own. He'd never see these people again, and, Jenna *was* an attractive woman.

Thorpe was to meet Jenna, Wyatt, Skull, and Hull in the hotel's bar to discuss what they'd uncovered. And like it does anytime you mix cops and alcohol, the gathering would dissolve into a liquor guzzling, "I've kicked more ass than you," war-story session. Thorpe would rather skip the drink fest and instead get on with his investigation but thought it best to keep up appearances. The Chicago cops wouldn't think anything of his absence, but he didn't want to stir Hull and Skull's insatiable curiosity. The two detectives were like flies. They swarmed to the smell of bullshit.

Wyatt had dropped Thorpe off at the hotel a few hours ago with files from CPD's Gangs Intelligence Unit. Armed with information gleaned from within, and what he'd learned during the day, Thorpe hoped to have a late and productive night. The session at the bar would only delay his plans.

A ping and an illuminated "L" let Thorpe know he'd reached the lobby. He stepped out of the mirrored coffin in pursuit of the house bar. Reaching his destination, Thorpe crossed the threshold, his pupils dilating with the depletion of light. Here classical music had been replaced by Billy Joel—though today's youth might argue the difference. A dark burgundy carpet adequately camouflaged the bar's accumulated spillage of drinks and stomach contents—because even wealthy folks over-imbibe from time to time. The room blended dark woods, dark paints, dark furniture, and subtle lighting.

Thorpe walked straight toward an attractive ginger-headed woman tending a large oval-shaped bar. His eyes adjusting to the cave-like conditions, he noticed the curvaceous woman, "Love in an Elevator", whom he'd encountered earlier. She sat on the opposite side of the bar with a commanding view of the room and its entryway. She was the meat in a suit sandwich—her two phallic bookends busy chatting-her-up.

Dressed to ensure she would not be ignored, Love in an Elevator appeared to be thoroughly enjoying the attention. Because of the height of the bar, Thorpe couldn't see below her sternum. She had on a tight, red outfit with a neckline that plunged well below the bar. Thorpe was curious what the lower half of the apparel had to offer, *or not offer*, but refrained from allowing voyeurism to control his actions.

Instead, he took a stool at turn four of the oval track with the trio to his left and the entryway to his right. Having spotted Stella on tap, he ordered a glass from Ginger, and made eye contact with Love—already on a first name basis. A faint smile indicated Love acknowledged Thorpe's presence, as he gave an almost imperceptible nod in return. Thorpe pretended to be interested in ESPN's SportsCenter as Ginger returned with his beer.

A name tag pinned to Ginger's shirt read "Sandy." *Didn't she know he'd already given her a nickname?*

"Sandy, your last name wouldn't be Rhoades or Banks would it?"

"Even worse; Forrest."

"Daddy had a sense of humor did he?"

"Nope, I did. Doss is my maiden name."

"Ah, see how I cleverly ascertained you were married without even asking?"

Sandy smiled, "Very clever. But you could have just looked at my finger."

"Too easy."

Speaking of easy, Love became more and more immersed in her performance. Laughs were amplified. Gesticulations drew the eye. Thorpe's occasional glances landed on unblinking attention and a practiced smile. Love wanted Thorpe to form a trio of competition for her affections. He wondered how many days of the year Love spent bagging men on business trips. He would have pegged her for a prostitute if he hadn't seen her getting off the elevator this morning. Her mannerisms echoed those of a hotel whore, except instead of money, she sought affection. *Or maybe she took in a double income—who knew?*

Movement near the entrance signaled the end of Act I. Thorpe turned to see Robert Hull walking to the bar with Chuck "The Skull" Lagrone in tow. Love would be happy for the growing audience.

"Hey, Bob."

"Hey, John. What you drinking?"

"Stella. What's up, Skull?"

"How you doin', Carnac?"

"Enjoying the show," Thorpe said, with a subtle head nod toward the woman in red. "Should provide some entertainment while we discuss things."

Hull and Skull looked over at Love and received a flirtatious smile in return. She liked being talked about.

Both men ordered Jack and Cokes before Skull suggested moving to a booth. The older detective led the group deeper into the lounge to a location that provided an unencumbered view of the woman in the red dress. Taking his seat, Thorpe noticed the hem of Love's dress was as high as the top was low.

"She a professional?" Hull asked.

Thorpe laughed, "I don't think so. Saw her get off the elevator dressed all respectable this morning, so she must be staying here."

"She's too good looking to be a professional." Skull offered.

"Skull, maybe Chicago pros are better looking than the ones you rent in Tulsa," Hull laughed.

"She's got a rockin' body, but I saw her get off the elevator under fluorescent lights," Thorpe added. "Her face showed some hard livin'."

"I'll give her some hard livin'," Skull smiled. "I might have to run off the two suits in an hour or so."

"Did you bring along your hard-on pills?" Thorpe laughed.

Skull answered with sincerity, "Damn straight I did."

Possessing an all-too vivid imagination, an image shot through Thorpe's brain like a lightning bolt. For a brief second his mind pictured Skull in the throes of passion. Now, while Lagrone was a nice guy, he wasn't called The Skull for nothing, and picturing his face contorted in ecstasy sent a shiver down Thorpe's spine.

"What's wrong with you?" Hull asked.

Apparently Thorpe's face had conveyed the frightening image to which he'd just been subjected, "Uh…nothing. This beer tastes like shit. Probably been sitting in the same tap for a month," Thorpe lied.

Skull held his glass up, "That's why we order whiskey. You don't have to worry about a damn born-on date."

The words "born-on" caused another lightning-bolt image to course through his mind forcing Thorpe to stand up, "I'm going to switch out drinks." He laughed at himself as he walked away from the table.

Thorpe stood at the bar shaking his head with a smile on his face. It didn't disappear when Jenna and Wyatt stepped into the bar.

"What can I get you?"

The bartender formerly known as Ginger had Thorpe's left ear, Jenna had his attention.

"Uh, *Missus* Forrest, can I switch this out for a bottle of Becks?"

"Sure, something wrong with this?" Sandy asked, holding up Thorpe's unfinished Stella.

"Nothing my imagination can't cure. Long story, the Stella's fine; I'll pay for both."

Sandy might have considered Thorpe's inattention rude if she too hadn't been watching Jenna cross the lounge's carpet like an unfed panther.

There's a saying you don't get a second chance to make a first impression. Whoever came up with that cliché never met Jenna in an Army field jacket, hair bunched under a stocking cap, undercover gangs investigator on the first encounter, and followed it up with her in a tiny black dress, hair long and flowing, lady, on the second.

As good as Jenna looked, Thorpe was self-aware enough to realize a potential problem and the likely reason he'd been instantly attracted to the woman. Her current dress and appearance only made the likeness more obvious.

Jenna held a resemblance to Ambretta. They were not identical in any sense of the word but shared several traits. Both had ink-black hair, mocha eyes, full lips over olive skin. Both possessed athletic builds. But where Ambretta was long and lithe, Jenna was more tight and compact. Both projected an aura of sure-footed strength and grace when they moved.

"Shit," Thorpe mumbled.

"Hey, cowboy," Jenna greeted him teasingly.

"You're not going to let it go are you?" Thorpe said as he shook both her and Wyatt's hands. "Whataya drinking?"

Jenna studied the taps, "I think I'll have a Stella."

Thorpe laughed, "Can I talk you out of that?"

She flashed Thorpe a questioning look.

"Long story, but I promise to tell you before the night's over."

"I guess I'll have what you're having then."

"Make it two," Wyatt chipped in.

"Why Wyatt, I apologize, I forgot you were there," Thorpe smiled.

"I'm your huckleberry," he answered with a laugh.

Thorpe raised his voice across the bar, "Sandy, make it three, please."

"What happened to your ear?"

"I fell down a ravine while I was hunting. Snagged it on a tree."

"Ouch."

Thorpe noticed the woman in red locked on Jenna's black dress. Love didn't appear to be happy with the competition.

When Sandy returned with the Becks, Thorpe flopped down cash and pointed to the booth housing Hull and Skull. "We're over there."

Having dispensed the beers, Thorpe extended his left elbow to Jenna and asked, "You want to piss-off the woman in red?"

Jenna looked over at the barfly and smiled. She returned her attention to Thorpe, rose to her toes, and whispered, "Oh, I just love to piss-off women in red dresses."

Thorpe wondered if the warm breath on his neck and the whispering voice were calculated to get under Love's skin or if *he* was Jenna's true target. She was no doubt effective in her intent with either scenario. Jenna looped her arm under Thorpe's elbow and wrapped her hand around his bicep as they walked toward Hull and the Skull. Wyatt trailed, Thorpe made introductions, the three became five and they all made themselves comfortable.

"Why do they call you Carnac?" Jenna asked.

"Because 'asshole' was already taken," Skull smirked.

Thorpe made air quotes, "Because I'm psychic."

Jenna smiled and stared deeply into Thorpe's eyes, "Oh yeah, then what am I thinking right now?"

"That I'm full of shit."

"Damn, you *are* psychic."

"He got that nickname," Hull interrupted, "because he saved his squad from getting their heads blown-off on a search warrant. He had a premonition something nasty waited behind a bedroom door and he was right. Turns out the 'something nasty' was a strung out crankster armed with a 12-gauge shotgun. The guy fired then came barreling out the room like a chimpanzee with his ass on fire. John put a round in his face and another in the back of the head before he hit the hallway floor."

Thorpe wanted to change the subject. His eyes locked on something in the room he knew would do the job.

"Enough about me," Thorpe said, then nodded at the woman in red, "I think we have someone's attention."

"She a pro?" Wyatt asked.

Thorpe, Hull, and Skull all laughed.

"What?"

"It doesn't matter where they're from, cops all think alike," Hull answered. "We've already had that discussion. We're leaning toward cheap and easy as opposed to professionally sleazy."

"And I've already called dibs," Skull smiled.

"A gentleman's agreement then," Hull announced while raising his glass. "We'll all work toward getting Skull laid tonight." Everyone nodded, including Jenna, as they clinked together bottles and glasses in a makeshift toast.

"Interdepartmental cooperation. Working hand-in-hand for a common cause," Jenna said, "Warms the heart, doesn't it?"

Hull tipped his glass at Jenna, "I like this woman already."

Not so long ago cops would have referred to this as choir practice or maybe roll call. The tradition was eroding. For good or bad, police officers today didn't carry the code of years past. The fraternity was not as tightly woven and continued to fray with every new academy class released onto the streets. Thorpe wasn't sure when it had started to unravel, but the causes were many. There was no longer a code of silence.

Thirty years ago departments didn't have black, Hispanic, Asian, or gay officers' coalitions. Only blue. One color, one identity. Cops didn't rat other cops out, didn't go out of their way to tear other officers down. But these days everyone had their own agenda. The "me" generation. *What do I get out of it?* Most municipal officers today held college degrees but lacked the blue-collar work ethic of generations past. They were the children of doctors and lawyers, not of plumbers, warehouse workers, and former cops. Many had never been in a fistfight or fired a weapon before getting on the department.

More health conscious, rarely were officers the doughnut eaters and whiskey drinkers of yesteryear. The change made for healthier cops but sacrificed the camaraderie sharing a beer and a story can achieve. Today, for the most part, officers finished their shifts and went home to their families. The badge used to be first, family second. Not anymore and not that it should be. But the blue line was much, much thinner these days—and still dieting.

Listening to the conversation, Thorpe realized he'd been spending too much time alone. He missed this; had been denying himself this. After his family's murders, he'd withdrawn into a protective cocoon sealing all others out. Perhaps it was time. Perhaps he could move on. He would always carry the pain. But maybe he'd lived in constant sorrow long enough. Maybe his wife and daughter would understand he still had a life to live. Maybe they would understand he would never try to replace them.

Then, as a guest in an unfamiliar city of nine million, in a hotel bar surrounded by four detectives using foul language and telling crude stories, some weight—not all—but some, lifted from Thorpe's shoulders. Through misted eyes, he looked into those of Jenna's and gave her something he hadn't given someone in a long time—a genuine smile.

AMBRETTA SAT INSIDE A HOTEL lounge similar to the one where Jonathan Thorpe currently held choir practice. Like him, she occupied a darkened booth. Unlike him, she drank alone and waited for another Thorpe—the father of the man she loved.

Largely left on the sidelines the last few days, Ambretta's only contact with Ben had been through radio communications and by telephone. "Operational integrity" dictated her lack of participation. Ben didn't want Saeed or one of his companions recognizing her so far from home. A bullshit excuse; there was plenty of work to be had behind the scenes. She supposed Ben was giving her time to recharge her batteries.

Undercover assignments are taxing. One doesn't punch a card after an eight hour shift. There are no weekends and holidays off. Toss in the constant pressure of potential death and it makes for one stressful occupation. At least Ambretta operated in her own country. She couldn't imagine working, totally dark, in a foreign land for extended periods of time, though she knew Ben had done just that. The problem with Ben, and also what made him so good, was he never let down his guard.

Having a moment to herself, she'd had time to think. She'd reached certain conclusions, had made a potentially life-changing decision. Reaching that decision, she'd requested a face-to-face with Ben.

Ambretta arrived first, choosing a corner table where she could see all points of entry and egress. And though there was little threat of danger here, she'd received enough mental beat-downs from Ben to always be cognizant of such things. Ben however, took matters to the extreme. The man bordered on paranoia.

Ambretta watched as Ben stepped into the lounge and casually scanned the crowd as if searching for his companion. His eyes passed over her as if unseen. Having taken in the landscape, Ben feigned as if he'd just discovered her and began his old-man-shuffle across the floor.

Ambretta had always attributed Ben's stiffness to arthritis from injuries incurred during his imprisonment. He certainly possessed the scars to justify his lack of physical prowess. But as she watched the older Thorpe labor his way through the room, she couldn't help but remember how the "old man" had ripped Saeed out the driver's side window like a rag doll, then drag Saeed's unconscious body across the pavement without so much as a hitch in his step.

Remembering that, and some of the other stunts Ben had pulled off, Ambretta realized the whole defenseless-old-man bit was an act. An act he rarely let down, even when the two were alone.

As Ben collapsed in the booth next to her, Ambretta smiled, "Does that ever get old?"

"Does what get old?"

"Acting twenty years older and half the man you really are."

Ben put on a rare grin of his own and leaned in, "You have no fucking idea."

"Oh, an honest moment. That must have hurt."

"My secret is safe with you," he winked.

"Bullshit. You just know I've seen your Clark Kent/Superman act so you figured there was no point in denying it."

"Well, there is that," Ben admitted.

"Why all the trouble?"

"Ambretta, no offense at all; but I've learned never to trust anyone."

"So you don't trust me?"

"As much as I trust anyone."

"That's a hard way to live. I don't think I could do it."

"Everyone talks, Ambretta; and everyone breaks. It's not about trusting you as you are now. It's about not trusting you after you've had weeks of sleep deprivation and are being raped by the twentieth man in twenty-four hours. What can you say if you don't know the answers? What can you say if even *you* don't know the truth?" Ben held her wrist, "You know all this, we've discussed it before."

"I know, but don't you ever have the need to…talk to someone? I mean an honest, meaningful discussion?" Ambretta asked, more for her own sake than Ben's.

"What's this really about?"

She let out a breath and gave a long pause before finally answering, "I love him you know."

There, it was out in the open. She'd never acknowledged she had feelings for John. She'd never even acknowledged she knew

Ben was his father. Though a month ago—inside a Tulsa cemetery where Ben's granddaughter rests—both had seen the truth revealed in the other's eyes.

Now, staring into those same eyes, she appreciated him not feigning ignorance. Instead, he simply nodded his head. "So, you know who John is."

Though not a question, Ambretta answered anyway, "He's your son."

Ben didn't verbalize a response but did offer an almost imperceptible nod.

"Look, Ben, I've got no problems with what we did and I'll never mention the incident to anyone. But John had nothing to do with national security. You used me, and you owe me the truth."

Ben sighed, "Sometimes the truth causes more harm than good." He returned her gaze, "What do you plan to do? About John, I mean."

THIRTY-FOUR

SALVATION, REAL OR IMAGINED, CAN be short lived—such is the human condition. Thorpe liked Jenna. She was a special kind of woman: strong, funny, interesting, and beautiful; the kind you don't share a weekend with then forget about. But as his adoration grew so did his apprehension. The load previously lifted, settled onto Thorpe's back like an old comfortable coat. *What life could he possibly offer her? What if he fell in love only to lose her like all the other loves of his life?* As the night continued and the closer Jenna drew near, the further he pushed away.

Thorpe excused himself from the table claiming exhaustion. A drunken Skull, only half-jokingly, called him "a pussy." Hull didn't say a word but a slight shake of the head expressed his disappointment; a few nights ago he'd witnessed Thorpe pull the same disappearing act under similar circumstances. Thorpe wasn't sure how Jenna reacted to his abrupt departure. He'd averted his eyes from hers entirely.

Thorpe left the bar having consumed a total of three beers. He returned to his room, changed into Under Armour heat gear, a pair of olive colored 5.11 tactical pants, and a black hooded sweatshirt. He threw a shoulder holster over the hoodie and covered it with a black fleece jacket. Transformation complete, he grabbed his GPS unit and a couple of bottles of water, hung the "PLEASE DO NOT

DISTURB" sign outside his door and headed to the parking garage.

Once in the Suburban, Thorpe released the retractable divider in the storage compartment, climbed over the rear seats, and disabled the flash bang. He then opened the lock box, retrieved a black duffel packed with weapons and equipment, returned to the front of the cabin and laid the pack on the passenger seat. He activated the GPS unit, and courtesy of Wyatt's files, entered an address.

Thorpe settled into his seat, engaged the gearshift, and prepared his mind—eliminating Jenna and her tight black dress from his thoughts.

SOLITARY, SEDENTARY SURVEILLANCE IS A better sleep inducer than any pill Pfizer could ever hope to formulate. Sitting upright in the back of the van, Carlos had succumbed to its effects not once, but twice. The first time, he awoke to find that the object of his diligent attention, the black Dodge Charger, had disappeared from the front of Luis Carbia's home while he'd been preoccupied with the backs of his eyelids. The faux pas had inspired a mild panic. *Had Alberto left? Should he enter the house while at least one of the guard dogs was away?* Ultimately, Carlos decided to remain in the van and continue with his surveillance.

In time, the sun slipped beneath the horizon and the Charger slipped back into its space. The driver—one of the soldiers—entered the home with a grocery bag. Carlos took that as a good sign. He hoped Alberto and Luis were the beneficiaries of the shopping trip. He also hoped that Alberto would soon show his face, otherwise, Carlos might be the first one to break. Alberto and his hired muscle sat comfortably inside a heated, furnished home. Carlos on the other hand, subsisted on protein bars and bottled water while hiding in the back of a freezing van surrounded by improvised waste containers. The men sequestered inside the home would lose vigilance with each passing hour, time does that. But Carlos wasn't immune to time's effects either; effects which are exasperated when one is uncomfortable.

So far, kinks, muscle stiffness, and aching joints were his only rewards for staring, nearly motionless, out the back window for an entire day. Carlos, in an effort to work out a few of those kinks, was stretching when a man passed southbound unusually close to the passenger side of his van. Ten minutes earlier, Carlos had seen the same man turn from the east-west street and walk north past the van on the opposite side of Hamlin. The man, now back up on the sidewalk, walked away from the van with his hood pulled over his head and his hands stuffed in his pockets.

Pedestrian traffic in the area was not uncommon, but something about the man bothered Carlos. Plus, he'd passed too close. *Off the damn sidewalk close.* If the man was one of Alberto's soldiers, Carlos might be compromised. He needed to move.

Mind racing, Carlos chose to turn a problem into an opportunity. Having already removed the cabin's overhead bulbs, Carlos didn't illuminate himself when he quietly slid open the passenger door. He slung a backpack over his shoulder, took another look at the hooded man, stuffed a silenced pistol in his waistband, and stepped onto the strip of grass that separated van from sidewalk.

The hooded man, looking straight ahead, passed by Luis' property. That meant nothing. If the guy worked for Luis, and if he possessed any street smarts, he wouldn't tip his hand by walking directly into the house. He'd wait until he walked out of sight and then make a phone call.

While the man continued on, Carlos eyed a darkened space between two houses. The location would provide an excellent view of the passenger side of his van. Ensuring he wasn't being watched, Carlos walked casually toward the potential hide. *Mistake.* Something big and dark, maybe a Rott or Bull Mastiff, let loose a flurry of deep barks that struck Carlos' chest like the sound waves from a Chicano's subwoofer.

A back yard chain-link fence contained the dog. Still, the beast was making such a racket it would surely draw the attention of the homeowners and/or neighbors. Carlos considered a well-placed, silenced, pistol round between the dog's black eyes but dismissed the notion. He had nothing against the dog, which was only doing his job, and shooting it might cause more problems than it solved.

He couldn't linger. He looked south to check on the hooded man and found him to be a shrinking shadow. Carlos left the yard, hit the sidewalk, and walked the opposite direction. He traveled a good distance allowing Devil Dog time to settle down, then doubled back and tried to find a new location on the opposite side of Hamlin Avenue.

THORPE WAS CONDUCTING COUNTERSURVEILLANCE outside the home of one Luis Carbia, the Chicago Latin King who'd somehow convinced a twice-convicted Tulsa loser, Lyndale Peterson, to take the fall on dope and weapons charges. The charges were Peterson's third strike, netting him a lengthy prison sentence. While Lyndale passed time behind bars, keistering contraband and drinking piss flavored Pruno (prison wine), Thorpe had killed Leon— Lyndale's younger, and only brother. Both had been involved in the murder of Thorpe's family.

Since the Latin Kings were unaware Thorpe prowled Chicago, his greatest concern was drawing the attention of fellow law enforcement officers. Neither Wyatt nor Jenna mentioned any ongoing surveillance of Carbia or his home but that didn't mean much. Even in Tulsa so many different investigative units operated that the left tentacles didn't always know what the right were doing. Between the Vice, Narcotics, Intelligence, Gangs, Homicide, Auto Theft, Burglary, and federal agencies, law enforcement sometimes, unwittingly, ran simultaneous investigations on the same target. The separate units were supposed to "deconflict" so officers wouldn't stumble over one another. In practice this safeguard was rarely utilized; narcotics investigators in particular clung to their secrets like a leprechaun does his gold. Two reasons for this: first, leaks were everywhere. TPD officers, civilian record clerks, cleaning crews, and a collection of others had gone to prison for providing information to their "old friends" from the hood. Second (and more importantly), like fishermen, when dope investigators found a good hole, they were reluctant to share their abundance with the competition. Thorpe doubted Chicago cops acted differently. Add to the equation a much larger police force and the problem likely increased tenfold. So, Thorpe was searching for any sign of surveillance, law enforcement or otherwise—and he'd just found it.

The brown GMC van first garnered his attention because of its fogged windows. Then he'd crossed the street and made a second pass closer to the van. The condensation and dark tint kept Thorpe from viewing the interior, but he didn't need to. He'd been nearly on top of the vehicle when he caught the slightest movement of the van itself. Someone was inside.

The nearest streetlamp—on the northeast corner of Carbia's yard—was unlit. Wyatt had told Thorpe the Kings sometimes purposely shorted-out the lamps. Whatever the cause, Thorpe appreciated the lack of light.

Eyes forward, a distant streetlight at his back, Thorpe continued down the sidewalk watching over his faint shadow. His companion lengthened, lost definition, dissolved into the concrete and as he passed a motion activated porch light, was reincarnated in the dormant grass. The weather both sharpened and dulled his senses. A persistent wind penetrated his hoodie and whispered into his ears. It masked sounds which could potentially save his life. The crisp morning air had bite. Deep inhalations stung the nostrils but kept one alert.

The hoodie was double-edged in its service. It shrouded his face from the occasional passing headlight, afforded a subtle swivel of the head, and disguised his wandering eyes. But the same veil that provided anonymity also reduced peripheral vision and diminished his hearing. The lack of sensory input from his flank induced an urge to turn. Instead, he relied on shadows and the hair on the nape of his neck.

Walking with the van at his back, the auditory suppression caused by the hood proved to be particularly bothersome. His overactive imagination conjured up a Latin soldier stepping from the van and framing Thorpe's shrouded head with iron sights.

Most likely the van was occupied by some kid banging his girlfriend outside her parents' home. Even if it was a Latin King, he or she had no reason to start blasting a guy just for walking down the street. *Right?* Thorpe eased up on his imagination but fought to hear through his hoodie at what may, or may not, be happening behind him.

Thorpe passed Carbia's home, his mind automatically gathering information on his target like an average man might commit a woman's cleavage to memory. He counted the number of windows, memorized their spacing, noted the barred screen door, the darkness the surrounding trees provided, the four foot chain-link fence in the back. The large dog house. Dogs always complicated matters.

As Thorpe pondered the dog conundrum, one of the neighborhood beasts started barking. However, the barks didn't come from Carbia's yard. They came from the direction Thorpe had just passed. He decided to risk taking the obvious glance. Besides, people turn and look all the time, especially at night. It was a dangerous world and everyone needed to look after one's own ass.

Well past Carbia's house, Thorpe spun and walked backward down the sidewalk. The GMC shrunken in the distance, he noticed a shadow leave the yard adjacent to the van. Instead of entering the vehicle, the shadow turned north away from Thorpe. *Could be nothing; could be something.* Thorpe decided to spend ten minutes watching from a darkened position.

While he waited, he considered the van problem. If in Tulsa, the solution would be easy; he'd simply...and then he had an idea. He'd let Chicago PD do his work for him. He'd call 911 and report a suspicious van. He'd provide a fake name, demand to be seen, and give the address of a nearby house. If the police never showed, or if they contacted the occupants of the van and left after a few seconds, then Thorpe had law enforcement on his hands. If some sweaty kid and his girlfriend were pulled out of the van, Thorpe would know he had nothing to worry about.

Never mind all that; the shadowy figure he'd seen leave the yard on the east side of Hamlin now walked toward him on the opposite side. The figure hesitated, then disappeared into a yard on the west. *Interesting*.

IN ADDITION TO PASSING SO close to the van, Carlos realized what it was about the man that bothered him so much. He'd been wearing tactical pants identical to the ones the Special Forces community were so fond of sporting in the military. If the guy *was* one of Alberto's military recruits, an impending assault on the van was almost assured.

Well screw that. Carlos would conceal himself in a place he could take out one, maybe two, soldiers with his silenced pistol. Then he'd be over a fence, through an alley and on the next street before they knew where the shots had originated. If only one or two men conducted the assault on the van, and Carlos took them both out, it might prove to be an opportune time to enter Luis' house. More than likely the two men he'd seen in the black Dodge Charger, Alberto's bodyguards, would be the ones attacking his van. That might leave Luis and Alberto alone in the house. A lot of "mights," but Carlos could live, or die, with those odds.

Now on the west side of Hamlin, Carlos picked an accommodating space between a house and its garage. There was no fence so he didn't have to worry about a noisy dog. Two large trees occupied the back yard, one providing plenty of darkness and an unencumbered view of the driver's side of his van. Carlos risked walking west, deeper into the yard. This would be his initial escape route and he didn't want any nasty surprises—like being garroted by a clothesline. He encountered a chain-link fence at the property to the west. Carlos grabbed the fence, shook it lightly and called out just above a whisper, "Here boy, here boy." Not getting a response, Carlos hopped the fence. Once inside the yard he plotted two escape routes. If chased by a pursuer within sight, he'd turn right and hit the alley. From there he'd have several available routes. However, if he managed to get to this point unseen, he'd turn left and head straight toward Luis Carbia's house.

Satisfied with his options for self-extraction, Carlos returned to his hide. He lay on the north side of a large tree which sat next to Hamlin, a northbound, one-way street. The tree would provide concealment from the headlights of approaching traffic. He stretched out on his belly with a silenced pistol in front of him. At this distance of twenty-five to thirty yards he could easily hit center of mass. Problem was, the two soldiers he'd encountered earlier, demonstrated a propensity for wearing body armor. A successful head shot would require concentration and a stationary target. On a positive note, he'd have his shots off before his quarry could identify the point of origin. By then Carlos would already be on the move.

BACK IN HIS SUBURBAN, THORPE drove northbound on Hamlin Avenue leaving Luis Carbia's property in his rearview mirror. Positive someone was conducting surveillance on the house, Thorpe kept slightly above the posted speed limit. In neighborhoods like this, slow moving cars attract more attention than speeders.

He didn't slow or turn his head as he passed the van; only used his peripheral vision to get a glimpse of the terrain. Though Thorpe's destination was an alley to the north, he drove straight through the next two intersections. He'd driven well out of sight before guiding the large Suburban around a corner. As he shuffled the wheel to the left, *Enter Sandman* played on the radio. Though not a fan of Metallica, the song seemed fitting to his mood and he found himself cranking the volume.

Two additional left turns put Thorpe eastbound in his chosen alley. The neighborhood was laid out in rectangular plots. The east-west streets long. The north-south avenues short. Alleys ran east-west and halved the rectangles. Except for corner lots, most properties had unattached garages facing the alley. Several houses short of his objective, Thorpe parked in front of one of those garages. He killed the engine, stepped through the captain's chairs, crawled over the back seats into the cargo area, and dug out a suppressed MP5. Still inside the cabin, he slung the weapon over his shoulder before stepping out onto the concrete alley. In an effort to help conceal the weapon, Thorpe tucked the MP5 close to his chest, and, as if he were cold, crossed his arms. Though most of the houses sat dark, one just never knew if eyes were watching. Leaving the Suburban and its freshly "borrowed" plates, he hoped the Chevy would still be there when he returned.

A short distance west of Hamlin, he ducked between two houses on the south side of the alley. If the man he'd seen earlier still lurked, Thorpe should be in very close proximity to his quarry. Between the houses, Thorpe went to the ground, pulled back his hood, and tuned himself to the environment.

Thorpe lay still for several minutes, eyes adjusting to the gloom, and ears adjusting to the rhythms of the neighborhood. Slowly he rose, taking measured steps. Move, stop, look, listen, repeat. Silently crossing the fence into the next yard proved to be a challenge. He found a section where a tree supported most of his weight and dampened the strain on the fence. Several minutes after having crossed, he spotted his target lying on the ground in the shadow of a large tree. Next, Thorpe spent what seemed an eternity covering the small expanse of yard—weapon up, heal to toe between fallen leaves, excruciatingly slow. Silent. During his approach, Thorpe determined one certainty; the man wasn't a cop. Cops didn't carry silenced pistols. They didn't lay in the dirt, weapon extended, while conducting surveillance. Thorpe felt confident he had a Latin King in his sights. Thorpe released a measured breath, placed his right index finger on the MP5's trigger, and steadily applied increasing pressure.

CARLOS WONDERED IF HE MIGHT have suffered a case of overactive imagination. Long periods of intense anticipation can have that effect on a person. If Latin Kings were going to fill his van with bullet holes, it would have happened by now. Carlos had been in his hide for nearly thirty minutes. He couldn't risk discovery by lying in wait all night, but returning to the van was not a viable option. Too dangerous. His imagination might be a bit overactive, but a good soldier doesn't dismiss intuition. Ignoring one's instincts was a good way to wake up dead.

Carlos had been formulating a new plan of action when all that went to shit. Now, the only thing going through his mind was how to extend the next few seconds of his life. A red laser had slipped off the back of his head onto the dirt in front of his nose. Carlos started to turn.

"You move another inch and you'll be shitting out the back of your head."

Son-of-a-bitch, the voice was right on top of him. How in the hell?

Sure and calm, the voice continued, "I have intimate knowledge of my weapon and how to use it. To quell your curiosity it is a Heckler and Koch MP5 in burst mode. You don't stand a chance, so don't start having James Bond fantasies. If you understand English, Latin Queen, open your hand and release your weapon. If not, well…"

The red dot disappeared. Though he couldn't see it, Carlos knew it had returned to the back of his head. The man spoke the truth, he didn't have a chance. If he was going to get out of this shit storm it wouldn't be now. Failure to comply meant certain death. Carlos opened his fingers, allowing the pistol to drop to the grass.

"Good boy. Arms out to your side, palms up."

Carlos did as told.

"Cross your left foot over your right."

Fuck! The guy knew his shit.

"Bury your face in the dirt. You turn it, you lose it."

Carlos stuck his face in the dead grass with the sobering thought it'd be the last smell he'd ever experience. *No, it was only one man and he hadn't yet killed him; they must want him alive for some reason. Maybe to find out where he'd hidden his family?*

One man. Carlos would try to overpower the man as he laid hands on him. It's hard to secure someone and keep a gun on them at the same time. If Carlos hoped to survive, that's when he had to make his move.

Carlos readied his body. As soon as the man grabbed a wrist, a leg, whatever, he'd uncoil his whole body unleashing everything he had.

"Bend your knees, keep your legs crossed and lift your ankles off the ground," the man ordered.

What the hell? Carlos had little choice but to comply. Before he knew what was happening his legs were stomped down and clamped together with flex cuffs, then two knees pinned him to the dead grass. With his legs bound in a crossed position he could offer little resistance. The man outweighed him considerably. Carlos lay there, powerless, cursing under his breath as his arms were brought behind his back and secured with another set of flex-cuffs. *Still alive; wait for a new opportunity.*

Carlos felt his pack being cut from his shoulders. Hands probed his body in search of additional weapons. He was rolled over onto his back with his bound arms pinned beneath him. Face to face with his attacker, he found himself peering into a pair of green eyes, eerily visible even in the darkness.

"Name?"

The question confused Carlos. Surely the man knew who he was? Perhaps Alberto didn't tell his guard dogs who they were up against.

"You know who I am."

The man rammed his fist into the soft spot below Carlos' sternum. Hard and fast. Something cracked. It drove the wind out of him.

"You little fuck, I'm not asking twice."

Carlos didn't respond. Not yet able to draw a breath, he couldn't even if he'd wanted to. His mind continued to function in spite of the pain. It seemed the man didn't know his name. No matter, as soon as he was dragged inside Carbia's house everyone would know.

"Carlos Benitez, United States Ranger," Carlos squeaked, then managed a question of his own, "Who the fuck are you?"

His inquiry earned him an elbow to the face. Carlos felt his nose explode and his vision blur. But through his tears, Carlos watched the man take in his surroundings, his head on a swivel. Strange, Green Eyes behaved as if he was the one expecting an ambush. Another thing: Green Eyes was white. The Kings had a few Caucasians as members but this guy was white, white. Nothing in his accent, mannerisms, or looks conveyed anything that said fellow Latin King. *Had Alberto recruited white soldiers completely outside the LK realm?* It would make sense; always good to have soldiers who can infiltrate the enemy's ranks. But something didn't add up.

"I have two men with me, both armed." Carlos bluffed.

Green Eyes saw through the bullshit and smiled. "You'd better start telling the truth Ranger. I don't have the time or patience. If you lie to me again, you're going to start losing appendages." The man pulled out a large serrated knife for effect, but his eyes said he wasn't bluffing. "How many men are in the house?"

What the fuck? How many men are in the house? Isn't that something I should be asking him?

"I don't know; I thought maybe you could tell me," Carlos answered honestly.

Looming over him the man settled the large blade on top of Carlos' left ear. "The name Van Gogh mean anything to you?"

"Singer or some shit. Look I don't fucking know who's in the house. I assume the two soldiers driving the black Dodge Charger are inside. I assume Luis Carbia's inside. And I hope my Uncle Alberto is inside."

Above him, for the first time, Carlos spotted a wavering in the man's eyes.

"Uncle Alberto?"

Carlos, perplexed, began to doubt this man worked for the Kings. *Another pissed-off soldier who'd been thoroughly screwed by Alberto?* For a second, Carlos thought of the Special Forces son of the old couple he'd meant to kill. *No, it wasn't him*; he'd seen pictures of that man who was obviously of Hispanic decent.

"Alberto Vega," Carlos answered.

"Who the fuck is Alberto Vega?"

What the hell? Was this guy a cop? No, cops don't run solo with silenced automatic weapons and an affinity for lopping off ears.

"He's a dead motherfucker is what he is," Carlos answered. "I don't know who you are mister, but I'm starting to think we may have a misunderstanding on our hands."

THIRTY-FIVE

THORPE—BACK INSIDE HIS TRUCK—had a lot on his mind. He wasn't prone to trusting people and saw no reason to make an exception for Carlos Benitez—if that was his real name. Still, the things he had related to Thorpe made sense, even if it did sound far-fetched. Then again, the story of how Thorpe wound up in Chicago holding a knife to a former U.S. Army Ranger's ear sounded no less fantastic. The thing that finally convinced Thorpe was Carlos' explanation of how he'd found Luis Carbia.

Carlos told of the men who'd been sent to his parents' home. He'd described how he'd followed one of the assailants to an apartment complex and tortured him for information. Carlos couldn't have known Thorpe had been to the crime scene of the slain Latin King. When Thorpe pushed for details, everything added up to what he'd seen. The silent car alarm, the gunshots to the legs, the insurance rounds to the brain and heart; while listening to Carlos' rendition, Thorpe yanked up on his bound legs and looked at the soles of his boots. The tread matched the print left on the Nissan's window. Carlos killed that man—no doubt about it. If the rest of his tale had been concocted, it was quite a story to make up on-the-fly with the serrated edge of a knife bearing down on his ear.

The smart move would have been to incapacitate Carlos. The man, perhaps only an expert liar, was a potential threat. Even if

Carlos had been telling the complete truth, their two objectives were not the same. Carlos was liable to kill Carbia and this "Uncle Alberto," before Thorpe had an opportunity to find out all the conspirators behind the attempt on his life. But Thorpe could never harm a possibly innocent man. He had to maintain at least one small scruple, though it carried potentially immense consequences.

It'd been easy to gain cooperation from Carlos when the man was restrained and had the constant threat of mutilation hanging above his head, literally. Now that Carlos' life wasn't in imminent danger, Thorpe would learn the man's true heart.

Before he'd left Carlos and returned to his SUV, Thorpe removed knife from ear and drove it into the ground just inches from the bound man's face. Then he'd written the number of his prepaid cell phone on Carlos' forehead. Hopefully, the man would be able to decipher it in his rearview mirror. If he couldn't, he didn't need the dumbass's help anyway.

He'd instructed Carlos to phone him as soon as he freed himself, otherwise the next time they met would be the last. If Carlos was indeed who he said, then the man would have more reason to trust Thorpe than the other way around; if Thorpe wanted Carlos dead, he already would be.

Thorpe was only a couple of minutes removed from Carlos when his cell phone rang.

"Yeah?"

"It's me."

"That didn't take long. By the way I want my knife back," Thorpe said, instantly regretting having used "knife" and "back" in the same sentence. He hoped the former wouldn't end up inside the latter.

"And I want my pistols back. Where we meeting?"

"I'll call you with instructions in five."

In truth, Thorpe didn't know where he wanted to meet. This wasn't his city and he didn't know a good location. At the same time he wouldn't let Carlos choose and wind up in a bad position.

Thorpe disconnected the call, pulled over to the side of the road and used his personal smartphone to find a suitable locale. Having found an acceptable meeting place, he punched the address into his handheld GPS. Then he picked up his throwaway phone, retrieved the last incoming call and hit send.

"Drive toward the east side of Marquette Park. I'll give you specifics when you get closer."

"How do I know I can trust you?"

"You're still breathing aren't you?"

"Point taken. I'm Oscar Mike."

Oscar Mike? A probe to see if Thorpe was military? It meant "On the move," in military slang. Thorpe disconnected without acknowledgement.

Thorpe wasn't headed to Marquette Park. At this hour, parks were too easy a place to get ambushed or stopped and questioned by the police. Thorpe needed a place that stayed open twenty-four hours, provided plenty of potential witnesses, and offered multiple avenues of escape.

A short drive later, Thorpe found himself circling his true destination, Holy Cross Hospital. The building bordered Marquette Park, separated only by California Avenue. He noted a few of the many exits in case he needed to "Oscar Mike" the hell out of there. Eventually he stashed his Suburban in a lot near 69th and California. Thorpe didn't like leaving his MP5 behind, but he couldn't exactly walk into an E.R. with a submachine gun draped over his shoulder. Instead, he grabbed a Sig Saur .45, and Carlos' backpack and took a sinuous route toward the hospital.

Having stashed both the pack and his own weapon, Thorpe stood inside the hospital's emergency room committing everything and everyone to memory. His phone rang.

"I'm here." Carlos announced, referring to the park.

"I'm not. I'll meet you inside Holy Cross Hospital. Inside the E.R."

"You going to change locations all fucking night?"

"Final destination," Thorpe assured.

"FINAL DESTINATION," CARRIED AN OMINOUS
connotation, Carlos thought. However, if the man wanted to harm
him, he'd have done so already. Plus, if he was to have an ear lopped
off, it may as well be in an emergency room—though he might have
to hold the appendage in his hand for a couple hours before being
seen.

The location change told Carlos a few things about his new
acquaintance. The man practiced caution. Meeting at a hospital was
a bit ingenious. Where else could one meet at this time of night that,
one: would be a secure and well-lit area; two, had plenty of
witnesses; three, had multiple avenues of escape; and finally,
provided a place where one could loiter without looking suspicious.
If anything, it was difficult to get anyone to acknowledge you in the
lobby of an emergency room. In addition, Carlos' askew and
bleeding nose afforded an excellent excuse to be there.

It would be virtually impossible to cover all avenues of egress
without twenty or so men. Plus, every hospital utilized armed
security. Most importantly it told Carlos the man was operating on
his own. He wouldn't need such precautions if he had a hoard of
men at his disposal. Carlos was unsure of the man's endgame;
maybe he'd find out inside the hospital. He just hoped he'd get his
weapons back—butt-first of course.

Carlos saw no reason to make a stealthy entrance into the
hospital. The green-eyed man already knew what he drove and his
safety wasn't a concern. He left his van in the emergency room
parking lot and made his way to the waiting room. He wasn't
surprised when he didn't find Green Eyes waiting for him. Carlos
casually took in his surroundings, spotted a chair in a lonely
corner—one that offered a view of the rest of the room, and sat down
to wait.

Seven other people occupied the waiting area. Three displayed no obvious maladies. Four clearly belonged. The afflicted consisted of a woman in her fifties with a disgusting wet hack of a cough. Another was an infant screaming his or her head off. The third, the infant's mother who managed to look both frantic and exhausted at the same time. The fourth, a scab-picking crankster in her early 30s, had a phone charger stuck in her noggin. The two prongs that fit into the power outlet were lodged in her forehead. A black cord led down to her lap. Carlos was surprised she didn't have a phone charging on the other end. *Jesus.*

A full ten minutes later, a man with dark green tactical pants and bright green eyes stepped into the lobby. Carlos watched as those eyes passed over his, then began studying everyone else in the room. He didn't even pause on the woman accessorized with a cell phone charger. Carlos bet Green Eyes had already been inside, had already seen the woman once before. He'd probably left and watched the entrance from the outside, watched Carlos park his van and enter the E.R., waited to see if any others had followed. He'd most likely memorized the faces in the E.R. from his earlier scouting mission to ensure no new ones had arrived.

Eventually, Green Eyes made his way to a seat next to Carlos.

In a voice altered by his blood-packed nostrils, Carlos asked, "So, what do I call you?"

"John will work."

A name even more common with Caucasians than Carlos was with Hispanics.

"Okay, 'John.' What's the situation?"

"You need to make me trust you. I want to know if things get reversed, if you have a weapon pointed at my head, you're not going to pull the trigger."

"And just how the hell am I supposed to do that? Unless you're willing to lend me your MP5 and the back of your head," Carlos smiled.

"We share common problems. If you want your pistols back, you're going to explain everything in your life that led you to your current predicament. Otherwise, you'll have an additional problem to deal with."

"John, if that's your real name, something tells me you're a problem I could do without."

"Carlos, if that's your real name, you sound like an intelligent man. And since you're so damned smart, I have a really important question I need answered."

"What's that?"

Thorpe nodded across the room, "Is that a phone charger sticking out of that woman's head?"

THIRTY-SIX

JENNA SMITH RARELY FOUND HERSELF smitten. She'd known men who were attractive enough, some who were interesting, and even a few that made her laugh. Seldom did she cross paths with a man who pulled the trifecta. Throw in an "X-factor" and she'd discovered her thoughts wandering back to Jonathan Thorpe like a pubescent ninth grader, a condition that was driving her half mad.

Jenna didn't give two shits about making men happy. She had at one time. Thanks to a piece-of-trash stepfather who beat her mother and once made an early morning visit to Jenna's room, she used to think that's what a woman did—make her man happy. *Screw 'em.* Unfortunately, screwing them is exactly what she found herself doing. Promiscuous as a teenager, she'd tried to find happiness by making happy men. A failed suicide attempt at age sixteen garnered the attention of a high school counselor. The counselor went well beyond her job assignment in getting Jenna the help she needed. She owed the woman her very life. The only thing the counselor asked was for Jenna to pay it forward. And the promise to pay it forward is why Jenna Smith became a Chicago police officer.

Since those days she hadn't given many men a second glance. On the other hand, nearly all men gave her a second, and a third. She wasn't accustomed to being ignored. Even while doing her best imitation of a flannel wearing, lesbian gangbanger, she usually had to fend off a few advances per shift—from the men she busted to her fellow officers. And when she wrapped herself in a little black dress, forget about it, men didn't stand a chance.

Last night sharing a table with four colleagues, dressed in her Saturday night best, putting out signals like a third base coach, the object of her advances up and left her with a half-empty beer in her hand and a stupid-looking smile on her face. She'd gone from shock, to embarrassment, to anger. Robert Hull must have noticed her discomfort. He apologized for his friend, and after a reluctant nod from Skull, explained the tragic loss of John's wife and daughter.

After relating the heart-wrenching story of John's life, Hull insisted she and Wyatt keep the revelation confidential—John wasn't a sympathy seeker. Clearly, Hull thought much of his friend and cared for his well being. Learning of John's unimaginable loss, Jenna couldn't help but feel for the man. *How could one not?* Her anger faded. John's past only fed the roots of her attraction, expanding, taking anchor. He was broken and she found herself, finally, wanting to make another man happy.

In an effort to avoid further embarrassment, Jenna helped close down the hotel bar with her fellow detectives. She allowed Wyatt to walk her to her car, and she'd driven away. Making the block, she'd returned, parked, and reentered the hotel. She'd flashed her identification and badge at the reception desk requesting to see the hotel's register.

She'd obtained John's room number and after a short stop to primp in the lobby's restroom, proceeded to John's floor. Despite a "DO NOT DISTURB" sign, she knocked repeatedly on his door. Either he'd gone out, or was intent not to answer. She ended up leaving the hotel in a sour mood.

Then this morning, under a pregnant sky, she'd pushed her way into work dressed much more sexily than the weather and her job assignment dictated. Ever the optimist, she also stuffed a change of clothing in a duffel bag.

On her way in, Wyatt phoned and explained he had a pre-trial conference with an assistant district attorney and asked her to escort John in his stead. Jenna figured Wyatt was full of shit and that he and Hull had conspired to play matchmaker. Whatever, she wasn't going to argue. With more anticipation than she would care to admit, she'd pulled up outside the hotel and phoned John only to have him blow her off yet again. "I appreciate you and Wyatt's hospitality, but I'm officially on vacation now," he'd told her. *Asshole.*

Jenna peeled out of the lot and spent her workday thinking about Jonathan Thorpe. Shift completed, she decided to return to the hotel and let John know of her interest in him. If he dismissed her again, so be it, she wasn't a pretty little wallflower who sat around waiting for a knight in ballistic armor to rescue her from a tower. If she wanted something she went after it—and damned if she'd play fair.

Jenna entered John's hotel, headed straight to the lobby's restroom, shrugged off her duffel, and selected the uniform she'd be wearing for combat.

OFFICIALLY ON VACATION, AND OFF the job, Thorpe had little doubt Carlos Benitez was telling the truth. Everything he'd said added up to what Thorpe learned from his day riding with Wyatt, from what he'd seen at the crime scene of the dead Latin King, and from the files he'd scoured. Thorpe, now saddled with a partner of sorts, was none too thrilled to have Carlos along for the ride. He was accustomed to working alone. Partners made mistakes. They got you caught. They got you convicted. They got you dead.

Too late now, it'd be impossible to convince Carlos to back down. The Kings were a threat to his wife and daughter. Whereas Thorpe failed to protect his own family, Carlos was determined not to suffer the same fate. Not that Carlos was aware of Thorpe's history. Carlos didn't know anything about Thorpe. The less the man knew the better. Hopefully, after the next few days, they'd never have contact with each other again.

Thorpe left Carlos with the number to his prepaid phone as well as the location of his silenced pistols. Their trust in each other worked this way: if Carlos took action without Thorpe's assistance, the man would have a new foe to worry about—Thorpe. If Thorpe acted without Carlos, the little shit promised he'd contact authorities with everything he knew about his new green-eyed accomplice, including telling them the name of a certain hospital where they could obtain video images.

Thorpe's assurances of personal safety had cost him his anonymity. Prior to separating, Carlos phoned Thorpe with one of the dead King's cell phones. Thorpe stored the number and would use it to communicate with Carlos. They were now an army of two. Two men against a nation.

Alone now, he faced three strands of barbed wire atop a chain-link fence of staggering height. He used a thrice folded army blanket to shield himself from the zinc-depleted, tetanus-inducing, rusted barbs. Safely over, he scaled halfway down before dropping to the ground. There he eyed three hundred yards of open field; nine hundred feet of pancaked earth, crisscrossed with high-intensity, human-seeking spotlights. Looming above the flat expanse, stone watchtowers of a bygone era kept a constant vigil. Those towers sheltered cold, expert marksmen, armed with sharp eyes and high-powered rifles. Three hundred yards separated the place where he knelt to the cover and concealment of a dark, lush, forest.

He studied the searchlights looking for a discernible pattern. Loose sod gave way as his right foot pushed off. Arms and legs pumped like pistons as he sought the darkness between streams of light. *Halfway there now; I might just make it.*

A siren pierced the night, spotlights narrowed, his legs turned to malleable lead, his speed dropped to a crawl. He risked a glance over his left shoulder. Impossibly, dozens of prison guards fashioned a skirmish line where none had been before. The guards worked feverishly to hold back large German Shepherds, each one straining on its leash, their barks and growls drowned out by the wailing siren.

He turned back to the woods. There, just in front of the black tree canopy, stood his daughter. *Alive!* Her arms reached out for him. From a hundred yards he read her lips, "Daddy, help." Concentrating on her pained face, he tripped and fell to the damp ground. The blanket he'd used atop the barbed wire entangled his legs. He turned to see two of the Shepherds closing fast. His dogs. Al and Trixie. Their large paws thundered with infeasible loudness across the soft grass.

He looked back to his daughter. She knew. She knew he wasn't going to make it. Knew he wouldn't save her—couldn't save her. He reached out as she receded back into the darkness of the forest. Spotlights blinded him. The damp grass soaked through his clothing. His legs were bound in the blanket. He heard the dogs nearing…

Thorpe woke with sweat-soaked sheets wrapped around his legs, alarm clock blaring, sun streaming through a crack in the curtains, someone pounding on the door. He was able to slap the clock into submission, but the knocking continued.

The nightmare had been vivid; dream and reality intertwined. It left him disoriented and sour. Untangling himself from the sheets, he scooped his pistol off the nightstand and staggered toward the door. Whoever had disregarded his "DO NOT DISTURB" sign was about to get an earful. Thorpe did have the presence of mind to conceal the weapon behind his thigh as he yanked open the door.

JENNA'S PREPARED WORDS WERE RIPPED from her like an umbrella in a thunderstorm. John stood just inside the room, naked, glistening with sweat. He was pissed. He was gorgeous.

Unconcerned, or unaware of his nudity, he stood; his muscular chest perched over a washboard waist narrowing to his hips. Muscle striations. No fat. None. Only scars. Crisscrossing scars over his ripped abdominal muscles, chest, and arms. Fresh stitches in his un-bandaged ear. *Why did these "blemishes" look so damned alluring?*

The visual impact was as disorienting as a blow to the face, yet

John appeared more off kilter than she. He looked like a wrung-out dishrag, mentally and physically.

Jenna lowered her gaze then brought them back up to his eyes, "Lose your underwear?"

Thorpe glanced down as if he'd just become aware of his nudity. The fact he'd been rousted from a deep sleep was obvious. Confusion painted his face. Finally, realization crept into those green eyes of his, yet he made no attempt to cover himself. His right hand lingered on the door—ready to slam it closed. His left remained concealed behind a glistening thigh.

"What are you hiding there, a jar of Vaseline?"

Capitalizing on Thorpe's still semi-dazed state, she walked through his extended arm in an x-rated version of Red Rover. Crossing behind him, she checked out his ass and the object concealed in his left hand. Alas he held a Glock, not petroleum jelly.

"Thought you were a righty," she said, nodding down at the pistol.

He turned, replacing her view with a very different weapon.

"When it comes to handguns and Vaseline, I'm ambidextrous," he said, the fog of confusion clearing from his eyes.

"Nice to see you have your sense of humor back," Jenna said, entering deeper into the room.

Thorpe remained at the door. "Come on in, make yourself comfortable." His words were laced with sarcasm.

Having been knocked loose from Thorpe's grip, the door clicked shut behind him.

Jenna peered down at the bed. The sheets were in disarray and soaked with sweat. John either suffered from night terrors or had an insatiable lover stashed in the bathroom. The dazed and confused look on his face answered that question. No doubt, the man had his demons.

His confusion had given way to anger and she knew no words would be effective in winning him over. Jenna had never been one for playing fair. Fair was for little old women destined to become cat food—dying alone in one-room apartments surrounded by unfed felines; their former master their only vittles. *To hell with that.*

Jenna possessed many physical assets, the least of which was not, well, her ass. The gentlemen with whom she worked described it as a "shelf." Fact was, it had angles approaching ninety degrees in all the right places and didn't acknowledge the words cellulite or gravity. Some of her more crude male friends sometimes asked if she wouldn't mind them setting their drink on it.

Jenna responded to John's sarcastic invitation, "Thanks. Don't mind if I do." As the words slipped off her tongue, her knee-length coat slipped off her shoulders onto the floor. Still facing the bed, back to her prey, she stood in black heels and bright pink, lace boy-shorts; the fabric riding high and stretched into the shape of McDonald's famous arches. The color accentuated her natural olive skin. The six-inch heels only lifted and accentuated a backside which already made a liar of Sir Isaac Newton.

Past the point of embarrassment if he rejected her, she pulled out all the stops. She looked over her shoulder, arched her back, reached down behind her left leg, and ran fingers painted the same color as her lingerie, up the inside of her thigh. The effect was both predetermined and immediate. Her victim never stood a chance.

THIRTY-SEVEN

EYES LOCKED ON LUIS CARBIA'S home, Carlos stewed inside the van he'd come to hate. Beside him sat a receiver for a tracking device. John—following their late night meet in the hospital E.R.—had attached the transponder to the Latin King's Dodge Charger and given Carlos simplistic instructions on the use of the receiver.

Having supplied the tracking device, John warned Carlos not to conduct visual surveillance. "If I found you, they can find you," he'd said. True enough, but "John" didn't have a wife and daughter he was trying to keep alive. *How could the man possibly understand?* Carlos' family's very lives depended on him getting his hands on Alberto. This was personal and he was not going to sit in some distant place where Alberto could slip between his fingers. Even now, Carlos didn't like his obscured view of the house. A cold mist and expectant sky shunned the moon and stars. The van's perpetually fogged rear windows created warped and wavering mirages that left him rubbing his tired eyes.

Carlos glanced at the receiver and wondered for the hundredth time who John really was. More importantly he wondered *what* he was. His mannerisms and speech reminded him of SF soldiers except he didn't speak the jargon. *Maybe he'd been out of the military awhile. Or maybe he purposely avoided military terms.* The tracking device suggested law enforcement. But cops don't sneak around, alone, shouldering fully automatic, suppressed weapons. They definitely don't return highly illegal silenced pistols to former Army Rangers-cum-gangbangers bent on vengeance.

Whatever his occupation, he was good. Carlos had never been bested before. Not like that. He'd never before allowed a man to control him—almost effortlessly. Carlos had been thoroughly embarrassed. He hadn't been given a sliver of hope of fighting his way out of the situation. No doubt about it, whoever John was, Carlos was glad to have him on his side. With one exception.

Carlos wanted to assault the house immediately and John talked him out of it. Worrying over his family, Carlos' reserve of patience was nearly bankrupt. "Impatient men are seldom rewarded in combat," John said. *Who the fuck says things like that?* Deep down Carlos knew John was right. It was smart to wait, watch, gather intel. But when trying to protect one's child, smart gives way to animalistic instincts. Carlos, aware of being wrong even as he'd made the argument, pushed for the element of surprise.

"So, you want to assault an urban home with your little silenced pea shooters? You want to storm a house occupied by at least two professional soldiers and who-knows-how-many armed gangbangers? You want to fight *their* battle on *their* turf?" John responded. "When those two Kings tried to kill you in your apartment, how'd that work out for them? Tell me Carlos, how does getting yourself killed help keep your family alive?"

It'd been the last sentence of John's argument that'd finally convinced Carlos to stand down. But the waiting was excruciating. *That fuck of an uncle had threatened to kill his wife and rape his daughter.* Carlos wanted the man's head, and he wanted it now.

Dwelling on such thoughts yet again, Carlos balled his fists in rage, his shoulders so tight they neighbored his ears. Then, when he thought things couldn't get any worse—they did.

He watched a white cargo van pull in front of Carbia's house. Struggling to define the misshapen images, he squinted through the mist-covered window out into the gloom. He observed a figure step out of the passenger side door pulling a smaller body by the scruff of the neck. The two met a third, probably the driver, at the rear of the van. The passenger dragged the smaller figure away as the driver opened the cargo doors. Three additional bodies piled out. As the group approached the front door, a porch light snapped on. The image froze Carlos in a constricted mass of rage and fear. The bastards had his wife and daughter.

A MISTAKE WAS IN THE making, Thorpe knew. But like a divining rod to water, he was led. Incapable of forming the word "no." Dismissed of free-will. Diminished mental capacity. The works.

Approaching Jenna from behind Thorpe wrapped his hands around her taut waist. Elevated by heels, her firm ass cradled the one thing currently making all of Thorpe's decisions. He felt the fabric of her shorts, the heat beneath, her shoulders on his damp chest. A foot of space separated her arched back and his quivering abdominal muscles. She turned and her lips found his. A dry first kiss, her bottom lip stuck to his as they pulled apart, the separation revealing a small triumphant smile.

Thorpe tended to attract a certain type of lover. He didn't have sleeves of tattoos, wear skintight Affliction shirts, or drive a Harley Davidson with un-baffled exhaust. He didn't try to project a bad-boy image, if anything he worked to tone it down. It didn't matter. Some just had the look. Danger oozed from their pores. Other men recognized it, particular women sought it.

He drew women on the fringes of society, ones who often proclaimed disinterest in relationships right before they morphed into borderline stalkers. If not them, then women who spent their days in the shallows—pining for a dip in the deep end of the pool. After having tread the deep water, these women always swam back to the relative safety of their accountants and bankers, two feet planted firmly beneath them, but one eye always on the other side of the buoyed rope.

Not all women Thorpe attracted were of these varieties. There had been exceptions, the most notable had been the one with whom he'd fallen in love, and by whom he'd been abandoned.

Jenna reminded Thorpe of Ambretta. Both were strong. And though he didn't know Jenna well, he suspected pride would keep her from falling prey to stalking. Still, despite promises to others and self, sex changes all dynamics in a relationship. Even the most balanced tend to lose a touch of their sanity. Expectations ensued; guilt and hurt felt when those expectations weren't met.

Thorpe's boundless guilt needed no supplementation. He had no time for emotional complications. He'd come to Chicago to end the threat to his life, period. Then it was back to Tulsa and his continued protection of the sheep from the wolves. He realized this, yet all it took was a fifty-dollar piece of lingerie and a half-naked body to toss reasoning aside. Granted, it was one hell of a body. One forever etched into his mind. Problem was, he also liked her.

"Cheater," he said in submission.

Thorpe's prepaid cell chirped on the nightstand. He reached around Jenna to answer when she snatched it up. She then took the term "throw-phone" literally, launching the device across the room, against the wall, and into pieces.

"Oh no you don't, cowboy," she whispered while turning into him. Reaching up, tongue finding his, she pulled away. "I just got off work. Join me in the shower?" Her left hand wrapped around his neck, her right around the decision maker. Leaving him in no condition to argue, Jenna strutted into the bathroom and started the water.

Thorpe looked down at the sweat-soaked, tangled sheets. *No wonder she opted for the shower.* Before joining her, he retrieved his phone from the floor and reinserted the displaced battery. The device took a few seconds to power-up. When it did, Thorpe discovered two missed calls from Carlos. The prepaid phone wasn't equipped with voice mail. He tried to call Carlos back but couldn't get a response.

"John, you coming?"

Damn near.

Thorpe stood naked in the hotel room—a beautiful woman calling from the shower—and struggled with a decision.

THE FEAR AND RAGE WERE all consuming. Everyone's seen it portrayed in the movies—a woman who can't perform the simple task of unlocking her front door from the inside. Behind her, the boogie man slowly descends the stairs. Paralyzing fear is real. Carlos was experiencing it. His fear wasn't for his own safety, but for his family's very lives. It'd taken Carlos a full minute of cognitive struggle to make a simple phone call to John, a call that'd gone unanswered. Somehow he'd managed to make a second with similar results. He was on his own.

Carlos walked with tension-laden, jerky steps, toward Luis Carbia's home. Arms crossed, Carlos concealed a silenced pistol under his left armpit. He had tunnel vision. His hearing was impaired. Higher thinking diminished, a singular thought became his mantra, "Save. My. Family." Even as he approached the home he fought back horrific images of his innocent daughter. He recognized he was not mentally prepared for what he was about to do.

Though drunk with adrenaline, Carlos processed that the front door might not be the best choice. Not taking the time to debate pros and cons, Carlos went left of the house and jumped a four foot chain-link fence. He landed in Carbia's back yard, pistol extended. Unconsciously, training kicked in; he "sliced the pie," weavering the corner before stepping onto a small concrete pad servicing the rear door.

An unthinking animal, Carlos didn't think to check the lock. He drew a deep breath and prepared to kick. As he raised his right leg, blood sprayed the door in front of him. His blood. Carlos slammed into the door, but not with his foot. His entire body collapsed against the wooden structure before crumbling in a heap on the concrete slab.

THORPE SPED TOWARD LUIS CARBIA'S home, two phones causing him much duress: his prepaid cell because Carlos wouldn't answer, his SID assigned phone because it wouldn't stop ringing.

Caller ID on the SID phone told him his incoming calls came from both his hotel room, and Jenna's cell. He'd stormed out without a word, leaving the woman alone in the shower. *How the hell would he explain his actions?* He wouldn't. He couldn't afford the distraction. Ultimately, he silenced his work phone and tossed it in the back seat, pushing Jenna from his thoughts.

Nearing Carbia's neighborhood, he picked up his prepaid phone and dialed Carlos one last time. *Finally!* The ringing ceased and clicked to an open line. Someone had picked-up, but wasn't speaking. Thorpe was forced to break the silence.

"Hello?"

Nothing.

"Who's there?" Thorpe inquired again.

A man answered, "Carlos. Who's this?"

The voice wasn't Carlos'. Carbia and Vega had him. *Stay on the line or hang-up?* Thorpe worried his call might raise alarms; he didn't want them knowing that Carlos had a potential partner.

"Carlos? Who's that? Is Shelia there?" Thorpe asked.

"Who the fuck is Shelia?"

"Sorry, bro. Wrong number," Thorpe offered and terminated the call.

"Shit," Thorpe pounded the steering wheel with the palm of his hand. *Did he owe it to Carlos to save his ass?* Even while he wrestled with the answer he knew what his actions would be. *He wouldn't allow the bad guys to win.* Then again maybe he wasn't all that noble. *Maybe he was just always looking for a fight.* If so, he at least tried to be on the right side of things, even if it sometimes involved Monday morning justification.

If he had to, he knew he'd give his own life in an attempt to save Carlos, though the life-for-a-life option certainly wasn't his first choice.

Thorpe's prepaid cell rang; the caller ID told him it was from Carlos' phone. His captors were concerned. *Not good, they'd be in a higher state of alert.* Thorpe chose not to answer.

A block from Carbia's home, Thorpe discovered Carlos wasn't parked at the agreed upon location. Rounding the corner, Thorpe spotted the van near where he'd first encountered Carlos. Despite Thorpe's warning, Carlos had chosen to conduct visual surveillance. *Damn it, the little shit was too emotionally attached.* And it cost him his ass.

At least the Dodge Charger still sat in front of Carbia's home. It had been joined by a white cargo van. As Thorpe passed the house his cell rang again, the caller ID displayed a number he didn't recognize. Carlos' captors might be calling him back from another phone. *Answer the call?* He couldn't see the benefit. They weren't going to provide intel, and he sure as hell didn't want to give any away.

Thorpe would like to have inspected Carlos' van to see if it offered any clues. But there were only two likely scenarios. Either they saw Carlos in the van and snatched him out of it, or Carlos lost his patience and assaulted the house. The only question that really mattered was whether Carlos had already been killed.

The presence of the cargo van also concerned Thorpe. If Carlos had indeed stormed the house, Thorpe could think of only one scenario that would have caused him to act so impetuously. The cargo van suggested just that—cargo. If Carlos saw something—or in particular *someone*—unloaded from that van, it would have driven him over the edge. *And what had Thorpe been doing at the time? Contemplating a screw in the shower? Damned if he'd be responsible for another wife and daughter getting murdered.* Almost without conscious thought, Thorpe slowed his breathing and heart rate. While others went to great extremes to get themselves "wired-up" for a fight, Thorpe relaxed. He morphed into a fluid yet calculating instrument of extreme violence.

DUCT TAPED TO A WOODEN chair, wounded but alive, Carlos wished for death. His right shoulder was a mangled mass of hamburger meat and shattered bone held loosely together by torn ligaments and tendons. To slow the bleeding, the sons-of-bitches had packed and wrapped his wounds. They didn't want him to die, not yet anyway. First they would make him suffer. Suffer for his disobedience to the Kings; for his betrayal of Alberto. He would be an example to others, though the worst of his suffering wouldn't be physical.

Carlos' death wish had nothing to do with the threat of pain. He invited death so he wouldn't have to see, so he wouldn't have to hear, so he wouldn't have to witness the butchery to be committed on his wife and daughter. He prayed silently for an act of God to kill everyone. A quick, painless, merciful, death for his family.

However, a single act wouldn't quite do the trick. Alberto was no longer present. Neither was his daughter. Alberto, and one of the soldiers, "Mongoose," had left the house with Celestina. They'd left with the excuse of cashing in on a large payday. But Carlos knew that wasn't the real reason. He fled because of a phone call; something had unnerved him.

Minutes before that phone call, Eva, his beautiful wife, had been stripped nude; her bleeding wrists secured to the wooden basement stairs. Alberto had beaten her unconscious; battered her delicate face. He'd ordered a junior King to rape her in front of an audience; an audience that included his young terrified daughter. The junior King had undone his belt and was in the process of unzipping his pants when Carlos' phone rang. At first, Alberto only stared at the phone, unsure how to proceed. Eventually, he'd snatched the cell off the cheap card table and pretended to be Carlos.

Carlos had only heard one side of the conversation, but Alberto had followed-up by redialing the number. Getting no answer, he'd ordered Mongoose to call using the house phone. When Mongoose couldn't get an answer, he'd directed the Kings back into their defensive positions. He'd grabbed Celestina by the hair and made an excuse to leave. Ordering Luis to stay behind, he'd left with Mongoose and Celestina. On his way out, Carlos heard Alberto call out to one of the soldiers, "Sauce, get back in the doghouse."

Carlos hoped it'd been John calling. Aspirations of death dismissed, he prayed John would come to their rescue. But time was running out. Alberto, Mongoose, and his daughter having left, Luis Carbia—pants around his ankles—had replaced the junior King behind his wife. And worse yet, she'd regained consciousness.

THORPE CONSIDERED CALLING THE POLICE and letting them handle the situation. He doubted, however, that anyone would take his anonymous call seriously. "Hey some soldiers and Latin Kings have another soldier and his family kidnapped over here. Would you please send SWAT?" He considered calling in a bogus domestic at the address but that might get an officer killed. If a cop knocked on the front door thinking they were handling another "anonymous third party domestic call," they could be in for one hell of a surprise when they entered the house. They would not be prepared for what awaited them on the other side. Thorpe had to handle matters on his own.

Outside, a cold mist was settling in. Thorpe walked heel-to-toe across the dampened earth. His left eye open but not seeing, his right eye peered through the rubber coned receptacle of his weapon-mounted forward-looking infrared scope.

Heel-to-toe, knees slightly bent, gliding; the platform of a moving shooter. He wore a black balaclava and body armor. He swept the weapon left to right, right to left; too vast an area for one man to effectively cover. Still, he was much better equipped than he'd been on similar scenarios. The equipment he'd taken off the Kings in Oklahoma was state-of-the-art.

Moon and starlight struggled to penetrate the steel wool sky. Distant street lamps barely pierced the thickening mist. Because of the equipment he carried, Thorpe relished the darkness. Darkness is one's friend when toting around military-grade night-vision gear. Operators own the night.

Thorpe had parked behind and to the west of Carbia's house. Because of all the damned one-way streets in the area, it'd taken him much too long to position his Suburban in the alley. No lights burned in the yard he occupied; nor were any lit in Carbia's back yard. He preferred the dark, yet at the same time the blackness caused him unease. It seemed too welcoming—like an invitation. Thorpe the mouse, darkness the cheese, a bullet the trap.

Thorpe squatted behind a chain-link fence at the back of Carbia's property. Poorly maintained and covered with thick brown vines, the fence offered concealment even after a long, cold, winter. In addition to looking for someone to kill, or be killed by, Thorpe eyed the terrain in and around Carbia's back yard. It was a mess of trampled mud.

Thorpe felt relaxed yet tuned to his surroundings. It was quiet; too much so, like silenced animals when a predator draws near. Hopefully, he was the predator they feared. Thorpe eased below the vine-covered fence but remained facing Carbia's property. He could no longer see the back yard. Nevertheless, he studied the mental picture he'd taken before dropping to a knee. *What had he seen?* Single story house maybe around 1500 square feet. Asphalt roof. A small, high-set window told Thorpe the bathroom was positioned on the west side of the house. From his earlier scouting mission he knew there was a basement with two windows facing Hamlin. Exterior issues: he'd seen a large doghouse. Dogs were loud. He'd also seen a trampled back yard absent of grass. This meant the dog(s) weren't likely chained to their house; he, she, or they, had free reign of the entire yard. Dogs bite. Dogs with houses that size maim.

No lights lit the yard and none were visible on the main floor of the house. He'd seen a small sliver of dull light coming from one of the basement windows when he passed by in the Suburban. *Lights on in the basement—its windows covered?* The basement would be his priority.

The doghouse sat on the far right side of the yard—farthest away from Thorpe. He didn't have a view of its interior and couldn't pick up a heat signature through the plywood—which didn't mean much; the FLIR he carried couldn't penetrate shit. Regardless, he couldn't cross here. He would be too exposed. Thorpe had to assume the soldiers inside Carbia's home were similarly equipped. One of them could very well be perched inside with a rifle trained on the back yard.

Thorpe continued to study the scene in his mind's eye. The safest route of approach would be at a ninety-degree angle. There, he'd remain out of view of Carbia's windows until nearly on top of the house. Thorpe shuffled west below the cover of the vines, and making more noise than he would have liked, rolled over the back fence of a neighboring yard. On the other side, he inched across the grass, careful not to step on any debris which would further announce his presence. Reconsidering, Thorpe selected a couple of sticks with enough heft for throwing. Left shoulder against the neighbor's house, he stayed below the windows; he didn't want to be mistaken for a burglar and get shot by a nervous home owner. *Wouldn't that be embarrassing?* He hoped the house wasn't owned by associates of the Kings. If so, he was screwed.

Thorpe reached the corner of the neighboring home. He studied Carbia's darkened back yard focusing on the doghouse. No heat signatures, yet the doghouse still bothered him. The trampled and muddy yard suggested a very large, noisy, hook-toothed dog roamed within. He had no desire to kill a dog. Dogs were guileless bystanders, protecting their loved ones—too stupid and loyal to know if their owners deserved such protection. But in this case, innocent human lives hung in the balance and he'd kill a dog if forced to. Thorpe thought it odd, these days killing a dog caused as much moral dilemma as killing a man. He knew he wasn't alone. Guys have shed more tears over the death of Old Yeller than any fictional human victim could ever elicit.

Because Thorpe excelled in shooting with either hand, but admittedly threw like a pre-K schoolgirl with his left, he switched hands with his weapon. He hurled a stick against the side of the doghouse. No reaction. That's why he'd picked up two. If the dog was sleeping, the first would wake his furry ass up. The second should bring him out of the house. Stick number two bounced off the roof. No reaction.

There had to be a dog. Thorpe couldn't find a heat signature through his scope, but he also didn't have a good vantage point to see inside. Still, he should have gotten a reaction. *Maybe the dog had been taken inside the house?* Just as Thorpe began to redirect his attention he glimpsed a white glow near the opening of the doghouse.

The dog was either very restrained, very chicken, or very *not* a dog. Thorpe still didn't have a good sight picture. But he now knew something large and alive dwelt within. Whatever it was, finally burst out of the door. The ball of white unfolded into a man. An armed man. Thorpe put three silenced rounds in the man's head then rushed forward before the body had time to settle in the mud.

Thorpe was a blur of movement. If the man in the doghouse had radioed or phoned the others, they'd be coming to investigate. *Speed.* Thorpe sprung over the remaining fence and took a position by the rear door, a rear door covered with blood. *Not good.*

He tried the knob. Locked. Thorpe kicked the door and the frame exploded. No bullets were sent his direction. Those inside had been counting on Doghouse Boy to provide protection. Thorpe remained outside and positioned himself near the shattered opening.

"Chicago Police, search warrant," Thorpe yelled, three times, loudly. "Come to the rear door."

He chose the search warrant ruse for two reasons. The first was to cause confusion. The Kings were not prepared for a search warrant. They'd been anticipating a lone gunman—Carlos. Thorpe's phone calls might have got them thinking about an accomplice, *but the police?* They weren't expecting cops. If the Kings had a wounded or dead man in their house, and two kidnap victims, they might decide to fight it out—even with the police. Whatever they decided, they'd have to think through the confusion. And confused decision making slows reaction time.

The second reason for faking a search warrant service was for the sake of the neighbors. If they heard Thorpe's announcements they'd be less inclined to call the real police. Thorpe guessed the neighborhood would be relieved to see this shit-hole raided.

Following his three commands, Thorpe tossed a stun grenade through the kitchen and into the next room. The force of the blast blew out the windows.

A corny line from a recent movie popped into Thorpe's head: *Once more into the fray...*

FILTHY COTTON STIFFLED CARLOS' SCREAMS. An inside-out sock was stuffed into his mouth and secured with duct tape. His wooden chair rattled atop the concrete floor as he struggled against his bindings and the vision before him. Luis Carbia knelt behind his wife, Eva, and in an attempt to achieve an erection, rubbed his flaccid penis between her buttocks. *Thank God Celestina was no longer here to witness this.*

Between whispered taunts into Carlos' ear, Sauce shouted words of encouragement to the would-be rapist. Sauce's presence violated his uncle's orders. Alberto had ordered him back into the doghouse—but hell if Sauce was going to miss all the fun. He'd delegated doghouse duty to another King then called for "seconds."

Deafened from screaming into the pungent sock, Carlos didn't hear the back door give way. He *did* notice both men glance upward and tune their ears to something unseen. Carlos stopped screaming in time to hear, "Chicago Police, Search Warrant!" *Thank God! Maybe they'd survive this after all.* Following the announcement he heard an explosion. Seconds later he heard what sounded like a body dropping on the floor above him. Then another.

Panic and confusion twisting the man's face, rape plans abandoned, Carbia backed away from Carlos' nude and sobbing wife and scrambled to buckle his pants. Sauce however, remained calm. He shouldered his weapon, knelt behind the stairs and waited. Carlos feared the first officer to descend wouldn't stand a chance. Sauce would kill him for sure.

The tin can flew up the wooden steps, flinging cartridges across the stairs and basement floor. *They were coming.* Carlos heard a click as Sauce disengaged the safety on his weapon. In an attempt to warn officers, Carlos bounced up and down in his wooden chair, creating as much noise as he could.

While Carlos struggled in his chair, Carbia stood frozen in the middle of the sparse basement—the epitome of indecision. Something metallic bounced off the concrete floor beside Eva, and despite his training, Carlos couldn't help but stare. Then his entire world left him: blinding light, concussive wave, ringing ears, loss of vision. His head swam. He felt as if he was deep in dark waters and didn't know the way back to the surface. Despite his havoc-wrought senses, Carlos realized he'd been on the receiving end of a stun grenade and was damned happy for it.

THORPE KNEW THOSE SEQUESTERED INSIDE wouldn't buy the police ruse simply because he'd yelled, "Search warrant." But the subsequent flash-bang would be much more persuasive. He'd even reapplied the Velcro "POLICE" patch on the front of his entry vest. He might have appeared very legitimate if he hadn't been alone. Major police departments don't conduct one-man search warrant services.

Having tossed the grenade, he passed through the empty kitchen low and fast. Then he'd encountered a small, darkened living room with an even smaller man backed into its corner. The man, frozen with terror, held a pistol in front of his open but unseeing eyes. A single silenced shot liberated the man from his fear.

A half-second of Thorpe's attention had been spent on the threat before another man burst from a bedroom into the hallway—weapon in hand. Thorpe fired three rounds—two to the chest, one to the head. The man fell forward on his face and skipped across the worn carpet like a fat stone on water.

Thorpe spotted a door between him and Skip that likely led to the basement. He thought of the light he'd seen while outside, and bet Carlos had been taken below. *No time to clear the rest of the upstairs.* Thorpe stepped to the side and pulled the basement door open. From below he heard a metallic crash. He saw a string attached to the doorknob. *Warning device.* It told Thorpe he'd made the right decision. Not looking, he tossed another stun grenade down the stairs, and closed the door for protection against the blast.

Stun grenades, more commonly referred to as "flash-bangs" in law enforcement circles, do exactly what both names imply. The device provides a brilliant flash meant to blind, and a loud boom meant to discombobulate.

The bang went off. Thorpe yanked open the door and descended the stairs two at a time. *Speed and aggression.* The lights, previously on, had been extinguished. Thorpe's night optics slid over a battered woman, either dead or unconscious, tethered to the stairs. Pivoting right, Thorpe spotted a shirtless man underneath a shattered light bulb—ass on bare concrete, hands on ears—unarmed. *His mistake.* Thorpe paused his descent and fired at the man's bare chest, then "walked" the shots upward. Shirtless man's head snapped back and Thorpe redirected his sights further into the basement. Amidst the sound of spent cartridges clinking down the wooden stairs he heard the dull thud of shirtless man's skull land on the cold concrete floor.

Stepping off the stairs, his optics passed over a flipped card table and found an unseeing man in tattered pants, ala a post-Hulking, Bruce Banner. The flash-bang had nearly blown off Hulk's pants. The man shouldered a weapon but pointed it harmlessly at a blank concrete wall. Behind the Hulk sat Carlos, bound to a chair. Alive.

Thorpe needed to keep a bad guy alive. He needed information. He needed to know all future threats against his life, and now Carlos' family, had been nullified.

Thorpe rushed Hulk, arced his weapon through the air and butt-stroked him across the base of his skull. Already out on his feet, Hulk crumpled to the floor, a pile of soiled laundry.

Reaching Carlos' side, Thorpe knelt, activated his weapon-mounted flashlight, and checked his condition. Carlos had suffered a nasty shoulder wound and though his eyes were open, they were unfocused. His mouth was taped shut and he struggled to breathe through a bloodied nose resting sideways on his face. He was badly hurt. Thorpe cut the tape and removed the sock. Carlos gasped for air then managed a single word, "Eva." Assuming Eva was Carlos' wife and the woman tethered to the stairs, Thorpe said, "Stand by," as he removed the last of Carlos' bindings.

Carlos appeared to still be suffering the effects of the flash-bang and probably hadn't heard him. Nevertheless, Thorpe left to check on the woman. She was breathing and had a strong steady pulse but was unconscious. Thorpe cut her loose from the stairs and helped her to the floor. She started kicking and clawing. *Very good sign.* Carlos, on his knees, used his uninjured arm to pull himself through the gloom toward his struggling wife and the only source of light.

As if trying to scream over loud music, Carlos called out, "Baby? Eva?"

"She's okay, Carlos. I need to clear the upstairs."

"John, that you? I thought you were the police."

"They'll be here soon. I gotta' get moving, Carlos."

"They've got my daughter, John. They have Celestina."

"Where?"

"I don't know. Alberto took her right before you hit."

"FFFFUCK!"

Carlos found his wife's side and called out to her. Thorpe didn't know if she could hear yet. The bang had gone off very close to the woman; she'd taken the full blast. Regardless, she apparently realized she was with her husband. She ceased her thrashing and clutched on to Carlos, sobbing in his arms.

Thorpe had much to do. If he didn't get it done quickly, he'd soon be locked in a CPD interrogation room. First he went to the man he'd stroked across the head, Hulk, and checked his pulse. He was alive. He took Hulk's weapon, slung it over his shoulder, and secured him with flex-cuffs, then grabbed his cell phone and stuffed it into one of the many pockets of his tactical pants.

Finished with the basement, Thorpe handed Carlos a handheld flashlight. "I have to clear the rest of the house. You think you can get her up the stairs?"

Carlos nodded.

"Meet you topside."

Surprisingly, during the bulk of search warrants Thorpe had been involved in over the years, few neighbors had ever called 911. Of course uniformed police officers were usually posted outside. Another reason they didn't call, Thorpe surmised, was because they were happy to see something "finally being done," about the neighborhood dope house. Thorpe hoped Carbia's neighbors fit into the latter category. But he couldn't count on it; by now a neighbor could very well be on the phone with the police calling in a disturbance or shots fired. He needed to hurry.

Thorpe searched the rest of the house with reckless abandon. He reentered the living room just as Carlos struggled up the stairs with his wife. They were speaking to each other and seemed to have regained their senses.

Satisfied the house was clear of threats, Thorpe looked out the glassless front window and noticed both the white cargo van and the black Dodge Charger were missing. Alberto and Mongoose left in the vehicles while Thorpe had been making his approach from the rear. One of them had Celestina.

"Carlos, the Charger's gone. Is the Birddog receiver still in your van?"

Hope flashed across injured man's face. "Yes."

Thorpe hated what he was about to do. No doubt neighbors watched through gaps in their curtains, others parted blinds a fraction of an inch; all wanting to see, none wanting to be seen. Thorpe bolted out the front, balaclava still in place, weapons bouncing off his heavy entry vest as he sprinted toward the parked van.

A few seconds later he yanked at the GMC's door. Locked. *Shit.* Thorpe pulled out a large knife and using the butt, struck the driver's side window. Stubborn, the glass finally gave way on his third attempt. He reached through the opening, snatched the receiver off the seat and ran back toward Alberto's house.

When Thorpe returned, he found Carlos kneeling by his wife. Nude before, she was now wrapped in a blanket. Carlos' bandages were soaked, no longer able to stem the tide. He might not survive the blood loss if he didn't receive immediate medical attention.

"We've got to get my Celestina," Carlos said, wilting before Thorpe's eyes.

"Not we, Carlos, me. I'll get her back. I promise."

"Bullshit, I'm going…"

"Carlos you're bleeding out, brother. Your wife needs a doctor. I'll get your daughter back." Thorpe pulled out a pouch containing a hemostatic agent. He carried the blood clotting compound in his entry vest for situations just like these. Thorpe tore off Carlos' makeshift bandages and poured the granules on his wounds. As he worked, Carlos used what little strength he had to pull himself up to Thorpe's ear.

"John, he said he was going to sell Celestina to men who like little girls. Said they'd fuck her till she was all used up." Carlos gripped his arm, "Get my little girl back."

Carlos collapsed back to the floor, tears streaming from his eyes. While his strength abated, his wife's was returning.

Wanting to make sure she could hear and understand, Thorpe shouted, "Get your husband to the front yard and apply pressure until medics arrive."

"Who are you?"

"I'm the man who's going to save your daughter. I was never here. You never saw me."

"But…" Eva started.

"You've never seen him," Carlos interrupted his wife with a shout.

Thorpe dialed 911 with a cordless house phone and left the line open. He handed the phone to Eva and pointed forcefully toward the front door. She didn't argue. She worked at getting her husband off the floor and out the door. The last thing Thorpe heard from Carlos was his repeated plea.

"Get her back, John. Get Celestina back!"

Thorpe snatched cells off the two upstairs dead men, then reentered the basement and found his bound prisoner moaning and stirring on the basement floor.

"You're coming with me, fuck nut."

THIRTY-EIGHT

HULL AND SKULL SHARED A hotel room, a bottle of Maker's Mark, and the spurious clarity-of-thought achieved by those who imbibe. Both men drank too much. Neither man gave a shit. Skull was drunk; Hull a tumbler away from joining his good friend.

Their topic of discussion? Jonathan Thorpe.

Hull dug two cubes out of the hotel ice bucket, dropped them in an empty glass, topped it with three fingers of both man's favorite whiskey, and placed the concoction in Skull's boney hand.

"What in the hell is that boy up to now?" Hull asked, as he poured himself a drink.

"Be damned if I know. Probably killing the fuck out of people."

"Skull, how exactly do you 'kill the fuck' out of someone? Drunk ass."

Skull acknowledged his boss's good-natured roast with a wet smile and by shrugging his gaunt shoulders, "I say we just ask him…point blank."

"Ask him? We can't even find him. Plus, I'm not sure we wanna' know the answers."

Skull raised his glass and tipped it toward his boss, "Here's to ignorance."

"Damn it Skull, I hate it when you get like this."

"Then quit feeding me bourbon! Probably take advantage of me

246

after I pass out," Skull said with a laugh.

"If I ever go gay it won't be with your bony ass." Hull shot back as he plopped down on an adjacent double bed. "Seriously, we need to find him."

"Well I don't know how we're going to do that without help from the Chicago P.D., and we sure as hell can't go to them with this."

Had his neck not been pressed up against the headboard, Hull would have nodded in agreement, "The understatement of the year."

The two homicide detectives had come across incriminating evidence while investigating "The Finger Basket Case." Technically not yet a homicide investigation (no bodies), the two detectives doubted a group of Latin Kings were driving around Tulsa searching for their missing fingers. No, all fingers pointed—pun intended—to a quadruple homicide; one with many mysteries, and mysteries were what got Hull out of bed every morning.

On this particular morning, Hull and Skull had been in "Area Central Homicide" poring over both paper and electronic files. They'd compiled a list of known associates of the now eight-fingered Latin Kings. Not surprisingly, many of those associates possessed NCIC criminal histories. The two detectives sent those criminal histories along with additional information to a detective in Tulsa. The Tulsa detective conducted a parallel investigation with TPD's database. Hull and Skull were looking for names that popped up on both departments' radar screens. The Tulsa detective found one such match and faxed the accompanying reports to Skull.

An associate of one of the eight-fingered men turned out to be a Latin King by the name of Luis Carbia. Carbia had prior contact with the Tulsa Police Department. Furthermore, investigators with TPD's Organized Gang Unit, supervised by Jonathan Thorpe, had arrested and released Carbia. Even more incriminating, Carbia had been the front seat passenger of a car driven by one Lyndale Peterson. Hull and his unit had an ongoing homicide investigation where Lyndale's brother, Leon, had been found tortured and murdered near an oil well in north Tulsa. Officially there were no leads. Unofficially, both Hull and Skull suspected—knew—Thorpe had snapped the little shit's neck. Leon had been a party to the murders of Thorpe's wife and daughter.

Cops aren't ones to believe in coincidence. Thorpe weaseled his way to Chicago under the guise of helping Skull and Hull investigate the Finger Basket Case. Both men now saw through the bullshit. Chicago was connected to Leon and Lyndale Peterson and Leon and Lyndale were connected to the death of Thorpe's family. Thorpe came here with ulterior motives.

Hull thought, or at least hoped, the carnage of last month was over. Thorpe had been provided an airtight alibi and it appeared all those responsible for his family's demise had been put in the dirt. That apparently wasn't the case.

Hull and Skull had still been inside Central Homicide discussing this new twist when they'd overheard a loud conversation between a rather obnoxious Chicago detective and couple of his associates. The detective was discussing "some Tulsa shit-kicker-of-a-cop" in reference to a dead Latin King found outside an apartment building. Hull and Skull injected themselves into the conversation. While they listened to the details, they'd looked at each other, both men recognizing their own fear reflected in the other's eyes. The bloodshed wasn't over.

They excused themselves, returned to the hotel, claimed a table at the bar, and began what turned into a lengthy drinking session. After much back-and-forth, they'd finally agreed to confront Thorpe about the events of February—though neither would take action against the man. *Those fucks got what was coming.* Men had brutally murdered Thorpe's wife and daughter and both detectives took it personally. No matter how many homicide scenes a detective worked, those with child victims always exacted an emotional toll. When the victim was a fellow officer's son or daughter, well, it was like losing one of their own.

The two detectives agreed not to act on the information they now possessed. Just one problem: Thorpe was beginning to leave a trail; a trail cluttered with dead bodies. If Hull and Skull had sniffed it out, others could as well.

By their sixth or seventh (or ninth) drink the men decided to confront Thorpe with what they knew, and offer their assistance— both fully aware of the possible repercussions. *But fuck it, sometimes justice is best served outside the courtroom.* They'd left the bar, tipsy already, and went to Thorpe's hotel room.

Set to knuckle the door, it'd flown open with a red-faced Jenna on her way out. They'd all startled one another.

"Sorry, Jenna, is this a bad time?" Hull asked.

"It's always a bad time with that son-of-a-bitch," she'd said while storming down the hall without explanation. Hull stuck his foot in John's door before it latched closed. He and Skull called out John's name and stepped into the room, discovering it empty. They noted the disheveled bed sheets and concluded Jenna and John had started on good terms before taking a wrong turn somewhere along the way.

They returned to their own room and made repeated calls to Thorpe's cell phone, all of which went unanswered. He'd disappeared. And when John disappeared, others tended to vanish along with him—permanently. Unsure how to proceed, the two men continued their drinking in the privacy of their hotel room.

Skull turned serious and asked a question he probably wouldn't have posed had he been sober, "You think John killed that Latin King Chicago PD is working?"

"Maybe, but I have a bigger worry. Who do you think left us the box fulla' fingers?"

"Fuck. But why get us involved?"

"Skull, I think I went and identified John's targets for him."

Skull regained his smile, "He's a crafty little shit."

"And now he's gone off the grid."

"Yeah, and I got a feelin' Chicago's about to have a spike in their homicide rate."

CHICAGO WAS TOO DAMNED BIG, the range on the tracking device too damned short. Heading in any given direction afforded Thorpe an eighty percent chance of traveling further from his target. Corkscrewing through the city in increasingly larger circles would take hours if not days. All of this on the assumption Celestina was near the transmitter-equipped Dodge Charger. Most likely she'd been transported in the cargo van and who knew if the two vehicles traveled to the same location. And what if they'd left Chicago altogether? Thorpe needed to find a different means of locating Celestina. He needed to act quickly. He had to get her back alive before something worse than death was perpetrated against her. The world was glutted with sadistic assholes, Thorpe flushed one—Jeremy Johnson—a little more than a week ago. Sadly, countless others would step forward to fill his shoes.

Luckily, Thorpe had another source of information in close proximity. His captive Latin King lay on the back floorboard wrapped with duct tape and secured to the seat rails with flex-cuffs. He'd looped one cuff around the King's neck. Too much struggling would result in self-strangulation. Once a flex cuff tightened it couldn't be loosened.

Thorpe felt uneasy with the man at his back. He'd searched him in haste yet still discovered two secreted knives and a pistol. The ex-soldier possibly possessed additional weapons and Thorpe found no enjoyment knowing the man lay less than a foot from his back and mostly out of view. He searched for a place to question his prisoner but his unfamiliarity with the city slowed his efforts. He'd like to use his smartphone but decided to keep the device powered down from this point forward. Smartphones are equipped with GPS and he didn't trust that his movements wouldn't be monitored or recorded.

The only semi-private area he'd seen was a railroad yard just west of the now ownerless white, Nissan Z. Thorpe wouldn't return so close to the scene of Carlos' crime, but it'd given him an idea. He used the handheld GPS to locate another railroad line to the east. After crossing the tracks, Thorpe turned north on a parallel street. At the corner of 52nd and Millard, he found a suitable location.

Turning east, asphalt gave way to gravel. On his right was a plain brick building, to his left a row of hedges. Forward, lay a wide expanse accommodating multiple sets of tracks. An enormous warehouse stood beyond the rails. Perfect.

Thorpe didn't want to remain in the Suburban and risk having his interrogation interrupted by law enforcement. He parked, grabbed his pack, and pulled the black balaclava down over his face. He took a quick glance between the captain seats at his prisoner. The man had either passed out or feigned unconsciousness. Thorpe stepped over the center console and between the two chairs, planting all of his weight on his captive's stomach. Reflexively, the man's abdominal muscles tensed; he was playing possum. Situated atop the man, Thorpe cut the restraints on his legs, opened the door next to his head, and cut his wrists free from the chair rail. The man's wrists were still bound in front with duct tape.

Thorpe climbed out, grabbed his prisoner underneath the chin with his right hand, by the hair with his left, and began tugging him out of the cab. The soldier decided this was a good time to drop the possum ruse. He grabbed Thorpe's collar with his bound hands and threw his legs up and over in an attempted leg triangle.

Thorpe's momentum prevented the maneuver. Possum man slid out of the cabin, his legs scissoring empty air, as Thorpe shoved the man's head straight into the gravel and followed it with an elbow across the bridge of his nose. The blow landed square causing an explosion of blood. The strike—momentarily at least—knocked the fight out of Mr. Possum. And because he wouldn't be drawing oxygen through his nose anytime soon, Thorpe tore the duct tape off of Possum Man's mouth, saving him from certain asphyxiation. A young girl's life depended on Possum Man living long enough to provide answers. Thorpe slammed the door on the Suburban locking it with a wireless remote. Then he dragged his bloodied possum across the gravel and out of view.

Around the corner of the hedges, Thorpe dropped the bloody

sack of a man to the ground and shone a flashlight on his face. A mess, he was missing two upper incisors and his pupils didn't react properly to the light. Well, he *had* been struck over the head at least three times in the last half hour. It was a miracle he was conscious.

"What's your name, Latin Queen?"

"Fuck you, shithead."

Possum's missing teeth created a whistling sound when he said "shit." Reminded of Gopher from Winnie-the-Pooh, Thorpe nearly laughed. Instead, he raised his knife for effect, and twisted the smile into his best Jack Nicholson impression.

Possum Man remained defiant, "Bring it, motherfucker."

Not being particularly careful with the serrated blade, Thorpe went to work removing clothing from the man's upper body. As he suspected, military tattoos covered Possum Man's torso and arms.

"Airborne, huh?"

"That's right, bitch."

"You graduate from SERE?" Thorpe asked, referring to the military's Survival, Evasion, Resistance, and Escape program. Most of the training focused on the SEE part of the acronym, not the R. It's difficult to replicate *Resistance* to torture. Not unless one wants to maim their all-volunteer army.

"Hooahh!"

Thorpe stuck the blade into Possum man's bloodied left nostril, "Well Airborne, let's find out if that shit really works..."

THIRTY-NINE

AWASH IN A SEA OF red and blue lights, Jenna pulled up to the crime scene. She'd been roused from bed by another Latin King homicide. Prior to arrival, she hadn't been told much, only that the scene was, "fucked-up." Coupled with the slain Latin King she'd worked earlier, signs hinted at a burgeoning gang war. Except so far, only Kings seemed to have found themselves on the business end of the barrel.

Bundled in layers, hands stuffed in pockets, Jenna treaded across the wet, but unfrozen pavement, toward the home of one Luis Carbia. The entire front yard of the residence was secured with yellow tape. Colder temperatures helped stave off rubberneckers but there were still ten to fifteen "citizens" eager to witness the events unfolding on the other side of the thin "POLICE LINE DO NOT CROSS," tape. As she neared, Jenna spotted her sergeant, Wyatt, huddled next to three detectives and a uniformed lieutenant who proudly wore his checkered blue and gold crown cap.

Wyatt saw Jenna approaching and broke free of the group.

"What we got, Sarge?"

"Wait till you see this," Wyatt replied with an unusual amount of enthusiasm.

"That bad, huh?"

"Umm, not bad. Precise."

Jenna gave a confused look.

"Never mind. You'll have to see for yourself. You know Luis Carbia?"

"Yeah, he's old-school Latin King and an asshole. Please tell me he's dead."

"He's dead."

"Well then, this day is starting off better than the last one ended." The tables turned, this time her sergeant offered a confused look and Jenna responded with a "Never mind" of her own. "Show me."

They skirted the tape's perimeter, heading toward the house's right side and a gate which led to the back yard. Jenna observed the front window's glass hanging by jagged shards. The blinds looked like they'd lost a battle with a rabid wolverine.

"Drive-by?" Jenna asked.

Leading the way Wyatt shook his head, "The glass was blown out, not in. Precise, remember?"

In the back, Jenna observed a small orange traffic cone in an adjacent yard. The cones were used by crime scene detectives to mark found evidence. Wyatt continued walking toward a dead man lying next to a large doghouse.

"Three shots. One directly over the heart, one in the throat, and one in his left eye."

"Not bad shooting."

"Not bad at all. Fucking remarkable when you consider the distance. See that cone?" Wyatt pointed back the way they'd come, "Three 9mm shell casings."

"Vertical shot pattern. Muzzle rise?" Jenna asked, referring to the tendency for shots to lift when shooting in rapid succession, especially with automatic weapons. The bucking of the weapon tended to make the muzzle rise with each successive shot.

"I don't think so. I think the bullets went exactly where the shooter wanted them to go. You'll think so too, after seeing the other bodies."

"Bodies? As in plural?"

"Yup."

"Holy shit! What happened here?"

Her question went unanswered. Instead Wyatt led Jenna through the kitchen and into the living room. He pointed out the remnants of a flash-bang and the precision kill shots that downed two more Latin Kings on the main floor. Then they approached the entrance to the basement. A string attached to the doorknob led down the stairs.

"Warning device. Appears they were expecting someone," Wyatt explained. "Didn't do 'em any fucking good though."

Descending, Jenna saw that the string led to a can dangling between the open-backed stairs. She also noticed bindings attached to the steps. Portable crime scene lights illuminated the basement. Detectives busied themselves with measurements.

Wyatt pointed, "Another flash-bang." Then redirected his finger, "And there is the artist previously known as Luis Carbia."

Carbia had a couple of wounds in his chest and one well-placed hole centered above his eyes. A large pool of blood surrounded his upper body.

"He's seen better days," Jenna remarked.

"Yeah, though I doubt he saw the end coming. Probably blinded by the flash-bang. Check that out," Wyatt pointed to a chair adorned with bindings.

"They had captives down here? Wonder who they were?"

"We *know* who they were…are. We have them in custody."

"No shit! Well?"

"Not gang members," Wyatt said, instantly dismissing the conclusion to which most would jump. "A wife and husband. Neither has a record except for some traffic bullshit. Both ex-military," he added with a smile.

Wyatt clearly enjoyed the bizarre circumstances. It might be hard for the average citizen to comprehend, but even murders get routine when you've seen enough of them. Unlike any scene either detective had ever encountered, it gave them sensations unfelt since they were rookie officers on their first homicide.

"They talking?"

"Not much. Uniforms are with them at the hospital. Both are pretty fucked-up. Tortured. Haven't had a chance for a formal interview yet. All they're saying is the Kings were trying to recruit them for their military skills. They refused and were brought here."

"That's bullshit," Jenna replied. "Probably a drug deal gone bad."

"Yeah, probably. But explain all this," Wyatt gestured.

"You summed it up before, precise. You said the kidnapped 'victims' were both ex-military?"

Wyatt nodded. "I think some of their military buddies came and saved their asses. And not just nut-tighteners. Whoever did this has experience with hostage rescue."

"Looks like fucking SWAT hit this place!"

"Jenna, you're reading my mind. We've got some professional trigger-pullers running around out there."

"What kind of units were they in? The wife and husband I mean?"

"The wife doesn't have any combat experience but the husband is an Army Ranger. Just back from Sand-land," Wyatt answered. "The thing is, Jenna, this isn't over yet."

"Yeah?"

"The son-of-a-bitches took the couple's three-year-old daughter."

EVERYTHING WAS STILL SALVAGEABLE, ALBERTO thought. Every plan encountered a speed bump or two. Carlos had turned out to be a disaster. *At least the little fuck was getting his—* witnessing his wife being repeatedly raped, retching over what would happen to his daughter. Alberto, set to make the call, would give Carlos some parting words over the phone before ordering

Sauce to put a bullet in the little fuck's head. Well, first he'd have Sauce shoot Carlos' foot, shin, and knee. Work his way up until Carlos either lost consciousness or died, whichever came first.

Alberto stood inside his living room accompanied by Mongoose and Celestina. He hated bringing the two here—his castle. Twenty-five minutes southwest of Crown Town, his home was nestled in Palos Park. He lived here because he couldn't stand the crushing weight of Chicago. A claustrophobe, he needed space which Palos Park provided. The home had been in foreclosure when purchased, and could use some work, but soon finances would no longer be a problem.

The Kings were not aware of this house, which was the precise reason he'd decided to come here now. His associates were disappearing at an alarming rate and he wanted a place far removed from gang business. *All this shit, just hours before the payday of his life.*

To get here, Alberto had driven Mongoose's Charger while Mongoose followed in the cargo van with Carlos' daughter secured within. *The hell if Alberto would be the one to get stopped by the police with a tied-up little girl.* Once they arrived, Alberto parked the Dodge in the driveway and directed Mongoose into the attached garage so they could unload the girl unseen. Before bringing the girl inside, he dismissed his semi-stoned girlfriend to the bedroom and told her if she didn't want to be beaten to death, she'd keep her ass and her business on the other side of the door.

So now he shared his home with two people who didn't belong. One, Celestina, lay curled up in the fetal position leaking tears on his leather sofa. Mongoose stood in the kitchen drinking a glass of water and awaiting further instruction. Alberto was glad to give it.

"Call Sauce. Time to put that little fuck Carlos out of his misery."

Mongoose fetched his cell phone out of his pants, hit a button, and put the device up to his ear.

"Put Carlos on the phone…What? Who is this? I said who *the fuck* is this? How do you know my…Goddamnit!" Mongoose went rigid as he clutched the phone. Face growing red, he tilted the mouthpiece away and breathed out heavily. Then he walked over to Alberto and held out the phone. "Trouble. It's not Sauce. Whoever it is, wants to talk to you."

What the fuck is it now? Alberto snatched the phone out of Mongoose's hand. "Who's this?"

"Hello, Uncle Alberto."

Alberto didn't recognize the voice, "What? Motherfucker, who are you?"

"I'm one of the motherfuckers who just cut through your men like a hot knife through butter. They're all dead; every fuckin' one of 'em. Guess who's next."

Alberto could feel the blood drain from his face; the room went askew, "Listen you fuck…"

"No, you listen you fuck. If you don't, you won't survive the night. Tell your little buddy Mongoose I'm a former operator and AFO team leader currently assigned to SOG, he'll know what it means. I want one thing, the girl. You take her to a hospital emergency room right now and leave a note on her to call the cops. If she isn't safely in the arms of the police in one hour you're dead and too stupid to know it. Everyone you've ever met is a walking corpse. You make her safe and you stay away from Carlos' family. You do that, and we might let you live."

The connection clicked dead. Alberto screamed in frustration and threw the phone into the couch, narrowly missing Celestina's head. Celestina let loose a scream of her own and began sobbing. Alberto's girlfriend came out of the bedroom in response to the commotion.

"You fucking bitch I told you to stay in your room," Alberto yelled as he gave chase. He managed to get a foot in the bedroom door before she slammed it closed, then shouldered his way inside and knocked her to the floor. He kicked her in the ribs and lost himself to blind fury. In his confused rage, he became aware of being restrained; Mongoose had wrapped him in a bear hug. His girlfriend lay in a bloody heap at his feet.

"Let me go you fucking…"

"You need to get your shit together. You have to tell me what the man said and we have to work through this," Mongoose said loudly, like a father disciplining his son. It almost sent Alberto off again, except he couldn't move—Alberto's worst fear.

"Fucking let me go," Alberto hissed.

Mongoose slowly released his vice-like grip. Alberto had half a mind to crack the man across the face, but before he could react, Mongoose knelt down and placed three fingers atop his girlfriend's throat. "She's alive." He said, matter-of-factly.

"Well, good for her," Alberto growled and strode out of the bedroom.

Mongoose followed, "What'd he say?"

"He said everyone at my brother's house is dead. He said they killed them and we were next if we didn't let the girl go."

"And you believe him?"

"He called from Sauce's fucking cell phone didn't he?"

Mongoose nodded, "What else?"

"Said he was an AFO operator and now he's an SOB, or something. Said you'd know what it meant."

"You mean SOG?"

"Maybe. What's it mean?"

Mongoose didn't answer immediately. He began pacing the room.

"Mongoose. What, *the fuck*, does it mean?"

"It means we're in some deep shit."

"What? He Special Forces or something?"

"He's the Special Forces of the Special Forces— A Delta operator who worked his way up to Advanced Force Operations. SOG means he's attached to the Special Operations Group."

"What the fuck is that?"

"Fucking commandos and professional killers for the

government is what they are. CIA assassins. Fucking bad-asses with a shit load of gear and resources. What else did he say?"

"He told us to drop the girl off at a hospital within the hour or we wouldn't survive the night."

Mongoose had become increasingly agitated as he listened to Alberto recite the phone conversation. The soldier sat down with his elbows on his knees and began rubbing his temples.

"What is it?"

"Before I handed you the phone, he used my fucking name. Not Mongoose, but my real fucking name."

Alberto didn't give a shit. That just meant Mongoose would be committed. "How'd he get your name?"

"They've either been surveilling us or someone from the house talked."

"What do we do?"

"We call him back. Set up a meet. We tell him the girl dies if he doesn't show."

"He kept saying we. Not me. I don't think he's alone."

"Goddammit!" Mongoose's pacing increased. "Doesn't matter, it's the only play we got. He's going to kill us whether we give the girl back or not. We might as well keep her around for leverage." Mongoose plucked the phone off the couch, "We call him back. Set up a meet. Get some guys, and take him out." Mongoose hit the number and placed the phone to his ear as he paced. "Fuck! He ain't answering." Mongoose tried several more times with similar results. "Fucker's smart. He's not allowing us to negotiate."

"What do we do?"

"I don't fucking know!"

"Maybe we should hide the girl," Alberto offered. "He won't kill us if he doesn't know what we did with her. He'll need to keep us alive."

Mongoose shook his head. "All that will do is get us tortured before he kills us. I ain't going out like that man. I watched two of those guys in action in Afghanistan. At least I think they were spooks; they don't exactly go around announcing who the fuck they are. They'd get us to talk. Everybody talks. Every fucking time."

"Then what the fuck do we do?"

Alberto watched Mongoose pace his living room like a cornered rat and realized the most unshakable person he'd ever met, didn't have the slightest clue.

FORTY

USING CARBIA'S HOUSE AS THE epicenter, Thorpe uncurled
through the city in increasingly larger circles. So far, he hadn't had
any luck with the tracking device and his desperation was becoming
unmanageable.

With each tick of the clock, his chances and options dwindled.
Thorpe cursed his selfishness. He'd placed his anonymity before the
young girl's safety. Unless Alberto heeded his warning and released
the girl—an unlikely scenario—Thorpe had to enlist help. Soliciting
aid might lead to a lifetime behind bars, but Celestina deserved his
everything. If his own daughter hadn't gotten his best then Celestina
certainly would.

Thorpe pulled over, dug his work phone out of the back seat
and punched in a number. Despite the late hour, his call was
answered. Four simple words ensured he would no longer fight
alone.

"We need to meet."

FORTY-ONE

TRUDGING THROUGH THE DAMP COLD, Jenna canvassed
Carbia's neighborhood. Uniformed officers had already performed
the task, unable to find anyone who would admit to having seen
anything. Jenna knew it was just a case of not wanting to get
involved. *The damned windows had been blown out for fuck's sake!*
People had heard and seen things.

Because Jenna had neither a penis nor a police uniform, citizens
were sometimes more receptive to speaking with her. If she let her
hair down, and batted her eyes, men could get downright chatty. But
tonight was too damned cold for the fluttering of lashes.

She'd already checked the houses on Carbia's Street. Most
residents refused to answer the door. Those who did insisted having
seen nothing. Jenna saw the fear in their eyes. Even she had been
unable to persuade them to talk.

Moving to the street behind Carbia's, she started at the corner
and worked her way west. On the porch of house number two, she
lifted the lid on a small mailbox beside the front door and was
rewarded with an outgoing letter. In the upper left-hand corner of the
envelope, above the address, was a name written with impeccable
penmanship, Mary Kay Masquelier.

Jenna knocked on the door, and with minimal guilt, called out
the woman's first name, "Mary. Mary are you home?"

"Who is it?" A female's voice replied from within.

Half the battle had been won; the woman acknowledged her presence. She'd most likely answer the door. "It's the Chicago Police, Mary."

The sound of turning locks and unhooking chains culminated in the appearance of an elderly woman's questioning face behind the rapidly fogging glass of a storm door. "I already told the other officers I didn't see anything."

Jenna displayed her credentials. At the same time she put on her best lady-in-distress look, "Mary, may I please come inside? It's freezing out here."

Jenna saw confusion give way to turmoil. *Almost in.* A feigned shiver knocked the woman loose of her hesitation. Mary unlocked the storm door and allowed Jenna inside.

"Honey, you're too pretty to be a policeman."

"Thank you," Jenna answered, though the comment seemed both a compliment and an insult.

"How do you know my name, honey?"

Jenna shrugged, "I'm the police." Then, "Mary, are you aware of what happened behind your house tonight?"

"You remind me of my little Juanita. She's about your age, and every bit as beautiful."

Jenna wondered if the woman was easily distracted or deliberately steering the conversation off track. Sometimes the elderly liked to play the dementia card and were acutely aware they could get away with it. "Thank you, Mary. Does Juanita live here with you?"

"Oh no, Juanita lives in California. She doesn't visit much anymore. She has two kids of her own. Her husband's left her. Can you believe…"

"I'm sorry, Mary. In other circumstances I'd love to sit and have a good chat. But I'm investigating a murder, several murders actually, that occurred in the house behind yours."

"Oh dear…" Mary placed her hand over her heart and slowly

sat down on the edge of an antique chair. "I didn't…"

Jenna interrupted before the woman had a chance to set her lie in concrete. "Mary, I don't care what you told those other officers. I swear whatever you tell me now won't ever be written down. I understand you're scared. I promise, what you say here stays between us."

Jenna could see Mary processing her response. If the woman hadn't witnessed anything her reply would have been immediate.

"Please, Mary. I promise. Whatever you tell me doesn't leave this house." Jenna would honor her pledge. Better to have the information even if she couldn't do anything with it, than to not have it at all.

Mary nodded and slowly stood. She walked to Jenna and took her hands before looking into her eyes. "There was one man. He wore one of those masks. He carried another man over his shoulder. Went right down the alley behind my house. I was scared; all the racket you know. Explosions. Yelling. I stood there." Mary pointed to her kitchen window facing the alley. "Watched the man carry the other one over to a big white truck." Mary squeezed Jenna's hands tighter, surprisingly tight for such a small woman. "You need to be scared too, honey. And you need to quit asking so many questions."

Jenna gave a questioning look.

"He was the police. The man you're looking for is a policeman. He's one of you."

FORTY-TWO

PROMPTNESS WAS CARVED HIGH ON Thorpe's totem pole of virtues, somewhere between trustworthiness and loyalty. Promptness let others know their time was of equal value. It told them you thought yourself no more important than they. But even though tracking Carlos' daughter seemed increasingly hopeless, Thorpe found it nearly impossible to pull himself from the task. Thorpe had called for a meeting with Hull, but unfulfilled prayers had kept him spiraling through the city. Now he was twenty-two minutes late for his own party.

Despite his tardiness he paused north of his destination. If you added them together, The White Palace Grill, along with the Dunkin' Donuts across the street, offered comfort food 48 hours a day, 14 days a week.

Thorpe's hesitation stemmed from Hull having none. The detective agreed to meet at the Palace Grill without pause or inquiry. Midnight dinner requests generally require an explanation. Hull's acquiescence had Thorpe's red flag flapping in the wind.

Navigating via side view mirrors, Thorpe backed the large SUV into a space along Canal Street. Behind him sat a "frost-turquoise," 1966 Ford Mustang; the same color, year, and model as his first car. The Mustang's rear passenger tire sat atop the curb. Thorpe fought back a mild touch of nostalgia, his battle aided by the still steaming pile of vomit next to the Pony's door.

Shoving the gearshift into park, his phone vibrated in the console. He snatched up the cell, recognized the number, and used an abbreviated ten-code upon answering.

"Ninety-seven," he said, which meant he had arrived on scene.

"See you inside," Hull tersely replied.

Still behind the wheel, Thorpe inspected his clothing while running his hands up and down the material. Next he pulled down the visor, flipped open a self-illuminating vanity mirror and studied his reflection. It seemed he recognized the image staring back at him less and less with each passing day. But he didn't peer into the mirror in introspection or out of vainness, he looked for blemishes. To be more precise, he searched for Sauce stains. Sauce, as in the late King Sauce, AKA Mr. Possum—former U.S. soldier, Latin King, and kidnapper—current railroad obstruction.

Satisfied, Thorpe climbed out of the suburban locking the doors behind him. Reconsidering, he ran his palms along the forearms of his black fleece jacket and felt something crusty. Pinching the material between thumb and forefinger he came away with a blackened substance that softened as he worked it between his fingers. Blood. Thorpe pulled off the jacket and shoulder holster at the same time, laid them in the backseat, then spread the jacket over the pistol and other exposed weapons.

Finished removing the tainted jacket, flexing from the cold, he started to walk toward the restaurant when he noticed a Styrofoam take-out container on the Mustang's hood. Curious, he paused and approached the car. As suspected, he found keys dangling from the ignition and a drunken man passed-out in the reclined driver's seat.

Thorpe walked around the hood of the Mustang, made sure he wasn't being watched, and went to a knee as if tying his boots. There, he shoved a blade into the front tire. He felt a bit sheepish at his act of vandalism but when the guy woke-up and drove the antique car into something, he wouldn't be traveling quite as fast.

Leaving the would-be drunken driver to nap, Thorpe crossed

the street and headed toward the Palace Grill's illuminated red, white, and blue signs. Pulling open the restaurant's condensation obscured glass door, he was blasted by heat and the aroma of coffee and bacon grease. Wavelike muscular contractions rolled through his abdomen. Until entering, he hadn't noticed his hunger. Famished, he tried to remember the last time he'd eaten.

Deeper into the restaurant, he wasn't at all happy with what he found. Instead of meeting *someone*, he was apparently meeting a threesome. Hull sat at a corner booth accompanied by Skull and Jenna. Skull didn't cause him too much concern, but Jenna certainly did. Furthermore, not one of the three seemed particularly happy to see him. He didn't have time for this bullshit. If this was some kind of relationship intervention then they were going to be sorely disappointed.

Thorpe wanted to turn on his heels and leave, but had the feeling escape wouldn't be so easy this time. The trio looked pissed. Ultimately, a young life teetered on his actions, and he'd do what was needed to save her. If that meant letting Jenna chew his ass for a few seconds before politely telling her to get the hell out of his life— so be it. Thorpe took a deep breath of resignation and marched across the tile.

"Look, Jenna, I'm sorry I walked out on you but I really need to talk to Bob alo…"

Jenna cut him off, "Shut up, John. This isn't about me."

Thorpe redirected his attention, "Bob, can I speak with you outside?"

"Sit down, John," Hull answered.

Thorpe paused, sighed, and sat, "Let's get this over with. I need to discuss something with Bob. It's important."

Jenna started right in but not with the subject matter Thorpe had anticipated, "I just came from the scene of a multiple homicide, John. Craziest fucking thing I've ever seen in my eight years on the department. Four people dead. Two wounded. The suspect, note the singular, hauled yet another victim away from the scene. Multiple witnesses. Care to guess what they all said?"

"Victim" my ass. Sauce was no victim. The man dug his own grave. Thorpe shrugged his shoulders and raised his hands as if to say the matter didn't concern him.

"The witnesses said one man did all that. Went through those guys like they weren't even there. You know what else they said?" Jenna paused, but only for a second. "Never mind, rhetorical question. They all said that man was you. Jonathan Thorpe, one-man-fucking-army."

Thorpe had played similar hands too many times to fall victim. Sure he'd usually been the dealer but he'd seen the cards enough to know Jenna was bluffing. Carlos wouldn't talk, and his wife wasn't privy. He'd been wearing a mask, so witnesses couldn't have seen much. Still, something had happened for Jenna to suspect him. Someone probably reported seeing the "POLICE" patch on his entry vest, or might have witnessed him get into his Suburban. *A Suburban with stolen plates.* Thorpe made a mental note to change the plates again after leaving the restaurant.

"Jenna, take the tinfoil off your head. I'm flattered you think I'm such a bad ass. Now, if you're finished with tales of fantasy, I'd like to have a few minutes alone with Bob."

Thorpe rose out of his chair, implying to the group the meeting was over.

Jenna didn't relent, "I've got enough to detain you, John. Search your Suburban and see what you've got inside. What I know, only the four of us know. So sit your smart ass down."

Thorpe paused and contemplated his next move. Leaving wouldn't stop her from putting out a BOLO, APB, ATL, COS, or whatever the hell acronym Chicago cops used to alert other officers. Getting detained by CPD certainly wouldn't help Celestina. He sighed and sat back down.

"What do you want from me? A confession? You sure as hell aren't getting one."

Jenna ignored him, "I hear a little girl is missing. That true?"

Bam. She'd hit him where it counted. *Lie now and put the little girl in jeopardy? Tell the truth and possibly get help saving her life?* There really wasn't a decision to be made. After a full minute of staring at the table, debating how much he wanted to divulge, he nodded. "I've got to get her back. She's a terrified three-year-old girl, taken by a bunch of sadistic gangbangers. Are you going to help me, or stop me?"

Bob finally joined the conversation, "John, it's more complicated than that. We need to know what the hell is going on here. This can't be like last time."

"Bob, no offense to these two," Thorpe said, gesturing to Skull and Jenna, "but they don't need to hear about that shit."

"Skull already knows. He worked by my side during the entire investigation. Jenna here is a finger twitch away from calling the dogs on you. Her knowing your motivation might make a difference in whether we work together on this, or if you tell your story from a Chicago PD interrogation room."

Shit. Thorpe operated on simple principles. Near the top of a short list, if not the very top, was trust no one. He always worked alone; like anchors in a bottomless ocean—accomplices would eventually pull you under. Now he was being forced to trust those around him or face their immediate disloyalty. *Be dragged down now—or later?* Since an innocent girl's life was tethered to his, he couldn't afford to drown. Not yet.

"What do you want to know?"

"I find the beginning is always a good place to start," Skull finally chipped in.

The beginning. The beginning was when he walked into his south Tulsa home and found his wife shot to death. It was when he ran up the stairs and found his precious, blood-drained, lifeless daughter slain in her own bedroom. It began when his old life ended. Thorpe looked at Bob, "This all comes back to the murder of my family. I thought it was over, but it's not. Doesn't seem like this shit will ever end." Thorpe directed his attention to Jenna, "Did Bob tell you how my wife and daughter died?"

"Only that they were murdered inside your home. That the killers were never caught."

Thorpe took a deep breath. Those events, though sixteen months ago, were still a fresh wound. Would always be an open sore. He was not the same man he'd been then. He wasn't even the same man he'd been a month ago. *Where to begin?* There'd be no turning back after disclosing the deeds he'd committed. His life—his free life—would forever be in the hands of the three people sharing his booth.

"Officially the killers were never caught. Unofficially, well, that's another story," Thorpe began. "About a year and a half ago, I came home from work a little after two in the morning and the first thing I saw was the back door. It'd been kicked in. Then I found my wife, dead. I ran up the stairs and found our little girl, Ella, shot to death in her own bedroom…"

Though constantly on his mind, the death of his family was something he never spoke of. Barely into the story, Thorpe heard his voice quiver, his eyes mist. *Damned if he'd cry.* He closed his eyes and took a deep breath. When he began again his voice was robotic; went from relating a personal tragedy to speaking with cop-like indifference—describing just one of the many crime scenes he'd investigated. "…Bob and Skull were already working a double homicide in north Tulsa when I discovered the bodies. Their crime scene involved a couple of local shitheads who'd been shot inside a car and set on fire. Hull and Skull had to break away from that scene and respond to my location…"

STUNNED, JENNA SAT AS JOHN recited the circumstances of his family's murder. She couldn't fathom what he'd gone through. *How could a husband and parent survive such a tragedy? How could one possibly move on?* She watched John almost crack; almost succumb to the emotion—almost. Then, like a flipped switch, he replaced all things personal. "Wife and Ella" became "the bodies." "My house" replaced with "crime scene." He had deftly acquired the fine art of repression. An art she knew first hand.

John was being devoured from the inside out, his soul a parasitic insatiable entity, that would leave nothing behind but an empty shell of a man. Though he'd successfully choked off his emotions, Jenna found herself openly crying. The men avoided eye contact with one another should one fail to hold back a tear. They stared at the table, likely reflecting on their own families; two probably thinking, "What would I have done?" John thinking, "What could I have done differently?" All tamping unwanted emotions to the darkened recesses of their hearts—unseen but skulking—ready to pounce if happiness came calling. *Cops. Men.*

"…Bob and Skull reached a dead end with both sets of murders. Not their fault. They had to play by the rules and their only leads were a bunch of gangbangers who'd rather catch leprosy than talk to the police."

Jenna caught John look at her then quickly turn away. *He probably saw her tears.*

"You know how it is," he added.

She nodded.

"Anyway, Bob and Skull, they had rules to follow. I didn't. The first guy I went after was a piece-of-shit gangbanger named Marcel Newman. Responsible for several murders including an innocent little girl who got caught in the crossfire. Everyone knew he was a killer, even the judge who had to cut him loose because of uncooperative witnesses and slimy defense lawyers. Anyway, I went after him. I had no clue if he knew anything about my family's murder. I got lucky." Jenna watched as John swiveled his head, checking to see if anyone had come within earshot, then he continued, "Seems like I always get lucky when it comes to killing people."

The statement caused Hull and Skull to finally lift their gaze from napkin-wrapped silverware. *People?* Jenna's primary thought was, *How many?* His words implied Marcel Newman wasn't the first or the last. Hull and Skull must have been sharing similar thoughts for now neither man fought to avoid eye contact. Their eyes locked on John. Their investigative ears zeroed in like a tuning fork, searching for answers, tics, signs.

"Marcel and I had a long talk. He said the two men who killed my family—the ones who actually pulled the triggers—were the DD brothers, Deandre and Damarius Davis. The DD brothers happened to be the same two gangbangers who were murdered and set on fire in their car the night my family was killed. The same murders Hull and Skull were investigating when I found my…"

John paused, probably not wanting to discuss, yet again, the grisly scene he'd found.

Instead, he asked, "The DD brothers killed my family. Then someone killed them immediately after. What does that tell you?"

A waitress in a red polo interrupted before Jenna could respond. "You ready to order?"

Three voices cried out in unison, "No."

John called back the chastened waitress, apologized for his friends, and ordered coffee, water, and an omelet platter.

"Anyone else?"

"Get that bag of bones the same," John said, pointing at Skull. "He needs to sober up."

John appeared to be appreciative for the interruption and unsuccessfully tried to interject humor into the conversation. Skull simply nodded to the waitress before she disappeared into the kitchen.

"It means," Jenna said, finally able to answer John's question, "someone wanted to keep the DD brothers quiet. It means others were involved in your wife and daughter's murder."

John nodded, "Marcel, turns out, had nothing at all to do with my family's murder. But he knew things because his best buddy, Kaleb Moment, couldn't keep his mouth shut. Marcel gave up Kaleb's name after some… aggressive questioning."

Aggressive questioning? Torture. Would she torture and kill someone to avenge the death of her own daughter? She thought she probably would. Most people give themselves too much credit; they've no idea what they're capable of until tribulation is upon them. Jenna had several high school acquaintances who expressed their utter condemnation of abortion, yet upon finding themselves with child, chose the procedure over teenaged parenthood. Righteousness abounds in those untested.

"After I finished with Marcel, I paid Kaleb a visit. Kaleb broke easy. He and the DD brothers were friends. Kaleb gave me the name of the man who sent the brothers to my house. Stephen Price."

The revelation brought simultaneous head shakes from Hull and Skull. "That fucking cocksucker," Skull mumbled.

"What? Who's Stephen Price," Jenna asked.

John's eyes no longer avoided hers. He stared, unblinking, tension visible in his muscular neck. "Stephen Price *was* a cop. A Tulsa police officer."

Jenna found herself mouthing, "Oh my God!" To lose one's family to an act of violence was horrific; for the perpetrator to be like family...such betrayal. "Why?"

"There is no 'why,' that could justify what they did. Fucking assholes," Hull shook his head.

"Price was part of a band of dirty cops. In fact, they referred to themselves as 'The Band.' In reality, I had no damn clue of their existence. But in my position as supervisor of the Organized Gang Unit, I'd been getting a little too close to some of their associates and family members. I don't know if they thought I was targeting them or what, but they, as a group, decided to remove me from the equation.

"They didn't send the DD brothers with the intention of killing my family. They sent them to plant dope in my house. They wanted to frame me to get me out of the way. They didn't realize my family was home. My wife surprised them; she had a gun. They killed her. My daughter witnessed her mom get killed. They chased my little girl up the stairs and shot her to death—right there in her pretty pink bedroom."

The last half of John's sentence came out in a convulsion. The dam had nearly burst. Then the transformation again. Jenna watched John close his eyes and take a series of breaths. Melting into his chair, bunched muscles became fluid. He appeared to be in the midst of a Houdiniesque relaxation technique—preparing himself for a five minute, underwater struggle for survival.

Metamorphosis complete, John's eyes opened and he resumed, "When I found them…I don't…something inside of me broke, got all twisted. I'm not making excuses. I'm fully aware of what I've done. But I'm not the same man who walked into that house that night." *He's not the man he was thirty seconds ago!* "Still, I'm no monster." John's impossibly green eyes looked into hers, searching for… *confirmation?* "I didn't kill Kaleb. I let that little snitch go, knowing my one good deed would probably land me in prison. I took what I learned from Kaleb and ended up identifying most of the players involved in the plot to frame me. And I'll tell you right now, I don't feel bad about what I did next. I started killing those sons-of-bitches. They killed my family. When the rest realized what was happening, they came after me. They didn't fare too well."

"You former military or something?" Jenna asked.

"Or something. It's complicated and not important," John said, deflecting the question. "Part of what instigated this whole mess was that I'd arrested two associates of The Band—Leon and Lyndale Peterson. Because of me, Lyndale got a prison stretch. He's still inside and will be for a long time. His brother, Leon, was involved in the plot against me. Leon is dead… I killed him."

Jenna watched Hull and Skull nod their heads as John made the admission, as if they'd already known, or at least suspected.

"The arrest of the Peterson brothers set everything into motion, probably even the killing of my family. But Leon and Lyndale weren't alone when I arrested them that day. They had a Latin King from Chicago with them."

Jenna found herself leaning forward. This was what brought John to her city. "Who was the Latin King?"

"Luis Carbia."

"So they're all associated?"

John nodded, "There's more. Lyndale was a two-time loser. We found a bunch of dope in his car and a couple of loaded handguns. Lyndale was screwed. And even though he faced some serious time, Lyndale took the hit for all the dope and both guns. We had to cut Carbia loose. Thing is, later we end up tracing one of the handguns to a sale in Chicago. One of those guns was Carbia's for sure."

"So Lyndale Peterson took the fall for Luis Carbia."

"Which means Carbia owes Lyndale big time," John added. He looked back at Hull and Skull, "And that leads us to the Finger Basket Case."

Hull shook his head. "Damn, John. That's four more homicides we're not going to be able to close."

"Didn't happen in Tulsa."

"Well, thanks for dragging their fingers inside the city limits."

Jenna blinked and shook her head, "Excuse me?"

"I thought all this shit was behind me. But last week a damned Airborne Ranger and three geared-out Latin Kings ambushed...correction... 'attempted' to ambush me on my property. Again, they didn't fare so well."

"You're telling me," Jenna began, "four armed men ambushed you at your house and you walked out without a scratch?"

John fingered his injured ear, "No, I got a scratch."

"Why the fingers?" Skull asked.

"I didn't know for certain who was after me. The men didn't have any identification on them. I had to make sure. I left you the fingers so you'd ID them for me, without me getting you...'involved.'"

"Well, we're sure as fuck involved now aren't we," Hull said a little too loudly. Realizing he'd garnered the scattered attention of several customers, he settled back into his booth.

The food arrived and despite the ongoing discussion, John tore into his meal. The waitress, having witnessed Hull's outburst and a table of sour faces, didn't linger.

Jenna thought she'd put the pieces together, "So Lyndale knows, or suspects, you killed his brother. He can't do anything himself because he's in prison. But he has a Latin King who owes him big time and you think the Kings tried to kill you to fulfill the debt?"

"That's the way I figure it."

"What a cluster-fuck. Where does this missing girl fit into all of this?"

"Alberto Vega. He's Carbia's half brother. He also has quite a bit of clout in the King's hierarchy. Alberto's been recruiting some of the brighter Kings, feeding them into the military, and getting back trained killers. I guess he's got grandiose plans of having a quasi-commando unit at his disposal. That's why an Airborne Ranger helped those three Kings ambush me at my house. Anyway, a man named Carlos Benitez refused to…"

Jenna interrupted, "Wait, Carlos Benitez is the name of the guy who was being held captive in Carbia's house. He's in the hospital now."

"How's he doing?"

"Going to live. Not talking much from what I understand."

"Good—on both counts. Carlos completed his stint in the Army but when he got out refused to work for Vega. "

"How'd you meet him?"

Jenna listened as John explained how he'd encountered Carlos outside Carbia's home and almost put a bullet in the man's head. How Alberto had been threatening Carlos' family.

"Carlos and I were going to take turns watching Carbia's house. He was conducting surveillance when you uhh… entered my hotel room. That was him calling when you flung my phone against the wall. Somehow Alberto got his hands on Carlos' wife and daughter. Carlos must've seen them drag them into Carbia's house—which is why I ran out on you. When I got to where Carlos was supposed to be, he wasn't in his van. I knew they had him. When I finally made it down into the basement, I found Carlos strapped to a chair. They'd raped, or were at least getting ready to rape, his wife. Alberto and a soldier who goes by the name "Mongoose" had already left with the daughter, Celestina. They would've killed Carlos and his wife for sure—maybe worse things for the daughter—and she's still out there. She's still in danger."

Jenna knew about the "worse" things; she'd experienced some of them.

"John, I went to Carbia's house. You mean to tell me you did all that by yourself?" Jenna asked, incredulously, "One man? Who the hell are you anyway?"

"I'm a man who's running out of luck. Vega told Carlos he was going to sell his daughter to men who liked little girls; rape then kill her. I've got to get her back and I can't do it alone. I need help." John held his arms out, palms up, "So what's it going to be?"

A lot to digest, if everything she'd seen hadn't corroborated his story she wouldn't have believed a word. How a simple car stop and arrest led to the murder of John's wife and daughter. How those murders led to many more. She still didn't know how many men had suffered Thorpe's vengeance. In the last week alone, he'd killed a minimum of eight men. Four perished during their attempted ambush at John's home, and four more in Carbia's house. How could one man do that, and only lose a piece of an ear in the process? Then there was this: if she helped John and ignored the fact he'd killed multiple people, she could be headed for prison herself. But, if she reported him, she'd be condemning a man who'd only sought retribution on the killers of his family. And now, if he spoke the truth, was only trying to save another man's daughter from a similar fate.

Jenna didn't need a degree in psychology to understand what was at play here. She remembered the sweaty, twisted, bed sheets in John's hotel room and thinking demons were at work in his head. He had, or felt he had, a chance at redemption. He'd lost his own little girl and now had the opportunity to save another man's daughter. Maybe he thought it would bring him peace. *Who knows, maybe it would.*

"I need time to think," Jenna finally answered.

"Celestina doesn't have time. Every minute we waste, is another minute her trail grows colder."

"We're both in," Skull said, answering for his boss.

"We are?" Hull replied, pushing back and staring at Skull.

"Hell yes we are. Those fucks had it coming. Bob and I, we've lived long enough. Fuck it, tell us what you need."

"How can we help anyway, John? What do you want us to do?" Jenna asked.

"I need to know where Alberto Vega lays his head at night. I need the addresses of his associates. I need everything you got on this Mongoose guy—I have his real name written down in the Suburban. But the first thing I need is to get their cells pinged. I have their numbers and I spoke to them on the phone."

"And why shouldn't we notify Chicago PD? Get a bunch of officers looking for her instead of just us?" she argued.

"Jenna, you just got the abbreviated version of what happened. It'll take two days of explanations before they'd be ready to act. That's even if they're inclined to believe me. Bob and Skull looked into my life for a year and a half. I've got a feeling this is personal for them as well." John turned to Hull, "If the tables were turned, and some Chicago cop showed up in your office with this story, what would you think?"

"I'd think he was full of shit," Hull answered.

"Exactly. Jenna you do these things for me and I'll keep your name out of all this. More importantly, I promise you I'll get that little girl back."

"And how many people will die in the process?" Jenna asked with a long stare.

John leaned right into her gaze, "Every single one who gets in my way."

"I've got some good news and some bad news," Hull said. "The good news is we're willing to help. The bad news is, pinging a cell phone is a process."

John looked surprised, "I thought you could get one up-and-running fairly quickly?"

"We can. But there's a paper trail. We have to fill out an emergency request and fax it to the phone carrier's compliance office. They'll need a reason why we're doing this. We can get the track going in a matter of hours. Problem is, most carriers will make you follow up with a court order."

Jenna interjected, "Surely we could fabricate where our information came from? Wait, how the hell do we justify Tulsa homicide detectives working a Chicago kidnapping case?" *What the hell? She sounded like she'd already agreed to participate.*

"We'd have to tie the Kings to the Finger Basket case," Hull said.

"Just fucking tell them already," Skull said smiling. He followed the statement with a heaping fork-load of omelet, ensuring Hull would be the one to expound.

Hull obliged, "When these get approved the service provider will hook you up with a guy they call a 'switch-tech.' The switch-tech conducts the actual tracking of the phone. The cell doesn't have to be in use, only powered up. Depending on how many cell towers are in the area, they can get pretty damned accurate pinpointing the location of the phone. If they're using a smartphone, GPS will pin them down."

"So how does that help us?" Jenna asked. *There she went again; when did she move from you to us?* Her subconscious already seemed resigned to assisting these men get the girl back.

Hull answered, "Because a lot of times we keep these switch-techs on the line for hours. You work with them enough and you start to develop relationships."

"In other words," Skull piped-up between forkfuls, "we know a few switch-techs who've given us their personal cell phone numbers. We can usually call them up, tell them what we got, and bypass all the rigamarole. Everything would be completely off the books."

"Perfect," John said. "I just hope I didn't screw up. Mongoose called one of his dead friend's phones. I answered and tried to scare them into releasing the girl. I might not have accomplished anything other than making them ditch their phones."

Hull nodded, "If they've turned off their phones or removed the SIM cards, we're screwed." Then, looking at his watch, "At this hour, it'll take some time to get things up and running."

"Then we'd better get started," John replied, as he stood.

"I'm coming with you," Jenna said, again surprised with herself.

"No, I need you to find Alberto Vega's address. I've got an RF tracking device on this Mongoose guy's car and I'm trying to reacquire the signal."

"We'll need to make one stop which isn't far. I'm with you."

"I work better alone."

"If you want my help, I'm coming along."

"Fine. Let's go." John turned to Hull, "Bob, I'll call you with the cell phone numbers and all the information I've got on Mongoose and Vega."

"Hey, Carnac?"

"Yeah, Skull?"

"You take any action. You let us know first, okay?"

"Don't worry; I'll warn you if blowback is coming your way."

"I didn't mean it like that," Skull smiled. "I'm tired of you having all the fun."

"You'd better sober up then," John said as he dropped cash on the table. He headed for the door and pushed his way outside. Jenna hurried to catch him.

"I've gotta grab something out of my car. If you take off on me, it's your ass."

John glanced back at her, "I understand you have me by the

balls."

Despite the circumstances, Jenna found herself smiling. Her adrenaline was spiking. She felt the high. "Damn right I do."

Jenna dug through her trunk while keeping one eye on John. She doubted he'd take off because he was right—she did have him by the balls. At least until she made an overt act to help him, then she'd also be culpable. Entry vest and Kevlar helmet in left hand, Jenna yanked her duty bag from the trunk, set it on the sweaty street, and slammed the lid closed as John pulled beside her. Jenna passed in front of the headlights and pulled open the rear passenger side door. Looking for a place to stow her equipment, she pushed aside John's jacket and uncovered a small weapons cache in the process.

"Holy shit."

Her own equipment situated, Jenna climbed into the front seat. Speaking on the phone with Hull, John read information from a sheet of paper. She waited until he finished.

"Who the hell are you?" She asked, throwing a thumb over her shoulder, "You've got some serious hardware."

"I'm nobody. I took that gear off the four goons who tried to ambush me."

"Nobody, my ass. The gear didn't kill those men at Carbia's house, you did. And if the four goons had that gear when they came after you, it didn't do them much good."

"They underestimated me."

"No shit. Well, I don't think they will again. Seriously, John, are you former military, or what?"

"No."

"If you think the mystery act is sexy, you're wrong," Jenna said, conceding to herself she may have lied.

"The last thing I'm trying to be is 'mysterious.' It's complicated, and I've got more important things to worry about."

Jenna hesitated, "Okay, but this conversation isn't over."

"My balls. You're going to enjoy leading me around by them aren't you?"

"Yes I am. Now, have your balls drive me to my office. I need to get that information on Vega."

"Yes ma'am."

Jenna directed John to turn right on Roosevelt Road. A couple blocks to the west he laughed.

"Something funny?"

He nodded forward.

Jenna looked at the direction of his nod and saw a Chicago patrol officer performing a field sobriety test on a very wobbly man with an undone fly. Both stood behind an old aqua blue Ford Mustang with a flattened front tire. *The drunk ass had probably hit a curb.*

"Are drunk drivers funny where you come from?"

John shrugged his shoulders, "Never mind."

Faintly illuminated by the dashboard lights, Jenna took in John's profile. His right arm rested on the top of the steering wheel, triceps displaying every muscle striation. *Damn.* She hoped some schoolgirl attraction wasn't causing her to act foolishly. *No, it was more than that.*

Jenna grew up in a lower-class neighborhood. She never went hungry, but she'd never known the finer things in life either. Her biological father had never been in the picture. Her mother, the sole provider, cleaned houses while Jenna was left in the care of an unlicensed daycare. Jenna's peers were of similar ilk so she had no idea she walked the poverty line. Life was okay.

The pendulum began its downward motion when her mother's incessant net-tossing landed a shark. The shark had a steady job, was mildly attractive and somewhat charming—when not drinking. Swimming in alcohol, the shark's dead eyes would roll back and reveal his deadly disposition.

The frequency with which her stepfather drank increased with each week of marriage. Jenna suspected he'd always been a drunk but did his best to curb his urges during the brief courtship. After she and her mother began sharing his apartment, he could no longer drink alone. Sober versus drunk, he was two different men, or maybe just one—the whisky melting away the mask.

On a night when Jenna was just twelve years old, the whisky breathing shark beached himself on her bed. During the brutal session he stressed how he'd kill both her and her mother if she talked. Only a child, she'd believed him. The next morning Jenna sat silently at the breakfast table while her mother asked what was wrong.

With the question still hanging, her stepfather walked into the kitchen and helped himself to a plate of eggs. He acted as if he hadn't a care in the world. Taking a seat across from her he asked, "Yeah, Jenna, is something bothering you?" *Had it really been him who'd visited her room and stolen her childhood?* But then she saw the flash, the finned shadow just below the surface of his eyes. The shark was there. Lurking.

Jenna had been lucky in a way. Her stepfather never entered her room again. Most deviants worsen with time, increasing the frequency of their abuse. She didn't know for certain why he stopped. Maybe he'd seen a dark seed in her eyes as well, because Jenna, age twelve, decided if he ever paid her another visit, it would be his last.

Twelve is too young an age to start sleeping with a rubber stopper barricading your door and a steak knife under your pillow. She was under no illusion the trauma hadn't led to repercussions in her personal life. Sexually active at fourteen, by fifteen she was promiscuous. Shortly after joining the department, she'd married a much older, self-loving Chicago detective. The marriage ended before it began; the only positive thing he'd given her was a daughter—the narcissistic father having little to do with his own child.

Jenna's abusive past and love for daughter were the driving forces behind her willingness to help. Celestina faced a hell no child should ever have to endure. The little girl represented the very reason Jenna had chosen to become a police officer—to help those unable to help themselves.

But she'd never before risked her career. For the most part, she'd always followed "the book." Unfortunately the bad guys didn't play by the rules. Killers, drug dealers, and child abusers walked the streets because lawyers stacked the deck in their favor. Suspects had all the rights while victims had none.

Still, would I be risking my career if John was a toupee wearing, overweight hobbit? Jenna didn't want to consider the answer.

"Screw me," she breathed.

"What's that?"

"Nothing."

THORPE STUDIED JENNA'S NEARLY FLAWLESS profile and felt a wave of guilt crash over him. Twelve hours ago she was just another woman living her life. As far as he knew, she lived a drama-free existence before being sucked into the black hole of a collapsing star named Thorpe. He had no right to ask her—or Hull and Skull for that matter—for help. He was putting them all in danger of losing their jobs and freedom. Jenna risked losing everything by helping him, and he hadn't been particularly kind to the woman. *He should turn himself in. Do this legal like. Take the fall and be a man.*

"Jenna, I'm sorry."

"Sorry for what?"

"I've got no right to ask you for help."

"You didn't. You asked Bob for help. I stuck my nose in."

"You know what I mean. I should turn this over to Chicago PD and the FBI. Get everyone looking for her."

"We may have to. But I want to try it your way first. Initially at least. You're right, doing it by the book would take more time. Just you giving your story would take hours before someone began to believe you. But if we don't come up with something PDQ, we'll do whatever we have to in order to protect Celestina, including getting official help."

"Agreed."

Thorpe took another long look at the woman beside him, she seemed to have acquired a bundle of resolve since their conversation inside the restaurant.

"If we do locate her, there's a good chance things will get ugly."

"I've noticed people's life expectancies take a sudden drop when you got a beef with them. These assholes are messing with kids. Whatever happens to them, they got it coming."

Eight minutes later, Thorpe exited I-90 onto 35th Street. There, they passed within fifty yards of U.S. Cellular Field, the home of the White Sox. Driving through a tunnel beneath a plethora of railroad tracks, they entered an industrial area. Not long after, Jenna guided him between two brick non-descript buildings. In a parking lot protected by a black iron fence, Jenna ordered Thorpe to stay put.

"We don't need to be seen together. I'll say it again, you take off on me and it's your ass. I'll be fifteen minutes, tops."

Cold damp wind slipped in as Jenna opened the passenger side door. Instead of climbing out, she slammed it shut and stared at Thorpe for what seemed an eternity. *Was she having second thoughts?*

Jenna reached over with her left hand, held the back of his neck and leaned into him. She planted her full lips on his then pulled away and gazed into his eyes—searching. Thorpe didn't know if she'd found what she was looking for, but she released her grip and offered herself to the cold. "Fifteen minutes," she repeated, and slammed the door.

If the eyes truly are the windows to the soul, then what had she seen in his? Had she only found empty pools of green? Thorpe had loved before: his mother, father, sister, daughter and wife. Four of the five were dead. He'd even been *in* love once. In love with a woman who'd purposely left him without a word or trace as to where she'd gone; had left him with no possible way of ever finding her again. *What did he owe Ambretta? He owed her his life for sure, but did he owe her anything else? Should he lead a life of celibacy in hopes of encountering her again? No.*

What did he owe Jenna? Much. She risked her career and very freedom to help him—a man she barely knew. *How could he allow her to risk so much?* People he cared about and people who cared about him always seemed to disappear, or worse—die. Ambretta simply left; his father, mother, wife, and daughter, all dead. Thorpe always seemed to sidestep life's bullets; the people he loved always stepped into them, leaving him to pick up the pieces. *Maybe the dead were the lucky ones.*

Thorpe considered leaving Jenna behind. He dropped the gearshift from park to drive just as she came bounding out of the two-story building, manila envelope in hand, looking jubilant despite the circumstances. She possibly held Celestina's life in that packet. Thorpe put the Suburban back in park as Jenna entered the SUV.

"Got it," she said with a smile.

She'd run a utilities check under Vega's name and pulled information gathered by the Gang's Intel Unit. Jenna opened the envelope and studied the contents. "Well, this is interesting."

"What?"

"Alberto lives in the 'burbs."

FORTY-THREE

NEARLY THIRTY MINUTES LATER, THORPE and Jenna approached an upscale community one wouldn't normally associate with gang members. During the drive, Jenna shared the contents of a relatively thin file devoted to Alberto Vega, AKA King Slick.

Though the packet lacked concrete evidence of specific criminal activities, various sources suggested Alberto was a reasonably important figure in the Latin King hierarchy. There had been few arrests. On most accounts, Alberto appeared to be a very careful man. He insulated himself from the dirty goings-on of the gang. Nevertheless, the Intel Unit had identified his position within the Kings and had subsequently conducted periodic surveillance operations into his activities. The Intel Unit also identified a home in Palos Park as his primary residence.

Traveling southwest on State Highway 7 they were rewarded with the first faint ping from the Birddog's receiver.

"Yes!"

"What's the range on that thing?" Jenna asked.

"In perfect conditions with no interference, about four miles. But two or three is average."

"We should be about two miles from Alberto's house."

Thorpe's hope grew with the strength of the signal.

"Should we call Hull and Skull?" Jenna asked.

288

"Let's confirm first."

The wooded and lightly populated area comforted and reminded Thorpe of home. Land area wise, the difference between Chicago and Tulsa was unremarkable. But where Tulsa housed approximately 2,000 citizens per square mile, Chicago managed to pile 12,000 bodies into the same sized space. Suffocating.

Off the highway and leaving behind a city of straight lines and right angles, Thorpe found refuge on an older blacktop road that actually had curves. A couple of bends later the Birddog was singing.

"It should be two or three houses up on the right side of the street," Jenna said.

Thorpe spotted the black Dodge in a drive, "That's Mongoose's Charger. Damn, the cargo van isn't here."

"Maybe it's in the garage."

Jenna could be right, he thought. Vega wouldn't unload the child where his neighbors could see. Not wanting to be seen himself, Thorpe didn't slow as he passed the house.

"What's the plan?" Jenna asked.

"I'm going in."

"That's your plan? 'I'm going in.'"

"Yup. Don't want anything bad happening to that girl because I'm off dickin' around."

"You're not going to wait for Hull and Skull?"

"No. Don't even call 'em. We don't have time to wait for them and they'd just get in my way. Besides, they need to concentrate on pinging those phones. We still don't know if the cargo van or Celestina is here."

Clear from the house, Thorpe guided the Suburban to the side of the road and climbed in the back to prepare. He continued giving instructions as he geared-up.

"You keep an eye on the house. If someone leaves while I'm gone, follow them. If you lose contact with me, call the police—anonymously. Here's my prepaid phone. It can't be traced."

"I'm not a damned paperweight. I'm going with you."

"No. This is non-negotiable. Alberto got out with Celestina last time because no one was guarding the front. They strolled right out of the house while I fucked around in the back yard. I don't want that to happen again. Plus, if we both get shot, who's going to call in the cavalry. You stay and watch the front."

He watched as Jenna processed the logic. She nodded her head.

"Turn us around while I get ready."

Thorpe put on his fleece jacket, fully prepared to add yet more stains to its material as Jenna got behind the wheel. He pulled his black entry vest over the fleece, adjusted the Velcro straps, attached a thigh holster, and shouldered an MP5. He topped it off with a black balaclava. Jenna turned the Suburban around and pulled up so she could watch the end of Alberto's driveway, but not his home. If someone looked out of the house they wouldn't be able to see the Suburban. If a vehicle left they wouldn't see Jenna until already committed to the street.

Thorpe returned to the front seat with a small headset that matched the one atop his balaclava. He handed it to Jenna.

"Coms. Here's how they work…"

Equipment strapped down to avoid unnecessary noise, Thorpe moved with haste toward Alberto's home. The lots here were large, at least half an acre and heavily wooded. The woods were the place Thorpe felt most at ease. He headed there now, seeking the concealment of the trees.

Alberto's home was built into the downward side of what Chicago would call a hill. A driveway sloped down from the street to an attached two-car garage. A large window sat to the right of the driveway. The curtains were drawn, but lights burned inside. Alberto wouldn't be sleeping; he'd be trying to ascertain how many of his associates kept his brother company in the afterlife. He'd be worrying about joining the party.

Based on information gleaned from Alberto's file, Thorpe agreed with Jenna that this place was the man's sanctuary. Alberto had gone out of his way to separate the residence from his gang activities. They also agreed his lifestyle appeared greater than his stature within the gang would warrant. It was possible, probable even, the Kings didn't know of this house. Surveillance teams had never observed any fellow Kings visit the place. In fact, except for a "surgically enhanced blonde," they hadn't noted any visitors at all. Thorpe decoded "surgically enhanced blonde" to mean large breasts. Hopefully, since Alberto had no reason to believe Carlos Benitez would possesses the wherewithal to locate his home, only Alberto, Mongoose, and Big Tits would be inside. Thorpe thought he could handle two men and a couple piles of silicone, even if one of the men was a professional trigger puller.

To avoid windows, Thorpe approached the house from the garage side of the home. He used the thermal scope to search the surrounding grounds. His encounter with the man in the doghouse had not been long ago, and the idea of an ambush lingered in his mind. There was no fence here and Thorpe hoped that translated into no dog. Keeping to the small band of trees dividing Alberto's home from his neighbor's, Thorpe inched forward, both eyes open, one peering through the scope.

Thorpe spoke into his throat mic, "Headed along side two, toward the rear."

"Copy," Jenna replied.

Three steps, heel to toe. Stop. Look. Listen. Four steps, repeat. Two steps, and so on; varied—no distinguishable pattern. Thorpe moved slowly, but faster than he would have liked. Unbearable thoughts of the little girl tore at him. They propelled him faster than was prudent. Though speed and aggression served one well once an assault began, patience and stealth was the rule prior to attack. Thorpe didn't have time to exercise patience. He prayed Celestina wouldn't be the one to pay for his lack of discipline.

The back of Alberto's property revealed a split-level home. A large wooden deck ran the entire length of the house. It jutted out over a smaller brick patio centered by a sliding glass door. The upper deck had two sets of French doors, one probably leading to a living room or kitchen, the other most likely to the master bedroom.

Between the patio and woods sat a sloping back yard, maybe fifteen yards deep. Lights from a neighboring home twinkled below and behind the property, the two homes cleaved by a thick stand of trees. Private. Thorpe continued working his way down the hill. Concealed in the trees, neighbor's house to his back, Thorpe took a knee and checked his watch. He'd already burned up seven minutes since exiting the Suburban.

He didn't have time to properly plan his assault. Celestina didn't have time. He brought the scope to his eye and tried to search the interior of the lower floor. The lights were off, and curtains drawn. He raised his weapon, bringing the upper floor into partial view. Because of the steep grade, and protruding deck, Thorpe could only see the top foot or so of the windows. Space enough to see the lights were on and curtains drawn on one set of French doors; the curtains standing open on the set to his right. That's where he would enter. He didn't have time for stealth. He'd have to go loud.

Thorpe used the quick-release mount to remove the thermal scope. He'd use open sights and an attached flashlight for darkened rooms.

"Two levels on rear of home. Lower level dark. Upper level lit up like a Christmas tree."

"Copy. No movement out front."

"Roger that. Making entry on upper level in less than thirty."

Thorpe inhaled deeply, closed his eyes, imagined his actions, and steeled himself. He breathed, "Screw it," as he rose and jogged, weapon up, across the small yard. He bounded up four brick steps to the lower patio, then the wooden stairs leading to the upper deck. He took those steps two at a time. Landing on the upper level, he bypassed the curtain concealed doors and hurried toward the glowing room to the right.

Thorpe was rewarded with an unencumbered view of a large, brightly lit, master bedroom. Each door had panes of glass enclosed by thin strips of wood and caulk. Peering through the panes, Thorpe saw something that turned his stomach sour. Once-white linens stained with fresh blood, covered the bed. *Motherfuc.....*

"Move up to where you can watch the front. Park so you don't get hit with stray rounds. I'm going in."

"Copy."

Thorpe selected full auto on his silenced weapon, depressed the trigger, and sent rounds into the glass panes. Wearing several layers of clothing topped with Kevlar, knowing windows like these were made of safety glass, Thorpe had little concern of being cut when he followed the bullets. He crashed through the wood and shattered glass onto the bedroom carpet staring up at a hideous velvet painting of a moonlit wolf. In a fraction of a second he was up and moving, scurrying into the master bath. He almost went down on the blood-slickened, tile floor. Towels, stained pink, hung on the side of the tub. Marble countertops were freckled with blood.

Jenna's strained voice came through his earpiece, "Car leaving in a hurry!"

Damn it, not again. "Follow it!"

Thorpe flew out the bedroom and scurried down a short hallway with his weapon shouldered. At the mouth of an expansive living room-kitchen combo, he lowered his weapon and sprinted through the house. Thorpe entered a utility room, yanked open a door to an already open garage and saw his own Suburban race past the driveway. The black Dodge Charger was still parked in the driveway. *Shit!* They'd left in a vehicle he couldn't track with the Birddog.

Whoever fled must have already been inside the garage and the car when Thorpe made entry. *Had they seen him approach or was his timing just that shitty?* It dawned on him that—in a panic—Alberto and Mongoose might have left Celestina behind.

"Just try to keep the car in view," Thorpe advised Jenna, "Don't do anything stupid. You're not equipped to deal with an armed soldier."

"Kiss my ass."

"I fucking mean it!"

"Okay, okay."

"Jenna, there's a lot of blood in the house. I hope we're not too late."

Her static laced voice crackled on the headset, "I'm stopping them."

"No!"

"I'M STOPPING THEM!" JENNA REPEATED. Thorpe's response had been a definitive "no." But, she couldn't follow the car on this desolate road for any length of time without being observed, and damned if she'd let them slip away with an injured or dying little girl. The car she followed was a newer Mercedes. It would easily outrun the Suburban if they noticed a tail—and they *would* notice. *It was now or never.* This might be her final act, but she couldn't live with herself if she let them escape with Celestina. The most she could really hope for was to delay them—give John a chance to catch-up.

Her vice-like grip left indentations in the soft steering wheel as she fed the accelerator. As the heavy SUV closed on the Mercedes, Jenna veered into the oncoming lane. Her unfamiliarity with the Suburban left her fumbling for the lever to the windshield wipers. The mist had thickened just short of being rain. Her visibility was for shit. The tinted windows of the sleek luxury car she chased only made her task more difficult; she had no idea if she was about to engage one man…or six. The potential consequences of her actions ripped through her mind. The Mercedes was traveling around 40 miles per hour. If it crashed, and Celestina wasn't secured in a child seat—a near certainty—the collision could be fatal.

Instead of slamming the Mercedes off the road, she'd try a pursuit immobilization technique, more commonly known as a PIT maneuver. Jenna slowly swerved into the Mercedes. The Suburban's right front bumper struck just behind the Mercedes' left rear tire. The sound of metal on metal infiltrated the quiet cabin as the rear end of the Mercedes slid out to the right and the driver's side contacted the front bumper of the ample SUV. Jenna braked to minimize contact. The Mercedes rotated 180 degrees. Now forward of the spun-out Mercedes, Jenna's right leg shook as the antilock brakes fought to bring the lumbering Suburban to a stop.

Jenna threw the gearshift into park even before the machine finished sliding to a stop. Out of the door, weapon up, the near freezing mist coated her face as her rubber-soled boots carried her across wet asphalt toward the stalled car. Everything oddly surreal, life moved in slow motion. The stillness eerie. Jenna parted the mist, aiming through night-sights at opaque tinted windows, ready to die for a little girl she'd never even met.

INSIDE ALBERTO'S GARAGE, THORPE STARED at a garish, bright orange custom chopper, and resisted the urge to kick the motorcycle on its side. He hadn't been able to raise Jenna, who, armed only with a handgun, had little hope of surviving an encounter with professional soldiers. If "Mongoose" was equipped as well as the men who'd ambushed Thorpe at his home, she didn't have a prayer. He began to pat his pockets for his cell phone then remembered he'd given it to Jenna before exiting the Suburban. *Stupid.*

Thorpe had long been liberated of fear for his physical self. It was the one freedom granted to him the night his wife and daughter were slain. Nothing much remained worth fretting over—including his life. But now, with both Celestina and Jenna in imminent danger, Thorpe felt something he hadn't in a long time—panic. Jenna might be fighting for her very existence and he was stuck in a garage with his thumb lodged firmly up his ass. The motorcycle had no keys.

Thorpe ran out of the open garage and returned to the Dodge Charger. Earlier he'd tried both doors finding them locked. Panic building, he no longer worried about neighbors and sent a silenced three round burst into the driver's side window. Pushing in the glass with his elbow, he reached inside and unlocked the door. He checked the ignition, above the visor, and under the carpet. No keys. Hotwiring today's newer cars is a thing of the movies. The Charger wasn't going anywhere.

Thorpe nearly shouted in frustration. His physical state a hindrance, he closed his eyes, concentrated on his breathing, and calmed himself. *He'd seen something? Where?* Thorpe continued with the exercise. Still sitting in the Charger, he felt his body floating down into the bucket seat—down into nothingness. Nearly free of the physical world.

Click. Earlier, when he'd charged through the house, he'd passed keys. Thorpe saw them clearly now in his mind's eye—three pegs in the utility room, one holding a ring of keys. Thorpe scrambled out of the Charger, reentered the house, and located the ring. He didn't find a Chrysler key but he found what looked like an ignition key with no markings.

Hurrying back to the bike Thorpe tried the unmarked key. It slid smoothly into the ignition and turned. He climbed aboard but couldn't figure out how to start the motor. Anxiety rapped on the door so recently closed. *Is Jenna fighting for her life? Is she dead? Did she have Celestina? So much blood in the bathroom...was Celestina beyond saving? Would he have two more deaths on his conscience?* Thorpe's emotionally bankrupt psyche couldn't survive another withdrawal. He pushed the thoughts aside. He'd have time to second-guess himself later.

Having located and opened the fuel line, when he thumbed the start button, the engine roared to life. The bike was deafening in the enclosed space. Thorpe rumbled out of the garage squinting into a sea of heavy mist.

Forks "raked-out" to the extreme, the bike had been built to command attention; just what Thorpe wanted to avoid. Close to ten feet in length, it sported custom pipes that shook the neighborhood as Thorpe thundered after Jenna. Add to the equation his weapon-adorned entry vest, and his only hope of going unnoticed would be empty roads and the concealment of the mist. Bad thing: slick roads, two wheels, and speed do not get along with each other.

Tracking the cars through Alberto's neighborhood proved simple. There were two sets of tracks on the wet blacktop—Jenna's and the vehicle she followed. Then he encountered a T-intersection and his first decision. Other vehicles had recently traveled the road. He couldn't discern which tracks belonged to the Suburban. Again he tried to summon Jenna on the coms but received no response. She must be out of range, occupied, or incapacitated. With a guess, Thorpe turned east. The 300mm rear tire almost slid out from underneath him as he yanked back on the throttle in the direction of downtown Chicago.

Near freezing temperatures stung his eyes. Mist conjoined tears ran down his cheeks, diminishing his already pathetic visibility. His attempt to catch Jenna on the bike was foolish; he couldn't continue like this. He had to summon help. Thorpe focused on a set of advancing headlights and made a desperate decision. He'd commandeer the approaching car…or die trying.

Thorpe crossed the center line, the light from his headlight reflecting off a wall of mist back into his wind-torn eyes. Playing a deadly game of chicken only he could lose, he drove toward the center of the headlights. The approaching vehicle traveled much too fast for the conditions. Maybe the driver didn't see him—it wasn't stopping—it wasn't even slowing. Thorpe closed his eyes, but could still see the lights through his eyelids. He felt calm. Perhaps the peace he'd been so desperately seeking would finally be delivered by a lumbering chunk of metal on a lonely, mist-slickened road.

FORTY-FOUR

"CALL JOHN, WE'VE GOT A signal!"

Skull's outburst caused Hull to slam down his own phone, disconnecting the call without explanation to the man on the other end. Skull had been working with a switch-tech in an attempt to get a fix on Alberto's cell.

"Hold on Skull, let's get some info before I call him."

Probably headed for a hangover, Skull had sobered, yet remained animated. The detectives were used to working homicides—they'd become routine. But neither had worked a case with such a personal connection. Jonathan Thorpe had somehow become like an adoptive child to both men. The realization caused Hull to shudder, because under this scenario, Skull would be his spouse.

"Is the signal moving or stationary?"

Skull repeated the question over the phone.

"Mobile."

"Location?"

Skull recited the general location back to Hull.

"How do you want to play this, Skull? We joining the game, or just coaching from the sideline?"

"Screw the sideline, boss. Let's get that little girl back."

Hull nodded. "Okay then." He picked up his cell and called the

298

number to Thorpe's prepaid phone. "I'm not getting an answer," Hull relayed to Skull. "Let's move. I'll call him again from the car."

Skull told the switch-tech he'd call him back in less than five. Both men tossed on coats and grabbed their weapons, painfully aware they weren't adequately armed. Hull had a Glock 27 loaded with ten .40 caliber cartridges. Skull, forever old-school, carried a five shot Smith snub-nose .38. Neither man brought body armor or additional ammunition. When they'd packed in Tulsa, they hadn't anticipated anything more dangerous than a cut finger—they'd come to shuffle paper.

An impossibly long ride in the hotel's elevator took them to an apocalyptic parking garage. Hull got behind the wheel keeping Skull free to speak with the switch-tech. Barreling out of the enclosed garage, the men found themselves ensconced in heavy fog.

"Holy shit, it's like soup," Hull said. The conditions would greatly diminish their response time.

Skull got the switch-tech back on the line, "It's me. Any change? Okay. This is life and death, brother. Stay on it."

"I'm going to try John again," Hull advised.

Hull found the contact and hit send. This time the phone clicked open but instead of reaching Thorpe, he heard a woman scream.

"Jenna!" Hull yelled into the mouthpiece, "Jenna is that you?!"

BACK IN THE SUBURBAN, JENNA was still alive. That could change in a hurry if she didn't reduce her speed through the sheeting mist. A cell phone sang its tune somewhere on the floorboard; it must have been thrown from the center console during the PIT maneuver. Fumbling for and finally locating the device, Jenna looked at the illuminated screen and read Hull's name. She used her bloody fingers to accept the call then turned her attention back to the shrouded road. *Headlights!* Actually just one headlight. Jenna dropped the phone, stomped the brake, veered right, and shrieked as the side view mirror was torn from the SUV.

What the hell! Out of the SUV, once again she ran through the mist, weapon out and ready. She found a motorcycle lying on its side, John lying beside it, SMG pointed at her face. He lowered his weapon as she approached.

Jenna rushed to his side, "Are you okay?"

Instead of answering, he slowly pushed himself up from the pavement and embraced her.

"I am now."

Standing on blacktop, waves of mist slapping her left cheek, Kevlar vest pinched between bodies, the hug wasn't the most comfortable she'd ever received, but she couldn't think of one better.

"Thank God you're alive," he said.

She watched his eyes change from relief to fear. He pulled away and looked at the blood on her hands and arms. "Celestina?"

"Not her blood. She wasn't in the car. I'll fill you in but we have to get off the road."

Jenna noticed John's first few steps were tentative, his right leg had a hitch. But like an NFL running back, shook off the limp as he increased in speed. The slickened streets had likely worked in his favor—his momentum carrying him forward instead of down into the pavement. He'd been lucky.

Back inside the Suburban, John shook violently. He was soaked. Jenna turned up the heat, shifted into drive and negotiated a three point turn on the narrow road. She headed back toward downtown Chicago.

"What happened?" Thorpe asked through clenched teeth. His hands held up to the heater vents.

"It wasn't the cargo van, it was a Mercedes. Alberto's girlfriend was driving. She was alone. Had the shit kicked out of her."

"Thank God."

"What?"

"I mean better than the alternative. I thought I was too late."

"The girlfriend is really fucked up. She said Alberto beat her ass."

"What about Celestina?"

"That's why she got her ass beat; for not minding her own business. She came out of the bedroom when she'd been told not to, and saw a little girl and another man—probably Mongoose—there with Alberto. She said Alberto went crazy; beat her half-to-death. I believe her; the girlfriend was pretty bloody. Afterward, she was cleaning herself up in the bathroom when she heard them leave. She waited a few minutes to make sure they were really gone, then took Alberto's Mercedes to drive to the hospital. Alberto, Mongoose, and Celestina were gone before we ever showed up."

"Damn it. Unless Hull and Skull come through, we've got no way of finding them now."

"Shit! Hull called. I was looking down at the damned phone when I almost ran you over."

Immediately, both started searching for the dropped cell. As if on cue, a ringing emanated from the floorboard between Jenna's legs. John placed his left hand on her inner thigh and stuck his head under the steering wheel in search of the device.

He rose with the phone propped against his right ear, his left hand— *absent mindedly?*—lingered.

"Skull? Yeah, Jenna's okay. What you got?"

Jenna could hear Skull's muffled voice but couldn't make out what he was saying. John slapped the dash.

"What? What is it?" Jenna interrupted their conversation.

"They've got a fix on Alberto's phone. We're still in it!"

FORTY-FIVE

THORPE LISTENED AS SKULL RECITED Alberto Vega's
direction of travel—or at least his phone's direction of travel.
Hopefully, man hadn't been separated from device. As Skull spit out
street names, Thorpe repeated them to Jenna who sat behind the
wheel. It was his SUV but this was her city. Skull's voice hit a
higher octave when the phone's signal finally came to rest.

Thorpe relayed the location to Jenna and asked how many
minutes away they were.

"In good weather, thirty minutes. In this…," Jenna shrugged
her shoulders, "who knows?"

Thorpe spoke into the phone, "We're about 45 minutes out.
This shit is starting to freeze. The bridges are getting slick."

"Same here."

"Skull…?"

"Yeah?"

"Don't get too close. I don't want them to get spooked. They
might smarten up and ditch their phones. This is our last chance."

"You think I'm too old and stupid for this?"

Skull seemed to be in an uncharacteristically good mood.

"Well, I don't think you're too old."

"John?"

"Yeah?"

"Fuck you."

"I love you too. Don't get your bony ass shot up before I can get there to save it." He terminated the call before Skull could respond.

Thorpe had been keeping an eye on Jenna. Her normally smooth skin was bunched around pursed lips, her knuckles white on the steering wheel. She needed to relax in order to think clearly, to react fluidly.

"I think Skull is enjoying himself."

"And you're not?"

Thorpe didn't take offense to her question. It was a legitimate inquiry given his sense of humor had no shut-off valve.

"No, I'm not enjoying myself. A little girl's life depends on me not fucking up. My stomach would be twisted in a knot if I didn't know how to control it."

"Sorry, I didn't mean to…"

Thorpe interrupted, "Don't be sorry, Jenna. If Celestina wasn't in the picture, you'd probably be right. I'm not sure anymore." Thorpe tapped his temple with his index finger, "I might have a few crossed wires up here."

Jenna glanced his way then back out the windshield. "Don't we all."

"Hull and Skull are close and they're good cops. We'll get there; take it slow and steady. We're not going to be any help if we slide off into a ditch."

Jenna nodded and let up on the accelerator, but her knuckles remained white on the wheel.

"You hear of tactical breathing?"

"Some."

Thorpe walked her through the diaphragm-employing, rhythmic breathing. He had her concentrate on specific muscles: contracting them, releasing them. He watched as her knuckles regained their color. "Use a word or phrase to repeat while you do the exercise. With about ten years of practice, just saying the phrase will work wonders," Thorpe smiled.

"What phrase do you use?"

"I usually say the words 'Fuck me,' over and over," Thorpe laughed. "A couple of other techniques and a finely tuned sense of humor will get you through most anything."

"So what do *you* use in place of a finely tuned sense of humor?"

Thorpe laughed again.

Jenna nodded at the array of weapons strapped to Thorpe's entry vest, "So are you ever going to tell me who you are; ex-SEAL or something?"

"That's an insult to SEALs everywhere."

Jenna's hair had fallen across her cheek and Thorpe found himself brushing the strands back behind her ear. Even under tremendous stress she dazzled. Scientists would probably call her symmetrical—eyes, ears, nose and mouth all properly aligned. *Whatever.* She had one of those faces. You'd think about it for the next hour after passing her on the street.

No matter her looks, she deserved an honest answer.

"My father was in the Army. Before that he was a fighter. It's the only skill set he ever really had. Instead of playing catch with a baseball he taught me how to pluck someone's eye out with a toothbrush," Thorpe laughed, only half joking.

"How adorable. What did he do in the Army?"

"Seems he did a lot more than I ever knew. He didn't talk about work much."

"What happened to him?"

"He disappeared when I was sixteen. Presumed dead."

"Presumed?"

"He's dead."

Perhaps sensing his reluctance to discuss his father, Jenna changed subjects. "So, cowboy, you have a woman back in Tulsa, or what?"

Images of Ambretta fluttered through Thorpe's mind. "No."

"You hesitated."

Ambretta had disappeared without as much as a goodbye. He'd likely never see her again. "There's no one."

"Yeah right."

"What about you, Ms. Smith?"

"Well, you were right about one thing. Smith is not my maiden name."

"You're married?"

"Was. Divorced. The only thing I got worthwhile was a precious little girl. Her daddy's a Chicago cop and an asshole."

Thorpe nodded his head, "That explains a lot."

"Such as?"

"For one, your willingness to risk your job to get Celestina back. And two, your reluctance to date fellow cops."

Jenna smiled, "You been asking about me?"

He only shrugged. "Was that your ex I met at the crime scene? The detective who made the Barney Fife jokes."

"No. He's just another asshole who asked me out and who I turned down. He probably didn't like the fact I was flirting with you."

"You were flirting with me?"

"You're a little thick aren't you?"

"I'm too stupid to try and argue otherwise. What's her name, your little girl?"

"Samantha."

"Jenna, do Samantha a favor and quit putting yourself in danger. Pitting that car was stupid."

"And just what would you have done?"

"That's different; I don't have anyone depending on me; just my two mangy dogs."

Though Jenna was confident she knew the way, Thorpe fed the coordinates Skull had given him into the GPS. The device told them they would arrive in twenty-four minutes. Its calculations didn't factor in freezing mist.

"How 'bout," Jenna began, "when this is all over—and if we're still alive—you take me on a legitimate date."

Thorpe extended his hand. When she took his, he simply stated, "Deal. But one that I'll let you break."

Taking his hand back, he fished out a box of cartridges, released the magazine on his MP5, and replaced the rounds he'd used to shatter windows on Alberto's home and on Mongoose's Charger. "If things go well we'll soon have Celestina back in the arms of her parents. But I swear if she's hurt, you're not going to recognize those assholes when I'm finished with them." Thorpe slammed the thirty-round magazine back into the receiver. "We'll see if you still want to date me when this is over."

FORTY-SIX

ALBERTO STABBED A CIGARETTE OUT in a sand-filled plastic bucket, then lifted himself off a disheveled couch. He'd wanted a few minutes alone in the office to gather his thoughts. The only thing he came away with was the stench of marijuana and stale beer trapped in his clothing. The couch left him scratching exposed skin and worrying about what else had been deposited on the upholstery over the years.

Alberto opened a door separating the office from the shop. The shop was full of auto parts, tools, stacked tires, and now—a white cargo van; the van straddled atop a service pit. The office and the shop were actually two separate buildings, the former being an afterthought. Both of the poorly insulated buildings nestled in the midst of a sprawling salvage yard.

Entering the shop, Alberto found three of his men standing beside the van, and despite Alberto's warnings, none appeared to be concerned with anything other than cutting jokes and farts.

"Where's Mongoose?"

"Here," came a voice from the corner of the garage. The soldier rose off the concrete floor from behind a stack of tires, automatic rifle strapped across his chest. The greasy floor was probably a cleaner surface than the one from which Alberto had just risen.

Alberto redirected his attention to the other three men, "You ready here?"

The shop manager, a squat man in his forties wearing greasy blue coveralls, answered. "All ready boss."

Alberto opened the rear of the van, ensured Carlos' duct taped daughter was still in good condition, then pulled her roughly out the doors. "Anybody touches the girl while we're gone, and my friend here," Alberto pointed to Mongoose, "will cut your dicks off with a rusty hacksaw." The statement earned a couple of forced laughs. "You think I'm fucking joking?"

The laughs stopped.

Alberto didn't give a shit about the girl's wellbeing. His concern was that used products weren't worth nearly as much as those still in their unopened, original packages. Plus, the girl served as his insurance policy against the unknown man, or men, helping Carlos.

Alberto pointed at the shop manager, "Something happens to her it's your ass."

Ready to leave, he tossed the keys to Mongoose who slid behind the wheel. The shop manager pulled a chain raising an aluminum rolling garage door. Cold mist drifted into the shop splattering the windshield.

Slowly, Mongoose drove down a weedy drive that hadn't seen fresh gravel since it was first laid. The van's headlights cut a swath through skeletonized cars lining their route like disinterested viewers of a one car parade. A sad passage to a glorious destination.

Mongoose fetched a vibrating phone from his jacket pocket, "Yeah? Good. Alright. Yes. I'll tell him." Mongoose lowered the phone, "King Ghost is ready to go."

"Let's hope he lasts longer than King Fubb and his dumbassed friends. I still don't know what the fuck happened in Tulsa. Too much shit to deal with."

"I did some checking while in the shop. Got some more bad news—Carlos is still alive. Wife too. They're both at Holy Cross Hospital."

"Can't neither one of 'em live."

"They're probably being watched by the cops."

"They talk yet?"

"Gotta assume they have."

Alberto paused, "Don't matter. Telling the cops something and living long enough to testify is different. Put out a kill order on both Carlos and his wife."

Mongoose nodded, "Your brother's dead. Your brother and everyone in that house. Everyone except Carlos and his wife, that is."

"Half-brother," Alberto corrected without a trace of emotion, "And we knew that already."

"All taken out by a single man," Mongoose said, with a hint of what Alberto thought was admiration. "From what I hear."

"One man? Good. We can handle one man."

"Never underestimate a highly trained and motivated individual."

Alberto stared at Mongoose, "You read that in a fuckin' Army manual? Besides, that's why I have you here."

"I'm almost looking forward to meeting him," Mongoose smiled. "Almost."

"You'll get your fucking chance," Alberto said, as a man with an SKS rifle draped over his shoulder let them out of the gate.

Alberto's mood was nearly as sour as the weather; the police undoubtedly had his name by now, some Special Forces friend of Carlos ran around with the intent of ending his life, and his Tulsa crew had up and disappeared.

Things had gotten out of hand. The time had come to sever ties with the Kings. *Blood-in, Blood-out? Fuck that!* Beatings were for assholes who didn't have his intellect and monetary means—means which were about to increase tenfold. When he had cash in hand, he'd set events in motion. Once underway, those events couldn't be stopped. Not by him. Not by anyone. And those events would be a continuing source of income. Best thing, he'd designed it to work totally independent of the Nation. Soon he'd be clear of the Latin Kings and making easy money. By day's end, he'd disappear with all the resources he'd ever need. Lost in thought, Alberto barely registered Mongoose's phone conversation. Carlos and Eva had just earned a "T.O.S." order—Terminate On Sight.

"I THINK I'VE SEEN THIS place in a movie," Skull joked.

"The Sandlot?" Hull replied.

"I was thinking of something a bit more ominous."

The two men were driving past "B&G Salvage," peering at a rusted, eight-foot, corrugated-steel fence, topped with barbed wire. Every twenty yards alternating metal signs issued warnings. One stated, "ATTACK DOGS ON PREMISES," the next, "NEVER MIND THE DOG, BEWARE THE OWNER." The latter message was accompanied by an illustrated hand holding a large revolver pointed at the viewer's face. Hull doubted the signs were idle threats. The front gate closed, it didn't appear the salvage yard was open for business. Somewhere inside B&G's perimeter was Mr. Alberto Vega, or at least the man's cell phone.

"What do we do?" Skull thought out loud.

"What can we do?" Hull replied. "We sit tight and wait for John to get here."

"It's going to be a bitch getting inside there unnoticed."

Hull watched Skull retrieve his Smith .38, flip open the cylinder, and check that each of the five chambers on the revolver held a cartridge.

"Shit. We're not ready for this," the older man mumbled.

Hull noticed Skull had lost his earlier swagger. The man had seen action in Vietnam and he'd been in multiple shootings on the department. But those had been years ago. He'd been a homicide cop for the last twenty, and unlike the movies, homicide detectives were not on the short list of police personnel likely to engage in a firefight.

Gunplay was akin to skydiving. It sounds romantic until one stands at the open door, wind clawing at the face, peering at the terrifying drop. And though Skull had made previous jumps out that open door, he'd forgotten what the view looked like. Skull was no coward but he wasn't stupid either. Because, sometimes, no matter how carefully packed, the chute just doesn't open. And in this case, neither man had packed their chutes with proper care.

Reading his partner's thoughts, Hull assured Skull—and himself—they weren't alone in what now seemed an improbable task, "If I know John, he probably has enough weapons and ammunition for everyone."

Skull pointed to a white pole rising from the backside of the fence. On top of the pole sat a plastic orb. Camera. "Better drive on by, boss. We're not alone."

Hull pulled around the block and parked at a considerable distance. The switch-tech assured Skull he'd notify them if Alberto's phone went mobile.

"Better tell Thorpe about the fucked-up situation," Hull told his long-time-friend.

Before Skull could punch in the digits, his phone began ringing.

"It's the switch-tech," Skull informed. Then, into the phone, "Talk to me…Shit."

"Vega's on the move again." Skull spoke as if discouraged, but Hull heard relief in the older man's voice. Both men knew assaulting the salvage yard would have been a bloody affair, and some of that blood would have been their own.

FORTY-SEVEN

THORPE HELD PHONE TO EAR with the realization
Celestina's very life teetered on cell phone technology. The cell
Skull tracked. The cell Skull used to communicate with the switch-
tech. And the cells Skull and Thorpe used to communicate with each
other.

He and Jenna had been ten minutes away from the salvage yard
when Skull called and informed them the signal was once again
mobile. The news elicited a frustrated growl, and Thorpe's growl
elicited a concerned glance from his chauffer. Based on Skull's
description, the yard would have been difficult to infiltrate. But
every time the van moved, it created new locations where the girl
could be unloaded, making her trail much more arduous to follow.

"They exited 94, east bound on 170th Street," Thorpe repeated
Skull's direction of travel to Jenna.

"Got it."

"North on Torrence Avenue."

Jenna nodded.

"He's pulling into a Walmart parking lot on the east side of the
road."

Jenna had been making up ground.

"We're less than five out."

"Skull, we're less than five out. Try to get a visual but don't get too close. I need the element of surprise." Thorpe looked at Jenna, closed his eyes and said, "Breathe." Then followed his own advice. "Remember our mantra—fuck me," Thorpe smiled.

"You're just trying to trick me into extending an invitation."

"You're on to me." Then, "Jenna, we're going to get her back."

She nodded but her movements were twitchy.

"Hey, look at me." Jenna turned and looked into his eyes. He smiled, "I'm pretty good, you know."

"At what?"

Thorpe laughed. "Well, now that you mention it, not a whole lot. But when it comes to violence, it seems I was born for it. I was definitely raised for it."

Skull interrupted their back-and-forth. "We've got eyes on. They're still in the white cargo van. It's parked on the northwest side of the Walmart lot. They're a good distance from the store so I doubt they're there to pick up toiletries. Hull and I are parked to their west in the lot of a UPS Store. Bunch of exits out of this place."

Skull imparted information rapid fire—his adrenaline spiking. Thorpe pictured his skeletal friend—a cell phone pressed against each hair-filled ear, veins pulsating on the sides of his head. Thorpe almost made the mistake of telling him to relax, which would have been similar to telling a woman to "calm down" during an argument.

"Okay, Skull, we're making the corner. Stay on…"

"Wait," Skull interrupted, "something's happening."

Jenna turned off Torrence toward the lot, as Thorpe listened to a few seconds of silence before Skull started back up again. "Exchange. A guy just left the cargo van and walked over to a pickup truck. Shit, *everyone's* moving."

"Who's everyone?" Thorpe asked.

Thorpe could hear Skull talking to several different people at the same time. He was talking to Hull and probably speaking with the switch-tech on another phone, all the while trying to keep Thorpe informed. Skull's stress was apparent in his voice.

"Talk to me Skull."

"Damn it, hold on," Skull shouted. "Okay, some guy walked away from a truck and one of our guys got into it. The guy who left the truck is walking into the Walmart store. One of our guys is driving away in the truck, a blue Ford F-150."

"What's going on?" Jenna asked.

"Some type of exchange. One of our guys from the cargo van jumped into a blue Ford F-150."

Thorpe pointed ahead, "Shit. The Ford's headed right toward us."

Skull continued, "The cargo van is following the truck."

Thorpe spoke to Jenna, "Just keep driving straight past. But see if you can spot the girl in either vehicle." Then into the phone, "Where's the little girl, Skull?"

"Don't know—haven't seen her. They didn't switch her here."

"You sure? The man who walked into the Walmart, was he alone?"

"Yeah."

"Which car is Vega in?"

"I don't even know what the fuck Vega looks like. And the truck and van are too close together for the switch-tech to pinpoint which car his phone's in."

"Damn it! Fall in behind them. If they split up you and Hull take the truck. Jenna and I will take the van." Since Skull hadn't seen them transfer the girl, Thorpe hoped she was still inside the cargo van.

"Get the fuck out of our way," he heard Skull shout over the phone.

Thorpe looked over to the lot and saw a large UPS truck had blocked in the two detectives. Then the phone connection turned to static. Murphy's Law—if something can go to shit—it will.

"Turn around," Thorpe hissed. "We're gonna' take that fucking van down in the middle of the street."

The pickup and the van turned south on Torrence Avenue. Both were already out of view as Jenna cut the wheel and stomped the accelerator. Fishtailing, she spun the large Suburban around and sped toward the exit. They slid sideways onto Torrence, Jenna working the wheel and accelerating hard.

"Get up beside them."

"John, I don't know if that's a good idea. We don't even know if…"

Jenna's head snapped to the right in mid-sentence. A violent jolt sent them into a clockwise spin on the slickened street. A fraction of a second and 360 degrees later, Thorpe was able to process they'd been struck—deliberately. Now they whirled down the street like a curling stone with too much English.

Thorpe spilled out of the Suburban as it settled from its spin. His equilibrium off kilter, he managed to raise his MP5 toward the silver SUV with heavily tinted windows and fresh front end damage. Street lamps provided a murky haze and barely illuminated the images Thorpe's eyes fought to stabilize. A ghostlike white female with black rimmed glasses and a stocking cap materialized above the hood. Her image froze Thorpe, and then she was gone. Again his vision wavered. He regained his composure in time to watch his reflection race by in the tinted windows of a silver Nissan Pathfinder.

Thorpe remained in the roadway, dumbfounded, weapon pointed at his feet.

"Get in!" Jenna's command snapped Thorpe back into action. She had the engine restarted.

Thorpe hadn't yet shut the door when Jenna fed the accelerator.

As she turned in the roadway, Thorpe tried to rationalize what he thought he'd seen. *No way that was her. His vision was awry from the spin. He only saw what he wanted to see.*

"John, you okay? You look like you've seen a ghost."

The silver Nissan turned right on 170th Street.

"Catch that damn Nissan!"

"She might not have anything to do with this."

"She's running from us isn't she?"

315

"You pointed a gun at her head. What'd you expect her to do, exchange insurance papers?"

"Jenna, that collision was perfectly executed."

"You think she's with them?"

Jenna made the turn, they were keeping up with the Nissan but not gaining on it. Thorpe removed his cell phone and called Skull, getting nothing but static. "Let me try your phone," he said to Jenna. The results were the same. "I don't like this."

"What?" Jenna asked. Then "Oh shit. Cop car behind us. We're toast."

Thorpe looked back and observed an unmarked car closing fast. The car didn't have an overhead light bar, but a driver's side spotlight was clearly visible. As it neared, overhead street lamps revealed an unlit dash-mounted light bar. Thorpe quickly began peeling off his weapons and tactical gear throwing them in the back. He didn't want to get killed by a nervous cop. The unmarked car slid in behind their Suburban.

"Maybe they're friends of yours."

"John, were not even in Chicago anymore. This is Lansing."

"Shit. We're done. They're going to get away."

"Maybe it's for the best," Jenna added. "Maybe the police can get Celestina back."

Thorpe was free of his weapons, "Maybe."

The unmarked police car traveled twenty feet behind. The occupants hadn't yet activated their lights. Thorpe watched them in the side view mirror.

"Jenna, stomp the brakes."

"What? I don't think that's a good idea. We're already in some deep..."

"Just do it, Jenna. Please. What more can they do to us? Arrest us for braking too fast?"

Jenna stomped on the brake pedal. The unmarked car reacted a second later. The police car had been gaining on them so it'd been traveling at a higher speed. Reaction is always slower than action.

The car slid on the slick road to within a foot of the Suburban's rear bumper. Thorpe peered into the side view mirror. The Suburban's brake lights illuminated the interior of the police car. Inside he saw two non-uniformed officers in load bearing vests. The passenger was speaking into a cell phone. That's all Thorpe needed to see.

Thorpe leapt out before the SUV had finished sliding to a halt. The unmarked police car kissed the rear bumper of the Suburban. Thorpe heard Jenna exit her door, screaming for him to stop. *Good. She'd provide a distraction.*

The driver of the police car exited quickly, but the passenger struggled with his seatbelt. The driver drew his weapon fluidly and ordered Thorpe to stop, then redirected his pistol toward Jenna as she continued to advance.

The officer on the passenger side finally cleared the car. Pale-faced and wild-eyed, he fumbled with his retention holster. Thorpe kicked the car's door. It flew back into the officer knocking him off balance. Thorpe pounced, taking him down beside the police car and out of view from the more experienced officer on the driver's side.

Thorpe could still hear Jenna screaming: "John! John, don't!"

He had the younger cop pinned and dropped an elbow on his face. Watched as the man's eyes rolled back in his head. Thorpe pulled a flex cuff off the cop's load bearing vest, wrapped it around his neck, and threaded it. He lowered his own head, saw the driver's feet retreating toward the trunk and coming around to the passenger side of the car. Thorpe rose, and, using the cop's vest as a handle, brought the smaller man up with him—a human shield. He spun the cop around so he'd be facing his partner. Thorpe smoothly drew the cop's own pistol from its holster.

His partner was forced to split his attention between Thorpe and Jenna—who now stood on the driver's side of the patrol car questioning Thorpe's sanity. The cop—in an unbelievably tense situation—looked unfazed. The man was accustomed to violence.

"John, stop it. What the hell are you doing?"

"These aren't cops, Jenna." Thorpe held the younger "officer" between himself and the other. "You're not, are you Scarface?"

The cop approaching Thorpe wore a thick beard, thick everywhere except on the scar tissue running from cheek to chin.

Thorpe nodded to the man he had in a choke hold. "This one here was on a cell phone when they stopped us. What kind of cop carries on a phone conversation during a high-risk car stop?"

Jenna began to inch forward.

Scarface finally joined the conversation, "You move another inch, bitch, and I'll drop you where you stand."

"Forget the poor police tactics, Jenna. Everyone's cell phone is being jammed except for these two knuckleheads. These two guys don't stop cars for a living. And if I were a betting man, I'd say they have orders not to harm us."

"You willing to bet your girlfriend's life on it?" Scarface replied. "You release him right now or your girlfriend dies."

"That statement just proved my point. You are not a cop." Thorpe tossed his weapon onto the street then yanked on the loose end of the flex cuff. He grabbed the back of the man's vest and flung him backwards into the ditch. The man grasped at the death band around his neck, his face already beginning to swell.

"You have a decision to make, tough guy. I'd say your partner has about a minute left in this world."

The man still had his weapon pointed at Jenna. He hesitated, sighed, and holstered his weapon. Scarface walked within arm's length of Thorpe, confident, seemingly unconcerned with him being a threat, and in no great hurry to get to his partner.

"Don't perform many car stops in Special Forces, do you?" Thorpe asked the man as he passed.

Scarface only smiled, "I'll see you again, Fuckhead."

"Looking forward to it."

"You can look all you want, you won't see me coming."

Thorpe dismissed the threat, walked around the trunk of the unmarked "police car," pulled out a pocket knife, and slit both driver's side tires. "Let's go."

"Are you crazy?" Jenna said incredulously. "I'm not going anywhere with you."

"These aren't cops, Jenna. Else I'd be dead."

"They're law enforcement of some kind."

"They're not even that. Come on, I'll explain in the car."

Jenna shook, but not from the cold. Thorpe hurried toward the driver's seat of the Suburban. He was leaving, with or without her. Back inside, he restarted the engine, looked over his shoulder, saw Jenna hesitate, then hurry past him and around the front of the Suburban. She climbed into the passenger seat and slammed the door.

As Thorpe drove away, he watched in his side view mirror as Scarface helped his partner to his feet then not so gently cut the flex-cuff off the man's throat.

"You're fucking crazy. You risked our lives on a hunch over a cell phone conversation?"

"I know the woman who hit us."

"The chick in the Pathfinder?"

"Yes."

"And...?"

"And she helped me out of a pinch one time."

"Helped you out of a pinch one time?"

"She calls herself Ambretta Collins, or at least, she did."

"Calls herself? Okay, I'll play your game. Who is Ambretta Collins?"

"If I had to guess, CIA."

"CIA? And why would the CIA be helping you out of pinches? And while you're at it, why is the CIA trying to stop you from rescuing a little girl? Are they here for you?"

"We had to of stumbled into something. I guarantee you they were responsible for blocking in Hull and Skull with that UPS truck. Ambretta's here, people imitating police officers, jamming cell phones. That's a big operation. We need to find out what's going on."

"And just how do you propose we do that? We've lost the van, the truck, and the SUV. And we can't communicate with Skull."

Thorpe pulled out a cell phone Jenna hadn't seen before. "I took this off Zip-tie Boy before I flung him in the ditch. He was using it when they pulled us over. Bet he was talking to little Ms. Collins."

AMBRETTA WIPED AWAY TEARS WITH her sleeve. Right hand holding cell phone to ear, she returned her left to the Pathfinder's steering wheel.

"What the hell is John doing here, Ben? Did you know?"

"I knew he was in Chicago. I had no idea he was involved in this shit. I didn't even know he was close. He must have his cell phones turned off."

"I thought you said the car you blocked in was talking to the Suburban with a cell phone?"

"They were, but not with John's phones. We thought they were local cops about to screw our operation."

"Jesus, Ben, I can't believe this. What is he doing here? What are you going to do about him?"

"Serpico is getting him stopped now. We'll detain him until this thing's sorted out. We're going to have to debrief him. I need to know how he's tied into all this—and what he knows. And Ambretta?"

"Yeah?"

"Did he recognize you?"

"I don't know. I'm wearing my half-ass disguise and he looked wobbly when he stepped out of the cab." Ambretta remembered the shocked look on John's face as she sped past. "Yeah, he recognized me."

Ben offered a long pause before responding. "That's a problem." Then, "Hold on, Ambretta. Serpico's calling in."

Ambretta could hear Ben talking on the other end, "You have

who on the line?" In the background, she heard the excited but muffled speech of one of the techs, then Ben again, "You have got to be shitting me."

"Ambretta, I'll have to call you back. Apparently, John has overpowered Serpico. He just called the command post with one of their fucking phones if you can believe it."

Did she detect admiration in the old man's voice? *Proud papa?* "He's loose?"

"He's loose and…and he's demanding to speak to *you.*"

Ambretta heard Ben breathe out in frustration. "Ambretta, keep your head in the game. We have important work to do. I'll call you back." Ben clicked off.

"Keep your head in the game?" She'd just collided, literally, with the man she loved and left him standing in the street. *How the hell is he mixed-up in this anyway? And what were the odds of them randomly meeting?* She didn't believe in destiny. And who in the hell was that woman with him? She found herself wondering if the two were romantically involved. *Should that surprise her? Did she expect him to lock himself in his home—staring out the window in hopes she would return? "Keep your head in the game."*

Ben was right. They had too much going on to let her feelings for John twist her thoughts. People's lives depended on her actions. She focused on her dash mounted GPS. The system was tied-in to the electronics laden UPS truck. She watched a red blip—Saeed's pickup—followed by a green blip—Ambretta. She traveled about a mile behind, and well out of visual range.

Others still conducted surveillance on Saeed himself, code-name "Betty," after the "Bouncing Betty" of World War II, a mindless mine that, when triggered, "bounced" into the air before it exploded, thereby increasing the likelihood of hitting vital organs. The moniker was an apt description for Saeed—a mindless weapon.

Other members of their team still followed the two men in the Honda Accord, who, in turn, had been following Betty since they'd left Atlanta. The team referred to the men as, "The Housewives." A name derived from the TV show "The Real Housewives of Atlanta," because they looked out for Betty like a worried parent. The code names kept all the moving pieces simple for radio talk.

Ambretta followed Saeed's F-150 now being driven by a yet-to-be-identified male. The F-150 was being followed by another unknown male in a white cargo van. Neither of these men had yet earned a code name.

The mist had turned to sleet, the sky to black. Dark clouds shielded the moon from the atrocities of earth. Ambretta's team would be without quality overhead surveillance for the foreseeable future. The lack of aerial oversight had already stretched resources to unacceptable levels.

The radio did little to mask the strain in the voices of those monitoring the chess pieces. Their chatter retreated to the background as Ambretta flashed back to her encounter with John—his weapon rising, those green eyes behind the optics, the paralyzing shock on his face. Afraid of crossing paths with Saeed, Ambretta wore black, lensless, librarian glasses, with her long hair tucked into a knit cap. Not much of a disguise, but effective at a distance while inside a car with tinted windows. The façade had delayed John's recognition for a split second.

What had she seen in John's eyes? Surprise? Hurt? Hard to discern—she'd jumped back into her Pathfinder in an instant, shock no-doubt evident on her own face. *What the hell was John doing here? Who was the woman accompanying him? "Keep your head in the game."*

Mr. Brown's radio traffic interrupted Ambretta's thoughts. "Mr. Brown" being the code name for the three men, including Ben, inside the mobile command post (MCP). The MCP masqueraded as a UPS truck. Mr. Brown—UPS—keep it simple stupid.

"Mr. Brown to all units, Alpha Charlie." The command directed all units to switch to the predetermined (A)lternate (C)hannel. Ben was obviously concerned John might have commandeered one of their radios. Ambretta noticed someone other than Ben had become the voice of Mr. Brown. *Ben couldn't have his son hearing his "dead" father barking orders over a government radio.* The voice repeated the order. Ambretta complied.

Having switched, Mr. Brown—still not Ben—continued, "Mr. Brown to Serpico: status?" Serpico was the code name for the two agents dressed as undercover cops. Their role was to stop and identify unknowns, run interference, and play the part of the police without having to get "real" law enforcement involved. Ambretta knew one of the faux cops, Zeb, was the shit—ex-Special Forces, quiet, unflappable. His "partner," nothing more than an analyst thrust into a field assignment because of a lack of resources. An explosion of surveillance targets coupled with the loss of satellite coverage had placed too many desk-jockeys into temporary field work.

"Serpico to Mr. Brown. We're Oscar Kilo but our ride will be out of commission for about thirty minutes."

Ambretta recognized the ex-commando's baritone voice.

"The Suburban remains in play. The no harm order still stands. I repeat, no one harms the occupants of the Suburban," Mr. Brown ordered.

"Magellan to Mr. Brown, what is the Suburban's current location?" Ambretta asked; her code name based on the model of vehicle she drove.

"Unknown at this time. We'll have thermal in place shortly. We'll also have a signal on the phone the occupant of the Suburban took off Serpico."

"It's not my fucking phone," the usually mute Zeb hissed.

Damn he's pissed. Ambretta thought with a smile. Only John—or his father—can set someone off that fast; John was a chip off the old block, except in this case the chip was considerably larger than the block. Still, there were numerous similarities, the most salient being their ethics. They both operated by their own strict, albeit slightly twisted moral code. And God have mercy on the man who violates that code—because grace will not be bestowed by father or by son.

Ambretta split her attention between the road, the red blip on her GPS monitor, and her rearview mirror. It appeared the man driving Saeed's truck had come to a stop.

The command post confirmed her observation, "Mr. Brown to Magellan, Betty's former ride has come to a rest. Remain out of visual."

Ambretta closed distance on her target but, cognizant of possible countersurveillance, used a different route than the pickup had taken. Using GPS overlaid with Google Maps, she found the red blip near a building in the center of a very large complex—possibly a salvage yard. Two turns later she encountered a rusted corrugated fence which confirmed what she'd seen on her navigational screen. "B&G Salvage."

Though the complex was enormous, there appeared to be just a single drive into the yard. Ambretta set-up south of the entrance, in a neighborhood both impoverished and sparse. From the position, she'd have quick access to any vehicles leaving the premises.

Parked under the drooping branches of a dying tree, Ambretta surveyed a street lined by houses in various stages of disrepair; some occupied, some abandoned, others hard to determine. She'd chosen a place in front of an obviously empty house with no glass in its windows. She didn't need homeowners coming out to investigate, or just as likely, try and sell her dope.

Ben suddenly resumed the voice of the command post, "Ambretta, get the hell out of there. The Suburban is about to drive up your ass."

FORTY-EIGHT

IF SOMETHING BAD WAS GOING to happen, Alberto knew it'd be during the next few critical hours. That's when the hammer would drop, erasing all his hard work with one crushing blow. In addition to a psychotic Special Forces fuck hell-bent on killing him, he had to worry about the very men with whom he did business—his fellow Kings and the ragheads who'd arranged the delivery. *What was to stop them from taking back their shipment after events were set into motion?* And he'd be doing just that very soon—at 6:00 a.m., the first round of devastation was scheduled to be delivered. America would have a lot to digest with her morning's coffee. But Alberto wasn't in this for the cause. His only cause was himself. Yet, he couldn't deny the excitement he felt for being the catalyst of such a historical event. It felt...*godlike.*

First things first. His number one priority was to free his cargo. Alberto sat outside the automotive shop of B&G Salvage in his newly acquired pickup waiting for the overhead garage door to rise and allow him entry. He checked his rearview mirror and studied the face of his guardian angel—Mongoose. The man idled behind him in the white cargo van. *Did he trust Mongoose? No.* Alberto didn't trust anything other than the almighty dollar.

Open the fucking door already! Alberto's fingers danced on the steering wheel; he was anxious to get out of the stinking pickup truck. *Fucking sand niggers.* The cab emitted a potpourri of foul aromas: ball sweat, rotting food, and *blood?* Alberto lowered his window letting in cold damp air to provide relief from the stench.

The metal overhead door finally rose allowing him to pull inside. His rear bumper barely cleared the opening when the door slammed closed. Alberto jumped from the truck seeking respite from the stink. A few seconds later, Mongoose entered the shop through the adjacent pedestrian door, rifle slung across his chest. Alberto gave instructions to two other men then ordered them outside. The fewer people present when the cargo was revealed, the better. He kept Mongoose inside for security purposes, and he needed the shop manager to free the cargo from the truck. The manager, a short pudgy man with a ring of black oily hair and matching coveralls, went by the unlikely moniker of "Whip."

As Alberto lowered the pickup's tailgate he instructed Whip to lock the overhead door. Once the man finished his task, Whip joined Alberto at his side and peered into the empty cargo bed.

"Peel it," Alberto ordered.

"The bed? What's underneath?"

"Cash. A lot of it. And if you set my shit on fire, I'll do the same to you."

The manager swallowed hard, "If I can't use a torch, it'll take a minute."

"How long?"

"It toward the cab or back bumper?"

"How the fuck I know?"

Whip nodded, "An hour maybe."

"Then get to it. And Whip…" Alberto pulled a large revolver from his waistband and pointed it at the man's face. "You wouldn't steal food from the man who feeds you, would you, Whip?"

Whip stared into the barrel shaking his head.

"I need you to verbalize. You know what verbalize means, don't you, Whip?"

"No, Mr. Vega. I mean yes." Whip cleared his throat and tried again. "I mean, I'd never steal from you."

"How much is it, boss?" Mongoose asked with a smile, clearly enjoying Whip's discomfort.

"Only the first of many payments," Alberto said as he slapped Mongoose on the shoulder. "You and I are going to be very rich, my friend."

Alberto wanted him to know more money would be coming and he'd get his fair share. Mongoose wasn't as easily intimidated as Whip and he didn't want the soldier getting any clever ideas; namely killing Alberto and keeping the money for himself. The agreed upon shipment was to be 1.2 million dollars. Alberto didn't want to say the figure out loud. Figures like that make smart men do stupid things.

Using an old drug smuggling technique, a false bed had been welded on top of the money. The bed now stood a few inches taller than it should; difficult to discern unless one is trained in trafficking techniques. The single cab and empty cargo area conveyed the illusion the truck couldn't be carrying anything of any significance. Once Whip freed the money, and Alberto surmised it totaled what was due, he'd make a series of calls. Then the proverbial shit would hit the fan.

Alberto turned to Mongoose, "You stay here. Anyone pokes their head inside this shop, put a hole in it."

THORPE EASED DOWN A QUIET street surmising only one car had passed this way before him. The temperature had plummeted. Even the arterial streets were frozen now, and looked like they'd been dusted with a fine powder. Tire tracks left in the sleet told him the car had continued on. The block was quiet.

Thorpe's newly acquired cell phone had been of no use. He'd hit send on the fake officer's last number received. The man on the opposite end of the line denied knowing an Ambretta Collins, refused to answer any questions, and ultimately terminated the phone call. Thorpe's subsequent calls went unanswered. Still unable to reach Skull with his other phones, Thorpe drove to B&G Salvage where his two friends first located Alberto's cell signal. The salvage yard was his only remaining link to the girl. He hoped she was inside—alive and well—if not, he hoped the location would at least offer clues as to where she might have been taken. And if he lost Celestina because of Ambretta's actions, the next time they met he'd stick his leather boot right up that beautiful ass of hers.

Thorpe unknowingly parked the battered Suburban in the exact spot Ambretta had just vacated, then climbed into the back to reattach his discarded weapons and Kevlar.

"I'm going alone and that's final."

Jenna had been arguing she should accompany him. It was an argument she wouldn't win.

"I'll communicate with you using the radios like before. If we get cut-off, call the police," Thorpe continued.

"You mean if you get killed, call the police."

"Non-negotiable, Jenna. I've always operated better alone and I always will. Besides, I need you to watch the exit. Let's move."

Jenna slid over to the driver's seat, pulled out, and drove toward the salvage yard. The entrance to the complex was near the southeast corner of the property. Just outside the gate sat a small parking area. Jenna passed both and took the street that followed the sprawling yard along its southern fence line. When she reached the west end of the complex she went by a small strip of trees and found another road heading north. She turned here and paralleled a larger band of trees separating the road from the salvage yard.

Thorpe cracked the tinted passenger side window. The wooded tract beyond was dark.

"Here," Thorpe instructed.

Jenna slowed and Thorpe sprung from the cab. He ran across a small open area and headed for the concealment of the trees. Running, he heard the engine fade then heard Jenna wish him well through his earpiece. It sounded like a goodbye. She didn't have a good feeling about this and hadn't been shy voicing her opinion. His sprint toward the woods reminded him of his dream he'd had only a few hours before. In the dream his daughter had been waiting for him in the trees. Now he sprinted toward the woods to save another man's daughter. If his dream had been foreshadowing then Jenna's feelings were well served—the night wouldn't end well.

Safely in the trees, Thorpe turned and looked the way he'd come. No skirmish line had gathered in the mist. Attack dogs did not pursue. So far reality proved kinder than his nightmare—something of a rarity for him.

Thorpe hoped he hadn't been spotted. He was equipped similarly as before, except now he also had a long, suppressed, sniper rifle strapped diagonally across his back. A sight definitely worthy of a 911 call had a nosey neighbor taken notice. The signs of his passing in the accumulated sleet were slight but present. Nothing he could do about them now.

Thorpe turned and crept toward the tall metal fence. A white sign fringed with rust warned in black lettering: "Attack Dogs on Premises." He noted wind breathing at his back and realized it would carry his scent across the yard, potentially alerting dogs, if there were in fact dogs to be found.

Thorpe looked down at his silenced MP5 and again questioned his motives. *Was he doing this for the girl or himself?* Either way, every minute she stayed in these monsters' arms meant further opportunity for harm. *So, in the end, what did his motivation really matter?* If he failed, Jenna could alert the police. *What did he have to lose? His life? No huge loss there.* His father always told him the most dangerous weapon was a man with nothing to lose. Thorpe fit the description.

Fuck it. The assholes on the other side of this fence are about to have a very shitty night. With the blade horizontal to the ground, Thorpe drove his knife into the corrugated metal. He'd soon discover if any dogs patrolled the complex—the hilt made a loud thwack on impact. Using the knife as a makeshift step, he raised himself so his eyes cleared the fence, and surveyed the vast yard. No toothy dogs were in sight; which didn't mean shit, but at least none barked an alert. Thorpe eyed the barbed wire at his forehead. Snipping it would leave obvious signs of his passage. Instead, he rose higher, pulled down the loose strands, and laid his chest on top. His Kevlar vest offered protection from the barbs as he reached down, grabbed a support post, and used his abdominal muscles to lift both legs over the fence and silently drop to the ground. He came away with a rip in his load-bearing vest but all of his appendages joined him safely this side of the wire.

He used the butt of his rifle to push the knife back through the fence before taking cover behind a row of cars. There, he listened for the padded footfalls of a large animal, happy to hear none.

Thorpe looked back at where he'd landed. *Footprints*. The good news was he didn't see anyone else's prints, dog or otherwise. The lack of tracks meant no one had been patrolling the perimeter. A vast complex, it was too large for a small group of men to effectively cover. They'd most likely be positioned near wherever Alberto was holed-up—if the man was even here.

"I'm in," Thorpe relayed to Jenna.

"Copy. I have eyes on the southeast exit."

"Roger that."

Thorpe scanned the darkened yard. Immense and carpeted with cars, there were literally thousands of hidden positions. Perfect for him to advance unnoticed. Perfect for others to lay in wait. Thorpe switched from MP5 to sniper rifle. Peering through the attached thermal optics he looked for hot spots. He also surveyed the yard for a location that would give him a better view of the complex. He found such a position and moved to an old windowless box van, and, as quietly as possible, climbed atop the roof, belly down.

Elevated, Thorpe turned his attention toward two buildings near the north fence line. The structures were about fifty yards north and a hundred yards east of his position. Because of the soup-like conditions, they stood at the outside limits of his visibility. The buildings appeared to be attached to one another. Bringing his head up from the optics and with his naked eyes, he could make out the outline of a window in the smaller building on the right. Shades or blinds shielded prying eyes. The larger structure on the left, most likely a shop judging by the bay door, stood dark.

Just west of the two buildings lay the only open expanse in the entire yard, around which cars were piled. Stacked high and in a semicircle, the piled cars resembled a small baseball stadium. The stacked cars looked down on two others in the middle of an otherwise open area. Thorpe briefly wondered why those two cars had been afforded an audience. He shrugged his mental shoulders then returned to his optics.

Thorpe had a poor field of vision to the southeast, and in his current location couldn't locate a sentry minding the gate. In fact he couldn't see anyone, anywhere. He forced himself to remain on the roof another ten minutes. Even with the self-administered, ten-minute requirement he almost missed it. Already sliding backward off the rear of the van, he spotted light with his naked left eye.

The light shone from the larger building on the left. A window peeled open for a second or two, then sealed closed. *Plastic sheeting? People were here, awake, and watching.* He took all this to be a good sign. Jazzed, adrenaline warmed his cold toes. This is what Thorpe lived for, and for what he'd probably die.

Encouraged by the sighting, an extra five minutes of waiting proved beneficial. A man stepped from between the baseball diamond stacked cars and the shop. He had possibly been there the whole time and all it took was a couple of steps forward for him to become visible. The man smoked a cigarette, ruining his night vision. The door to the smaller building on the right swung open and another man, clearly armed with a long gun, walked toward the southeast gate. A minute later, a man topped in a cowboy hat came from the direction of the gate and approached the man smoking the cigarette. The smoker went inside and Cowboy Hat took his place. *Sentries.* Thorpe checked his watch. The men were likely on a relief schedule, letting some of the men take turns in the warmth.

More jazz; Thorpe wasn't aware the corners of his mouth had twisted into the slightest of grins. He did realize he was about to "get in the shit." He was also confident he'd find what he came for. At the very least, he'd find the man who could tell him where the girl was being held.

He slid off the rear of the van, now knowing the approximate location of three men. *But three of how many? At least four.* In addition to the sentries, he'd seen movement in the building on the left. There were probably more, but he couldn't spend the entire night lying on top of a van in an attempt to acquire their positions.

Thorpe notified Jenna of his observations, "Armed sentries. At least four bad-guys on premises. I'm heading toward two buildings near the middle of the yard and near the north fence line."

"Copy."

"You also have an armed guard with a long gun at the southeast gate, so keep your ass out of visual."

"Yes, daddy."

Thorpe's grin widened. Staying low, he crept north. He moved slowly, wary of unseen adversaries hidden in their lairs. He himself utilized the rows of cars for concealment. Dead, un-mowed grass separated muddy tire tracks—old ruts carved out by customers searching the yard for used treasures. Thorpe continued to look for fresh signs—from man or beast—in the powder Mother Nature had been kind enough to sprinkle about. He found none. If either patrolled these grounds, they hadn't done so in the last thirty minutes.

Thorpe took a knee and listened to his environment. The ground frozen, stiff grass offered a faint crunch when stepped upon. Depending on his adversaries' deftness, he might, or might not, hear approaching footfalls.

As Thorpe neared the buildings he heard coughing. It came from the replacement guard on the west side of the shop. Based on the rattling phlegm, Thorpe figured this man to be a smoker as well, his hack no doubt exacerbated by the damp cold. Thorpe estimated the distance to his position to be slightly less than fifty yards. And though he couldn't yet see the man, he placed him somewhere between the quasi baseball stadium and the shop, shielded by a wall of pancaked cars.

Reaching a critical point in his advance, Thorpe paused. A wider passageway, probably used by tow trucks, separated him from the concealment of a row of cars and the buildings. He was close enough now to see footprints, though they didn't look recent; they'd been left in the mud before it'd frozen. Most led from the area of the two buildings to the two cars in the middle of the "baseball diamond." The men either liked to sit on these cars or they kept something stored inside. If Thorpe were executing a search warrant for dope, it would be the very first area he'd search. But he didn't give a shit about dope. He was here to rescue a little girl, and not playing by search warrant rules. People would die tonight and Thorpe didn't want to be first on the list. He knew if he crossed this road he'd be exposed. He'd also leave behind fresh, visible tracks— if any of these assholes were observant enough to notice.

Here, Thorpe had a better view of the buildings. They were of different heights, but definitely attached. He didn't know if an interior door connected the buildings, but thought it likely. The structure on the left was obviously an automotive shop; it had a large rolling overhead door to allow vehicles in and out. A steel, windowless, pedestrian door stood to its left.

The overhead door had two rectangular windows about five feet off the ground. The windows didn't show a hint of illumination, but Thorpe knew it was from these openings he'd earlier seen light. They were likely sealed with heavy plastic, a tactic methamphetamine cooks often employed to mask their activities. Meth cooks were some of the most ignorant animals wandering the earth. Through the simple act of hanging plastic on their trailer windows, they posted a sign that might as well read, "Dear law enforcement, we are currently manufacturing methamphetamine.

Please prepare a search warrant on our stupid asses."

Thorpe noticed flood lights attached to the sides of the buildings. Once again he was reminded of his dream: the run to the woods, the fence, and now the floodlights. *When would the dogs make their appearance? When would he realize he didn't have a chance at reaching the girl?*

The lights were extinguished now, but if turned on, the immediate area would only more resemble a baseball stadium, and Thorpe didn't want to get caught alone on the field. If equipped with motion detectors, they were deactivated; earlier, when the guards had moved about, they'd remained dark.

On a positive note, he hadn't seen any surveillance cameras except those along the front fence line, but cameras were so easy to conceal these days, one just never knew.

In lieu of crossing the open expanse, Thorpe considered leaving the way he'd come and crossing the fence behind the building, but for all he knew, a man was positioned there. Plus, it'd be noisy; the man on the west side of the building would surely hear him scale the metal fence. Besides, if Alberto slipped out the front again, Thorpe would lose his damned mind.

No, this was it. He'd cross the road, sprint toward the edge of the stacked cars, round the corner, and fill the guard with silent lead. Subjugation was not an option, and hitting a person over the head to "knock them out" for a few minutes a thing of fiction. He'd use speed to eliminate the first guard, then find concealment and evaluate.

Without thinking, Thorpe slowed his breathing, relaxed his muscles, and readied for battle.

His body and mind prepared, Thorpe keyed his mic to advise Jenna of his intent, "Eliminating tango on west side of building."

"Stand down, John."

Barely audible through his ear bud, the command pushed Thorpe back down to his knee with an unbearable weight. The reply hadn't come from Jenna. *Ambretta?* He should hardly be surprised.

He wondered if Ambretta had commandeered Jenna's radio or only cracked their "secure" channel.

Thorpe whispered into his mic, "Jenna, you still over here?"

"She's a little tied up at the moment, John," Ambretta's voice whispered back.

Was she mocking him?

"Ambretta, no offense, but you can kiss my ass." She'd managed to do what an impending gun battle hadn't—spike his heart rate. "I don't know what your fascination is with me, but there's a little girl who needs my help."

"John, stand down. That's an order."

"Sorry, darlin'. I'm done following orders from you."

Again Thorpe rose from the ground. This time, he wouldn't allow her pleas to stop him.

"John, behind you."

Behind me what?

Weapon at the ready, Thorpe turned.

There Ambretta stood, ink-black hair flowing over black fleece, black nylon strap separating her breasts, empty hands at her side. Beauty ensconced in a junkyard.

Pink lips moved behind a black microphone that projected her whisper directly into his ear. "Please."

FORTY-NINE

ALBERTO VEGA LOOKED DOWN AT the peeled truck bed in amazement. He'd never seen so much money at one time in one place. He reached for one of the vacuum sealed bags slicing it open with a chrome-plated pocket knife. Ensuring the bundles weren't counterfeits covered with genuine bills, he held Benjamin after Benjamin up to the light checking the paper, watermarks, portraits, security threads and color-shifting ink. He opened another bag from a different location and repeated the process. The money was real. He was flush. And this was only payment number one.

Mongoose crawled out of his darkened corner for a look-see. "Fuck n' A!"

"Fuck n' A is right," Alberto agreed. He turned to Whip, "Bag it." Then back to Mongoose, "Stay alert, we're almost home free."

"What about the girl?"

"Fuck the girl. We don't need her anymore." Alberto dismissively flipped his wrist in the air, "Let the boys do what they want with her. But she doesn't leave here alive—she's seen our faces."

On a tight time schedule, Alberto checked his watch. He pulled out a phone he'd only used once. Ten separate numbers were stored inside. He selected the first contact and hit send.

A man picked up on the second ring and answered with a single word, "Chicago."

"Chicago, it's a go."

"Acknowledged."

Alberto clicked off and continued with the next contact.

"Kansas City."

"Kansas City, it's a go."

"Roger it's a go."

Alberto would repeat the process eight more times, to men in eight different cities.

It had begun.

A HALF MILE AWAY TWO olive-skinned men sat in a black Honda Accord. Their assigned code name—though they didn't know it—was "The Housewives," and they'd followed Saeed and his money-laden truck all the way from Atlanta.

Saeed no longer concerned them; the man was an idiot and would soon be dead. Their concern was the money, and only the money. This operation was years in the making, and the result of relationships developed with Mexican drug cartels. Terrorism and cartels—a natural relationship from which both organizations would benefit. The cartels had access to military-grade weapons (ironically, courtesy of the U.S. government), they had long established smuggling routes into the United States, and they loved money.

The cartels were in business with numerous American street gangs. The gangs made the least amount of money and took nearly all the heat. And the sons-of-bitches were downright crazy. The Zetas employed terrorism techniques that would make the average Islamic terrorist blush with pride. *Skinning men alive? Removing their hearts?* They were serious about intimidation and were willing to do *anything* for a buck. In a nutshell, they were perfect.

The Housewives' relationships—or more precisely their bosses' relationships—with the cartels had filtered down to several street gangs including the Latin Kings and one Alberto Vega. The

Housewives didn't trust the cartels, the Kings, or Vega. Distrust is why Vega had been put on an inflexible schedule and why the truck and one of the bundles of cash were equipped with GPS. If news reports didn't begin surfacing in Midwest cities by daybreak, the Housewives would open up the trunk of their Honda, equip themselves with the weapons it contained, and do everything within their power to get their money back.

The Housewives knew they had associates on the East Coast operating under similar orders. Neither man knew an entirely different cell had similar arrangements with MS-13—a crazily violent Hispanic street gang. That cell was responsible for a five-man West Coast team, and a five-man team in the Mountain States. All attacks had been scheduled to occur simultaneously, the United States would wake up to one hell of a bloody morning.

Upon hearing the news, most Americans would decide to call in sick and stay home to mind the family. The great machine known as the United States of America was about to grind to a halt.

FIFTY

THORPE STOOD, MP5 DANGLING AT his side, sniper rifle slung across his back—dumbfounded. Ambretta had a way of making an entrance. He'd half a mind to turn away from her and continue with his assault. But she'd momentarily rendered him useless. No longer mentally prepared, he stood erect, in full view of the buildings he'd been set to aggress.

"Please," she mouthed.

Her eyes conveyed sorrow, sympathy, and sensuality, yet he was reminded of her exceptional acting abilities. As likely to taser him as offer a hug, a welcoming embrace might come with a sedative-filled syringe. Thorpe cursed under his breath and moved cautiously toward the vision in black.

Ambretta turned and walked away, retracing Thorpe's footprints in the fallen sleet. Her back to him, he saw the strap across her breasts led to a suppressed FN P90 submachine gun. His eyes slid from the rigid lines of the weapon to the gentle curves of an ass snugly wrapped in black running pants. Again he cursed.

She walked upright showing little concern of being seen.

"A bit nonchalant aren't we?" Thorpe whispered into the mic.

Ambretta continued on but pointed her right index finger up into the night. He looked. The clouds impenetrable, he couldn't see anything; couldn't hear a helicopter or plane, but deciphered some type of surveillance patrolled overhead. *Satellite? UAV?*

"Don't walk your pretty little ass too far. I'm still assaulting those buildings."

Moving with purpose, Ambretta ignored him. It took them seconds to cover the same ground he'd so painstakingly crossed earlier. She reached the spot where Thorpe had dropped from the fence. A large canvass bag sat where he'd landed. Thorpe stopped well out of arm's reach and took in his surroundings. He looked for signs that others had crossed the fence but the only tracks he saw were Ambretta's and his own.

"Relax, I'm alone," she said, trying on a reassuring smile.

"That smiling bullshit isn't going to work this time, Ambretta. Or whatever the hell your real name is. 'Ambretta'—why'd you choose her name anyway? Was it all part of your plan to reel me in?"

Ambretta was the middle name of Thorpe's slain daughter. He'd chosen the name himself. And just like his daughter the name was unique. He'd never met another who shared it. Not until this woman inserted herself into his life.

"I didn't choose the name. It was given to me."

"You're telling me Ambretta is your given name?"

"No. Not given in that way."

"Given? Do you even know whose name it is?"

"It was your daughter's. I didn't know then. I know now."

Was your daughter's. The "was" stabbed at him. "Why was the name chosen, to get under my skin?"

"I was just doing my job, John. It was my assignment."

"Say what you mean, Ambretta. *I was* the assignment."

"Yes, John, you were my assignment. I never meant to fall in love with you."

Love? The word knocked him backwards, stunned him. He wanted to believe but was determined not to fall under her spell yet again. He brushed aside the comment.

"Why was I your assignment, Ambretta?"

"You know why, John. You've always known."

"I don't know shit. Quit playing games and just tell me."

"You do know, John. Who would step in and save your ass from that mess? Who cares that much for you? Who do you know who has those capabilities?"

"I have no fucking idea what you're talking about. You need to answer *my* question."

"But you already have the answer, John. You already know."

"No."

ALL AMBRETTA COULD SEE WAS pain. Six feet and nearly two hundred pounds of raw emotion. John bathed in it, oozed it, and was about to spill over the edge into a great truth. She watched him struggle to accept what he'd always suspected but had refused to acknowledge.

With the disappearance of his father, John had been marooned in the five stages of grief. He never reached acceptance because he never *really* knew. Now he raced through many of those stages bringing his father back—though in this case acceptance wouldn't be the final stage. The final step would be reserved for anger. Anger, because he would have to accept his father had abandoned him.

John's eyes were bridled pools. Ambretta's tears fell freely on her cheeks.

"No."

He turned away from her. She watched his back expand with a deep breath.

She stepped forward, reaching out to him.

"Don't."

She withdrew her hand.

"He's dead," John said quietly.

"John…"

"He's dead…to me."

Ambretta didn't respond. *What could she say?*

"Why?" John asked.

Why? Why did Ben abandon his son? She didn't know the why. She couldn't provide the answers he needed. There's only one thing she knew for certain.

"He loves you, John."

Ambretta watched as John's one deep breath became many. They lengthened, slowed, became rhythmic. He tilted his head forward as if in prayer. A final deep exhalation and John turned to face her. His eyes dry. His face blank, almost robotic. She'd been trained in similar techniques to the one she'd just witnessed—no doubt from the same teacher—though she didn't possess John's mastery. Then again, she hadn't been taught from birth, father to son.

"I'm not your mission this time," he said. "Why are you here?"

And just like that, John slammed the door on the news of his father. She wanted to embrace him. Wanted to kiss him. Wanted him to acknowledge her love for him. And she desperately wanted for John to love her back. But it was too late for any of that now. Emotions locked safely away, he morphed from man to machine. A machine ready for battle.

FIFTY-ONE

THE SUFFOCATING BLACK MADE IT hard to determine his predicament. The pain only amplified his disorientation. Robert Hull wore a hood of heavy fabric over his throbbing head. His hands were bound behind him and secured to the floor. If forced to guess, he figured he was inside a van. The incident with the UPS truck hadn't ended well; he and Skull lured in and quickly disposed of. If his chest didn't hurt so damn bad he'd be embarrassed. But embarrassed was a whole lot better than being dead.

Hull hadn't paid much attention to the UPS truck. *It was in a UPS Store parking lot for Christ's sake! Had the truck been running?* Hull couldn't remember. All he knew is one moment it'd been parked nearby, and the next the damned thing had blocked them in. Hull had cursed the truck while Skull cursed his phone and its dropped connection. *Dropped connection.* It was all very plain to see in retrospect: *Their phone call turning to static the instant the truck pinned them inside the lot?*

An old man had come limping around the corner of the UPS truck, arms raised as if Hull had been the one driving like an idiot. Hull got out and ordered the old man to move the truck. He'd even shown his badge, though his jurisdiction didn't extend beyond Oklahoma. The old man picked up on it immediately, "Tulsa? What the hell is a Tulsa cop doing flashing his badge in Illinois?" he

343

yelled, and began poking Hull in the chest with his finger.

Skull, having little reluctance to kick the ass of a man his same approximate age, came barreling out of the car. The next thing Hull saw was a blur of movement. He felt the strike hit his sternum more than he'd seen the punch. Then the world turned upside down. The last thing he remembered was Skull's face landing beside his, followed by a jab in the back of the thigh. He awoke in darkness.

He and Skull had been perfectly played. Hull saw the signs clearly as he replayed events in his mind. The UPS van parked in a UPS Store lot—*perfectly logical.* Looking back he recognized the red flags he'd missed. The old man hadn't been dressed in UPS clothing. He was too old to be a driver. The limp in his gait implied he was incapable of hauling heavy boxes for a living. The limp had been to draw Hull in, make him feel as if he couldn't possibly be a threat. *The old man.* The old man looked damned familiar now that Hull had time to reflect. He'd seen him before. Well, he'd seen photos of him before—photos of a younger man in military garb; some with his young son at his side. *John.*

Hull struggled with his restraints but his efforts only caused them to tighten. Then he heard the working of a metal latch and a door slide open. *Definitely a van.* His hood removed, he found himself squinting despite the dim conditions. Pupils having adjusted, he looked into the eyes of a bearded man with a scar from cheek to chin. The man smiled broadly stretching a linear scar into the shape of a boomerang.

Hull cleared his throat, "I want to speak with Benjamin Thorpe, and I want to do it right fucking now."

The bearded man's scar snapped back into a straight line.

FIFTY-TWO

THORPE DIDN'T TRUST AMBRETTA. IF successful
relationships were built on foundations of truth, then theirs would
surely crumble. Everything he knew of Ambretta constituted a lie.
But as he listened to her relate how she'd come to be in Chicago,
Thorpe felt the puzzle pieces falling into place. Some were missing,
but enough gathered that a picture began to take shape, and it wasn't
pretty.

Ambretta's people had followed a "potential threat to national
security," Saeed al-Haznawi, from Atlanta, Georgia to Chicago. The
apparently empty pickup Saeed had been driving was equipped with
two separate tracking devices—neither of which had been applied by
Ambretta's team. Additionally, two body guards shadowed Saeed
and his truck the entire distance. So, even though the truck appeared
to be without cargo, it seemed very important to someone. When
Thorpe suggested Saeed might be the one of importance, Ambretta
laughed. "The truck is smarter than he is," she said.

Ambretta's team followed Saeed from Atlanta all the way to the
aforementioned Illinois Walmart when Thorpe had inexplicably
driven into the middle of their operation at a critical moment—an
exchange. Ambretta's team had picked up the cell conversation of
the car next to them (Hull and Skull) and thought them to be local
law enforcement. Afraid locals were about to compromise their

investigation, Ben used the mobile command post to block in the two detectives and ordered other units to remove "the Suburban" from the equation.

Things went to shit after that. Upon exiting the UPS truck, Ben immediately recognized Hull, and Ambretta had been the only one in a position to stop the Suburban before it potentially bungled the op. She'd already been in the process of spinning out John's SUV before Ben could offer her warning.

"I answered your questions," Ambretta finished. "I need to know why you're here, John. I need to know who it is that intercepted the truck. Lives are at stake."

Lives are at stake. Thorpe considered the professional soldiers and the soldier's relationship with the Kings and now with possible terrorists. "You're not going to like where this is headed. You can't let anyone leave this property."

He began to relate what he knew. Ambretta gestured for him to pause by holding up a hand, then she flipped a switch on her headset and told Thorpe he was broadcasting. The mobile command post would hear everything he related to Ambretta.

He told of the Army Airborne soldier and three Kings who'd tried to ambush him at his home. He told of their ties to his family's murder and the connection to Chicago. He explained how he'd met Carlos Benitez, and how Carlos related how the Kings had been funneling gang members through elite military units in order to provide them with combat experience. Finally he told them how Alberto had taken Carlos' little girl and how he was trying to get her back. Ambretta interrupted from time to time with questions. Thorpe wasn't sure if the inquiries were hers or from people listening in. When he finished, Ambretta shook her head, realization in her eyes.

"You thinking what I'm thinking?" Thorpe asked.

"I am if you're thinking we've got a terrorist cell that's contracted local street gangs who's been funneling members through elite combat units. Something very shitty is about to happen."

"And I don't have time for governmental red tape, Ambretta.

There's a terrified little girl who might be in one of those buildings. If she's still alive she's in danger and I plan on getting her back."

"John, you don't know the whole story…"

"Ambretta, you're not talking me out of this. I plan to…"

"Shut up, John. Let me finish. I'm not here to push you away. We need your help."

Thorpe waited for the "but," surprised when it didn't come.

"We're pretty sure the little girl is inside."

"How?"

"Audio we've been picking up." Then she added in a grim tone, "I'm also afraid we're too late."

Ambretta must have seen a reaction in Thorpe's face. "Jesus, I'm sorry; not too late with the girl. I mean whatever their plan is, we're fairly certain it's already in motion. One of your bad guys just made ten phone calls to ten different cities. Each call lasted only a few seconds. Every call went to a prepaid cell phone and then those phones went dead. Now it's my turn; you thinking what I'm thinking?"

Thorpe nodded, "Ten men or ten separate cells just got the green light to do something in ten different cities. The players shut down the phones so they couldn't be located. Not good."

"Very not good. The only way to locate them is if they power the phones back up and that's not going to happen." Ambretta took a deep breath, "It gets worse; in addition to the Chicago cell, a similar group traveled to New York City. A man on the other end of a similar exchange made ten calls to cities across the East Coast. Same deal—all prepaid phones that went off line."

"Shit. Twenty different cities?"

"At least twenty cities. There could be other cells."

"What's their end-game?"

"No idea. That's why we need to hit this place now. But our people are spread all over, following Saeed, his bodyguards, and babysitting your friends." Ambretta pointed in the sky. "This weather has limited our surveillance. It's like soup out here. All we have is thermal."

"You can cut my friends loose to free up your people; they're tight."

"We don't like it but we're going to have to. They're all getting the 'It's national security/we can make you disappear' speech."

"You might want to consider using them instead of dismissing them. They're all sharp."

"Not my call. One thing, John: if you help us, we need intel. We need the man who made those phone calls taken alive. And alive isn't exactly your specialty."

"Not so," Thorpe said evenly. "It just isn't my preference."

Ambretta stared at him hard. It was her time not to trust. "I'm not kidding, John."

"I realize the consequences, Ambretta. There are more lives at stake than just the little girl's. 'The greater good' and all that bullshit. I get it."

She nodded, reached behind her back and handed him a knife— his knife, the one he'd used as a makeshift step to cross the fence.

"Don't make me regret returning this to you." Then she knelt, reached into the bag lying on the ground, and came out with night-vision optics and a headset that matched her own.

Thorpe switched coms, but declined the optics. "I have some I'm already acquainted with."

"Not like these you don't. Try them."

Ambretta showed him a set of simple controls. The optics were unlike anything he'd ever seen. They weren't the four-tube panoramic night-vision goggles made famous in Zero Dark Thirty. In fact, there were no visible intensifier tubes at all; boxy, the contraption didn't extend as far from the face. He slipped the gear over his head while Ambretta made several adjustments. A lever allowed him to move the optics from forehead to eyes without having to adjust the headgear. He experimented with the device.

"Latest generation," Ambretta said. "They're being tested by an AC-130 Spooky crew. You're wearing a couple hundred grand on your head. Light amplification with thermal overlay capabilities. Field of view is about ninety degrees. Parallax-free, hydrophobic, perfect visual acuity with little depth distortion. Turns night into day."

"What are you, a freakin' engineer?" Thorpe looked around the yard, "This isn't playing fair."

"Only play fair if dealt a winning hand."

Thorpe's familiarity with the quote stirred a pang of jealousy. He'd often heard it recited by his father. *Had son been replaced with daughter?* Thorpe pushed away the frivolous thought, disappointed with himself for having cared. Then he pulled the lever that pivoted the goggles to his forehead. The optics were impressive but he was reluctant to use unfamiliar equipment. For now, he'd operate without the NVGs.

Ambretta pulled additional stun grenades from the bag and handed two to Thorpe. "Be careful with the fat one, it projects rubber coated pellets. You'll lose an eye, or the girl's if you're not careful."

Thorpe nodded and stuffed the bangs in his load-bearing vest.

She showed him around the headset. "Switch to 'cont' if you need hand's free communication. If you do, your mic will always be live so limit your speech and…"

Thorpe looked at her impatiently.

"Right. Not your first rodeo. That's what you like to say isn't it?"

Thorpe powered up the headset. Both he and Ambretta selected PTT, push-to-talk, so they could speak to each other without broadcasting over the radios.

"Mr. Brown is calling the shots," Ambretta advised.

Mr. Brown— UPS—clever. "Is my fath…who is Mr. Brown?" Thorpe refused to say the words, "my father."

"It's the call sign for the mobile command post. But your father is inside and running the show."

Just fuckin' great. "Does anyone else on your team know who he is?"

"That he's your father? Are you serious?"

"Right." *His dad never shared anything with anyone.*

Thorpe pressed the transmit button, "John to Mr. Brown, radio check."

He received the response in his ear bud, "Mr. Brown to John, you're five by five." Thankfully, the voice was not his father's.

"Back at ya."

Then he heard Ambretta in both ears—in person and electronically, "We're ready to proceed."

Mr. Brown broadcast, "Serpico is en route with equipment. Do not assault the building until he is on scene; you are free to soften the perimeter."

"Magellan copies," Ambretta answered.

Thorpe shook his head, "Aren't all these code-names kinda childish?"

"What can I tell you, it's a male-dominated profession."

"Humph."

"Who is Serpico?"

"The guy in the unmarked police car; bearded, had a long scar on his face. You stole his partner's phone," Ambretta explained.

"Ah, I hope Serpico doesn't 'accidentally' shoot me in the ass."

"He's a professional." Ambretta smiled, "He'd shoot you in the head."

"Comforting."

The man *was* a pro. It was his partner who'd screwed-up. But he also knew guys like "Serpico" couldn't stand to lose. Most had the need to prove themselves the better man. Hopefully, Serpico had put the incident behind him.

"Rules of engagement?" Thorpe keyed.

A pause, then, "You are weapons-free on exterior tangos."

This meant they were allowed to use deadly force on exterior sentries. The freedom simplified matters. It'd be difficult to approach and subdue without the guards getting off an alert, most likely in the form of gunfire.

Perhaps in an effort to demonstrate who was in charge, Ambretta wordlessly started off to the east. She moved faster than Thorpe would have preferred, relying heavily on information provided by overhead thermal imaging. Old school, Thorpe didn't trust anything but his own senses. Then again, he'd never had access to such high-tech equipment.

Headed toward the front gate, they took an easterly route slightly south of Thorpe's original approach. Following Ambretta's footsteps, he found himself questioning her experience. Women aren't allowed in combat units so she most likely hadn't seen action there. *Ex-cop? Maybe. Had she killed before?* He realized he didn't know anything about her. He didn't know if he could depend on her to do what needed done. This could be *her* first rodeo. Hell, he'd seen grown men succumb to buck fever the first time they pointed a rifle at a deer—let alone at a human being. Similarly, shooting at paper silhouettes versus pulling the trigger on a real person are worlds apart. Some people just don't have it in them, even when their own life or those of others are at stake.

Thorpe reached out and touched Ambretta's shoulder. She took a knee, he knelt beside her.

"Have you killed anyone before?"

Ambretta hesitated, and he knew the answer.

"Let me take the lead," he said.

She remained silent, thinking.

"It's not something you want to do if you don't have to. Believe me Ambretta, you don't ever want it to become easy."

Instead of answering, Ambretta keyed her mic, "Magellan to Mr. Brown, can Gatekeeper and Jessie James see each other's position?"

"That's a negative, Magellan."

She turned her attention back to Thorpe, "No need for a *sims-shot*. I might end up giving you the trigger but I still have the lead."

Before Thorpe could argue, she'd pushed herself up and started moving again.

Using a common sniper team tactic, they'd named the two exterior tangos for simplicity's sake. Gatekeeper was the man guarding the front gate, Jessie James the man wearing a cowboy hat who stood near the buildings.

If Jessie James and Gatekeeper were positioned so they could see each other, the best tactic would have been a simultaneous engagement, or a "sims-shot." A sims-shot was accomplished with two or more shooters firing on one or more targets simultaneously, usually with one of the shooters counting backwards to a designated fire number; a critical tactic in taking out multiple sentries with line-of-sight positions. Since Jessie James and Gatekeeper couldn't see each other, the tactic wasn't needed. Ambretta had just told Thorpe she knew her business and was thinking clearly.

Their movements directed by Mr. Brown, they continued on a southeasterly route through the yard toward Gatekeeper. Drawing near, they were advised to keep low. Finally, Mr. Brown told them to turn right between rows of rusted cars. When they reached the end, they'd have a clear field of view of the Gatekeeper approximately one hundred meters forward. Making the turn, he and Ambretta went to their bellies, army crawling into position.

Ambretta motioned Thorpe forward to her side.

"A hundred meters is pushing my effective range with this weapon." She nodded at the long gun on Thorpe's back, "You any good with that thing?"

A hundred meters represented a chip shot for the rifle he had strapped on his back. "Very."

Ambretta keyed her mic, "John will engage Gatekeeper."

Another pause, then, "Mr. Brown copies." Thorpe figured the man on the radio had just consulted his father. And his father was the man who'd taught John how to shoot. Benjamin Thorpe was well aware of his son's capabilities with a firearm.

Thorpe propped his MP5 against a treadless tire and shimmied forward. A tan Buick well past its prime sat to his left. Thorpe stopped short of its front bumper. Even though Mr. Brown assured them they were alone, Ambretta spun around so her weapon covered their six. Thorpe prepared his rifle then settled in below the bumper and just forward of the Buick's flattened front tire.

Gatekeeper stood a hundred meters away and about ten meters north of the gate. A nearby streetlamp illuminated much of the man's immediate area and provided Thorpe with an excellent sight picture. The light would also destroy Gatekeeper's night vision. Nevertheless, the human eye is very adept at picking up movement, so, even though Thorpe was ensconced in darkness at a distance of a hundred meters, he kept his movements slow and methodical.

Right hand on stock, index finger on trigger guard, right thumb releasing the safety, Thorpe spoke into his mic. "John is in position."

"Mr. Brown copies, you are clear to engage."

Trying to warm himself, Gatekeeper bounced up and down on the balls of his feet. Thorpe took even breaths. His pulse slowed. The crosshairs of his sights steadied on a man unknowingly spending his last few moments on this earth. Thorpe wondered if Gatekeeper deserved what was about to befall him. He wondered if Gatekeeper would soon be standing outside a very different gate and if he'd be turned away or allowed inside. That certainly wasn't Thorpe's call. He was only here to arrange the meeting.

The man's cold feet—not Thorpe's—delayed the appointment. Gatekeeper's continuous bouncing and shuffling kept Thorpe's finger from retracting—but the wait was short. Gatekeeper stood flat-footed, retrieved a pack of cigarettes from the inside of his coat, then turned toward the fence and offered a view of his right side. Head pitched forward, left hand cupping the flame of a lighter, he lit a cancer-stick—but the cigarette would never get the chance to kill him. Gatekeeper inhaled deeply and the cigarette burned red. Then the man tilted his head back to release the smoke.

At the same time, Thorpe released four grams of precision manufactured lead. The suppressed rifle's bark was slightly louder than a pellet gun. Slamming forward in the quiet, the action proved a bit more noticeable. Pink mist. His target dropped in a straight line, only spreading out when meeting resistance from the frozen ground. Cigarette smoke rose from the dead man's nose.

"Gatekeeper down."

"Mr. Brown confirms, tango is down."

There was no need to approach. Gatekeeper was dead before his knees hit the ground; he never saw death coming. Thorpe fleetingly wondered what the man saw now. A quarter-second lost on the thought before rising and moving toward the next target.

"Jessie James" was currently positioned at the rear of the automotive shop, or as Mr. Brown referred to it, "Building one, side three." Tactical teams use a numbering system for structures. Generally side one was the front of the structure, with each side labeled sequentially in clockwise order. Openings like windows and doors were numbered sequentially from left to right. In this way it was easy to communicate a specific area to everyone on the assault team, as in, "I saw movement on level two, side three, opening four."

If he and Ambretta were to address Jessie at the back, that would leave the front unprotected, and backup still hadn't arrived on scene. Things would get considerably more complicated if their targets went mobile. Here inside the salvage yard, everything was nicely contained from public view.

A new voice came over the radio proclaiming she and her "package" had the front gate covered. Thorpe assumed the "package" was Jenna. Perhaps his father had decided they were in desperate need of more help.

Now that they'd already taken direct action, he and Ambretta moved with purpose. The potential for premature discovery of Gatekeeper's body was a concern. Additional threats entering the front gate and finding a guard with a crater in his head would raise the alarm. So far, they had the element of surprise on their side.

Thorpe didn't care for haste but took comfort in the fact big brother hovered above watching theirs, and others' movements. Nearing the structures, he and Ambretta jogged, legs bent, backs nearly parallel to the ground, toward an outcropping of cars about twenty yards east of the buildings.

Ambretta slowed as she reached her destination. Informed by Mr. Brown it was safe to look, she peeked around the cars and behind the building.

"You see any video?"

Thorpe scanned the structure for cameras. He couldn't find any, but video systems had become so advanced they were nearly impossible to detect if hidden well. But, as a general rule, people wanted you to see the cameras, because they didn't want you to break-in in the first place.

"Don't see any."

"Moving up to the three-four corner," Ambretta advised. "Let us know if Jessie changes position."

"Mr. Brown copies."

"Serpico to Magellan, be advised we've rigged the transformer for your grid. We're two minutes out."

"Magellan copies."

Ambretta turned and explained, "Before the assault we'll blow the transformer. The whole neighborhood will go black. It will also help explain any explosions the neighbors might report to the police."

"So that's what Serpico's been doing. And I've been feeling bad because I thought he was waiting on Triple A."

Ambretta smiled, "Well the flat tires didn't help matters."

Thorpe ditched his sniper rifle. Anything that happened now would be close quarters. He followed Ambretta silently toward the structure. They reached side four of building two, then crept to within six feet of the three-four corner.

"Status?" Ambretta whispered over the mic.

"Unchanged."

Ambretta didn't hesitate. Thorpe watched her shoulder her weapon, creep to the corner, bend forward at the hips, and spit three rounds from the muzzle. Though he should've been watching the one/four corner, he found himself transfixed on a woman who continued to amaze him.

"Target down." Her voice in his ear bud, as calm as he'd ever heard her; like an operator on his tenth deployment.

"Mr. Brown confirms, Jessie James is down."

Ambretta didn't move forward to check her work, she simply turned and walked toward Thorpe. Her eyes were covered with night-vision goggles but the lower half of her face displayed no signs of strain. He wanted desperately to remove her optics. To look in her eyes. He hoped they were filled with remorse. He hoped they wouldn't harden. He hoped they didn't look like his. Shaking his head, he reminded himself of his mission.

Of the two attached structures, the one to the west, building one, was obviously a garage of some sort. The east building—against which they stood—likely office space. Overhead surveillance indicated at least five individuals inside the two structures. Two heat sources were inside the office area and one of those was possibly that of the girl—it hadn't moved since they'd been on scene. Just a little ball of heat; it could be a dog curled up on a cot for all they knew.

Intel streaming into his ear, it occurred to Thorpe his father was about to assist him on his quest to save someone's daughter. *Happenstance?* Thorpe had never been one to believe in destiny; too many shitty things happened to good people for it to be "God's plan." If it was God's plan for his daughter to be gunned down in her bedroom, then he didn't have much use for Him.

But Thorpe couldn't ignore his personal quest for retribution had walked him straight into the path of his long-lost father; how all the deadly skills passed down from father to son were about to be used to save another little girl. How those same skills might intervene to prevent a plot designed to take untold innocent lives. It was enough to make his head spin. It was enough to make him question if things really did happen for a reason.

Bullshit. Other paths could have led him here. Sacrificing his daughter's life wasn't necessary. Too much to process now, Thorpe bowed his head, breathed, and prepared his mind. But it was the toe-curling scream of a terrified little girl that put him into motion.

His body already leading him down the side of the building, Thorpe heard Ambretta speak into the mic, "We have screaming inside. Talk to me Mr. Brown."

"Someone is next to who we think is the little girl," Mr. Brown responded.

Fuck! The screaming continued from inside the building. Thorpe barely recognized the presence of Ambretta's hand on his shoulder. She uttered something he didn't bother to decipher. His thoughts a mix of images: his own daughter's futile escape from a killer, Celestina sharing his daughter's fate. *Not again.*

Thorpe stifled his fear and concentrated on what needed to be. A lifetime of training filled him with calm, clarity. He became aware of the finest detail.

"Don't move. Serpico is nearing the gate."

Bullshit. We'll be too late.

Mr. Brown's pleas went unanswered.

Thorpe felt Ambretta on his heels. She no longer tried to stop him. He heard her speak breathlessly into the radio, "Shit, blow the transformer. We're going in."

"John wait!" His father had finally come over the radio. Thorpe ignored his father's pleas as well. He wouldn't lose another little girl.

They'd already been advised the door to the office wasn't likely barred or locked. Relief guards hadn't hesitated when walking in and out.

Thorpe moved fast. He switched his radio to continuous, "Going in, in six, five, four..."

Thorpe heard the transformer blow. The few lights around the yard snapped off. The interior would be ink black. He pulled the NVGs over his eyes.

"two...one."

Thorpe turned the knob, pulled open the metal door and burst inside.

The optics were excellent. A man blindly backed up in the room. In the man's right hand a knife—in the crook of his left arm a screaming little girl. He'd been cutting her loose from restraints. Duct tape hung in flaps from her wrists. *Keep the bad guys alive,* Thorpe told himself.

To avoid being backlit, Thorpe sidestepped the entry and approached at an angle. He closed the distance in four long strides. The man swung the knife, protecting himself from unseen assailants. Thorpe allowed his MP5 to dangle from its sling. He wrenched the knife from the man's hand then gave it back to him, jamming the blade into his right shoulder. Thorpe twisted the handle with all his strength, felt the man's tendons and muscle stretch, tear, snap.

The man released the girl. His screams of anguish so loud they drowned-out hers.

"Get her out," Thorpe yelled to Ambretta.

His shout interrupted by popping noises. Metal on metal. Lead slicing through tin and sheetrock.

"We're taking fire," Ambretta screamed.

Thorpe used the knife like a handle. He was about to take the suspect to the ground when he saw the man's head lurch sideways, the left side exploded against the wall in a clump. Then Thorpe felt his own head snap around and all went black. Through the fog he heard Ambretta let out a gasp as if she'd been punched in the gut. He heard her drop to the floor and knew she'd been hit.

Thorpe realized that he too had fallen to his knees. He could no longer see. The girl screamed. *Good, she was alive.* A bullet had struck his optics and snapped his head around. It'd momentarily stunned him. Thorpe tore off the useless equipment; tangled, the communications gear went with it.

Like a stalled disco ball, light from the accompanying shop streamed into the office via multiple bullet holes. *Light from a flashlight?* The illumination allowed him to see Ambretta; she was on her hands and knees pulling the kicking and screaming girl to her. The incoming fire ceased. Trying to soothe the girl, Ambretta mouthed words but no sound escaped her lips. She was badly hurt.

Despite her wounds, Ambretta managed to scoop up Celestina and start for the door. Again, incoming rounds raked the office. The shooter's weapon silent; only the impact of the bullets could be heard. Ambretta gave her back to the incoming projectiles, protecting Celestina with her own body.

Ambretta had been wounded because of his actions; might die because of him. Thorpe stood and ran toward the fury of incoming bullets, not caring in the least if one found him.

TWO MINUTES PRIOR, WHILE ALBERTO prepped to leave, Mongoose stood concealed in the corner of the shop. He'd been behind three stacks of worn tires pondering recent events: the disappearance of his counterpart in Tulsa, the total dismantling of the men at Luis Carbia's house, and the phone call from a self-declared special ops soldier.

From what he'd been able to glean from his brother Kings, it appeared as if one man had entered Carbia's house and killed the four men who'd been lying in wait—one of whom was King Sauce and no slouch—before walking away without so much as a scratch. Someone was hunting them, and whoever that someone was, he wasn't fucking around.

Before, Mongoose doubted the man's claims of being a Delta operator. D-boys didn't walk around bragging about their identities. One usually found out who they were the hard way. Mongoose figured the man had used the Delta tag to intimidate them into releasing the girl. It'd almost worked. But the more Mongoose contemplated how his associates were disappearing in rapid order, the less sure he was about anything.

Mongoose checked his automatic rifle for the hundredth time. Locked and loaded. He hadn't even bothered engaging the safety. If he were still in the army, the infraction would have an NCO all over his ass. But what's the worst that could happen here? *That he accidentally shoot Alberto? More money for him.*

The cash finally bagged, Alberto pulled open the connecting door to the shop's office and stuck his head inside.

"Get rid of the girl, we don't need her anymore. I don't care what you do with her; just make sure she's never found."

Alberto turned away, closing the door behind him and sealing the girl's fate. "Let's go, Mongoose. We're fucking gone."

Mongoose left his hide and immediately heard the girl's screams. Fucking with little girls was chickenshit, but not his problem. Walking toward the pedestrian door Mongoose heard a distant explosion and found himself ensconced in darkness. *Blown transformer?* He hesitated. *That'd be some fucking coincidence.* Mongoose activated the flashlight on his weapon and concentrated on his hearing. He heard the office's exterior door slam open against the side of the building. He heard Alberto's man join the girl in her screams. *That motherfucker's here!*

Mongoose returned to the cover of the tires, and on full automatic, let loose an entire magazine in the direction he'd heard the voice. He flooded the connecting wall with thirty rounds of armor piercing ammunition and was rapidly depleting a second mag. He didn't give a shit if he killed his own man, the girl, Alberto, or everyone. *There was only one "rule of engagement" in this fucking war. Win.*

Mongoose tried not to succumb to tunnel vision. He was somewhat aware the outside pedestrian door just flung open. He redirected his rifle toward the door only to see Alberto — moneyless—running for his life. *Good fucking riddance.* If Mongoose was able to survive the next few minutes, he'd have all the money to himself. But before he could get his sights back on the connecting door, it slammed open. He heard something large crash into the opposite side of the truck and a metal object strike the concrete floor not far from his position. He was a millisecond from realizing he should look away when a blinding flash and deafening boom blasted him backward. A projectile caught him below the right eye; another punched him in the left thigh. Knocked to his ass, Mongoose felt like his orbital bone had been crushed.

THORPE LAUNCHED HIMSELF INTO THE shop releasing the rubber-raining stun grenade in mid-flight. He bounced off the side of a pickup, landed in a heap, and curled into the fetal position—fingers in ears. Rubber pellets struck his back, layers of Kevlar absorbing most of the energy. Up in an instant, flashlight activated, he started toward the rear of the truck where he found a short fat man in greasy coveralls impersonating a June bug—on his back, limbs twitching.

Thorpe soccer kicked him in the side of the head, hard, and kept moving. *Keep the bad guys alive.* He rounded the tailgate and spotted stacked tires in the northwest corner of the shop. Shooter's nest. *We need them alive. There are more lives at stake than just the girls. Twenty cities.*

Thorpe sprinted toward the tires, finding his way with the MP5's mounted flashlight, but determined not to use the weapon. As he neared the tires, a man in combat gear stood up armed with an assault rifle. Thorpe let his weapon hang as he flung himself into the dark. Beams of light from the MP5 bounced through the air, catching glimpses of the shop as the two men collided.

His weapon bouncing off flesh, equipment, and concrete, the light was extinguished. Thorpe found himself fighting for his life in total darkness.

Control the hands, Son. The hands are what will kill you.

His father's voice spoke to him; had never left him. Thorpe managed to gain control of a wrist with his left hand. His adversary had the same idea and held Thorpe's right wrist. On top, Thorpe dropped his head violently toward where he thought his opponent's face should be. He struck something, unsure what, and heard a grunt. Thorpe felt the man's left leg fling over his shoulder looking for a leg triangle. Thorpe postured out of it and went crashing down into the darkness with an elbow. It glanced off the man and struck the concrete floor. The impact caused his entire right arm to go numb and his opponent took the opportunity to try and roll him, fighting for top position.

Struggling for his very life, Thorpe remembered the front door slamming shut when he'd first launched himself into the shop. Someone had made it outside. Ambretta was outside with the girl. They were in danger. Somehow, he managed to twist his deadened right arm loose, felt along his load-bearing vest with his injured arm and grabbed what he thought was the handle of his knife—the very one Ambretta had reluctantly returned to him—afraid he'd kill someone with it.

The man secured his wrist again. The length of Thorpe's arm tingled and he feared he'd lose his grip on the knife. *"Don't make me regret returning this to you."* Images of Ambretta and the girl flared in his mind: Ambretta with possible mortal injuries, Celestina scared and unprotected.

Fuck it. Thorpe released the man's left wrist, regained top position, put both of his hands on the knife's handle, and pushed. His opponent must have realized Thorpe held a weapon, for his hands now worked to keep Thorpe's from descending.

"Motherfucker." The man hissed.

Thorpe felt the man's breath—smelled it. It told him the exact location of his head. Thorpe slid his body forward, putting his own bodyweight behind the knife. He pressed down with both arms and his chest. He heard the blade scrape against something hard. *Teeth?* Felt it push through flesh. Warm blood sprayed his face. Inch by inch the resistance from his opponent's arms lessened, but the friction from the blade increased until its momentum stopped completely; the eight-inch blade buried to its hilt. The man's body shuddered and was still.

Thorpe pushed up, staggered back into shelving, and activated his light as he ran toward the pedestrian door. He snapped the light off before bursting outside where he nearly fell in not-yet frozen mud. Thorpe recovered, looked to his left and found Ambretta on her back, badly hurt but alive. He started toward her but she silently waived him off, pointing down the drive that led to the front gate.

He hated running past her; felt as if he was leaving her to die. He charged down the path trying to keep his weapon up, his right arm nearly useless. Thorpe rounded an abandoned Cutlass and found a man, his back to Thorpe, standing in the darkness, a body strewn at his feet.

Thorpe raised his weapon and activated the flashlight. The optics swam back and forth across the man's head, Thorpe's injured right arm unable to keep steady. The man turned to face Thorpe, a little girl in a tattered dress draped across his arms. Thorpe's legs went as weak as his battered arm.

Thorpe found his voice was as shaky as his limbs as he cried out to his father, "Ambretta's down."

FIFTY-THREE

JENNA WASN'T FREE TO LEAVE nor was she free to enter the salvage yard, a point made perfectly clear by the woman— "Johnson"—who'd been "protecting her" the last half hour. Never mind the protection began with a pistol pointed at Jenna's face.

Johnson followed two other "agents" inside the salvage yard, leaving Jenna alone with her thoughts and a view of a rusted metal gate. Jenna might not be alone for long; two sets of headlights quickly approached. *Screw this.* She stepped through the opening.

Inside she found Agent Johnson relieving a dead man of his weapon, a cigarette still smoldering between the cadaver's lifeless fingers. Seeing Jenna, Johnson rose and pitched open her mouth to object but stopped short. Maybe it was Jenna's look of steely determination, or maybe the woman simply calculated priorities. Whatever the reason, Johnson clenched her jaw, slung the dead man's weapon over her shoulder, and hustled toward two men engaged in a standoff in the middle of a muddy drive.

Jenna followed Johnson into the gloom. The agent stopped and attended to a darkened mass at the nearest man's feet. As Jenna drew near, she recognized the mass as Alberto Vega, now secured with disposable restraints.

The man standing above Vega whispered words of comfort down toward his chest—a little girl cradled in his arms. Twenty yards away, arms dangling at his side, stood John, his face blackened, his eyes and teeth brilliant in contrast. *No, his face wasn't blackened. It was painted with blood.*

Jenna started toward him but something in his eyes gave her pause. The green orbs appeared backlit with fiery anger and burning pain. Instinctively, she realized his anguish wasn't physical, the blood coating his face not his own.

The other man turned to her and spoke, "Please, take the girl."

The frightened girl lifted her head and peered into the darkness with teary eyes. Confused, she murmured, "Mommy?" and reached out. Jenna couldn't deny her. As more bodies rushed past and up the drive, Jenna took the girl into her arms.

"No baby, I'm not your mommy. But I am a friend of your parents. They sent us to come get you. You're safe now, Celestina."

The girl shuddered and expelled a gush of air. Her sobs deepened, but Jenna felt her emotions had morphed from ones of terror to hope. *We did it. We found her safe and alive!* Jenna looked up to offer John a smile—an acknowledgement of a life saved—only to find his back. Running away, John didn't possess the demeanor of a man who'd accomplished his mission—of a man who'd just saved the life of a little girl.

Jenna followed but at a much slower pace. Running was associated with panic, and for Celestina's sake, Jenna needed to appear calm and steady. Walking, Jenna assured Celestina she'd soon be reunited with her parents and that Jenna herself would make the delivery. It was a promise she intended to keep, no matter what the cloak-and-dagger assholes had to say about it.

Jenna stepped to the side at the sound of approaching vehicles. She continued to a cluster of activity near two buildings. A car's headlights illuminated four people huddled over a figure. Drawing near, Jenna cupped the back of Celestina's head, pressing the girl's face into her bosom. The little girl had seen enough; she didn't need to see this.

Two men worked feverishly on a raven-haired woman. She lay

exposed from the waist up, her pale body atop the dark muddy ground. The man who'd handed her Celestina quietly issued orders, yet his eyes remained locked on the injured woman and the man kneeling above—John.

John cradled the woman's head, smoothed back her hair, lowered himself and kissed her forehead. Jenna circled, looked into his face, and knew. She knew John loved this woman. A wave of hatred and guilt crashed over her. She hated a woman who might be dying before her very eyes; she hated her own tears running down her neck and mixing with those of Celestina's.

Men lifted and carried the injured woman toward a waiting car. John, his face contorted in anguish, trailed at her feet. They placed the woman in the backseat and John was pushed away. A physical altercation appeared imminent. The older man—the one who seemed to be in charge—wrapped his arms around John, restraining him.

"I'm going with her."

"She's in good hands, John," the older man said, strangely reassuring for a supposed spook.

"I'm going with her," he insisted, pushing away.

"I need you, John."

"I've needed you for the last ten years, Father. Where the fuck were you?"

The word "father" caused everyone within earshot to stop what they were doing, pausing momentarily before a glare from the old man snapped them back to work.

"They're killing people, John. They're killing people in Tulsa. Son…I need you."

FIFTY-FOUR

Thursday
19 hours later

KING GHOST LOOKED DOWN AT the Tag Heuer watch
strapped to his wrist and was reminded of Carlos "Too Tall" Benitez.
Ghost had supplied Too Tall, Loc, and Speedy with weapons for
some "work" to which Ghost hadn't been privy, and promised the
diminutive Too Tall he'd get his watch back after the job was
finished. Turns out, Too Tall wouldn't be getting his watch back; the
man had managed to earn a "terminate on sight" order for himself
and his entire family. Too Tall must have thoroughly pissed-off
Alberto, a mistake Ghost was determined not to duplicate.

Carlos' death sentence would be dealt by someone else. Ghost
had bigger concerns; he was to replace King Fubb, who, along with
three of his "trainees," disappeared right here in Tulsa, Oklahoma.
Their first mission had been to kill some local cop, and not one of
them had been heard from since.

Unless affecting him personally, Ghost usually enjoyed others'
mistakes—they only made him look better in comparison. But
Fubb's disappearance affected him alright—right up the ass. Ghost
had been sent to Tulsa to try and figure out what happened to Fubb.
There'd been no reports of the man or his associates being arrested,

nor news of a Tulsa police officer having an attempt made on his life. The four men had simply vanished.

Upon arrival, Ghost located the motel room the four men rented and thoroughly searched it. At Alberto's direction, he also wiped it down, "just in case." Ghost uncovered no clues to the men's whereabouts. They seemed to have found the land variant of the Bermuda Triangle.

Unfortunately for Ghost, the screwing didn't end there. Alberto ordered him to remain in Tulsa. Apparently Fubb had assignments in addition to the cop. Ghost inherited those duties. But whereas Fubb was a professional soldier and had been given weeks, even months, to prepare, Ghost was given little time. He'd been provided money, unfamiliar equipment, and thirty minutes of instruction from King Mongoose over the phone. That was it. According to Mongoose the disappearance of the four Kings blew a sizeable hole in Alberto's plans, and Ghost's job was to help fill it.

At first, Ghost was enraged to have been put in such a position. But one doesn't say "no" to the Kings and one surely doesn't say "no" to Alberto Vega. *Any doubters please refer to Carlos Benitez and family.* But, after giving the assignment some thought, Ghost became increasingly excited. *I'm smart and I won't get caught.* After all, like Mongoose said, "When people kill they get caught for two reasons: they know their victims, and they have motive. You won't have either."

How hard could it be anyway?

His assignment: kill at least two people per week, "The greater the distance, the better." Mongoose informed him how militaries used snipers to paralyze entire companies with fear. Ghost didn't know how many men were in a company, but he assumed it was a lot. Mongoose also reminded him how the Beltway Snipers paralyzed Washington D.C. for weeks. His true assignment was the instilment of terror, and he would immobilize Tulsa in its grip.

Ghost made his first kill, well, attempted kill, less than twenty-four hours ago, and despite six more days left in the week, here he was the very next morning on the hunt for victim number two. If he didn't find an easy target tonight, he still had till midnight Wednesday. *Piece of cake.* And in four weeks he'd receive additional funds. Four weeks—eight random shootings.

Not modest by anyone's interpretation, even Ghost possessed enough self-awareness to know his first foray as a sniper hadn't been a smooth one. He'd picked a location not far from Fubb-and-friends' motel, where he parked his rented car behind a restaurant on the western fringe of the city. There, he crossed a small wooded area, maybe twenty yards wide, to reach his destination—a bank under construction, its skeletal frame jutting out of a fresh foundation.

The night cool but not cold, he'd lain prone on the bank's concrete floor, his rifle protruding between wall studs as he peered through a scope at a well-lit gas station. The station sat on the opposite side of a four-lane road and at a slightly lower elevation.

Ghost, though he'd been lying still, remembered his heart pounding as if its host were being pursued by a pack of wolves. The thumping seemed so thunderous he half expected customers to look across the street in an attempt to find the source. He became aware of his ragged breathing while peering through his scope. The damned thing bobbed up and down, swaying back and forth like a pendulum. He couldn't keep the crosshairs steady for shit.

Recalling Mongoose's brief instructions, he calmed himself by taking long, slow, deep breaths. While he worked on his breathing, a gray Dodge Stratus pulled up to one of the gas pumps and a black man stepped out. He parked on the opposite side of the pumps but Ghost still managed to acquire a clear sight picture of his head. Ghost held his breath and placed his finger on the trigger. The swaying continued but not as bad as before. Determined to shoot, the crosshairs wouldn't cooperate. *Pull the trigger when the crosshairs are in the center of his head.*

Ghost nervously yanked the trigger, and though he heard no gunshot, the man completely disappeared from view—trigger jerk. *What the fuck?!* He'd said those exact words—*aloud no less.* He remembered looking down at his weapon as if it disobeyed him only to discover an engaged safety. *Thank God no one had been around to see that.*

Following his little faux pas, Ghost rolled to his back and wiped his sweaty brow. *Fuck, Fuck, Fuck, FUCK!* He'd killed before, spraying wildly with a handgun, but had never used a precise weapon.

Ghost rolled back to prone, closed his eyes and took three deep breaths. He opened them, disengaged the safety, and peered through the scope. The man returned the gas nozzle and climbed into his Stratus.

"Your lucky day, asshole," Ghost mumbled under his breath, then set down the rifle and awaited his next potential victim.

Fifteen minutes, and three customers later, Ghost selected his next mark. Parked on his side of the pumps, he'd never get an easier target. A white woman stood big and tall; ten years and fifty pounds ago she might have been the starting center for her high school basketball team.

Ghost tried to calm his mind as he set his sights on the new target. The woman fetched a squeegee from the fuel island and went to work on the driver's side windshield. Ghost felt steadier than before as he watched her through the scope. Busy wiping the windshield, the car's hood shielded her lower half. Finished, she walked around the front and began to squeegee the passenger side in all her glorious girth.

Ghost abandoned his dreams of a head shot and centered his crosshairs on the woman's back. Then, remembering something else Mongoose said, adjusted his aim. He couldn't remember the exact terminology but knew if he fired from a higher position, his bullet would strike higher than where he aimed.

He re-sighted just above the woman's buttocks, took a deep breath, and squeezed the trigger. Again the scope jumped but this time an enormous report accompanied the movement. The woman fell.

"Fuck yeah!" Ghost cried aloud.

Then he scrambled to his feet and ran the opposite direction; getting about twenty yards before realizing he'd left his rifle in the unfinished bank. Ghost ran back, tripped over construction equipment, and landed beside his rifle. He retrieved the weapon and sprinted back to his rental car, twice falling in the wooded area. *But he made it out. And damn it'd been a rush.*

Tonight, Ghost vowed not to make the same mistakes. He looked at his eyes in the rearview mirror of his rental car and saw a professional assassin. His first attempt might not have been textbook, but this one would be different. He was hooked; hooked with the process, the hunt, the control over who he let live or die. Unable to sleep all day, the events of last night played over and over in his mind—what he'd do differently, what he'd do better. Ghost discovered he liked to hunt humans.

The gas station had been perfect. People stop there in the early morning hours and they have to remain stationary while they use their credit cards, put a nozzle in the tank, and so forth. But Ghost had been advised not to keep a pattern. "Be unpredictable. Change your targets, times, locations, and your appearance," Mongoose had told him.

It was Wednesday night, early Thursday morning. The bars would be letting out soon. It didn't matter that a national catastrophe was underway, nothing would keep Americans from their alcohol. If anything the bars might be more crowded. People would gather to discuss the day's events over a beer, or two, or ten; drink their sorrows away, or talk about how if they were in charge they'd drop nukes on the entire Middle East and erase all their country's problems with the push of a button.

Ghost selected a small bar in deep, South Tulsa, situated in the midst of an expensive looking neighborhood. It'd be occupied by folks with money. *That's good.* When people of means are killed it instills more fear. When lower-class citizens are gunned down, the masses tend to believe they are immune, that the person killed must have got what was coming. But when middle class fucks are killed, they think, "If it happened to them, it can happen to me."

Ghost already cased this morning's location. Again he'd be firing across a major street. Again—because of the hour—there'd be little traffic. And again, he'd be firing from an elevated position. He'd learned from his first attempt a small elevation difference doesn't alter round placement to such a large degree. The news reported the woman he shot last night was in critical condition having been struck in the lower back. He'd meant to strike her much higher. He learned from his mistakes. This time his victim would not survive.

Ghost parked in a nearby neighborhood, walked west toward a major north-south street, and entered a thick stand of trees on a morning more mild than the day before. Pausing, he took a deep breath and stretched his arm parallel to the ground; his hand was steady. *This time would be different. He was a killer. King Ghost— assassin!*

Wearing black jeans, black boots, a gray t-shirt, and a black hoodie, Ghost would be invisible in the trees. He scanned his surroundings, confident he couldn't be seen. On his back was a black, padded, nylon case. Inside the case was death.

He walked north toward his destination. Paralleling the street, he stayed well inside the tree line. Ghost found himself ensconced in darkness. Though the canopy was barren, the trees here were so tightly knit he couldn't see more than a few feet. Though the darkness would hide his activities, it would also slow his retreat. Following his shot, he needed to get to his car as quickly as possible. Last night he'd fallen twice while fleeing the scene and was lucky to escape uninjured. *Smarter now, he thought more clearly than during his first hunt.*

Ghost turned back toward the north-south street. There, he'd be able to skirt the tree line and move with more speed. Retracing his steps through the woods, his excitement grew—excitement, not fear. The rush manageable, he felt alive; alive in taking others' lives from them. Ghost wasn't sure if he'd ever be able to stop. Even when some day this assignment ended, even if he ceased being paid, he didn't think he'd be able to stop. Violence is addictive. *Surely, there will always be business opportunities for a man with my new skills.*

Lost in perverse, grandiose, thoughts, Ghost caught a flash of movement to his left. The little light available to him swirled, his body twisted in the air, he landed on his back, the air knocked out of his lungs. Like a drunk in a pitch black room, his vision swam. He couldn't breathe.

Ghost felt things happening to him but couldn't make sense of them. Unable to move his arms he was aware of being lifted. Air returning to his lungs, he heard a disconnected moan—*his own?* More light became available. His senses were slowly coming back. Slung over someone's shoulder, he was being carried through the woods. Then, flung backward, darkness again swallowed him whole. Hands moved over him; his vision went in and out of focus. He saw a street. He couldn't move. A man worked on something in front of him.

Ghost vomited, the warm bile running down his chin. He was standing. *What kept him upright?* He was bound to something by his chest. *A tree?* Shirtless, Ghost could feel the bark on his back. *Yes, a tree.*

A man in a black ski-mask stepped up to his face. Framed within the mask were a set of unnaturally green eyes that seemed to peer into his very soul…searching. They burned with hatred and judgment. Ghost wanted to look away but was seized by his gaze.

The man pulled out a large knife and grabbed Ghost's head. Ghost tried to scream but realized something had been stuffed in his mouth. The knife carved into his forehead; blood ran into his eyes. Then a searing pain across his abdomen and the man in the mask was gone without a word. Strapped to the tree, unable to look down, Ghost felt his belly give way, heard its contents spill onto the ground, felt them splash on his bare feet.

FIFTY-FIVE

GRIPPING A WRISTWATCH, THORPE STUDIED his ghostly reflection in its blood splattered crystal. In turn, his dark expression reflected the mood of a nation. Less than twenty hours ago the United States suffered its second "nine-eleven." This time fewer innocent lives were lost, but the ordeal would be longer lasting, the fear more penetrating. Yesterday morning, just before dawn, thirty people were shot down—most on their way to work. Thirty people. Thirty different cities. Thirty shooters had managed to terrorize an entire nation.

Thorpe knew many of the answers the nation's citizens were now demanding of its government. The media again paraded a litany of "experts" before the twenty-four hour news stations, every one of them droning on with their theories and hypothesizing the government's response. In this case the experts correctly surmised a few generalities. After all, thirty men in thirty different cities—all coordinated to attack at the same time took considerable resources and planning; the shootings were obviously an act of terrorism. Their initial educated guesses that the trigger-pullers were home-grown extremists or terrorists in the country illegally, is where their theories fell apart. The street gang element was just now being made public. The experts were also mistaken with their theories of the government's response. If citizens knew what a small group of dedicated men and women were doing to protect this country, the ACLU would fall down kicking, screaming, and sucking their collective thumb.

Thorpe knew of the government's response. He was, for a short time at least, a combatant in the war on terror; a war being fought on friendly soil and in this instance, in Thorpe's own backyard. Because of his skill set and his familiarity with Tulsa, Thorpe had been briefed into the code-worded operation. Much of the intelligence they now possessed had been made possible because his father accomplished something John couldn't—leave someone alive worth interrogating. That someone—Alberto Vega—probably wished he hadn't survived.

After the assault on the salvage yard, Thorpe had been given a modified Iridium satellite phone and driven directly to O'Hare. There he boarded one of the last commercial flights to leave Chicago before the president, as a precaution, shut down U.S. airspace. Much of the intelligence bled from Alberto had been relayed to Thorpe before the pilot issued the order to turn off all electronic devices. By the time he arrived in Tulsa, news of the killings played on every television and radio station across the world. The shootings had been random and carried out from considerable distances. Thirty snipers were actively engaging targets across America.

"One man with a rifle can terrorize an entire enemy force," his father used to say—that had been before two idiots with a rifle paralyzed the Washington Metropolitan Area for nearly a month.

One man with a rifle. John shook his head. Thirty men, thirty rifles, thirty cities. Thirty men had effectively pinned-down a nation. The morning of the initial shootings, parents who'd already made it to work immediately left to collect their kids. Those who heard the news while still sitting around breakfast tables never ventured from home. Twenty-three people murdered, six critically wounded, one had escaped with a shattered hip. Thirty casualties—three hundred and twelve million people paralyzed with fear.

Alberto was responsible for ten of those shooters. Apparently a severe claustrophobe, in custody Alberto was singing like a canary and eventually he'd die like one—in a cage. Interrogators obtained the name to the Tulsa shooter before Thorpe had even departed Chicago.

Although the public would never know, Alberto's New York counterpart—responsible for a cell operating along the East Coast—had also been taken into custody; his "cooperation" helping to dismantle the ten-man team.

Unfortunately, there had been no prior intelligence reference the simultaneous actions along the West Coast and inside the Mountain States. For purposes of expediency, officials began with the assumption the shooters there operated under similar parameters as their East Coast and Midwest counterparts. The assumption was proving to be true—Latin street gangs were involved. As a result, both political parties were calling to plug the porous Mexican border. Terrorists had cozied up to Mexican cartels and used their long established drug routes to their advantage. Before these attacks, municipal police officers weren't even allowed to contact illegal aliens, let alone take law enforcement action. Politicians were finally forced to admit not all illegal aliens, Hispanic or otherwise, enter this country to pursue the American dream.

It was difficult to affix blame for America's complacency; she had plenty of warning. Not a year after nine-eleven its citizens were already bitching about inconveniences at airports. How quickly they forget. Perhaps now America would learn to be vigilant and proactive. But as a forgetful and reactive country, she will more than likely require additional acts of terrorism before learning what Israel did so long ago.

America's enemies were no longer on the other side of a great ocean; they were neighbors, visitors, and sometimes her own citizens. It was one of the cornerstones of guerilla warfare—Ground Level Embedding and Integration. The enemy within.

Yesterday, when Thorpe arrived at Tulsa's mostly empty airport, he took a moment to search the eyes of people he passed. In those eyes he saw all of his emotions reflected back: sadness, fear, anger, and yes, hate. Women wept, men clenched their fists. There would be no shortage of volunteers in the military's recruiting offices. People would want payback. But unlike the wars of yesteryear there'd be no clear enemy. No established battle fronts. No identifiable targets. The enemy was everywhere yet nowhere. Walking through the airport he stopped to watch a story on a news station. A reporter interviewed a stunned woman who'd just lost her husband to twisted ideology and a bullet, one of hundreds who now felt the weight Thorpe had been carrying for a year—the loss of a loved one to senseless violence. Millions more would be determined to avoid the anguish.

Thorpe walked out of the airport knowing more innocent lives would be lost in the days ahead. Peace-loving Muslims would be beaten down in the streets. The extremists had declared a holy war; the call would be answered and in the process many innocent people of all races and religions would get caught in the crossfire.

A Honda Accord had been left for Thorpe outside Tulsa International Airport. Inside the car and away from prying eyes, he'd powered up his secure phone. Information and a photograph of his assignment glowed on its screen: Hector Costilla, AKA King Ghost. His father, Ben, had obtained the names of all ten of Alberto's shooters. Six were operating under aliases complete with false identification. Those aliases were yet to be uncovered. But, thanks to Thorpe having killed four of the men in the woods beside his house, those replacements hadn't yet been provided false documents. Those men would be using real drivers' licenses, credit cards, etc. They'd be much easier to track down. One of those men, King Ghost, was in Tulsa; the man had shot a woman at a West Tulsa gas station. The kindergarten teacher clung to life, her husband and three young children no doubt bedside clutching her hand and praying to God for Him to save their mommy.

Not surprisingly, Ghost proved to be stupid. He continued to contact his known associates—all of whom under electronic surveillance—via a prepaid cell phone. He readily identified himself during those calls, as in, "Hey this is Ghost," etc. It didn't take long to isolate his phone and triangulate his signal. Thorpe had been directed straight to Ghost's hotel room. After that, it was just a matter of when.

Before Thorpe spilled Ghost's intestines on the forest floor, he'd stripped the man for intelligence. As part of Ben's plan to plant misinformation, the only thing he'd left behind was the man's rifle.

One of the items he'd taken from Ghost, which he now held in his hand, was a black Tag Heuer wristwatch. Thorpe turned over the watch, used his thumb to wipe clean the casing, and read three inscribed words above the Tag Heuer shield: "Counting the time." Below the inscription were two names: "Eva and Celestina."

Thorpe strapped the watch to his own wrist and took comfort knowing a friend would get his timepiece back and Ghost would never haunt anyone else again—not in this world.

FIFTY-SIX

HULL'S "WORKING VACATION" WAS OVER. Following the Wednesday morning, nationwide sniper attacks, his major had phoned telling him to get his ass back to Tulsa. One of the fallen was a Tulsan; the woman alive but clinging to life. Even those not informed of the situation realized the shootings weren't over. Thirty people shot in thirty different cities—not one of the suspects yet caught. There would be more murders. This was just wave one. Though the investigation would largely be federal, Hull and the homicide unit would use their local expertise to assist the FBI.

What his major didn't know was Hull already had the name of the Tulsa shooter. Hull knew far more than would ever be released to the news media. The "situation" that occurred at the salvage yard never happened. The two men taken alive would never be afforded attorneys. Lawyers wouldn't be screaming for the men's fair treatment. The government would never acknowledge having those men. For the most part the government wouldn't be lying because only a select few would be informed of their imprisonment. Certain agencies might become recipients of the intelligence gathered, but the origin would not be released. "Sources," would be a common term used in many future intelligence reports. Alberto and the shop manager would be bled for information. What happened to them afterward, Hull didn't know and wasn't sure he wanted to.

Hull rubbed at his eyes. All flights had been grounded so he and Skull took turns driving back home. Just outside of Tulsa, both men were eager to climb into their beds and get some much needed rest. A phone call from the deputy chief of investigations put those hopes on hold. There'd been another murder, but not by a sniper. The victim had been bound to a tree, gutted with a knife, and left in full view of a busy, South Tulsa street.

Exhausted, the last thing Hull wanted to do was investigate a homicide scene, particularly one unrelated to the terrorist attacks that scarred his city and his nation.

Exiting the Creek Turnpike for a bustling four-lane, north-south avenue, Hull tried to shake the mental fog of driving half asleep. He turned north catching a glimpse of Skull, head against window, snoring, his mouth agape. Reminded of the painting "The Scream," Hull chuckled before realizing how long his day was about to become.

Northbound, Hull peered across the busy intersection at his destination. Police cruisers, fire trucks, an ambulance, and a cluster of detective units awaited him. Thinking that too much of his life had been surrounded by flashing lights, grim faces, and dead bodies, he nearly turned left. Instead, he sighed and drove forward toward the scene.

Hull approached a marked unit blocking the northbound traffic. Looking inside the patrol unit, he saw the face of a crusty, thirty-year veteran contort with disgust. The officer had likely turned away dozens of citizens who thought they were of such importance a murder investigation should be halted to save them an extra ten minutes of commute time. The older officer was halfway out his door when he recognized Hull, nodded his head, plopped back down, backed up his cruiser, and allowed the supervisor over Homicide into *his* office.

Hull parked the rental car along the shoulder and jabbed Skull in the side.

"We're here you old fart. Wake up."

Too drowsy for a comeback, Skull mumbled "Okay," ran his fingers across the stubble on his chin, and reached for the door handle. Hull took a deep breath and stepped out into the street. In his right ear, he could hear Skull cursing him for having to exit the car into a ditch.

"You look like shit."

The compliment came from the deputy chief of operations. Hull noticed him, the police chief, and the deputy chief of investigations huddled on the street not far from a hastily cordoned off area in the woods. *Three chiefs at a crime scene? Not good.*

"Chief, what brings you out here?"

"Heard about it. Had to see it."

A curtain had been hung to shield the public from the gruesome scene. Approaching the three chiefs, Hull's angle changed so that he had a view of the carnage.

"Holy shit," Hull offered.

"Holy shit!"

"I just said that, Skull."

"Sorry boss, seemed worth repeating."

A naked man stood bound against a tree, his arms wrapped around the trunk behind him. Head-to-toe coagulated blood made it difficult to see the duct tape encircling his hips, chest, and neck. He'd been disemboweled. The man's guts lay at his feet, a rope of intestines led up into his mostly voided stomach cavity. His innards lay atop a rifle.

"He pissed somebody off," the chief declared. Then he pointed up a hill and across the street, "Scared the living shit out of a motorist this morning. Poor bastard drove straight into the ditch."

"Holy shit." Hull said yet again.

"Yeah, you've both said that already. We were hoping for a more professional opinion."

"Got an ID on the body?" Skull mustered.

"Everything was stripped and taken from him except the rifle and an Illinois driver's license. Looks like whoever killed him wanted us to know who he was. Strange they didn't take the rifle though." The chief pointed to the tree. "The guy's ID is stuck between the bark and the duct tape around his neck. It's sticking out so you can read his information without having to touch it. Hell it's on display."

"That is strange."

"The name Hector Costilla mean anything to you?" The chief asked.

Damn right it means something to me, Hull thought. *Jesus, John. What the hell?* He shared a look with Skull. The chief caught it.

"What?"

Hull answered his ringing cell phone, happy for the interruption, "Hull."

"It's me." The "me" being Benjamin Thorpe. "Sergeant, when you arrive in Tulsa you're going to have a bit of a situation on your hands."

Hull stepped away from the gathered men and spoke softly into the phone. "Thanks for the fucking warning. I'm already standing in the middle of your 'situation.'"

"I *have* been a little busy."

"What the fuck?"

"It's a message to the shooters. The ballistics on the rifle will check back to the shooting of the mother at the gas station. You can tell the media one of the nation's terrorists has been found—dead."

"Yeah, but I don't understand why..."

Ben interrupted, "If you haven't discovered it yet, you'll find a crown has been carved into that asshole's forehead. We'll make sure that detail, and other circumstances of his death, are leaked to the media."

The crown was a sign of the Latin Kings. Their members often spray-painted the symbol to mark their area. *They're going to make it look like the Kings are killing their own men*, Hull thought. The shooters won't know who to trust.

Ben continued. "Another shooter just met a similar fate in Chicago. Hopefully two others will be 'crowned' before the day's end."

"Trying to make them go into hiding?"

"That, or come forward—ask for protection. Just as long as they stop killing people."

"Fucking hard core, brother."

"Desperate times."

"How the hell am I going to explain this?"

"You're not. The FBI will help you develop Alberto Vega as a suspect. Of course, he'll never be found."

"Shit."

"Thanks, Bob. We owe you. We'll help you make the pieces fit."

"I didn't say yes."

The phone clicked dead. Hull looked at the Chief and Skull. Both men were intently staring at him. The chief's eyes were suspicious, Skull's questioning.

"Family shit," Hull said, stuffing the phone into his pocket.

The chief nodded and returned his attention to the body, "Jesus Christ, what the hell's happened to this country?"

No one offered an answer.

FIFTY-SEVEN

PROPPED UP AND ALONE IN his hospital room, Carlos stared in horror at the wall-mounted television. Every news channel carried the same story and showed the same disturbing images albeit from different angles. Even the talking heads seemed genuinely disgusted with their own news reports. Experts talked about the "new America" and government officials pleaded with citizens to carry on as usual. Watching the reports, Carlos saw his own fears realized in the loved ones of the victims. While his daughter had been returned unharmed, others weren't as lucky. Family members had been ripped away from them and they'd never get them back.

Only yesterday Carlos feared he'd never again hold Celestina. He'd been in a post-op ICU room; analgesic drugs dripped into his arm, but did nothing to quell his emotional anguish. His wife sat at his side, equally distraught. Police officers questioned them both and they'd told everything; everything except the man they knew as "John."

Carlos in bed, Eva beside him holding his hand, both prayed for John to make good on his promise. Their heads had been bowed, eyes closed, pleading for God to answer their prayers. He did. Two black-haired angels entered their room. One had exchanged her halo for a Chicago P.D. badge. In that angel's arms a cherub. Their daughter.

Celestina shrieked. Eva stood from her chair like a shot, and just as quickly lost her legs. The officer released Celestina who ran into her mother's arms. Carlos managed to work his way off the side of the bed and all three were filled with warmth on the cold tile floor.

The unknown officer stood silently as the three reconnected, managing to look both happy and sad at the same time. The woman noticed Carlos' attention and tried to slip out of the room.

"Officer, what's your name?"

"Jenna."

"How?" Carlos managed with a creaky voice.

The woman paused at the door, "John," she said. "The reports will say that I found her wandering around in the parking lot of the hospital. But it was John."

Then she left without another word, leaving the three on the floor crying and hugging.

They had food brought in for Celestina. Physically she seemed fine. Mentally…who knew? Carlos expected for her to cry more, for her to show more emotion. Instead, she silently clutched her mother, wrapping those tiny arms around her neck like she'd never let go.

Confident the kidnappers had already paid dearly for their acts, Carlos denied detectives permission to interview Celestina; their reunion only interrupted by a medical examination. Even then, Eva refused to leave Celestina's side. It appeared no sexual abuse had occurred—one more thing for which Carlos was thankful.

During these happy hours, Carlos heard of the tragedy unfolding outside the hospital doors. He overheard conversations between nurses, had seen them in the hallway shaking their heads. But Carlos kept the television off in their room, and the nurses—respectfully—didn't speak of the situation around his daughter. Celestina had seen enough violence. She didn't need to be exposed to more.

For only the second time since being reunited with his daughter, Carlos sat alone in his room. A specialist had requested to see Celestina on another floor and Eva accompanied her. Watching the television and the carnage occurring across the nation, Carlos wept. He knew Alberto had been an integral part of the devastation wrought on so many families. Carlos wept because he knew how close he'd come to participating in those events.

Tears flowing, good arm across his eyes, he never noticed the man slip into his room.

"There's an order out to terminate you on sight."

The voice had come from beside his bed. Carlos' arm flew from his face. His anguish forgotten, adrenalin-fed muscles lifted his back from the bedding as the man belonging to the voice came into focus through tear-blurred eyes.

"Relax, Carlos. If I was here to kill you, you'd already be dead."

An older man sat in the same chair his wife and daughter occupied only minutes before.

As if reading his mind the old man spoke, "Your wife and daughter are fine." The assurance was accompanied by a disfigured smile.

"Who the hell are you?"

"Who I am isn't important. What I've come to offer is."

There was something familiar about the man but Carlos couldn't place it.

"Do I know you?"

"No. I think I'd remember you, Too Tall."

"Old man, are you trying to piss me off? Because you're doing a damn good job of it."

Standing, the old man laid a card on the nightstand and jabbed at it with his index finger. "I don't have time to discuss my offer with you now. I'm busy and your wife is on her way back. Apparently the specialist who called for Celestina isn't even in the building."

"What? What are you talking about? What offer?"

"A new start. Alberto Vega ordered you and your family killed.

He might not be in a position to carry out that order himself but the command has already been given. I can protect you and your family for twenty-four hours, after that you're on your own. If you're interested in what I have to say, you'll call that number." The old man nodded at the television while walking toward the door, "We're very busy right now. What you and I will be discussing is your continuing service to your country."

"And I can trust you?"

The old man hesitated at the door. The light from the wall-mounted television illuminated his unusually bright green eyes. He shrugged his shoulders, "Can you trust anyone?"

FIFTY-EIGHT

PROPELLED BY A SENSE OF destiny Saeed al-Haznawi marched forward. Chest bowed out, lats flexed, he snarled at passing motorists. *They no doubt recognized the cold, hard eyes of a killer.* Two days ago this journey might not have been possible but his genitals were healing nicely. *No injury could stop him. He was a killer of men. Unstoppable. Invincible.*

Though Saeed always suspected he was meant for greatness, the last few days made him worry his glory would never be realized. That was, until he sat behind the computer monitor of a downtown Tulsa library, where his destiny with grandeur was confirmed.

The days leading up to that moment had been less than inspiring. His Greyhound trip from Chicago to Oklahoma suggested he'd not be a player in the drama unfolding across the nation. The shootings began before he'd even boarded the bus. He was in transit when the media started to put things together. A few murmurs from his fellow passengers soon turned to a quiet roar. The bus was equipped with multiple power outlets and a wireless router. Those with laptops were favored by their travel mates. Small pockets gathered around HPs, Dells, and Sonys to witness America's latest terrorist attack. Most passengers expressed disgust and fear; others beamed with excitement—an unmistakable sparkle in their eyes. Saeed had no need to feign being angry, shocked, or depressed; he was all those things. He was supposed to have been an integral part of history. Instead, he'd driven an empty fucking truck to a Walmart parking lot, where he'd been ordered to walk away and destroy his cell phone. As the bus trip continued and the news stories poured in, Saeed grew more and more frustrated.

Upon arrival, Saeed took a short cab ride from Tulsa's downtown bus station to the Central Library where his role in history became clear. There he used a public computer to access the internet. Email—if utilized correctly, it was one of the most secure ways to communicate. The procedure was simple: all parties shared an email account and password. Messages never needed to be sent to be read. Bad guy "A" simply typed his message into an email account and saved it to drafts. Bad guy "B" pulled up the same account, looked in the draft section and voila—message received but never cast into cyberspace where it could be intercepted.

As Saeed read the email he'd felt his face flush, and quickly glanced around at his fellow patrons to ensure no one could see his screen. Not only was he a part of the attacks, he'd been the catalyst. And it seemed his mission wasn't finished; he was to be the grand finale. Nestled deep in America's heartland, he'd been sent to Tulsa, Oklahoma, for a reason. He would soon be famous. Believers would revere him. Infidels would fear him. Everyone would remember his name.

The taxi dropped him off a half mile away from his destination—a motel on east Admiral where he would receive his final instructions. He'd been directed to walk to the motel. His movements before the attacks were not to be traced. Saeed strode confidently down the street. *Did this evening's motorists recognize that a great man walked their streets? Did they know? Would they brag of having seen him just before "the event?"*

Having arrived at his destination, Saeed approached room 114 and knocked five times as instructed. *Would the men inside know of his accomplishments? Would they know whose company they shared?*

A dark-haired man with a dour expression cracked open the motel door. Upon seeing Saeed, the man's mouth transformed into a wide grin—teeth white behind his black stubbly beard. *Yes, they knew.*

The man wrapped him in an embrace and called him "brother." Deeper in the room, another man called to him by name. *Soon, many would speak his name.* This man also smiled broadly, his arms outstretched, summoning Saeed forward, welcoming him.

Yes they knew of his deeds; of his greatness.

Light on his feet Saeed floated across the room buoyed by pride and two layers of carpet, the top layer recently laid and ill-fitting.

THIRTY MINUTES LATER AND HALF a block away, a tired-looking man in a blue Honda Odyssey watched as a black Chevy Caprice backed into a parking space in front of room 114 of the Cherry Blossom Motel. Two olive-skinned men, struggling with a roll of carpet, exited the room and stuffed their burden into the Caprice's open trunk.

The tired man jolted awake, he cursed under his breath before keying up his mic, "Homer to Mr. Brown: we have a situation."

FIFTY-NINE

NINETY-ODD MILES SOUTH OF TULSA, Lyndale Peterson paced his living room, bedroom, kitchen and bathroom, his tour complete with two strides. Though his residence sat on nearly 1,600 acres, he was mostly confined to a mere eighty-one square feet. Thanks to Jonathan Thorpe, he called Oklahoma State Penitentiary his home. Located in McAlester, the prison was commonly referred to as "Big Mac." Lyndale shared his residence with 1,200 others, all male, and most classified as maximum-security inmates.

As Lyndale paced his cell, his thoughts were not on his surroundings or the freedoms he'd lost. He had many years left in this hell-hole and those kinds of musings would drive a man crazy well before his release date. His thoughts were on the man who'd put him in this predicament and who'd put his younger brother in the grave. By now Lyndale should have been reading a newspaper article pinned above his bed with the headline, "Tulsa Police Sergeant Slain," or something similar. The article would help make his stay here more bearable.

For several days, Lyndale had been using the prison's illicit, but very real communications system in an attempt to contact Luis Carbia. Luis was not returning his phone calls—so to speak. The prison's phones were all monitored of course. Therefore, inmates used a fairly sophisticated code to communicate with those outside its walls. But when conversations involved planning the assassination of a police officer, it was best to use other methods. Sometimes those methods included illegal cell phones, though there had been a crackdown of late. One of his stupid-assed fellow inmates had been using a smartphone to update his Facebook page, complete with photos of him smoking marijuana inside his cell. His little escapade had been very embarrassing to prison officials. Because of that stupid fuck, everyone's cells had been torn apart, contraband and additional phones confiscated.

It was nearly impossible to keep the devices out. Guards brought them in and sold them for astronomical profits. Other phones entered the prison via stretched-out orifices not properly probed. Plus, there were ways to have associates outside the walls make calls for you. Bottom line: it wasn't difficult for Lyndale to communicate with the outside world.

Luis Carbia—that fuck owed him. Sure he would've gone to prison anyway, but that fucking beaner would be sitting right beside him had Lyndale not taken the fall for both guns. Luis owed him. He owed him Jonathan Thorpe. That fucking cop killed his brother and he wanted the pig on a spit.

Lyndale heard a folded piece of paper strike the concrete floor outside his cell. He stepped up to the aging bars, squatted, reached through and picked up the kite—a written communication between inmates. Notes were passed back and forth using a variety of methods: hand-to-hand, anus-to-hand, "note-on-a-rope," any way one could imagine. This kite was attached to a string and addressed to his cellmate, Reggie White, not of football fame.

Big Reggie was a lifer; in prison for beating to death the love interest of an ex-girlfriend. Big Regg wasn't a bad roommate and Lyndale got along fairly well with the man. Not that Lyndale had much of a choice. Reggie stood six and a half feet tall and barked at 300's door—yet another resemblance to the Reggie White of the NFL.

"You gotta Kite, Regg," Lyndale passed the note off to the

mammoth man lying on his concrete bunk.

Big Regg unfolded the note, studied it for a full minute then said, "Well ain't that something."

"What?"

"My momma done hit the lottery."

"No shit?"

"No shit."

"How much?"

"Twenty Gs."

"Motherfucker! That's good Regg."

"Hell yeah, my momma deserve it."

Lyndale should have thought it odd Reggie received a kite for legitimate news. Family would call, visit, or write a real letter. But Lyndale wasn't thinking straight. He wanted Jonathan Thorpe's neck. It was all he could think about.

Lights out. The lights started clicking off around the rotunda. Lyndale wanted to receive a similar note. His good news would be learning that Luis had carved up that puke of a cop who ended his brother's life.

Lyndale continued to stand at the bars of his darkened cell, livid, unable to rest. *Luis, call me back, motherfucker.*

"Hey, Lyndale?"

Lyndale registered that Reggie had risen off his bunk. He turned and looked up into his eyes, "What man?"

"Sorry, bro."

"Sorry fo' what, Regg?"

"You the lottery."

EPILOGUE

SERGEANT JONATHAN THORPE BROUGHT HIS eyes down from the desolate highway to the soft green glow of his dashboard lights. Five minutes till four. Out late, rather than up early, he enjoyed this time. His time. He owned the early morning, was one with it. No distractions, only solitude; nothing but the humming of tires on blacktop. It was easy to think.

Already things were returning to a "new normal" in T-town. While other cities were still under siege, Tulsa's shootings ended with the discovery of a mutilated body found tethered to a tree. Like Tulsa, the nightmares had also ended in Chicago, St. Louis, and Dallas. In those cities, three other men had been discovered, the condition of their bodies similar to that of King Ghost. Disfigured, crowns carved into the thin flesh of their foreheads.

The killings ended in those cities with the media reporting the mutilated gunmen worked for one Alberto Vega, a certified gang member in the Latin King hierarchy. "For reasons unknown"—the media reported—Vega had turned on his own men, methodically executing them in horrific fashion. Talking heads speculated Vega was cutting loose ends, but who really knew? If law enforcement could find the man they'd ask, but he seems to have disappeared.

Fertilized with blood, Ben's plan was bearing fruit. It'd been two weeks since Thorpe spilled Ghost's intestines onto Tulsa soil.

Ghost's death and those of the three other slain snipers received plenty of air time on local and national news channels. The six living snipers under Alberto's control had undoubtedly seen those news reports. The cities in which they worked hadn't had another killing with the same M.O. in the past week. They feared both the police and their own gang. With no one to trust, they were all alone and most likely in hiding.

The East Coast shooters were still wreaking havoc; each of the ten men committing at least four murders in their respective cities. Only one of those terrorists had been identified—killed just last night. The man was an Almighty Latin King from New York City. Operating in Charlotte, North Carolina, he'd shot a nurse outside a hospital emergency room. So close to medical care, she'd died instantly in front of her colleagues. A witness walking through a multilevel parking garage had heard the shot, saw a man running with "something long" in his hands, and watched the man enter a car. The witness provided a vague description of the suspect's car to the 911 dispatcher. A lone officer spotted a potential suspect vehicle two miles from where the shooting occurred. The officer pulled behind the car, notified dispatch he was behind a possible suspect, and advised he'd follow until backup units arrived.

That was the last radio traffic the officer ever provided—apparently the suspect didn't wait for the officer to initiate a stop. When the first backer arrived—a K-9 unit—she spotted the suspect vehicle driving away at a high rate of speed and the initial officer's patrol car filled with bullet holes. The K-9 officer had a difficult decision to make, render aid to her comrade or engage in a pursuit. If she didn't stop the suspect, more people would die. She chased. Later, it was determined the first officer had died instantly from well-place high-caliber rifle rounds; the K-9 officer made the right choice.

The K-9 unit closed on the suspect and the pursuit ended quickly. The suspect deployed from his car with an assault rifle and killed the k-9 officer—a mother of two. He also wounded her trapped dog and two additional officers before being killed by a responding unit armed with a patrol rifle. In a sick twist of fate, the suspect and the initial fallen officer had both been Airborne soldiers in the United States Army. One died protecting his country, the other betraying it. One citizen and two officers dead. Three families crushed.

Meanwhile, Thorpe had been ordered back to work. Despite the death of Tulsa's shooter, the entire department had been denied leave. Unsure of how to proceed, TPD's leadership instructed Thorpe to start "fucking with" Tulsa's Latin street gangs to see if his unit could identify members with links to Middle Eastern terrorists. Then the feds finally recognized they needed help from local law enforcement and Thorpe's Gangs Unit began working directly with Immigration and Customs Enforcement agents (ICE) and the Joint Terrorism Task Force (JTTF).

Almost overnight, immigration laws were deemed worthy of enforcement. If caught committing a criminal act, violators could now expect more than a bus ride across a border only to return the next day. Laws were being drafted so these people would be given real time. Efforts were underway to double the number of agents assigned to the U.S. Border Patrol.

Weapons, money, and the low-level fanatics controlling the money had entered the United States by way of Mexico's border. So far, only one of the shooters was determined to have entered the country illegally. The most caustic thing to have crossed the border wasn't physical; it was the connections drug cartels maintained with American street gangs and the street gang's willingness to do anything for a buck.

The new task force concentrated on Latin gang members and those who'd entered this country to prey on others. Unconcerned with working-class illegals, the unit pursued real bad guys, though most constituted street-level narco traffickers. Thorpe figured the major players would be handled by men like his father. Men who would make the Zealots hell-bent on destroying this country disappear. Sometimes battlefields need to be leveled, especially when those battlefields and their depraved enemies aren't easily discernible. Though he hadn't yet been asked, Thorpe would play a part in this war. The request implied when he'd returned home from work one evening to find his once-wrecked Suburban sitting in his drive, all the damage repaired, his weapons and equipment stashed neatly inside. Additional supplies had been provided as well: communications gear, tracking devices, phones, and more weapons. Everything needed to wage war packed into the weighted down Suburban.

Most importantly he received word Ambretta would be fine. She'd been suffering from tension pneumothorax when loaded into the car but the sucking chest wound had been "burped" and covered with a HALO Seal while en route to the hospital, where she reportedly recovered nicely from a punctured lung. *Thank you, God.* He wouldn't be responsible for the casualty of yet another loved one.

Thorpe eased off the blacktop and tucked his pickup in an RV park just north of a four-lane road. He grabbed a small pack off his front seat, slung it over his shoulder and stepped out into the brisk, still, morning. He crossed a private drive and approached a tall chain-link fence concealed in a stand of trees. Thorpe took in his surroundings, listened to the stillness, effortlessly scaled the fence and dropped to the other side.

Shielded by the darkened shadows of a moonless night he moved deeper into the property. Thorpe easily found his way in the darkness; he'd been here before. Arriving at his destination, he lowered himself and sat cross-legged on sacred ground, the air deathly still. Thorpe closed his eyes. His heart rate decreased, his breathing became as silent as his environment. He sat between his two fallen loves. His wife to his left, his daughter to his right. He came here, trespassing after dark so he could sit in silence, so he could listen, so he could learn what his wife and daughter thought of the man he'd become. *Were they embarrassed? Disgusted? Did they pity him? Were they pleading with God to save his soul? Or were they simply no more?*

Thorpe remained still, continuing his relaxation techniques as though preparing for battle. In the ensuing silence, he strained to hear words unspoken.

"Please," he heard himself whisper, "talk to me."

His daughter's headstone stood pale in the gloom; its black engraving readable even in the dark:

Ella Ambretta Thorpe
My World

Thorpe unslung his pack and pulled at the nylon zipper. Inside were two yellow daisies; his daughter's favorite flower. Today would have marked her seventh birthday. He placed one flower on each grave. A small grin creased his lips as the flowers brought forth a memory. The image of his little girl's mischievous smile—her hands hidden behind her back.

Memory becoming tangible, the background peeled away leaving only his luminescent daughter standing in front of him in a glowing Easter dress. Her hands revealed a bouquet of flowers— picked for her daddy. Now, just as then, they were only a bundle of dandelions. Now, just as then, they were the color of the sun and equally beautiful to any collection of expensive flowers. The only thing shining brighter than those dandelions—her radiant smile. So vivid.

"Are those for me?" Thorpe whispered, his hands reaching for flowers he knew he wouldn't find. As quickly as she'd appeared Ella's image turned to vapor, leaving him with the darkness of the graveyard. He'd give anything, everything, to have her again for a few more minutes. To thank her for the bouquet; to tell her how beautiful she was; to let her know how much he missed her.

"Happy birthday, sweetie. Daddy's sorry."

He remained the epitome of calm: heartbeat in the 40s, breathing slow, but losing a river of tears. A silent waterfall.

Time passed and the tears dried. He looked up at the sky, the lump in his throat gone. He wouldn't hear his daughter tonight. His questions wouldn't be answered. But he'd seen her, and that was enough for now. However fleeting, he felt a measure of peace.

He felt something else as well. Something he'd felt often over the course of his life; the feeling of not being alone. Maybe the sense was caused by a shifting of the wind, a noise or smell. The sensation wasn't as grandiose as knowing his wife and daughter lived on beside him—it was something physical, something real. Something behind him.

"How long have you been watching me," Thorpe called out, not bothering to turn.

It hadn't been his imagination. He sensed movement. Finally he heard soft footfalls on the dead grass as someone approached to within a few feet.

"Your whole life."

Benjamin Thorpe moved to his side, "Your whole life, son."

John resisted the urge to look up into his father's eyes.

"May I?"

John found himself unable or unwilling to answer. In the silence his father eased to the ground.

"She was beautiful."

John nodded. *She was indeed.*

"It wasn't your fault."

John didn't respond.

"If I'd only," his father said. "It'll kill you, son."

Finally John looked into his father's eyes—his own eyes.

Ben continued, "If I'd only taken a different street. If I'd only left five minutes earlier. If I'd only left five minutes later. If I'd only been an accountant instead of a cop. If I'd only let that maggot go, he would've never killed my family. If I'd only stayed home, they'd still be alive."

Did his father realize how many times he'd repeated those last two sentences?

"It's true, they would be," John finally responded.

"Maybe, but when you do the jobs we do, the 'If I'd onlys' pile up." His father looked away, staring straight ahead, his eyes unfocused. "If I'd only went in first. If I'd only not issued that order…"

John realized his father was talking about himself now; remembering things past.

"…If I'd only *not* gone on that last deployment." His father shook his head then returned John's gaze, "The 'If I'd onlys' will kill you, son; not as quick as a bullet, but dead just the same."

"So what, I chalk it up to destiny? God's plan? Random bullshit?"

"I don't have the answers. I do know if your daughter hadn't been killed, there'd be four more trained snipers still alive and killing innocent families. And their six buddies would still be out killing others instead of hiding from fear of losing their own life. All those lives spared. Carlos' own daughter would be dead…or worse."

"You're trying to tell me my daughter was sacrificed for the greater good? That's a bunch of bullshit. If those sick fucks needed stopped then drop a tree on their heads, don't take my little girl down with them."

"Again, I don't have the answers, son. All I know is your daughter saved a lot of lives. Bad things happen to good people. 'For He gives His sunlight to both the evil and the good, and He sends rain on the just and the unjust alike.'"

John shook his head in disbelief; he'd never before heard his father utter a word from the Bible. "What was that? Since when did you quote Scripture over Sun Tzu?"

"When you get to my age, and you've see the things I've seen, you look for answers anywhere you think you might find them. My whole life is a 'If I'd only.' If I'd only come back into my son's life, I would have been there for my granddaughter, my daughter-in-law—and my son.

"In trying to prepare you, I doomed you. 'Always protect your family.' That's what I used to say. I know you feel like you've failed me, but I failed you, son. I didn't protect *my* family. I wasn't there for you, Johnny. But I'm here now. You're not alone anymore."

I'm here now? John clenched his jaw. *What excuse could his father possibly offer?* He didn't want to hear, yet had to know.

"Why'd you leave us?"

His father let out a long sigh, "Let's just say me and a couple other men were someplace the U.S. had no authority to be. We got caught. Neither government acknowledged our existence. The country that captured us pretended they didn't. Our own government pretended we weren't there. I have no bitterness; we knew the score going in.

"I was badly injured during my capture; nursed back to health only to be tortured half to death again. But I survived." His father took a deep breath, the pain apparent in his eyes. "The two men with me weren't so lucky. Damn good men. 'If I'd only' had my head on straight in the first place, we would have never been captured; those two men would still be alive and their kids would still have a daddy."

Head on straight? His father and mother had a huge falling out before Ben left on his last deployment; the marriage in jeopardy because John had killed a man in self-defense. His mother learned Ben had been teaching him 'real-world' hand-to-hand combat— teachings that resulted in her son being slashed and stabbed.

"I know what you're thinking, son. If I'd only not killed that man. How can you blame yourself? I mean what kind of father drives his son around getting him into street fights? You were better off without me. I should've been taking you to baseball or basketball practices, not teaching you warcraft. Jesus." His father paused, shook his head, and continued, "After a few years in a shithole of a prison, I was exchanged. Exchanged for some assholes who probably went on and killed more innocent people—still more blood on my hands. Our government should have left me to rot. When I finally got back stateside your mother had already passed and I spent another year in the hospital recovering from my injuries. You and your sister had moved on. I'd caused enough destruction in your lives. I saw no reason to inflict more harm. But I always followed your life, son."

John studied his father. Some of the damage inflicted in prison was visible on his face; deep scars that would never completely fade. "Mom told us you were dead. Did she know the truth?"

"She'd been told I went missing during a training exercise. Standard bullshit. We'd discussed it before. Captive or dead she would have received the same notification. The government can't have widows on the six o'clock news discussing how their husbands were being detained by country X. Especially when we had no business being inside country X. She sure as hell wasn't going to tell you and your sister I might be alive and being held captive someplace. Have you picturing some asshole drilling into my molars with a Black and Decker. Believe me, son, its better believing someone died a quick death than thinking they're in a foreign prison—forgotten and in pain. Your mother not knowing is probably what killed her. One more 'If I'd only' on my never ending list."

It was a lot for Thorpe to digest. He realized he shouldn't hold his father responsible for being captured and held in a foreign prison while serving his country. If ever there was a good excuse, that one would have to rank near the top. But John had held on to his anger for so long he found it difficult to let go.

"You saved my ass last month, didn't you? You have me under surveillance?"

His father nodded. "My only way of being close to you. I don't have men watching you, but cell phones and what not—Yeah, I almost always know where you are and what you're doing. When your wife and daughter got killed, I stepped it up a notch. I assumed you'd been the actual target—because of your job—and the bad guys fucked it up. I was worried they might try again."

"But how'd you see it coming so fast?"

"I've been doing what I've been doing for a long time. I have access to a special set of analysts at NSA. I had them put your identifiers into the system. If someone uses your name and words from a canned list, it triggers an alert similar to how they monitor threats against government officials. If the president is mentioned in a phone conversation along with certain words, like, bomb, kill, shoot, etc. it triggers a response. Analysts retrieve the recording and review it.

"The only real difference is when your alarm goes off, I'm the only person designated to be notified. One day I got an alert pairing your name with about every trigger-word in the system. Except you weren't the target. The conversation originated from a cell phone in Tulsa to an FBI office in Texas; some guy talking about you and the people you were about to kill."

John nodded his head, "Kaleb Moment." John's friend, Jeff, told Thorpe of the phone conversation. Kaleb called an FBI office in Dallas, telling them a Sergeant Jonathan Thorpe planned to kill fellow Tulsa Police officers. The Dallas agent hadn't taken Kaleb seriously, at least not until the deaths of several TPD officers made the news.

"I pulled Ambretta off the Atlanta cell and sent her to Tulsa with FBI credentials. Believe me I did some fudging and burnt a few favors on that one. Meanwhile, I tagged Kaleb's phone and intercepted it just south of the Oklahoma border. That's where I met the little shit. He had a face full of stitches and one hell of a story to tell."

"I shoulda' killed him."

"But you didn't. Because you knew it was wrong."

John shrugged. "You kill him?"

"I have to admit I considered it. But no, he's alive and he's free. But he won't be a problem."

John ignored his father's ambiguity. He really didn't care what happened to Kaleb. "Did Ambretta know the whole time?"

"No. Our folks operate off the books, but this was even off those books. I didn't want to get her involved but I couldn't do it alone. She operated in the dark most of the time she was with you. I told her you were an asset who needed kept alive."

"And she didn't know you were my father?"

Ben shook his head. "Not until she came with me to this very cemetery. I told her to stay in the car when I walked down here, so she didn't know then either. But she put it together when you showed up and damn near caught me visiting."

John remembered the day. He'd walked down to where he sat now, clueless as to being watched. He didn't visit often and when he did he always came alone. Now he sat between his wife's and daughter's graves with his father beside him. And though he wasn't quite ready to forgive, Ben's explanation relieved his sense of abandonment. With many of life's questions finally answered, John felt a deeper sense of calm—a calm he hadn't had to achieve through physiological manipulation.

"Daisies were your daughter's favorite, right?" Ben said looking down at the flowers, one on each grave.

The statement caused John to realize how much his father knew about his life. Never a man to engage in physical contact—unless one counted grappling—John was surprised when Ben took his hand. Surprise turned to shock when his father prayed aloud. He'd never before seen him bow his head, not even during church service, always assuming his father attended only at the insistence of his mother.

Ben prayed over his family's graves asking for peace and forgiveness—it seemed a prayer he was accustomed to delivering.

"I'm tempted to pull off your mask."

Ben smiled, "Never too late to change, son." Then, "You've been struggling. You think you're condemned?"

"I'm fairly certain 'thou shall not kill' was near the top of Moses' to-do list."

"I believe the correct interpretation is 'Thou shall not murder.' There's a difference. Then again, folks like to interpret the Bible to fit their own agenda." Ben sighed. "Here's what I think. If God is the

Shepherd, and the people His sheep, then we're the sheepdogs. And fear of the sheepdog is the only thing keeping the wolves at bay. The trick is for us to not bite the flock."

"I don't think revenge fits into your analogy."

"There's no doubt you've exercised your share. Ask for forgiveness and move on."

"I can't ask forgiveness for something I don't intend to stop doing."

"Son, you've been the same since I can remember; probably even before I started passing my warped view of the world on to you. Once, when you were about six years old, you were playing on a tractor with some new kid in the neighborhood when your friend, Cole Freeman, came along. Remember Cole?"

John nodded his head. Cole had been his next-door neighbor when they lived in Kansas City, Missouri.

"I never liked Cole but you two were buds. He was a bully and treated you like shit. For some reason you put up with him—never lifted a finger, no matter how angry he made you. But on this particular day he slapped that new kid and told him get off 'his' tractor. You remember what you did?"

John couldn't recall; he'd been too young and it'd been too long ago.

"You punched Cole right in the nose, which started bleeding like a sieve. Cole ran off and told his parents. I had to deal with Cole's daddy who was probably the one who taught Cole to be a bully in the first place. Two Thorpes punched a Freeman in the nose that day."

John found himself smiling. He remembered Cole's dad as a drunken asshole.

"My point is, you've always looked out for those who couldn't look out for themselves. That's not revenge. That's being a sheepdog. What you've done in the past—I don't know, son. Forgive yourself and move on. You're a good boy, Johnny. "

You're a good boy, Johnny. Words he'd often heard during his childhood. His father stood and John pushed up to meet him.

"I'd like to be a part of your life, son, if you'll let me. But right now I'm about as busy as I've ever been. Innocent people are still dying. I should have pushed to end this op earlier. One more 'if I'd only.'"

Though physically a much smaller man, his father stood larger than life. His greatest hero extended his hand and John accepted. The handshake of two men. When his father pulled away, John held a white card with a handwritten phone number.

Walking away with the fluidity of a younger man, his father spoke over his shoulder, "That number will reach me anywhere, anytime."

"Ambretta?" John called out to his father.

Ben stopped and turned with a slightly deformed grin. "Took you long enough to ask. She said this wasn't the time," Ben nodded toward his family's headstones, "or the place."

John felt his heart sink.

Ben's crooked grin became a full blown smile, "I said bullshit. No more secrets." Ben looked up the hill.

John turned and followed his father's gaze toward a circle drive and behind it, a lit marble fountain. The fountain was far enough away the falling water fell as silently as Thorpe's tears had. On its rim sat a backlit woman with long dark hair.

"Does she...?" John began to ask, turning back toward his father.

Ben had already resumed his retreat. "Love you? I think that's something you should ask her," he answered, not bothering to look back.

Thorpe drew a deep breath and took to the hill. He'd been mistaken—one of his life's most important questions had yet to be answered. His throat tightened, his palms grew moist, his apprehension increased with each step taken. As he neared, Ambretta rose off the fountain and stood motionless. As he drew within arm's distance, he saw his same worries and fears reflected in her expression. In her beautiful dark eyes, he found the answer to his unasked question.

Ambretta accepted John's extended hand as he pulled her into a long kiss. Their lips parted with a single tear rolling down her cheek. Without words they walked hand-in-hand, fingers interlaced, back down to his wife's and daughter's headstones.

"Erica, Ella, this is Ambretta. I think you would have liked her."

ACKNOWLEDGMENTS

Thanks to:

My 800,000 brothers and sisters.

The United States military—because cops need heroes too.

Katherine Benight, Cole Butler, Greg Matthews, David Rhoades, Daryl Webster, and Steve Wood for your editing and honesty.

Officer Dan O'Connell with Chicago PD's Deployment Operations Center for your insight into the Chicago Police Department and the Latin King Nation.

God for my many blessings.

ALSO BY GARY NEECE

Tulsa Police Department Sergeant Jonathan Thorpe finds his wife and young daughter slain in their home. Frustrated by the department's failure to solve the crime, Thorpe conducts his own covert investigation that requires Thorpe to mete out a very personal form of justice. A lone man against a rogue group, Thorpe sets off a controversy that brings the FBI into the midst of the city's police department. And the FBI's beautiful Ambretta Collins seems to have zeroed in on him as the prime suspect. Still Thorpe fights on. But is he really alone?

For more information about Gary Neece and his books, follow him on Facebook:

https://www.facebook.com/GaryNeeceAuthor

Editorial Reviews for
Cold Blue by Gary Neece

"Not only is it written well and suspenseful, the end of the book has an amazing twist!"
Savilla Cribbs, via Amazon review

"I'd love to see the main character, Jonathan Thorpe, in future stories!"
terri horner, via Amazon review

"Great read. Neece is the real deal. I like this book better than any of Lee Childs "Reacher" novels. The only problem with this book is there isn't another five of Neece's books ready to read."
Tony Latham, via Goodreads review

"A gripping tale written by someone who [knows] the inside workings of a major city police department. A real page turner. Gary Neece is the next Nelson DeMille when it comes to police thrillers."
Craig Roberts, author: *One Shot--One Kill* and *Police Sniper*

"Thorpe is brilliant, broken, and real. I was hooked from page one, and surprised by the twist at the end. Gritty, witty, and gripping; an exceptional debut novel."
Garda 1967, via Amazon review

"Raw and gritty. Only a co can write about the cop's real world. Neece is the next Jospeh Wambaugh - with more edge."
Charles W. Sasser, ex-cop and author: *Homicide!, Shoot to Kill, No Gentle Streets*, and *At Larger*

CPSIA information can be obtained
at www.ICGtesting.com
Printed in the USA
LVHW03s1600160618
580973LV00001B/209/P